Ellery Queen's Book of First Appearances

ELLERY QUEEN'S
Book of First
Appearances

Edited by
Ellery Queen *pseud.*
and Eleanor Sullivan

The Dial Press

Davis Publications, Inc.
380 Lexington Avenue
New York, New York 10017

COPYRIGHT NOTICES AND ACKNOWLEDGMENTS

iv

CONTENTS

"Q"

DOUBLE FOREWORD

I. Preface

Dear Reader:

One day early in 1951, at a monthly board meeting of the Mystery Writers of America, the subject of MWA's 1952 anthology surfaced on the agenda. Which angle this time, which gimmick? The MWA usually based its annual anthology on a specialized detective or mystery theme, and the selected concept not only dictated the choice of stories but gave the book a pattern or unity, a cumulative reading impact.

Now, it happened at this time that E.Q. was also planning an anthology for the next year, a collection based on an idea never before used to connect a group of mystery and detective stories. Well, MWA needed a new approach to its forthcoming collection, and E.Q. being young and prodigal at that time, and bursting with ideas that could easily be replaced (they thought) from a bottomless trunk of plots and tricks—well, in a cavalier disregard of our own future requirements, we offered the previously unused theme to MWA, complete with a book title.

The title was MAIDEN MURDERS, and the book did appear in 1952. The theme was classically simple: famous and well-known mystery writers would contribute their first-published short stories—hence, MAIDEN MURDERS, although MAIDEN MYSTERIES would have been more precise. Like the anthology now in your hands, MAIDEN MURDERS contained a double foreword—a Preface by Lawrence G. Blochman, creator of medical detective Dr. Daniel Webster Coffee, and a "wise and witty" Introduction by John Dickson Carr, creator of Gideon Fell, Sir Henry Merrivale, and Colonel March.

Plus ça change, plus c'est la même chose—the more it changes, the more it's the same thing. True. About mystery stories too. The more the mystery story changes, the more it's the same. The style of the mystery does change over the years, but the substance of the mystery story remains the same—exciting tales of impossible murders, of historical detection, of pure deduction—tales of horror and humor, parody and pastiche—psychological thrillers and stories of everyday-gone-wrong—of sleuths and supersleuths, amateur and official—the gamut, the spectrum, the variants of crime, mystery, and brain-testing, brain-tingling suspense . . .

After this biblio-history of ELLERY QUEEN'S BOOK OF FIRST APPEARANCES, after this brief inquiry into its beginnings, its thematic origin, we now pass the baton to co-editor Eleanor Sullivan who will give you more details about this anthology. So doff your deerstalker, and salute the brilliant newcomers who have brought honor to our genre.

E.Q.

II. Introduction

The 27 stories in this collection range from a detective debut in 1943 to a first appearance in print in 1979, a span of 36 years. The opening "first" was written by a 15-year-old schoolboy, and the closing "first" by a retired schoolteacher who gave her age as "plenty plus." In between are three *EQMM* first stories that were awarded Edgars by the Mystery Writers of America for best mystery short story of the years in which they were published—Joyce Harrington's "The Purple Shroud" (1972), Etta Revesz's "Like a Terrible Scream" (1976), and Barbara Owens' "The Cloud Beneath the Eaves" (1978).

Other writers included in this anthology went on to receive honors from MWA as well. Three have won Edgars in the Best First Novel category—Robert L. Fish (*The Fugitive*, 1962), Harry Kemelman (*Friday the Rabbi Slept Late*, 1964), and Kay Nolte Smith (*The Watcher*, 1981)—and Mr. Fish also received an Edgar for Best Short Story ("Moonlight Gardener," 1971). Francis M. Nevins, Jr. was given a Special Award in 1974 for his book, *Royal Bloodline: Ellery Queen, Author and Detective*. In 1980 William Link and Richard Levinson, still writing in tandem, were awarded an Edgar for Best Television Program (*Murder by Natural Causes*). Jon L. Breen, just this year, won an Edgar in the Critical/Biographical category for *What About Murder?* And Stanley Ellin has received not only three Edgars—two for Best Short Story ("The House Party," 1954, and "The Blessington Method," 1956) and one for Best Novel (*The Eighth*

Circle, 1958)—but also MWA's highest honor, the Grand Master Award.

Six stories in this collection are the first appearances of well known series characters—James Yaffe's Paul Dawn, Lillian de la Torre's Dr. Sam: Johnson, Harry Kemelman's Nicky Welt, Robert L. Fish's Schlock Homes, Alice Scanlan Reach's Father Crumlish, S. S. Rafferty's Jeremy Cork. And Jon L. Breen's pastiche of Ed McBain's 87th Precinct is the first in his highly successful series of parody/pastiches of major mystery writers.

Speaking of pastiches: in his Introduction to MAIDEN MURDERS John Dickson Carr wrote, "Is it possible that you are not an admirer of Dr. Johnson, as presented either by James Boswell or by Miss de la Torre? If not, I am sorry. But, if anyone had told most of us that a writer could turn the Great Lexicographer into a detective and get away with it, I am sure we should not have believed it—until we read the first story." Well, would you believe this? We recently received an excellent pastiche of Miss de la Torre's Dr. Sam: Johnson stories—written by her brother, Theodore de la Torre Bueno! And it is his first fiction! It will appear in a forthcoming issue of *Ellery Queen's Mystery Magazine* as #600 in *EQMM*'s Department of First Stories—exactly 40 years after Lillian de la Torre's first story.

E.S.

"Q"

James Yaffe

D.I.C. (Department of Impossible Crimes)

B lank blank blank blank t.
     If he could only find those first four letters everything would be all right. He was sure of it.

"What's a five-letter word meaning 'to fall prostrate'? The last letter is 't'."

"I'm sure I couldn't tell you," said Inspector Stanley Fledge, of the New York Homicide Squad. "Now suppose you listen to me for a minute. We've got a case on our hands. A murder. It's running the force ragged. And you're just the man to solve it."

Paul Dawn was flattered. He liked it very much indeed when they came to him for advice, though he would have cut off his right arm rather than admit it. He took a cigarette from the box on his desk and lit it. He shook out the match and tossed it neatly into the wastepaper basket. "Neat shot, eh?" Paul was a rather nice-looking young man. There was a faraway expression on his face most of the time. Paul could have the most rousing adventures in the barren ice-stretches of the North Pole, while his body was firmly implanted in his office chair.

"Look here, Paul," Inspector Fledge insisted, "this isn't funny business, you know. We don't bother you very often, do we? Only in cases of emergency. So put away your crossword puzzles and whatchamacallits and listen to me."

Stanley Fledge was a grizzled old veteran of the Homicide Squad. Paul Dawn didn't mind Fledge, it was just that he couldn't understand him. Fledge was a Man of Action, and this jarred Paul's scheme of things. Paul's idea of action was to sit in an easy chair, fondling a bottle, and do nothing more than let his mind wander.

He saw Fledge's peering little rabbit-eyes focused anxiously upon him, so he deposited himself back in this world.

"Is this crime in my department?"

"You bet. It's one of the most impossible crimes we've ever come across."

"Go ahead then." Paul leaned back in his chair, and as he listened he tapped the point of his pencil absently against the desk. It was because of his passion for impossible crimes—crimes which couldn't have happened—that he had persuaded the Commissioner to let him take charge of an obscure little office connected to the Homicide Squad, known as the D.I.C.—the Department of Impossible Crimes.

"Here's the problem," Fledge said. "A rich old stockbroker named George Seabrook was killed last night. He'd been spending the evening with some of his poor relations—his nephew Philip and Philip's wife, Agnes.

"Around nine o'clock Seabrook got up to go. He wanted to be back at his home by ten. They said their goodbyes and walked their uncle to the elevator."

Paul's attention was caught by Stanley Fledge's large and protruding Adam's apple. It bobbed up and down in a little bouncing motion as the Inspector spoke. And on the word "elevator" Paul received a special treat. The Adam's apple, caught up by the flow of syllables, not only bounded back and forth but wobbled slightly to the side.

If only Fledge would say "elevator" a few more times.

"The Seabrooks," continued the Inspector, "live in a small apartment house called the Lexington Arms. They have a couple of rooms on the fifth floor. The Lexington Arms has only one elevator—" hurray! "—and it's one of those automatic, push-button affairs. You know. You push the button for the third floor and the elevator goes to the third floor.

"Anyway, George Seabrook got into the elevator—" again! "— and pushed the button for the first floor. Philip Seabrook and Agnes Seabrook both saw him push the button for the first floor. So did Mrs. Battleman, a woman who lives in one of the other apartments on the fifth floor. Mrs. Battleman had just opened the door of her apartment in order to take in the evening paper, which was lying on the mat. She saw Seabrook getting into the elevator. She saw him push the button. And Mrs. Battleman, Philip Seabrook, and Agnes Seabrook can testify that when that elevator started to go down George Seabrook was in perfectly good condition."

Something Fledge said made Paul switch his attention to the matter at hand. He would return to the elusive little Adam's apple later. "What do you mean by 'perfectly good condition'?"

"I mean alive." The Inspector cleared his throat and went on. "At the same time, Paul, two tenants of the Lexington Arms were waiting for the elevator on the first floor. One of them was a Dr. Herbert Martin, who was coming back from a call, and the other one was a stenographer, Miss Flora Kingsley. Incidentally, this Kingsley woman used to work for Seabrook years ago.

"These two waited at the first floor. Around nine o'clock this was. They saw the indicator above the elevator door stop at the fifth floor. Then they saw the indicator move from the fifth floor to the first floor. They were both watching that indicator all the time, and they swear that it didn't stop once on its way down to their floor. In other words, from the time George Seabrook got into that elevator on the fifth floor to the time that elevator reached the first floor, it made no other stops.

"Now just a little about the construction of the elevator. It's made of good thick wood. The walls, floor, and ceiling are absolutely solid. There are no secret doorways or hidden entrances in it. The only way of getting into that elevator or out is by the door. And the mechanism is such that the door won't open if the elevator is in motion. Since the elevator *was* in motion from Floor 5 to Floor 1, the door couldn't have been opened. And since that door was the only entrance to the elevator, nobody could have possibly entered it or left it while George Seabrook took his trip down. Get the picture?"

Paul nodded. "But I don't see what you're leading up to, Fledge."

"Just this." The Inspector leaned forward and spoke intently. "George Seabrook was alive when he entered the elevator. No one else was in the elevator. It traveled straight down without any stops. And yet, when that elevator reached the first floor, Dr. Martin and Miss Kingsley pulled open the door and found George Seabrook lying dead on the elevator floor, *with a knife in his back*."

Fledge slammed the palm of his hand down on the surface of the desk to emphasize his point. "And if that isn't an impossible crime," he said, "I don't know what is!"

A loud silence filled the room.

Paul Dawn was thinking. In a slow, lazy fashion, of course—but for him any form of concentrated thought was an effort. He usually got better results by giving his mind a free hand and letting it spread out in whichever direction it liked. But now he was thinking about the Impossible Crime in the elevator. Paul always tabbed his cases with titles. The labels helped him keep everything straight.

He kept on tapping his pencil lightly against a blotter that lay on his desk. Stanley Fledge's Adam's apple was entirely forgotten.

"Well, Paul," Fledge asked eagerly. "What do you think of it?"

"Think of what?"

"The case. The impossible murder."

"I try not to," said Paul. "It's interesting, though."

"It'll interest me when we clear it up."

Paul blew a nearly perfect smoke ring, a feat which gave him a great deal of satisfaction. "I have visions," he said suddenly, and Fledge looked at him queerly. Paul closed his eyes. "I see our victim, George Seabrook. He stands in the elevator, probably with the idea that he is completely alone. And then without warning something happens. The machinery begins to turn. The automatic thingamajig, whatever it might be, starts to whirr, and a knife is plunged into George Seabrook's back. Then our murderer vanishes. Very melodramatic. Especially melodramatic since, from what you've told me, it couldn't have happened that way."

"And yet," said the Inspector, scratching his chin contemplatively, "it looks like it couldn't have happened any other way."

"I wonder how it did happen," Paul said. "Pigs don't fly. Automobiles can't change into kangaroos. And murderers don't disappear up elevator shafts whenever they please. This case is riddled with complexities."

"It's riddled with something, all right." Fledge shook his head gloomily. "How about it? Does it appeal to you?"

"Oh, vaguely." Of course it appeals, Paul thought. He hadn't had a case for weeks that appealed half as much. But it wouldn't do to show he was too anxious. Bored and superior. That was the proper effect. "By the way, Fledge, have you thought of a five-letter word meaning 'to fall prostrate' yet? Remember, the last letter is 't'."

"No, I haven't given it a thought," the Inspector said irritably. "Will you take the case?"

"I'll take the case."

He blew another smoke ring, which, he was glad to note, was up to his usually high standard.

"This," said Paul Dawn out loud, though he meant it to himself, "is going to be good."

The remark was prompted by his first glance at the automatic elevator in the Lexington Arms. A second glance was unnecessary. The elevator was solid, all right. Impenetrable even. No suspicious cracks in the wall. No out-of-place bumps in the ceiling. No concealed crevices in the floor. With the door closed, Paul reflected, a bug would have trouble sneaking into that elevator. He thought of all the trouble it would have saved him if only the builder had obligingly placed a few trap doors in the floor, or several sliding panels in the wall. But this was the kind of difficult problem he liked, something like that troublesome five-letter word meaning 'to fall prostrate.' He wondered whether, if he tried falling prostrate once or twice, it might not give him the answer.

With effort he pulled his mind back to more immediate things.

"Tight as a drum, isn't it?" Stanley Fledge said. "It doesn't look as if there's any way at all to get into it. But someone did. It's frightening, Paul. Can't say I'm particularly comforted by the idea of an invisible murderer running around loose. Come on, now. Let's get busy."

The Fledge philosophy in a few short words, Paul thought. Inspector Stanley Let's-Get-Busy Fledge. These get-up-and-go men upset Paul's nervous system.

"Let's get busy at what?" he asked.

"Questioning suspects! Hunting for clues! Solving the case! That's what. Come on."

Paul puffed tranquilly at his cigarette and seated himself on the one chair in the cramped lobby of the Lexington Arms. "I'll get busy right here," he said. "I have a few questions to ask of *you*."

"I didn't commit the murder."

Paul let that one pass. "First, what about fingerprints? Have you found any?"

Fledge snorted indelicately. "Too many. Just about everybody in the building rode up in that elevator yesterday. But the clearest sets are made by George Seabrook."

"Did you find his thumbprint on the first-floor button?"

"Sure we did. That's the first place we looked."

"Did you find Seabrook's print on *any of the other* push buttons?"

Fledge looked at him with a puzzled expression. "Why do you ask that?"

"Did you?"

"Yes, as a matter of fact we did."

If Paul felt any great interest or eagerness his face didn't show it. His expression was placid and mild. His eyes looked rather sleepy. He completely skipped over the obvious question. "What does the Medical Examiner say?" he asked instead.

"Death due to stabbing. Died instantly. Say! Hold on a minute." Fledge's face was a study in bewilderment. "Aren't you going to ask me on what button we found those other fingerprints of Seabrook's?"

"The fifth-floor button," said Paul absently. "What did the Medical Examiner say about Seabrook's general physical condition?"

Fledge's neck was reddening. "How did you know Seabrook's thumbprint was on the fifth-floor button?"

"Use your logic," Paul explained patiently. "When he came down from the fifth floor he pushed the first-floor button. Therefore, earlier in the evening, when he went up from the first floor he must have pushed the *fifth*-floor button. Does it penetrate?"

Fledge nodded his head doubtfully. Paul blew another smoke ring. "I'll repeat my other question. What did the Medical Examiner say about Seabrook's general physical condition?"

"He said it was rotten. Seabrook was a sick man."

"What does his doctor say?"

"Seabrook's doctor? That's this Dr. Herbert Martin, who found the body. I haven't asked him yet."

"Why haven't you asked him?"

"I didn't think it was important."

"You didn't think it was important!" Paul gave him one of those very annoying and-you're-supposed-to-have-brains looks and Fledge's face turned a livid shade of scarlet. Good tactics, thought Paul. Get him embarrassed. Impress him with his mediocrity and your own superiority. Mentally he patted himself on the back.

"When do you start questioning the suspects?" Fledge asked timidly.

"As soon as I find out what kind of a knife Seabrook was stabbed with."

"An ordinary pocket penknife. The murderer jabbed it in a few times."

"Fingerprints?"

"Not a single one. Only a few smudges, as if the man who handled the knife had been wearing gloves."

With a great deal of painful effort Paul pulled himself out of the chair. Inspector Fledge greeted the news that they would now question suspects with a great deal of pleasure. Paul knew why. The Inspector was known on the force as a suspect-pounder. He liked to squeeze information out of hostile witnesses. Sometimes he liked it even better than having the witness offer him the information in a perfectly friendly, cooperative manner.

"I've given instructions that no one in the building is to use the elevator," Fledge said. "But we can go up in it ourselves." They stepped into it, and Fledge pulled the door shut and then the steel elevator gate. His thumb stabbed the button marked five. "First, Mr. and Mrs. Philip Seabrook."

On the way up, Fledge pointed to a large X mark drawn in the very corner of the elevator in white chalk.

"That marks the spot where the body was found."

X marks the spot.

"Seabrook's body," the Inspector went on, "was kinda slumped up in the corner when Dr. Martin and Miss Kingsley first saw him. His back was against the wall, and the knife was sticking out his back."

The elevator had come to a stop. They walked out into the fifth-floor hallway.

"Five-E," said the Inspector, pushing a doorbell. "Now we can get busy solving this thing." Paul winced.

Paul Dawn had a way with suspects. He managed to extract more information from witnesses in his own quiet, unintentional way than the bulldozing, browbeating Stanley Fledge. Paul explained it by saying that he "caught them off guard," which is probably just as good an explanation as any.

Agnes Seabrook was a cute little blonde with a nice smile and a vacant head. Her husband was more the studious type. He was a short young man, slightly pudgy in spots, with big eyes peering out from behind dark-rimmed glasses. With the appearance of two representatives of the Law, he appeared to be rather flustered.

"And I'll say right now," he said hotly, "that this is getting to be downright annoying. Police dropping in every minute of the day to ask me stupid questions. I couldn't even get down to the office today."

"I'm really very sorry, Mr. Seabrook," Fledge said soothingly, "but routine is routine. I think I can promise you that this will be the last time we question you."

"It better be. Enough is enough. I'll say right now that—"

Fledge cleared his throat. "Now, Mr. Seabrook, will you tell me again what happened last night?"

"For the five-thousandth time—we had dinner with Uncle George, at nine o'clock he had to leave so we walked him to the elevator, the elevator came, he said goodbye, he pushed the button for the first floor, he said goodbye again, the elevator door closed. And that was that."

"Your neighbor, Mrs. Battleman, saw all this too?"

"Yeah. Old leather-puss came out to take in her evening paper.

Only I think she really wanted to catch a look at Uncle George. Big financier and all that. She's an old sneak, anyway."

"She is not an old sneak, Phil!" Mrs. Seabrook spoke up for the first time, indignantly. "She's a charming and cultured woman. And she's one of the nicest girls I know."

"Girls," Philip sneered. "If that 'girl' is a day under seventy-five I'll eat her bustle."

"You're absolutely certain that Mr. George Seabrook was alive when that elevator door closed?" Fledge asked.

"He didn't *look* dead," Agnes Seabrook said tentatively.

Philip drew himself up in what he meant to be a haughty manner. "I can still tell a live man from a corpse, Inspector," he said.

"Now," said Fledge, veering off on another tack, "what about motive? Mr. Seabrook, can you think of any possible reason why anyone should want to kill your uncle?"

"I'm sure I can't tell you." Philip glared at Fledge defiantly. "Seems to me that's your job, Inspector."

"So it is." Fledge turned to Agnes. "Can you think of any reason?"

"Of course," she said. "There are a lot of people who'd want to kill Uncle George."

"Ah! Who?"

"Well, Philip and myself, for instance."

Philip's face grew red. "You're a fool, Agnes!" he exploded.

"No, I'm not." She faced the Inspector. "You were bound to find out sooner or later. We didn't like George Seabrook. Not many people did. He was horribly conceited, pompous, self-righteous, possessive—that's about all the words I can think of. Anyway, that's the kind of awful old man he was. He didn't like Philip getting married to me, and when he did he decided he was going to give me a sort of six months' period of inspection. For the last six months, since we were married, George Seabrook has been inviting himself up to the apartment for dinner almost every week. And you know why? Just so he could look me over and see if he approved of me. Well, we didn't like that. We don't like being pawed over and dissected by a rich relative. There were times when I felt like killing him myself."

Here was a phenomenon, Paul thought. A dumb woman with brains. For lack of anything better to do, he decided to ask a question. "You'll pardon me, Mrs. Seabrook—" His voice was quiet enough but they all started at the sound of it. "I was just wondering—if you really detested your uncle so much, why did you tolerate him all this time?"

"Just what I was about to ask," Fledge said.

"Money!" Philip Seabrook burst out suddenly. "What did you think? Uncle George was a rich man and I'm not. But I was his only living relative. And if you can't follow it from there—"

"You stood to gain everything?" Fledge asked.

"I stood! I do get everything. Uncle's lawyer phoned me this morning. And I'm not particularly sorry or humble about it either. As a matter of fact, it's a relief that he's dead. I never did get Rockefeller's salary."

There was a strained pause.

Well, now, this is nice, thought Paul Dawn. It isn't often that he had a perfect motive, wrapped in a neat little bundle, deposited in his lap. But Inspector Fledge was hesitating. Under ordinary circumstances, a police officer would arrest a suspect on an admission like that. But not in this case. Fledge could do nothing. Paul smiled as he wondered how the Inspector was going to charge anybody with a murder that nobody could have committed.

With a sudden pang of worry, Paul wondered how he himself was going to figure this thing out. The fact remained. Somebody must have got into that elevator—except that nobody *could* have got into it.

"Have any questions before we leave, Paul?" said Fledge, rising.

"Uh—yes. Just one." He looked at the Seabrooks with that same sleepy expression. "Mr. or Mrs. Seabrook—perhaps you can tell me one thing. Can you think of a five-letter word meaning 'to fall prostrate' and the last letter is 't'?"

The very puzzled Seabrooks stared blankly and the two detectives left.

Out in the hallway, Fledge was completely bewildered. "Listen, Paul, are you sure you know what you're doing?"

"Maybe it was suicide," Paul muttered.

"Suicide!" Fledge spoke in a murderously calm voice. "And how, tell me, did our suicidal corpse *stab himself in the back?*"

"Perhaps," said Paul maliciously, "he was a contortionist."

Dr. Herbert Martin was one of those big, hearty, robust physicians who are never without their bedside manner. Paul and Fledge found him in his downtown office and were treated to an effusive greeting.

"Sit down, gentlemen! Glad to see you. Anything I can do to help?

Horrible affair, isn't it? Well, well, well. What is it you want to know?"

The doctor had a trick of rubbing his big hamlike hands together in a businesslike manner while speaking.

"We'd just like to know once more what happened, Doctor." Fledge was polite but still official.

"What happened? Now let me see." The doctor paused thoughtfully. "I'd just come back to the apartment from a call I'd been making. Patient was an old woman I've been treating for years. She's a hypochondriac and pays me a lot of money to tell her there's something the matter with her. She's as healthy as a horse, really. Healthier. But I've got to make a living. At any rate, I arrived at the house just as the elevator door was closing. I pushed the button and waited. The indicator started at the first floor and went up to the fifth. Then it started down again. Around that time, another tenant—a woman—arrived and we waited together."

"Miss Flora Kingsley?"

"So I discovered later. I'm new to the building and I don't usually get very friendly with neighbors anyway. Trouble with all us New Yorkers. Stick to ourselves too much. But that's beside the point. Miss Kingsley and I waited till the elevator reached our floor. It stopped and I pulled open the door. Then—I saw him." It seemed to Paul that Dr. Martin was trembling just slightly. "He was bunched up in the corner of the elevator, his back to the wall. I rushed toward him, but I told Miss Kingsley to stay back. She waited in the doorway and watched. I bent down by the body and saw the knife. She screamed. 'He's dead,' I said. 'Go phone the police.' At first she was frozen to the spot. I didn't want her to get hysterical, so I ordered her to phone the police. In a few minutes she returned and we waited together. Then you arrived, Inspector."

Convincing enough, Paul thought. "Doctor," he drawled, "you were George Seabrook's physician?"

"Yes. I was." Martin's gaze was level and unflinching.

"Wasn't in good health, was he?"

"No, he wasn't. He had heart trouble. Bad kidneys. Fainting spells. Bad headaches. A great deal of pain, I imagine."

"Enough pain, do you think, to make him commit suicide?"

The doctor hesitated a moment. Then finally he said, "Perhaps."

"That's not very definite."

"That's as definite as I care to be."

"Thank you, Dr. Martin."

"Oh, by the way," Martin said. "That's a puzzler, isn't it—how the murder was committed?"

"Certainly is," said Paul. "Talking of puzzlers, do you know a five-letter word meaning 'to fall prostrate'? The last letter is 't'."

"Crossword puzzles?" Martin said jovially. "Used to work them. I'm out of the habit these days."

"Do you know the word?" Paul inquired.

"No."

Paul could understand why Miss Flora Kingsley had remained a spinster all sixty years of her life. She had tight lips, a drawn white face, and two piercing, highly menacing eyes. She looked to Paul as if she had escaped from a Boris Karloff movie. And the fact that she wore her hair in a very modern fashion only served to increase the ghoulish effect.

"What do you want to ask me?" Miss Kingsley asked in a flat, metallic voice.

"Miss Kingsley, we'd just like your story of what happened last evening."

She told them in short, precise sentences as if she knew it by heart. It corroborated what Dr. Martin had told them almost exactly. Paul especially noticed how she described her reactions to the murder.

"I was quite broken up," she said. "Dr. Martin said that the man was dead, and after that I must have screamed. An exceedingly undignified thing to do."

"You used to work for Mr. Seabrook, Miss Kingsley?"

"Yes. I did." Her lips tightened. "Many years ago."

"Why did you leave him?"

"He retired from business."

"Do you know why?"

"No."

Paul spoke suddenly in a lazy voice. "Miss Kingsley, is it possible that Mr. Seabrook retired because his business failed?"

Her fingers gripped the side of her chair.

"Yes. That's possible."

"And wasn't there a rumor at the time that the reason his business failed was because Mr. Seabrook had been drawing illegally from the funds of his stockholders?"

"It was never proved!" she cried, jumping to her feet. It was her

first sign of emotion. She subsided wearily into the chair. "I'm sorry,"
she said. "Yes. I'd heard that."

"You believed it?"

She nodded her head.

"Thank you. Uh—do you ever do crossword puzzles, Miss Kingsley?"

She looked at him with a very suspicious expression for a moment.
Then her face hardened. She rose to her feet and faced both of them
squarely.

"Would you gentlemen leave now?"

"You didn't answer my question," Paul said gently.

"No, I didn't, did I? Good afternoon."

They were in police headquarters that evening.

"Blind alleys!" Stanley Fledge shouted. "Dead ends!" Stanley
Fledge yelled. "Stone walls!" Stanley Fledge screamed. "And elevators! Damn it all, that's what gets me. I could take each one of
them and sweat it out of them—if I only had some sort of a clue
about the elevator. How did the murderer get into that elevator?
What happened? Am I going nuts? Am I dreaming all this? *How did
the murderer get into that elevator?*"

"The murderer didn't get into that elevator," said Paul very
calmly.

Fledge's mouth fell open; his eyes bulged.

"What?"

"I said the murderer didn't get into that elevator."

"Do you know how it was done?"

Paul Dawn lit a cigarette with a steady hand. He puffed once and
let the smoke pour out of his nostrils. "I knew how it was done some
time ago. The question was," he said, "to prove it."

"And did you—" Fledge gulped helplessly "—did you prove it?"

"I did. Come up to my office tomorrow morning and find out all
about it." He rose from his chair. "You'd better come early. At ten-
thirty the morning paper arrives, and I'll be very busy—doing the
crossword puzzle."

Paul Dawn kept a bottle of scotch in his desk drawer—for medic-
inal purposes. After he learned what the real solution was, Inspector
Fledge was astounded enough to dispose of half the bottle in three
large gulps.

"It's so simple," Paul said. "So easy. I really saw it all the time."

And it *was* simple. Very simple. But ingenious, Paul hastened to add. It was especially ingenious the way he explained it.

"All you've got to do is look at it with imagination. That's why these impossible crimes are right up my alley. I might not have a lot of things. Initiative or energy. But I certainly have imagination."

Inspector Fledge would be the last to deny it.

"Here's the way it really happened," Paul said. "In solving these impossible murders we've got to take a hard, unsentimental view. You've got to discount ghosts, or invisible men, or complicated contraptions operated by radio control. You've got to get it into your head that *there is no such thing as an impossible murder.*

"That's what I got into my head right from the start. George Seabrook was killed. Someone entered that elevator and shoved a knife into his back. In order to enter the elevator the murderer had to come in, obviously, by an entrance. There is, however, only one entrance to the elevator. You searched it through and through yourself. You found only one entrance. I searched it through and through. I found only one entrance. That entrance is the elevator door. Therefore the murderer must have entered when the elevator door was open.

"But it's impossible for the elevator door to be open while the elevator is in motion, and in the course of this affair the elevator door was open only twice. It was open while the elevator was on the fifth floor, and while the elevator was on the first floor. Therefore George Seabrook was killed while the elevator was either on the fifth floor or on the first floor.

"Well, let's see about these two times. When Seabrook got into the elevator he was alive. When he pushed the elevator button he was alive. When the door closed he was alive. Three different people confirmed that, including a woman who can be considered an outsider. From this we conclude that Seabrook couldn't have been killed while the elevator was on the fifth floor.

"So he must have been killed while the elevator was on the first floor!"

"But as soon as the elevator door opened at the first floor," objected Fledge, "two different witnesses *saw* Seabrook lying on the floor with a knife in his back!"

"Did they? That is where we've been making our mistake all along. What do we know, and what are we only surmising? The witnesses say that Seabrook was lying on the floor with a knife in his back. But the witnesses only saw Seabrook from the elevator doorway.

Seabrook's back was toward the wall. Actually all that *both* of these witnesses saw was Seabrook lying on the floor. Miss Kingsley was standing in the doorway all the time. Contrary to what she says, she couldn't possibly have seen that knife in Seabrook's back."

Fledge waved his hand at Paul like a child asking to be called on in class. "Hold on!" the Inspector said. "The action is moving too fast for me. So what if Miss Kingsley didn't see the knife—Dr. Martin did!"

"Did he?" Paul paused and smiled with satisfaction. "That's exactly my point, Fledge. Did Dr. Martin see the knife in Seabrook's back, or did Dr. Martin merely say that he saw a knife in Seabrook's back?

"Let's piece together the facts. Martin says that Miss Kingsley screamed and then he said, 'He's dead!' Miss Kingsley says that Martin said 'He's dead!' first, and *then* she screamed. Why should one of them lie? It's my guess that Martin lied because he made that exclamation 'He's dead!' for a purpose. He cried out 'He's dead!' in order psychologically to plant in Miss Kingsley's mind the false idea that she had seen Seabrook dead, when all she had really seen was Seabrook lying on the floor.

"Well, knowing that Seabrook wasn't dead, what *was* wrong with him? And there comes one of the greatest twists of fate that I have ever encountered in my life. Remember my five-letter word meaning 'to fall prostrate', the last letter a 't'. Well, that's exactly what Seabrook did. He gave me my definition. He 'fell prostrate'. He *fainted!*

"Don't you see? Seabrook had one of his fainting spells while going down in the elevator. Dr. Martin said he was subject to them. When the elevator reached the first floor, Martin saw Seabrook lying there. He realized instantly what had happened. An idea sprang to his mind. He saw how he could take advantage of the fact that Seabrook had fainted in an elevator.

"Immediately he began to play up the idea that Seabrook was dead, all for Miss Kingsley's benefit. He rushed over to the body. He shouted 'He's dead!' He pointed to an imaginary knife in Seabrook's back that Miss Kingsley couldn't possibly see because of the body's position. All the time he kept her at a safe distance from Seabrook. He made it all seem very cold-blooded and realistic. By the time Dr. Martin had finished his little scene he had poor Miss Kingsley actually believing she had seen a corpse.

"Then he got rid of her—he ordered her to phone the police.

"This is another point against Dr. Martin. He was the only one in the whole bunch who was alone with Seabrook from the moment the old man got into that elevator.

"While Miss Kingsley was phoning, Martin bent down beside Seabrook and put on his doctor's rubber gloves. He had them in his medical bag. And we know he had his medical bag with him because he had just come back from a call. He put on the gloves, stabbed Seabrook in the back, and put the gloves back in the bag.

"Martin probably felt absolutely safe. As long as Miss Kingsley held up—and he was sure she would—he had nothing to worry about. Because she could always alibi him by testifying that Seabrook was dead at a time when Martin couldn't possibly have killed him. Get it?"

Inspector Fledge was breathing deeply, and he started to mop the sweat off his brow. "Now only one more point. Tell me the motive and I'll put the handcuffs on Dr. Martin."

"The motive," Paul Dawn said, "was staring us in the face all the time. Miss Kingsley confirmed the fact that Seabrook's business had once gone bankrupt owing to Seabrook's shady dealings. A lot of stockholders lost money in that collapse, and it's conceivable that one of them would hold a grudge for a long, long time. Look up Martin's past, why don't you?"

"I'd better hurry off now," said Inspector Fledge heartily, "and do my duty. Oh, by the way, this has been somewhat of a strain. You don't happen to have a bit of liquid refreshment, do you?"

Paul did. And that was when the Inspector emptied half the bottle.

Lillian de la Torre

Dr. Sam: Johnson, Detector

(As related by James Boswell in 1784)

On the night of March 23, 1784, the Great Seal of England was stolen out of Lord Chancellor Thurlow's house in Great Ormonde Street, and was never seen again. In August of that year, Lord Chancellor Thurlow very graciously intimated to the friends of Dr. Johnson that that learned philosopher might draw against him at need for as much as £600.

The connexion between these two events forms a part of secret history. In that history I, James Boswell of Auchinleck, advocate, played a not inconsiderable part; and my learned friend, Sam: Johnson, displayed at large his inimitable powers of ratiocination and penetration, the more that he was then confined to his dwelling with a dropsical condition, complicated by asthma, that was soon to prove mortal.

In early March I was at York, and in two minds whether to press on to London or to retreat to Edinburgh. News that Parliament was about to be prorogued, with a general election to follow, inclined one of my broad principles to return to my home port to weather the storm; but then I should miss seeing Mannering hang. Mannering was the last of the Tyburn hangings, a gallant and a duellist, and he was to hang for spitting his man and missing the French packet.

I sat long in the ordinary at York, weighing my principles against the last of the Tyburn shows; and in the end I rode post for London to be in at the death. I rode up to Tyburn as dawn was breaking, and saw all from the spectator's gallery.

Had I not done so, I had missed the greatest of Dr. Johnson's feats of ratiocination. For coming away from the gallows while the mob was still shouting, I encountered George Selwyn in the press, and he carried me in his coach as far as St. James's Street; and there I met Lord Chancellor Thurlow coming out of Brooks's arm in arm with Charles James Fox; and that in itself was a portent of stranger things to come.

The Tory Chancellor was composed and sardonic. His swarthy

skin was cool and his black eyes were watchful under their bushy brows. The Whig leader was deucedly foxed, his usual condition at that hour of any morning. He was rumpled and bleary, and his bushy hair stood on end. He was also in a complaining frame of mind.

"Look at him," he complained, gesturing at Thurlow in a way that threatened him with immersion in the kennel. "Look at 'm. Been standing by the gaming tables all night long. Wha's he got? Got his pockets full, tha's what. Looka me. Been standing by him all night long. Gaming? No. Mustn't game, Mrs. Armistead says. Gaming's ruin. Me, I been drinking. Stanning right by him, he's gaming, I'm drinking. Wha's he got? Got his pockets full. Wha've I got? Got my snout full. Armistead's all wrong. Never make that mistake again. Whoosh."

A final windmill gesture set him on his broad rump on the pavement. His grievances continued to run through his head.

"Pocket full o'money, and going to pro—prorogue Parliament tomorrow an' send all the Whigs home to stay."

"You say true, Mr. Fox," replied Thurlow icily, "for there's not a borough in England will return a Whig to the new Parliament."

Fox slewed him a quick look. It occurred to me that he was not so incapacitated as he seemed.

"A wager," he cried. "A rump and dozen that I'm returned for Westminster. Guineas to shillings Parliament an't prorogued. My head to a turnip you lose the seals, you trimming half-faced Tory."

He swayed to his feet. His contorted face was diabolic in the red light of dawn. Then it dissolved into a silly grin. He wagged his head to himself.

"These proposals," says Thurlow, still calmly, "would hardly meet the approval of Mrs. Armistead."

"Keep your tongue off Armistead," said Fox surlily. "Who are you to talk?"

Thurlow's eyebrows went up; then he shrugged and turned his back.

"A night at Brooks's," he remarked, "is a night wasted among Whigs and scoundrels; and a pocketful of guineas off the gaming tables is poor enough pay. Pray, Mr. Boswell, will you ride along with me to Great Ormonde Street and break your fast?"

I accepted with alacrity; and so it fell out that I played a part in the strange events of secret history which I am about to narrate. The Chancellor entered his coach, and we were carried at a smart pace toward Great Ormonde Street.

As I drove along at Thurlow's side, I reflected with some awe on the inscrutable ways of Providence, that I, a poor Scotch advocate, should be breaking my fast on terms of intimacy with the Lord Chancellor of England and the Keeper of the Great Seal. I thought with indescribable emotion of the sacred nature of the Great Seal, and I resolved to beg a sight of it, that I might record for posterity the feelings of a man of sensibility on beholding that aweful symbol of Kingly authority.

Accordingly I led the discourse subtly in that direction.

"Pray, my lord," I began, "inform me whether the Great Seal is not necessary to the dissolution of Parliament?"

"It is always affixed to the King's writ of whatever kind," replied Thurlow. "Ha! 'Twill *seal* the fate of the d——d dastardly Whigs, I promise you."

Lord Thurlow is noted for his profane swearing. I ignored it, and followed him as he stepped from his carriage and mounted his elegant stair in Great Ormonde Street.

"Pray, my lord," I continued as best I could for climbing, "could you not gratify me with a sight of the Great Seal, for I have never seen it?"

"Nothing is easier," replied Thurlow, "for when all is said and done 'tis no more than a handful of soft metal, and I always keep it by me. Pray step this way."

I followed the saturnine Chancellor into a study on the first floor. The walls were lined with elegant authors in calf bindings. Opposite the door stood a graceful writing bureau, its drawer half open. Beside it stood something covered with a green baize cloth. Thurlow twitched away the cloth, and with an easy movement handed me a heavy club surmounted by a crown. My wrist snapped with its weight.

"'Tis the Mace!" I cried between awe and delight.

"'Tis the Mace," assented Thurlow carelessly, "and well it is that 'tis borne before the Chancellor by a bravo with a porter's knot, for I've known many a d——d puny little monkey of a Lord Keeper who could not have wielded it to save his life. Now the Seal is lighter."

He drew out the half open drawer, and his face changed. A sickly green came up in his swarthy cheeks, and his voice dried in his throat. I made bold to peer over his shoulder. The drawer was empty.

Or rather, not quite empty. In it lay two bags, turned back and tossed down like carelessly drawn-off gloves. One bag was of leather;

the other was a precious and costly purse of silk, richly embroidered and bejewelled.

Both bags were empty. The Great Seal was gone.

The Lord Chancellor stood like one struck to stone while one might have counted to three. Then he damned the Whigs. He damned them for a thieving, scoundrelly pack of highway robbers, with no fear of their God or their King. He damned them for breaking and entering, for debauching the electorate, and for picking pockets. He promised to have them pilloried, lampooned, and disfranchised. All the time he was turning out the drawers of the bureau and searching the room. 'Twas useless. The Great Seal of England was gone.

"Boswell," cried Thurlow, "do you mount guard here, lest the d——d thieving Whigs come back for the Mace. I charge you, don't stir for your life. If the dogs are in the house, I'll rout them out." With a solemn sense of responsibility, I kept close watch over the sacred symbol of majesty.

I thought long till Thurlow returned. The house was quiet as the grave. Once I thought someone stood in the doorway behind me; but when I whirled, there was nothing. Once I thought Thurlow had apprehended the Whigs indeed, for there was a great clatter belowstairs and the sound of Thurlow swearing. But again the solemn silence supervened; and in a few moments more the troubled chancellor returned.

"All is clear, Boswell," said he, his old truculent composure restored. "The miscreants have escaped. Come with me."

He dusted the rusty streaks from his palms, locked the drawers of the cabinet, and led me below to the domestic offices. There he showed me how the bars of the back kitchen window had been wrenched loose. I looked at the loosened bars lying in the court below under the open window, and shook my head over the pools of plaster lying on the kitchen floor.

"With bars at every window, surely a man ought to be safe from the d——d Whigs," he muttered.

"This is clearly a matter for the philosophical mind of Dr. Johnson," I cried. "I will wait upon him at once."

" 'Tis a matter for the bailiffs," responded Thurlow surlily, "they shall wait upon the b——y b——y Whigs at once."

I wondered if he meant Mr. Fox, and so my mind turned to Parliamentary affairs.

"What will come of this?" I queried. "How is Parliament to be prorogued?"

"I'll prorogue 'em," cried Thurlow grimly. "I'll find a way to send the scoundrels home. But I must search out precedents. I'll go straight off to Downing Street and consult Pitt."

"And I," said I, "will go straight off to Bolt Court and consult Dr. Johnson."

"Do so," responded Thurlow, "and I'll come after you as swiftly as I may."

I found Dr. Johnson lying late in his bed-gown, with a kerchief on his grizzled head. He stared as I burst into his chamber.

"Bozzy!" he exclaimed, "What brings you to London? 'Pon my life, 'tis some weighty affair of state. By the bulging of your eyes, you are big with news of the great world. Well, well, I will hear it."

The tone of raillery piqued me. Composing my countenance, therefore, I seated myself and enquired politely for my venerable friend's state of health.

"The indisposition is abated," replied Johnson impatiently. "Come, Bozzy, your news! What brings you to London?"

"To see Mannering hang."

JOHNSON: "And did he hang with a good grace?"

BOSWELL: "He did not hang."

JOHNSON: "So you were cheated of your entertainment after all."

BOSWELL: "No, sir, my entertainment was very well. All the world and his wife was there, with my Lady Lanchester that Mannering fought for supported by three gallants in the forefront, and the dead man's brothers glowering at the gallows foot. 'Twas a noble sight to see Mannering smile on them and never turn a hair, with his arms bound at his sides and the man of God mumbling beside him and the cart ready to move off and leave him dangling."

JOHNSON: "Why, is not this better than turning a man off huggermugger at Newgate, as the new law requires? Why must we do without the procession to Tyburn? The public is gratified with the procession; the criminal is supported by it. Why must it be swept away?"

BOSWELL: "I know not; but so it must be."

JOHNSON: "But come, Bozzy, be not so close-mouthed. How came Mannering so near the other world, and yet remains in this?"

I own I was tired of my tale, and longed to astound my friend with the grave news which was agitating me. I had no more time for Mannering.

"Why, sir," said I, "thus it was. At the very point when Mannering had perforce to give over his strutting and his ogling and let the handkerchief fall, comes a cry from the crowd *A reprieve, a reprieve;* though 'twas in truth no reprieve, but the King's pardon engrossed at large with the yellow wax on the tapes; and Mannering kissed the boy that had brought it, and rode away in his coach as he had come, with never a glance at my Lady Lanchester. As for her, she let out a screech and fell into a swoon; and 'tis all the talk that it has come to mortal hatred between them, and that the dead man's brothers will kill Mannering sure if he remains in England."

"Why, so," says Dr. Johnson, "this is a docket indeed, and George Selwyn himself could not have told it better; though indeed it falls something short of the great affairs I thought you big with."

This was my opportunity.

"Pray sir," I said quietly, "what news would content you? How if I tell you that the Great Seal of England has been stolen, and that I was by when the loss was discovered?"

Dr. Johnson was thunderstruck. A staunch Tory, and a great supporter of Kingly authority, he appreciated to the full the infamy of the deed. I presented Lord Thurlow's request for the assistance of my friend's known acumen; to which he replied:

"I am an old man, Bozzy, and my infirmities gain upon me; but I solemnly declare that I will neither repose nor recruit till I shall have put the Great Seal of England into Lord Thurlow's hand."

Rising, he summoned Francis Barber to bring his clothes; and as he dressed and broke his fast with me, I told him all the circumstances of the audacious theft.

He heard me through in silence, shaking his head and rolling his great frame the while. Only when I had finished did he question me.

"The domestic offices are on the lowest floor?"

"Yes, sir."

"And the writing-bureau on the floor above?"

"That is so, sir."

"The bars of the window were dislodged and fell to the ground?"

"Yes, sir. I ought to say that the window faces the open fields, whence the house-breakers are supposed to have come."

"And plaster and rubbish lay on the kitchen floor? Sparse, or thick? Under the window, or more generally dispersed?"

"Thick, sir, under the window, and sparser where it had been tracked into the passage."

"Footprints?"

"No, sir, only a line of faint smudges, as it might be off the boots of a man who had stood in plaster; and indeed Lord Thurlow and I made such another track when we came away from the window."

"The servants?"

"All in their beds on the lowest floor. Lord Thurlow rouzed them as we came away."

"Had they heard aught in the night?"

"Nothing, they said."

"Yet a band of Whigs broke in and abstracted the Great Seal. Pray, whom of his household has Lord Thurlow about him?"

"I know not. His irregular connexion with Mrs. Hervey is well-known; but I never saw her, nor any of her children."

Dr. Johnson shook his head in dissatisfaction. There was a summons below, and my friend's black servant announced Lord Thurlow. We descended to him in the panelled drawing-room, where the sage and the politician greeted one another with great mutual respect.

Though separated in age by upwards of twenty years, these two famous men were not unlike: Thurlow tall, strong-built, of a saturnine cast, with sharp black eyes under beetling brows; Johnson as tall, but more massive, his heavy face marred by the King's evil. If Johnson roared, Thurlow thundered. The one had met his match in the other, and they were mighty civil and polite together.

"Well, Dr. Johnson, what think you of this outrage?" demanded the Lord Chancellor. "But the d——d thieving Whigs shan't make good their purpose, I promise you. I have taken the opinions of Gower and Kenyon; a new Seal is making, and Parliament shall be prorogued tomorrow. So all is happily resolved, and we'll send the d——d Whigs home to stay in spite of their teeth. Mr. Boswell, Dr. Johnson, I thank you for your good offices in this matter, and beg that you'll discommode yourselves no further over it."

"Surely, Lord Thurlow," protested my Tory friend, "the matter is not to end thus. Have you taken no steps for the apprehension of the thief?"

"You mistake me, Dr. Johnson," replied Lord Thurlow. "One Lee, a notorious receiver of stolen goods, is under our eye. We think to take him in the fact, if we but have patience. But my first care is to send the rascally Whigs packing; and this we may do, for the new Seal will be ready by nightfall."

"Pray, Lord Thurlow," replied Dr. Johnson, "indulge me. I am no thief-taker, but I have had my successes as a detector of problems, and I have sworn to lay the stolen Seal in your hand. Pray let me have your answer to a question or two."

"I will do so, Dr. Johnson; but pray be brief, for I have yet to wait upon his majesty."

"Tell me, then: the Great Seal was customarily preserved in a bag?"

"Two bags, Dr. Johnson, of silk and of leather, the one within the other."

"How were they secured?"

"With a thong or draw-string."

"The silk bag was costly?"

"That is so. It is enriched with gems and bullion, and cost upwards of fifty guineas."

"So that the thief," said Dr. Johnson meditatively, "though 'twas worth his life to be found there, lingered so long as would serve to untie, not one bag, but two, that he might leave behind him fifty guineas worth of booty; when he might in a single motion have pocketed bags, Seal, and all, and made good his escape. This is a strange sort of thief, and one who cannot hope to rise in his profession. A practised thief will disdain no loot that comes to his hand."

"Nor did he so," said Lord Thurlow quickly, "for he carried off my silver sword-hilts, and a matter of £35 in fees, that were laid up in the writing-bureau."

I looked my surprise at this news.

" 'Tis a bagatelle, to the loss of the Seal," continued Thurlow, "and I have given it scant attention; but such is my personal loss, out of the drawers that were ransacked."

"One more question, then," said Dr. Johnson. "Who of your family were at home with you in Great Ormonde Street?"

Thurlow looked like a thundercloud.

"How can this be to the purpose, Dr. Johnson?" he enquired stiffly.

"Pray, my lord, do not hinder me," said Dr. Johnson firmly, "for I am resolved to get to the bottom of this matter, whatever I may find there."

Thurlow looked blacker still, but he replied to the question:

"Why sir, Mrs. Hervey is taking the waters at Bath, and my little girl with her. My household at present is only my daughters Catharine and Caroline, and my cousin Gooch's boy, Ned Durban."

"What's he?"

"Why, sir, he's a young springald come to me for old times' sake to be made a man of fashion; though indeed 'tis all in vain, for the d——d stubborn young dog is a Whig and a gamester, and I can make nothing of him."

"Pray, Lord Thurlow, make these young people known to me."

Lord Thurlow rose from his place.

"Very well, Dr. Johnson, if you wish it. Will you come down to Great Ormonde Street?"

"No, sir, I will not. I am a dropsical old man, and I cannot gallop about London like a Bow Street runner. You must be my courier, and send Great Ormonde Street to me."

"Let it be as you wish," said Lord Thurlow coldly; and left us with scant ceremony.

The morning was half gone when a hackney coach deposited a young lady and a young gentleman at the mouth of Bolt Court. I watched them from the two pair of stair windows as they crossed the court. The young lady was sombrely dressed and cloaked in black to her heels. Her companion, thin and shambling, was gorgeous in mulberry brocade from his wig to his buckled shoes. He made play with a muff and a clouded cane. He handed his companion carefully up the steps and supported her into the withdrawing room, where Dr. Johnson received them.

"Your servant, Dr. Johnson," lisped he of the clouded cane, and made a leg, "Ned Durban at your service. Here's Caroline."

"Miss Thurlow," said Dr. Johnson gently, "I bid you welcome."

The girl in the black cape looked at him mutely. She was very young, not more than fifteen, with pale ivory skin showing dark shadows under the eyes. She wore her own soft dark hair, not a made head, but swept back any how. She was dressed in gray tabby, without ornament.

Gravely Dr. Johnson led her to his deep wing chair. She sat gingerly on the edge, and looked at Ned Durban. The exquisite youth came to her, and took her hand.

"Never fear, my dear," he said gently, "you are to answer what Dr. Johnson asks; he won't hurt you. He only wants to find the Great Seal."

The dark eyes turned to Dr. Johnson.

"Truly, truly, sir, I know nothing of the Seal."

"Nor I, sir," added Durban; "but ask me what you please."

I was liking the shambling exquisite a little better, when he fell to sucking the head of his cane.

"Then tell me, pray," began Dr. Johnson, "how you have spent your time since yesterday."

Durban left off sucking his cane, and replied:

"Strap me, sir, 'twas a rare night for me, for I never once saw the inside of Brooks's, though I have a card there, and seldom miss. But last night I carried my cousins to sup at Ranelagh, and so on to the masquerade in Oxford Street; and so it fell out we three were together till the east showed gray."

"All the time?"

"From supper till morning."

"Pray tell me, sir, is it your custom to squire your ladies so closely?"

Durban cackled, and replied:

"There you have me, Dr. Johnson. 'Twas the first masquerade from which I have failed to follow one or other devastating little mask and let the rest go hang. But, d'ye see, sir, little Caroline here was half beside herself, and Cathy and I in dejection, and we just sat one by another and watched the masquers, until near dawn we could bear it no longer and came away home together."

"How late?"

"Perhaps an hour before sunrise."

"And you then retired?" enquired Dr. Johnson.

"Yes, sir. I had half a mind to the hanging, but the thought of it was so deuced dumpish and depressing, in the end I carried a bottle to bed with me, and the next thing I remember my Uncle Thurlow was shaking me and bidding me rise and come down to Bolt Court."

"And you, my dear?" Dr. Johnson turned to Caroline Thurlow.

She looked at Ned, and he squeezed her hand and nodded at her.

" 'Twas as Ned said," she faltered.

"And after? When you came home?"

"I went to my bed."

"Do you lie alone? Or with your sister?"

"With my sister," whispered the white-faced girl.

"Well, my dear, and so you fell asleep and slept till mid-morning."

"No, sir. I lay awake and watched the day break. I couldn't sleep."

"And you heard nothing?"

"Yes, sir, I heard a great clatter and a rending sound. It made me afraid. My window fronts the fields, and sometimes men fight there."

"Did you look out?"

"Oh, good lack, no sir. I hid my head under the counterpane."

"What an unlucky chance," I exclaimed. "You might else have detected the thieves."

"When was this rending sound, my dear?" enquired Dr. Johnson.

"I cannot say, sir. I had lain awake for hours, and the sun was risen."

"And your sister slept by you?"

"All the night, sir. But it was morning before I slept, and when I awoke she was gone."

"Whither?"

Caroline looked at my benevolent friend without speaking. Durban answered for her.

"O lud, sir, who knows where a lady goes o' mornings? To the milliners, to pay calls, I know not what. She is to follow us when she returns."

"She comes pat upon her cue, sir," I reported from the window, "for here is Lord Thurlow crosssing the court, and with him a most exquisite lady of fashion."

" 'Tis Cathy," said little Miss Thurlow wistfully, "for Cathy's eighteen, and a reigning toast."

Cathy came into the sombre panelled room like a queen. She wore lavender lutestring, and a made head full twelve inches high, powdered and picked out with plumes. She was a sparkling girl with her father's eyes. I bent over her hand as Dr. Johnson saluted the Lord Chancellor.

"Why, Cathy," said Caroline. "Where ever have you been? All the time I lay awake you were snoring, and as soon as I slept you rose up and left me."

"Nowhere," said Cathy. "Everywhere. What do you think, Cathy, the mantua-maker has the impudence to be indisposed! What am I to wear to the ball tonight?"

Thurlow greeted his little daughter tenderly.

"What, poppet, look up, my dear. Never fret about the Seal. The new one is as good as made, and there's no harm done."

"Nevertheless the Seal is to be found," said Dr. Johnson. "I have taken so much upon myself."

"I take this resolve very kindly of you," said Thurlow cordially, "nevertheless I would not have you fatigue yourself unduly."

"Nay, sir," replied Dr. Johnson, "we progress, and without fatigue. I have learned much about this strange thief, who does his housebreaking by day-light, who takes the Seal and leaves the Mace and the jewelled bag. Pray, answer me one question more: when did you last see the Great Seal?"

"Why," says Thurlow, "last sealing-day."

"Recollect yourself, sir. I think it was when you sealed Mannering's pardon."

"That is so, sir," replied Thurlow instantly.

"And I think that was done last night, else how comes it that it nearly came too late?"

"Prodigious, Dr. Johnson! Again you are right. The document came late from the engrosser's. 'Twas close on midnight, and I sealed it then and there and sent it by hand to the unfortunate man's friends."

"And did you then deposit the Seal in the bureau?"

"I did, sir," replied Thurlow.

"And was anybody by to observe these transactions?"

"Sir!" began Thurlow angrily.

"Pray, Papa, no heroics," said Cathy languidly. "I was by, Dr. Johnson. I helped. I served as chaffwax, as I have often done before—haven't I, Carly —*Carly!*"

Every head turned to the winged chair. Caroline's face was the colour of lead. Her eyes were closed, and her breath came shallow.

"The child's fainted!" cried Thurlow angrily. "Come, Dr. Johnson, a truce to this inquisition."

Catharine moved stiffly to her sister—stiffly from the effort of carrying her stately powdered head—and cut her stays with despatch and decision. Ned Durban laid her tenderly on the sofa, and gradually her breath and her colour returned. She opened her eyes, looked into his face above her, and burst into a storm of weeping. As he smiled tenderly into Caroline's eyes, muff or no muff, I liked the boy.

Miss Thurlow's indisposition put an end to my acute friend's researches for that while. Catharine donned a green baize apron belonging among Francis Barber's kitchen gear, and with her own hands made a posset for her sister; and very strange she looked in her lavender lutestring with the plumes in her powdered head.

Soon Caroline was sitting up. Her weeping fit had done her good. There was pink in her cheeks, and a smile began to play about her lips. Nevertheless, Dr. Johnson swore that she must not be moved, but the whole company must stay and dine. Thurlow excused himself on the ground of much business; but Caroline consented, and Ned and Catharine elected to stay with her. Francis Barber was to be sent to the ordinary to bespeak chickens and sweetbreads.

The Lord Chancellor then took his leave, promising Dr. Johnson a sight of the new Seal before suppertime. I offered to accompany him, if I could be of use; and he gratefully closed with my offer. So I departed with the Lord Chancellor; and of my doings that afternoon suffice it to say that my usefulness was all in fetching and carrying, fetching and carrying.

I returned to Bolt Court as evening was falling. I found Dr. Johnson on the step taking leave of a visitor; and so I greeted for the second time that day Charles James Fox, the fascinating and beloved Whig leader.

This was a different Fox, however; fresh from the hands of his man, wigged and point-device; with his irresistible smile on his broad lively-looking face.

"You may set your mind at rest, sir," Dr. Johnson was saying. "I promise you no one shall suffer for the sequestration of the Great Seal, save alone him who destroys it."

"Then I will promise you," rejoined Fox in his rich voice, "that no Whig has it, no Whig took it, and no Whig will destroy it. 'Tis my belief, Dr. Johnson, that the surly Chancellor himself could tell us much, if he would."

"Lord Thurlow has already told me much," replied Dr. Johnson, "and the matter approaches its end. But pray gratify my curiosity in one particular. Boswell here tells me that Thurlow spent last night with you at Brooks's. How can this be, that a staunch Tory should be found in the Whig stronghold?"

Fox laughed.

"He came by that way after supper," he replied, "to threaten me, in his amiable way, about Ned Durban, who is personally attached to my party, and of great use to me. When he was announced, Jack Wilkes tipped me a wink, and laid me guineas to crowns I could not make so good a Whig of him as to keep him in the club till dawn. Well, sir, I never refuse a wager; and a hundred guineas is more than curling-paper money. It took all my finesse to get him to the tables; and there I guarded him like gold till the night was spent. 'Twas hardest of all to see him winning, and lay no stakes myself, but I dared not. Had I begun gaming, he might have walked away, and I would never have followed. Jack Wilkes was by, and saw fair play; and when the light began to come in at the windows, he paid down my guineas on the nail, and I got Thurlow out of Brooks's and consigned him to the devil, for I don't like the man."

"You never left his side?"

"I stood by the black-browed Tory from ten in the evening till daylight, and 'tis a task that's ill-paid at a hundred guineas."

"One question more: how knew you that I was employed in the matter?"

Fox smiled blandly.

"Nothing Thurlow does," he replied, "is unknown to the Whig leaders; and at this very moment, I'll lay a guinea, someone is telling Thurlow that Fox has called at Bolt Court."

"Well, sir," says Dr. Johnson, "I will serve you, if I may serve justice at the same time."

" 'Tis all I ask," replied Fox, "for indeed whether the old curmudgeon has made away with it himself, and blames the Whigs, or whether a thief has it indeed, and Thurlow has put about this Whig story to turn it to his own ends, 'tis all one to me; the Whigs have it not."

"You may set your mind at rest, sir," replied Dr. Johnson; and the Whig leader took his leave.

"What, Bozzy," exclaimed Dr. Johnson, peering into my face as he gave me welcome, "you're again great with news."

"That is so, sir," I exclaimed eagerly as we mounted the stair.

"Stop, I will tell you," said Dr. Johnson, "there was a felonious entry at the Petty Bag in Rolls Yard last night."

"There was indeed," said I, dumbfounded, "but—"

"But nothing was taken," finished Dr. Johnson.

But I still had a couple of crumbs.

" 'Tis thought," I told him, "that they looked to find the Great Seal there, for 'tis there they have the engrossing of pardons and such-like; but they had their labour for their pains, and so went away to the Chancellor's house, and there fared better."

"Do you say so?" said Dr. Johnson politely.

"Furthermore," I concluded triumphantly at the drawing-room door, "Lee, the receiver of stolen goods, is taken, and will be arraigned for purchasing the stolen Seal. 'Tis said he had it of a woman for forty guineas."

"So the Seal is found!" exclaimed Johnson, thunderstruck.

"No, sir. 'Tis feared it is into the melting-pot already."

Johnson opened the panelled door, and we entered the room. I bent low over Catharine Thurlow's hand. She had been crying, but she was more beautiful than ever with a last tear sparkling in her eye, and her glossy dark hair in little ringlets all over her proud little head. She reminded me of an ancient statue—or a portrait—what was it?—something I had seen recently.

Dr. Johnson was most assiduous in his attentions to both the ladies. The Whig Maccaroni fondled his muff and smiled at vacancy. I had my mouth open to sound the opinion of the Great Cham on the strange events just passed, when Francis Barber announced Lord Thurlow, the latter coming in briskly on his heels with a leathern bag in his hand.

"Now, sir," said Thurlow, "we'll prorogue 'em—" he brandished the leathern bag "—we'll prorogue 'em and send the d——d dog-stealing Whigs back to their kennels. Here's the little beauty will do it."

"The new Seal!" I exclaimed.

"Ay," said Thurlow, handing the leathern bag to my learned friend, "the new Great Seal. 'Tis a replica of the old one, and equally as handsome, brass though it may be."

My near-sighted friend carried the bags to the window. The leathern bag yielded a silk purse of exquisite workmanship; the silk purse yielded a heavy disc of yellow metal.

"You say true," remarked Dr. Johnson, hunching his shoulders as he peered at it in the light from the sky, "this is not to be told from goldsmith's work."

He passed the heavy thing to me, and I at last beheld, albeit of brass and hastily constructed, the GREAT SEAL OF ENGLAND.

I gazed with indescribable emotion on the sacred person of George III, represented as seated on a charger; on the obverse the same, seated in state. I handed the heavy metal disc to the young ladies. Caroline regarded it with wondering eyes; but Catharine shrugged her slim shoulders.

"This is no nine-days' wonder," she said indifferently. " 'Tis no different from the other one."

She yielded it back to my friend.

"Francis," called Dr. Johnson from the passage, bagging the Great Seal the while, "pray let us have our tea."

"I cannot drink tea with you," said Thurlow instantly, "for I am on my way to Downing Street with the new Seal; but my daughters may do so, and I will send the carriage back for them."

"Very well, my lord," responded Dr. Johnson, "I rejoice that the crisis is happily over, and we may drink our tea with light hearts."

"So?" says Thurlow, "have you, then, given over your determination to lay the Great Seal in my hand?"

"Sir," says Dr. Johnson. "The Great Seal is but metal, till the King's will gives it life; and so I hold that the disc you carry there in its bag is in very truth the Great Seal and no other; and in that belief I rest from my labours."

"Now," says Thurlow, "you speak like a man of sense. Sir, I am obliged to you. Pray command me. Give me the pleasure of serving you to requite your trouble in this matter."

"I thank you, my lord," replied Dr. Johnson. "I have but one request: freedom for Lee the receiver."

"Freedom? For the tool of the Whigs? The man who melted up the Great Seal of England? Sure, sir, you jest."

"Not so, my lord. I counsel you, Lee must not be brought to trial."

"Not? When twenty witnesses stand ready against him?"

"No, sir. There might come a twenty-first witness you would not wish to hear."

Thurlow looked sharply at Johnson. Then he lifted his shoulders.

"I can see," he remarked, "that I am in your debt indeed. Lee shall go free."

"I thank your lordship," said Dr. Johnson; and Thurlow took his departure. I attended him into Fleet Street and so we parted.

As the Lord Chancellor mounted his coach, I took note of a young man who was lounging in front of the Dolphin, smoking a church-warden and watching the mouth of Bolt Court. No sooner had the Lord Chancellor driven off, then he shook out his pipe and put himself in motion. To my surprise he caught me up at Dr. Johnson's door. I stared at him. It was Mannering.

Mannering had elected to hang in peach-coloured velvet, picked out with gold. He was still in peach-coloured velvet, and he was still smiling.

"Exit the heavy father," he murmured; "enter the lover. We should all make our fortunes at Drury Lane. Pray sir, is this the right stair for Dr. Johnson? And who are *you*?"

"James Boswell, at your service, Mr. Mannering. Pray come with me."

"Oons, nothing like hanging to get oneself known," drawled Mannering, mounting the stairs before me. There was no handsomer man in England. He carried himself like a grenadier; his handsome sallow face was like a player's, melancholy and sentimental, with shades of sensibility constantly playing over it.

Like a player he threw open the drawing-room door and stood motionless on the threshold. He got his effect.

The languid Durban leaped to his feet, crying:

"Tom! Stap me, 'tis Tom!"

Catharine Thurlow applauded softly, saying,

"Bravo, well timed, Tom!"

But Caroline Thurlow crossed the room in one motion, and threw herself on his breast. Dr. Johnson peered at the newcomer, who seemed to be mightily relishing the scene.

"Permit me," said Catharine sedately, "to make Mr. Mannering known to Dr. Johnson." Though Caroline's head was pressed tight against the peach-coloured chest, Mannering managed a graceful salutation.

He touched Caroline's dark hair gently.

"Be satisfied, little one," he said, "they can't hurt Tom Mannering." He set her gently in her chair.

"How come you so pat, Tom?" said Durban.

It was Catharine who answered.

"I sent to him," she said, "by Francis, when he bespoke the chickens at the ordinary."

"And I," said Mannering, "came when dusk fell. I have enemies in England."

"Had you but come a little sooner," said Caroline in a dreamy voice, "you might have thanked Papa for your pardon."

"Papa!" cried Mannering. "Trust me, I will give Papa a wide berth."

"Pray, sir," said Dr. Johnson, "be seated and take a dish of tea with us."

"I thank you, no. I ride for Dover in an hour, and so over into France. 'Tis safer so, I think."

He looked directly at Catharine Thurlow.

"I had not looked to speak before an audience," he said (I thought he minded us little enough), "but time presses. I thank you for my life. Will you marry me and come with me into France?"

Catharine Thurlow returned as level a look.

"I have not changed my mind," she said. "I couldn't see you hang; but I will not marry you, Tom, tonight or ever."

Mannering scowled.

"You'll be the death of me," he said, "whose fault was the Lanchester affair?"

"I've made amends, I think, for driving you into her arms," replied Catharine. "Go over into France, Tom, and God take care of you, for I won't again."

Caroline stood up. "I'll come with you, Tom."

Mannering looked at her.

"No, no, little one, you're too young and tender. I'll go alone." He touched her hand; looked a long moment at Catharine's vivid face; bowed, and was gone.

Catharine Thurlow went to her sister and set an arm about her shoulders.

"Catharine," said Caroline wonderingly, "what did he mean, about Papa?"

"Why, you little goose," cried Catharine, "where did you think I went when I left you weeping your heart out in the darkness and went off dressed like a link-boy?"

"You said you were going to fight a duel," said Caroline doubtfully.

"That was to keep you quiet, you little moppet," said her elder sister. "I lay there in the dark listening to your sobs, and wished I could have got father to save Tom; and it came over me that if I were bold enough I could do it myself."

"How?" said Caroline.

"By sealing a pardon and carrying it myself. It wasn't hard. I carried the Seal to Rolls Yard, and engrossed a pardon in form as best I could. 'Twas a botch, but a bold botch. I sealed it with yellow wax, and then I had to run all the way to get there in time. The hangman never looked at it; how could he, with the press shouting *A reprieve, a pardon,* and Tom Mannering getting into his coach as cool as a cucumber?"

I stared at the intrepid girl.

"All had gone well," she continued, "had my father not taken a freak to look at the Seal at six o'clock in the morning."

" 'Twas I," I said, "who took that freak."

"You have given me a bad day, Mr. Boswell," she replied; "but all's well that ends well."

"Yet give me leave," I begged, "to know the answer to a question or two. Pray how had you a boy's suit by you?"

"I had gone to the masquerade as a link-boy."

"Did your father know of this?"

"Not when 'twas done; but like Dr. Johnson he saw that 'twas not the work of a thief, but of a member of his household. Therefore he wrenched out the bars of the kitchen window, that it might look the more like a house-breaking."

"And therefore he was so fierce against the Whigs?" I added.

"No, sir; he is fierce against the Whigs from long practise."

"Pray, Dr. Johnson, was this known to you?"

"Sir, by little and by little. At your first account I saw plainly, from the rust on his palms, from the clatter below-stairs, from the plaster *inside* the window though the bars had been cast *outside,* that 'twas Lord Thurlow himself who had breached his own defenses. Therefore I summoned to me all who lived above-stairs, and learned that all had been in company with others till nigh on dawn. I was puzzled to know which of the young people had abstracted the Seal upon their return home, and why. Then I mentioned Mannering's pardon, and father and daughter immediately lied in concert. Lord Thurlow claimed to have sealed Mannering's pardon and Miss Catharine to have served as chaffwax. Obviously both lied, for Lord Thurlow was at Brooks's all night long, though he knew not that I knew it and Miss Catharine was at the masquerade. Then Mannering's pardon was forged. And by whom? Not Lord Thurlow—he could have procured a genuine pardon, had he so wished. Therefore Miss Catharine was the forger; Lord Thurlow guessed so much, and lied to cover her. 'Twas all news to Miss Caroline that Mannering had got off; she fainted away with the revulsion of feeling."

"Pray, Miss Thurlow," I enquired, "did you indeed steal £35 and two silver sword hilts?"

"No, indeed, Mr. Boswell. I now hear this accusation for the first time."

" 'Twas a detail your father invented to lend verisimilitude to his version of the house-breaking," explained Dr. Johnson, pouring his fifth cup of tea.

"Now, sir," said I, rallying him, "what's this supping of tea? Did you not swear not to rest nor recruit until you had laid the Seal in Lord Thurlow's hand?"

"Why, sir," returned Dr. Johnson, "you saw me do so."

I stared.

"Why, Bozzy," exclaimed Dr. Johnson, "did you think I would let the King's writ pass under base metal? Here is the brass one." He drew it from the capacious old-fashioned pocket of his snuff-coloured suit.

I continued to stare.

"But, sir, how came you by it?" I exclaimed, "without stirring out at the door all day."

"I detected its hiding-place, and asked for it."

"Where—?"

Catharine Thurlow laughed aloud.

"Pray, Mr. Boswell, is it the custom in Scotland for ladies of the *ton* to wear a made head before breakfast? 'Tis not so here; but when a lady has chopped off her hair in a hurry to pass for a boy by daylight, she must needs don a wig; and what better hiding-place for a thing she must conceal on her person till the hue and cry is over than the inner reaches of that same wig?"

"Pray, Mr. Boswell," said Dr. Johnson, "accept of the brass seal as a memento of this day's transactions. As for me, I desire no better reward than to have saved a lady from the consequences of her rashness."

In fine, Dr. Johnson was true to his word; for though all became known to the Chancellor through the agency of his younger daughter and though he made the proffer with the utmost delicacy, Dr. Johnson was steadfast not to touch Lord Thurlow's £600.

Harry Kemelman

The Nine Mile Walk

I had made an ass of myself in a speech I had given at the Good Government Association dinner, and Nicky Welt had cornered me at breakfast at the Blue Moon, where we both ate occasionally, for the pleasure of rubbing it in. I had made the mistake of departing from my prepared speech to criticize a statement my predecessor in the office of district attorney had made to the press. I had drawn a number of inferences from his statement and had thus left myself open to a rebuttal which he had promptly made and which had the effect of making me appear intellectually dishonest. I was new to this political game, having but a few months before left the Law School faculty to become the Reform Party candidate for district attorney. I said as much in extenuation, but Nicholas Welt, who could never drop his pedagogical manner (he was Snowdon Professor of English Language and Literature), replied in much the same tone that he would dismiss a request from a sophomore for an extension on a term paper, "That's no excuse."

Although he is only two or three years older than I, in his late forties, he always treats me like a school master hectoring a stupid pupil. And I, perhaps because he looks so much older with his white hair and lined, gnomelike face, suffer it.

"They were perfectly logical inferences," I pleaded.

"My dear boy," he purred, "although human intercourse is well nigh impossible without inference, most inferences are usually wrong. The percentage of error is particularly high in the legal profession where the intention is not to discover what the speaker wishes to convey, but rather what he wishes to conceal."

I picked up my check and eased out from behind the table.

"I suppose you are referring to cross-examination of witnesses in court. Well, there's always an opposing counsel who will object if the inference is illogical."

"Who said anything about logic?" he retorted. "An inference can be logical and still not be true."

He followed me down the aisle to the cashier's booth. I paid my check and waited impatiently while he searched in an old-fashioned change purse, fishing out coins one by one and placing them on the

36

counter beside his check, only to discover that the total was insufficient. He slid them back into his purse and with a tiny sigh extracted a bill from another compartment of the purse and handed it to the cashier.

"Give me any sentence of ten or twelve words," he said, "and I'll build you a logical chain of inferences that you never dreamed of when you framed the sentence."

Other customers were coming in, and since the space in front of the cashier's booth was small, I decided to wait outside until Nicky completed his transaction with the cashier. I remember being mildly amused at the idea that he probably thought I was still at his elbow and was going right ahead with his discourse.

When he joined me on the sidewalk I said, "A nine-mile walk is no joke, especially in the rain."

"No, I shouldn't think it would be," he agreed absently. Then he stopped in his stride and looked at me sharply. "What the devil are you talking about?"

"It's a sentence and it has eleven words," I insisted. And I repeated the sentence, ticking off the words on my fingers.

"What about it?"

"You said that given a sentence of ten or twelve words—"

"Oh, yes." He looked at me suspiciously. "Where did you get it?"

"It just popped into my head. Come on now, build your inferences."

"You're serious about this?" he asked, his little blue eyes glittering with amusement. "You really want me to?"

It was just like him to issue a challenge and then to appear amused when I accepted it. And it made me angry.

"Put up or shut up," I said.

"All right," he said mildly. "No need to be huffy. I'll play. Hmm, let me see, how did the sentence go? 'A nine-mile walk is no joke, especially in the rain.' Not much to go on there."

"It's more than ten words," I rejoined.

"Very well." His voice became crisp as he mentally squared off to the problem. "First inference: the speaker is aggrieved."

"I'll grant that," I said, "although it hardly seems to be an inference. It's really implicit in the statement."

He nodded impatiently. "Next inference: the rain was unforeseen, otherwise he would have said, 'A nine-mile walk in the rain is no joke,' instead of using the 'especially' phrase as an afterthought."

"I'll allow that," I said, "although it's pretty obvious."

"First inferences should be obvious," said Nicky tartly.

I let it go at that. He seemed to be floundering and I didn't want to rub it in.

"Next inference: the speaker is not an athlete or an outdoors man."

"You'll have to explain that one," I said.

"It's the 'especially' phrase again," he said. "The speaker does not say that a nine-mile walk in the rain is no joke, but merely the walk—just the distance, mind you—is no joke. Now, nine miles is not such a terribly long distance. You walk more than half that in eighteen holes of golf—and golf is an old man's game," he added slyly. *I* play golf.

"Well, that would be all right under ordinary circumstances," I said, "but there are other possibilities. The speaker might be a soldier in the jungle in which case nine miles would be a pretty good hike, rain or no rain."

"Yes," and Nicky was sarcastic, "and the speaker might be one-legged. For that matter, the speaker might be a graduate student writing a Ph.D. on humor and starting by listing all the things that are not funny. See here, I'll have to make a couple of assumptions before I continue."

"How do you mean?" I asked, suspiciously.

"Remember, I'm taking this sentence *in vacuo,* as it were. I don't know who said it or what the occasion was. Normally a sentence belongs in the framework of a situation."

"I see. What assumptions do you want to make?"

"For one thing, I want to assume that the intention was not frivolous, that the speaker is referring to a walk that was actually taken, and that the purpose of the walk was not to win a bet or something of that sort."

"That seems reasonable enough," I said.

"And I also want to assume that the locale of the walk is here."

"You mean here in Fairfield?"

"Not necessarily. I mean in this general section of the country."

"Fair enough."

"Then, if you grant those assumptions, you'll have to accept my last inference that the speaker is no athlete or outdoors man."

"Well, all right, go on."

"Then my next inference is that the walk was taken very late at night or very early in the morning—say, between midnight and five or six in the morning."

"How do you figure that one?" I asked.

"Consider the distance, nine miles. We're in a fairly well-populated section. Take any road and you'll find a community of some sort in less than nine miles. Hadley is five miles away, Hadley Falls is seven and a half, Goreton is eleven, but East Goreton is only eight and you strike East Goreton before you come to Goreton. There is local train service along the Goreton road and bus service along the others. All the highways are pretty well traveled. Would anyone have to walk nine miles in a rain unless it were late at night when no buses or trains were running and when the few automobiles that were out would hesitate to pick up a stranger on the highway?"

"He might not have wanted to be seen," I suggested.

Nicky smiled pityingly. "You think he would be less noticeable trudging along the highway then he would be riding in a public conveyance where everyone is usually absorbed in his newspaper?"

"Well, I won't press the point," I said brusquely.

"Then try this one: he was walking towards a town rather than away from one."

I nodded. "It is more likely, I suppose. If he were in a town, he could probably arrange for some sort of transportation. Is that the basis for your inference?"

"Partly that," said Nicky, "but there is also an inference to be drawn from the distance. Remember, it's a *nine*-mile walk and nine is one of the exact numbers."

"I'm afraid I don't understand."

That exasperated schoolteacher look appeared on Nicky's face again. "Suppose you say, 'I took a ten-mile walk' or 'a hundred-mile drive'; I would assume that you actually walked anywhere from eight to a dozen miles, or that you rode between ninety and a hundred and ten miles. In other words, *ten* and *hundred* are round numbers. You might have walked *exactly* ten miles or just as likely you might have walked *approximately* ten miles. But when you speak of walking *nine* miles, I have a right to assume that you have named an exact figure. Now, we are far more likely to know the distance of the city from a given point than we are to know the distance of a given point from the city. That is, ask anyone in the city how far out Farmer Brown lives, and if he knows him, he will say, 'Three or four miles.' But ask Farmer Brown how far he lives from the city and he will tell you. 'Three and six-tenths miles—measured it on my speedometer many a time.' "

"It's weak, Nicky," I said.

"But in conjunction with your own suggestion that he could have arranged transportation if he had been in a city—"

"Yes, that would do it," I said. "I'll pass it. Any more?"

"I've just begun to hit my stride," he boasted. "My next inference is that he was going to a definite destination and that he had to be there at a particular time. It was not a case of going off to get help because his car broke down or his wife was going to have a baby or somebody was trying to break into his house."

"Oh, come now," I said, "the car breaking down is really the most likely situation. He could have known the exact distance from having checked the mileage just as he was leaving the town."

Nicky shook his head. "Rather than walk nine miles in the rain, he would have curled up on the back seat and gone to sleep, or at least stayed by his car and tried to flag another motorist. Remember, it's nine miles. What would be the least it would take him to hike it?"

"Four hours," I offered.

He nodded. "Certainly no less, considering the rain. We've agreed that it happened very late at night or very early in the morning. Suppose he had his breakdown at one o'clock in the morning. It would be five o'clock before he would arrive. That's daybreak. You begin to see a lot of cars on the road. The buses start just a little later. In fact, the first buses hit Fairfield around 5:30. Besides, if he were going for help, he would not have to go all the way to town—only as far as the nearest telephone. No, he had a definite appointment, and it was in a town, and it was for some time before 5:30."

"Then why couldn't he have got there earlier and waited?" I asked. "He could have taken the last bus, arrived around one o'clock, and waited until his appointment. He walks nine miles in the rain instead, and you said he was no athlete."

We had arrived at the Municipal Building where my office is. Normally, any arguments begun at the Blue Moon ended at the entrance to the Municipal Building. But I was interested in Nicky's demonstration and I suggested that he come up for a few minutes.

When we were seated I said, "How about it, Nicky, why couldn't he have arrived early and waited?"

"He could have," Nicky retorted. "But since he didn't, we must assume that he was either detained until after the last bus left or that he had to wait where he was for a signal of some sort, perhaps a telephone call."

"Then according to you, he had an appointment sometime beteen midnight and 5:30—"

"We can draw it much finer than that. Remember, it takes him four hours to walk the distance. The last bus stops at 12:30 A. M. If he doesn't take that, but starts at the same time, he won't arrive at his destination until 4:30. On the other hand, if he takes the first bus in the morning, he will arrive around 5:30. That would mean that his appointment was for sometime between 4:30 and 5:30."

"You mean that if his appointment were earlier than 4:30, he would have taken the last night bus, and if it were later than 5:30, he would have taken the first morning bus?"

"Precisely. And another thing: if he were waiting for a signal or a phone call, it must have come not much later than one o'clock."

"Yes, I see that," I said. "If his appointment is around five o'clock and it takes him four hours to walk the distance, he'd have to start around one."

He nodded, silent and thoughtful. For some queer reason I couldn't explain, I didn't feel like interrupting his thoughts. On the wall was a large map of the county and I walked over to it and began to study it.

"You're right, Nicky," I remarked over my shoulder, "there's no place as far as nine miles away from Fairfield that doesn't hit another town first. Fairfield is right in the middle of a bunch of smaller towns."

He joined me at the map. "It doesn't have to be Fairfield, you know," he said quietly. "It was probably one of the outlying towns he had to reach. Try Hadley."

"Why Hadley? What would anyone want in Hadley at five o'clock in the morning?"

"The *Washington Flyer* stops there to take on water about that time," he said quietly.

"That's right too," I said. "I've heard that train many a night when I couldn't sleep. I'd hear it pulling in and then a minute or two later I'd hear the clock on the Methodist Chuch banging out five." I went back to my desk for a timetable. "The *Flyer* leaves Washington at 12:47 A.M. and gets into Boston at 8:00 A.M."

Nicky was still at the map measuring distances with a pencil.

"Exactly nine miles from Hadley is the Old Sumter Inn," he announced.

"Old Sumter Inn," I echoed. "But that upsets the whole theory. You can arrange for transportation there as easily as you can in a town."

He shook his head. "The cars are kept in an enclosure and you have to get an attendant to check you through the gate. The attendant would remember anyone taking out his car at a strange hour. It's a pretty conservative place. He could have waited in his room until he got a call from Washington about someone on the *Flyer*—maybe the number of the car and the berth. Then he could just slip out of the hotel and walk to Hadley."

I stared at him, hypnotized.

"It wouldn't be difficult to slip aboard while the train was taking on water, and then if he knew the car number and the berth—"

"Nicky," I said portentously, "as the Reform district attorney who campaigned on an economy program, I am going to waste the taxpayers' money and call Boston long distance. It's ridiculous, it's insane—but I'm going to do it!"

His little blue eyes glittered and he moistened his lips with the tip of his tongue.

"Go ahead," he said hoarsely.

I replaced the telephone in its cradle.

"Nicky," I said, "this is probably the most remarkable coincidence in the history of criminal investigation: *a man was found murdered in his berth on last night's 12:47 from Washington!* He'd been dead about three hours, which would make it exactly right for Hadley."

"I thought it was something like that," said Nicky. "But you're wrong about it being a coincidence. It can't be. Where did you get that sentence?"

"It was just a sentence. It simply popped into my head."

"It couldn't have! It's not the sort of sentence that pops into one's head. If you had taught composition as long as I have, you'd know that when you ask someone for a sentence of ten words or so, you get an ordinary statement such as 'I like milk'—with the other words made up by a modifying clause like, 'because it is good for my health.' The sentence you offered related to a *particular situation*."

"But I tell you I talked to no one this morning. And I was alone with you at the Blue Moon."

"You weren't with me all the time I paid my check," he said sharply. "Did you meet anyone while you were waiting on the sidewalk for me to come out of the Blue Moon?"

I shook my head. "I was outside for less than a minute before you joined me. You see, a couple of men came in while you were digging out your change and one of them bumped me, so I thought I'd wait—"

"Did you ever see them before?"

"Who?"

"The two men who came in," he said, the note of exasperation creeping into his voice again.

"Why, no—they weren't anyone I knew."

"Were they talking?"

"I guess so. Yes, they were. Quite absorbed in their conversation, as a matter of fact—otherwise, they would have noticed me and I would not have been bumped."

"Not many strangers come into the Blue Moon," he remarked.

"Do you think it was they?" I asked eagerly. "I think I'd know them again if I saw them."

Nicky's eyes narrowed. "It's possible. There had to be two—one to trail the victim in Washington and ascertain his berth number, the other to wait here and do the job. The Washington man would be likely to come down here afterward. If there were theft as well as murder, it would be to divide the spoils. If it was just murder, he would probably have to come down to pay off his confederate."

I reached for the telephone.

"We've been gone less than half an hour," Nicky went on. "They were just coming in and service is slow at the Blue Moon. The one who walked all the way to Hadley must certainly be hungry and the other probably drove all night from Washington."

"Call me immediately if you make an arrest," I said and hung up.

Neither of us spoke a word while we waited. We paced the floor, avoiding each other almost as though we had done something we were ashamed of. The telephone rang at last. I picked it up and listened. Then I said, "O.K." and turned to Nicky.

"One of them tried to escape through the kitchen but Winn had someone stationed at the back and they got him."

"That would seem to prove it," said Nicky with a frosty little smile.

I nodded agreement.

He glanced at his watch. "Gracious," he exclaimed, "I wanted to make an early start on my work this morning, and here I've already wasted all this time talking with you."

I let him get to the door. "Oh, Nicky," I called, "what was it you set out to prove?"

"That a chain of inferences could be logical and still not be true," he said.

"Oh."

"What are you laughing at?" he asked snappishly. And then he laughed too.

Jack Finney

The Widow's Walk

I'm so mad I could spit.

I walked into her room that morning as always; quietly, though not on tiptoe. The loose board creaked, but she didn't move, of course: she sleeps like a pig. At the side of her bed I stood looking down. She lay flat on her back, her skin, even her eyelids, yellow and wrinkled, her skull showing behind the sagging old flesh, and her mouth, without her teeth, puckered to a slit. How I hate it when I have to kiss her. It takes a day for the feeling to leave my lips.

Her pillow was on the floor. It always is, though I've often spoken about it. I wore gloves and my suede jacket and skirt. I picked up her pillow and held it tightly at each end, stretched between my hands. I edged closer to her bed, almost touching it. The rest I went through only in imagination, for I was rehearsing: I had to be certain, first, that I could really do it. But I saw it in my mind as though it were happening. I could even feel tentative little muscle movements.

Down with the pillow, flat across her face, a knee on the bed, shoulders hunched over my arms, the knuckles of each fist pressed deep in the mattress. A moment of utter silence, then her bony hands shoot out, clawing rapidly, senselessly, at my arms and hands, scratching at the leather. Then they tug purposefully at my wrists. A silent, almost motionless struggle—and now her old hands begin to relax.

Suddenly a new picture flashed through my mind, and up to that moment this possibility had never occurred to me. Suddenly, and I could hear it in my brain, her feet began to drum on the mattress. Fast! Fast as a two-year-old's in a tantrum, and loud!

I couldn't stand that. Not even in imagination. I could feel the blood drop from my face. Perhaps I made a sound, I don't know. And I don't like to think how my face must have looked. But when I turned it to hers—I'd been staring straight ahead—those mean blue eyes were boring into mine.

"What are you doing?" she said in her flat, cold voice. The panic remained for a moment. Then I could speak.

"Nothing, Mother," and my voice was easy. "I decided to shop

44

early." That explained my jacket and gloves. "And I thought I'd tidy up your room first."

"Can't do much tidying while I'm still here."

"No, I guess not. It was foolish of me. I'm sorry I disturbed you. Try to sleep some more."

"Can't sleep once I've been waked up; you know that." She was trying to prolong the conversation, alert for a clue.

"I'm sorry, Mother. I'll be back in a few minutes and get you some breakfast." Then I went out to the stores, though there was really no shopping to do. I bought a few staples.

It's infuriating, though. So perfect, so simple—and I just can't do it. She wouldn't be smothered, you see. Her creaky old heart would give out! Her doctor has warned us, and he'd be the doctor I'd call. Then I'd phone Al: "I tiptoed into her room to see if she wanted breakfast, and she looked sort of funny, and—oh, Al, she's dead!"

Almost true, and it would have been true, really, by the time they arrived. I'd have run it over and over in my mind, like a film, till I believed it myself, almost. I know how to lie. But I'm just not a murderer, that's all. I'm simply a housewife.

I'm thirty-two years old, five feet five inches tall, wavy hair, dark-blue eyes, reasonably pretty, and I'm in love with my husband. I'm a homemaker, much as I dislike that word, and I want my home the way it was before she came.

We didn't do much then, Al and I. Evenings mostly at home, reading in the living room. In the spring and summer, the garden till dark. Bridge with the Dykes fairly often: we hardly see them now. And occasionally a movie. Daytimes I cleaned, I shopped, I cooked. That's all. But I liked it. I made a home—for my husband and me. And I want it back.

But now it's like this. The other morning I was doing the dishes. She sat on the back porch, "taking the air"—unpleasant phrase. I couldn't see her, actually, but I could see her in my mind, staring out at the pile of new lumber in the yard, hands folded in her lap. And thinking of me. As I was thinking of her. For a long time she made no sound, and then she cleared her throat. That doesn't mean anything to you, does it? But it did to me. And she knew it. It was a nasty, deliberate, spiteful reminder that she was present and existing, sharing my house and my husband. Do you see now what I mean? I can feel her, actually *feel* her, in every room of the house at all times, day and night! Even in our bedroom, which she never enters.

Oh, I'm going to kill her, all right. Al will get over it. He *must* hate it as much as I do. We've had four years of it. And it started as soon as she came.

We'd had a date with the Crowleys, made just before she arrived—a weekend at their cottage on the lake. And we kept it. She insisted. "You children go ahead. I'll be glad to get rid of you!"

"Sure now, Mother?" Al asked. "You know, a weekend's not important, and if—"

"Of course I am! I won't hear another word—you're going!"

The doctor was there when we returned Sunday evening. An ambulance in front of the house, a nurse inside with an oxygen tent. A heart attack. I know she did it deliberately; not faked, exactly, but somehow self-induced. She'd phoned a neighbor in the late afternoon, hardly able to talk. Our neighbor hurried over, called the hospital—and that's what we came home to. She's never had another attack, and we've never had another weekend.

I mentioned it again a few days ago. "Yes, I'd have got over it," Al said. "You can't foresee and guard against everything. But you have to try. I have to see that she has as long and happy a life as she can." And then he startled me by adding this, "But I know it's hard on you sometimes, Annie."

I'd thought he didn't realize, wasn't aware. Of course he must have been—a little, at least. But he'll never know how I really feel, that I'm sure of.

My new plan is so perfect, you see. It's going to be a push, a sudden push from a high place. So simple, but it took me a long time to think of it. I was afraid I couldn't trust myself to go through with any of the plans I was able to think of. And then it came to me. There's nothing, really, to go through with in a push! It's over before you can think, over the moment it's started! And then—well, I heard her gasp, turned around, and there she was, disappearing over the edge! Her heart, I suppose.

But what high place? She never leaves the house. The stairs, from our second floor to the first, turn at a landing; not much of a fall. It wouldn't be certain. I wish I could plan ahead and think more logically. Al says I'd be out of house and home in a month if he weren't here to plan for me. Maybe he's right, but I've always found, it seems to me, that things work themselves out in the long run.

And sure enough. One night Al and I were reading in the living room; his mother had gone to bed. One of my magazines had come that day. I was leafing through it and I came to an article on widow's walks—photographs of the originals in New England, sketches of modern adaptations. So cute. Perfect little porches, the article said, for sunbathing and for sitting of an evening. Perfect: a widow's walk with a knee-high railing.

Al's set in his ways, though, and I could just hear what he'd say if I suggested a widow's walk on *our* house!

I did, though. "Look, dear," I said, and he glanced up from his book. "Aren't these darling?" I held up the article.

"Uh huh," he answered. I smiled expectantly and didn't move. "Yeah, they are," Al said. I continued to wait, still smiling, still holding my magazine up. I know the game: we've been married six years. He was hoping I'd consider his comment sufficient and let him get back to his book. Or that I'd be the one to get up. So I waited. Al is a polite man, and he started to rise. In an instant I was on my feet, carrying the magazine over to him. And because he'd kept his comfort, I'd earned my interruption. He laid his book in his lap and took my magazine.

"Aren't they darling?" I knelt on the floor beside Al's chair. "Widow's walks, they're called."

"Yeah, I've seen them," Al said. "The old whaling days. The women watched for the men at sea."

"So that's what they're for!"

"Sure. That's why the name. Half the time the husbands never came back."

"Well, no danger of your drowning at the office, dear. And I could watch for you to come home after work. How about building one on our roof?"

That half irritated, half pitying look men reserve for women's impracticality came over his face, but before he could turn to look at me I was smiling. He grinned then. "Oh, sure," he said, "I'll start tomorrow."

I waited three nights before I mentioned it again. We were walking home from the movies. And I waited till we were less than a block from home; just time enough to voice his objections, not time enough to get dead set against it. "I've been thinking, Al. It *would* be nice to have a widow's walk. It'd be easy to build," and now I was excited and enthusiastic. "You're so handy with tools and the plans are all in the magazine. It'd be *so* nice in the evening. I'll bet we could see the river, and—"

"Oh, Annie," Al said, "in the first place—" And I listened, and nodded, and agreed.

"It was just an idea," I said. We had reached our porch and he took out his keys. "But you're right, it wouldn't be practical." And as we entered the house, I added only this, "Your mother would like it, though." Then we had to be quiet: she was asleep.

It took less than two days. Spring came to stay on a Thursday. The sun was warmer, closer, the ground moist and crumbling, and the air was alive. Al, I knew, would be aching to build something, anything. He's a marvel with tools and loves to work with them. The lumber was delivered on Friday, dumped in the back yard, and I signed the receipt.

I grinned when Al came home. "What's the wood for?" I asked, and Al grinned back. His mother had to be told, then, and I let Al tell her. She mumbled and muttered about the lumber on the flower beds. Was there anything she liked, anything that met with her royal approval? But I didn't care, not this time.

Sunday, it happened again. That damned unexpected panic! Maybe I relaxed too much—it was that kind of day. Everything green and alive, the outdoor sounds so new and clear and soft; the sort of day you think of when someone says Spring. It should have been perfect.

Al was working on the roof in the sun—no shirt. His mother and I on the lawn in canvas chairs, she with the Sunday paper, while I shelled peas. Dinner was a comfortable two hours off, the meat was on and needed no attention. You could feel the air, soft and cool, moving across the back of your hands. And it carried sound as it never does otherwise. A dog barking, many houses away, the chitter of birds, and the soft, clean sound of the wood as Al worked on the little, half finished platform he'd built on the roof. A pause, then the sudden loose clatter of light new planking as it dropped on the heavier timbers already in place. A grunt from Al as he got down on his knees, then the skilled tap of his hammer, nudging a board to position. The tiny rattle of nails, the sharp ping, pong as he set one in the wood, then the heavy, measured, satisfactory bang, bang, bang, on a rising scale, as he drove it home.

"He's going to fall," she said nastily.

"Oh, no, Mother, Al's light as a cat on his feet." I spoke gently, kindly and I smiled. She didn't answer directly, didn't look at me.

"Don't see the use of it, anyway. Porch on a roof!"

"But, Mother," I said, "you'll love that porch!" That was a mistake. Her face set. Any urging from me is like pulling a mule with a rope. I said nothing more, but I was annoyed at myself and at her. If you only knew, I thought, and then, without warning, the panic broke. I hadn't expected it, hadn't allowed for it, but suddenly the sound of that hammer, bang, bang, bang, was the sound of a hammer building a scaffold. The next plank scraped and bumped hollowly over the others, then dropped into place. And I couldn't bear to hear the next nail, to hear the sound of her scaffold moving nearer and nearer to completion. I rose, turned, set the bowl carefully on my chair, and ran to the house.

Al called to me, "What's the matter?" Then he yelled. "Annie!"

"The meat!" I shrieked, and yanked the screen door open.

I leaned on the kitchen table, hands flat on the top, my eyes closed. "Take hold of yourself, take hold of yourself," I muttered senselessly, and then, in a moment or two, I was all right. The heavy, hollow hammer sound began again and I listened. Yes, I thought, a scaffold. For her. Make it good and strong.

What a ridiculous weakness, though, not to be able to count on yourself, to trust yourself! Oh, I *wish* she'd die of her own accord!

She won't though. She knows I want her to. Yes, she's that stubborn! Al finished the porch—it's really very cute—but she wouldn't use it. He painted it Sunday night, a light green, and we went up next morning before he went to work. His mother, too: trust her to be in on everything. But she wouldn't go back. I'd try to keep from urging her, but sometimes I couldn't help it. Then she'd smile, stay just where she was, and answer, "No, you go up, dear. I'm comfortable right where I am." Then I'd have to go up there and sit.

Things work themselves out, though. I stopped talking about the porch and spent a lot of time there. It *was* rather nice, and presently she began to suspect that I liked getting away from her. And maybe she was a little lonely. Then, one evening at dinner, Al mentioned the porch. I told him how much I liked it, how quiet and so sort of away from things it seemed. Maybe it was my speaking of the pleasant quiet that gave her the idea. She thought it would be so nice to have a radio up there—the one from the kitchen, perhaps. She knows I use it when I'm cooking. I wanted her to start using the porch so much that I nearly agreed with her. But I caught myself.

"I don't know that a radio would be so good up there, Mother. It's—"

"Don't see why not!" she answered instinctively. "Like to hear a few programs myself sometimes, and if we're going to sit up there all the time—"

I was elated. "We'll see," I said coldly, and later when she'd gone to bed I told Al, "Put the radio up there tonight—from the kitchen. I hardly ever use it."

"You're sweet," he said, and kissed me. He's a darling.

Now she likes the porch. Loves it! She puffs and mutters her way up to the attic, rests for a few moments on the old cedar chest, then pulls herself up the new flight of stairs to the roof. And there she sits, with her fan and her handkerchief, all morning long, till the sun gets at it from the west. Of course she has me on the jump all the time. Downstairs for the mail, for her glasses, for a drink of water, for anything and everything she can think of. "Do you mind, Annie? I'd go myself, but—"

Sometimes I'll say, "In a minute," and then let her wait. But usually I answer, "Of course not, Mother, I have to go down anyway." And I don't mind. Not in the least. Because it makes me madder and madder every time she does it. And that's what I want.

I know I can't trust myself, can't be sure I won't stop an instant before it happens, unable to go through with it—unless I see red. I really do see red. Some people think that's a figure of speech, but it isn't. When I get really furiously angry, it's as though a sheet of red cellophane were in front of my eyes. I actually see red, and then I can do anything.

I think it's going to happen soon, now—about the radio. Things work themselves out, you see. She had to use it, of course, once it was up there. And she's discovered a particularly unpleasant program. It comes on at ten; old-time songs played on an organ, and an obnoxious-voiced man reading bad poetry. Ten, she knows, is when I've always listened to "Woman of Destiny." I asked her the other day if she'd mind my occasionally hearing it just to keep up with the story. She guessed not. But when I get up there, after breakfast dishes and the beds, there she sits listening to *her* program. Never a move, never a suggestion to change it to mine. I haven't said any more. I just sit there, seething. She knows it, too, and likes it.

One other thing has been happening lately. I've forgotten several times to fold the canvas chairs when we leave the porch for the day. Then next morning the seats are damp from the dew and she has to sit on the rail till the chairs dry. She's complained about it.

Oh, things do work themselves out. One of these mornings the chairs will be damp again. I'll come up at ten and there she'll be,

sitting on the rail listening to that sanctimonious fool on the radio.
I'll sit down beside her. She'll complain in that nagging voice of hers
that I forgot the chairs again yesterday. I'll suggest that she might
think of it herself occasionally. Then that sullen silence. I'll glance
at the radio, then back at her, hinting that she *might* just suggest
hearing my program for a change.

She'll ignore that, as always. My blood will start to boil. And I'll
let it. I'll feed the flames, remembering everything she's ever done,
and that's plenty. I'll start back through the years and remember
them all. And suddenly—I'll see red. Really *red,* just for an instant.
Then, afterwards—panic? Well, let it come! Who wouldn't be panicky
when she'd seen her mother-in-law fall two and a half stories to a
cement driveway? Things, you see, do work themselves out. And it'll
serve her right. It will! It'll—serve—her—right! The old *bitch!*

I don't know, now, why I wrote what you've read. I started, I
remember, with some idea of getting all my plans on paper. It became
something else, of course, but I continued to write just the same. I
meant to burn it, but I never have. I've kept it and read it, many
times, over and over again.

Somehow I didn't think much about Al's using the porch. Naturally he did, on weekends especially. He went up one Saturday morning, shortly after his mother. I'd forgotten the chairs again, the night
before, and she was sitting on the railing. I suppose, this time, her
attack was a real one. Al sat on the opposite rail, the width of the
porch away, and she couldn't have been sure he'd be able to reach
her in time. He almost did, though. When she started to fall, he shot
across that porch faster than I'd ever seen him move before. I was
watching; I was coming up the stairs and my eyes were level with
the floor of the porch.

He got a hand on her skirt, a tight, strong hold, reaching way over
the railing a split-second after she was clear of the porch. And then,
as she plunged, her skirt went taut, yanked on his arm with the
force of a whip, and the precarious balance he held, leaning way
over the rail, was gone.

Things do work themselves out, I suppose. Long after their husbands were dead and gone, the old seafarers' wives must have continued pacing the floors of their widow's walks. The name says that.
Back and forth, back and forth they walked, day after day after
hopeless day. As I do.

Stanley Ellin

The Specialty of the House

66 **A**nd this," said Laffler, "is Sbirro's." Costain saw a square brownstone façade identical with the others that extended from either side into the clammy darkness of the deserted street. From the barred windows of the basement at his feet, a glimmer of light showed behind heavy curtains.

"Lord," he observed, "it's a dismal hole, isn't it?"

"I beg you to understand," said Laffler stiffly, "that Sbirro's is the restaurant without pretensions. Beseiged by these ghastly, neurotic times, it has refused to compromise. It is perhaps the last important establishment in this city lit by gas jets. Here you will find the same honest furnishings, the same magnificent Sheffield service, and possibly, in a far corner, the very same spider webs that were remarked by the patrons of a half century ago!"

"A doubtful recommendation," said Costain, "and hardly sanitary."

"When you enter," Laffler continued, "you leave the insanity of this year, this day, and this hour, and you find yourself for a brief span restored in spirit, not by opulence but by dignity, which is the lost quality of our time."

Costain laughed uncomfortably. "You make it sound more like a cathedral than a restaurant," he said.

In the pale reflection of the street lamp overhead, Laffler peered at his companion's face. "I wonder," he said abruptly, "whether I have not made a mistake in extending this invitation to you."

Costain was hurt. Despite an impressive title and large salary, he was no more than clerk to this pompous little man, but he was impelled to make some display of his feelings. "If you wish," he said coldly, "I can make other plans for my evening with no trouble."

With his large, cowlike eyes turned up to Costain, the mist drifting into the ruddy full moon of his face, Laffler seemed strangely ill at ease. Then, "No, no," he said at last, "absolutely not. It's important that you dine at Sbirro's with me." He grasped Costain's arm firmly and led the way to the wrought-iron gate of the basement. "You see, you're the sole person in my office who seems to know anything at all about good food. And on my part, knowing about Sbirro's but not

52

having some appreciative friend to share it, is like having a unique piece of art locked in a room where no one else can enjoy it."

Costain was considerably mollified by this. "I understand there are a great many people who relish that situation."

"I'm not one of that kind!" Laffler said sharply. "And having the secret of Sbirro's locked in myself for years has finally become unendurable." He fumbled at the side of the gate and from within could be heard the small, discordant jangle of an ancient pull-bell. An interior door opened with a groan and Costain found himself peering into a dark face whose only discernible feature was a row of gleaming teeth.

"Sair?" said the face.

"Mr. Laffler and a guest."

"Sair," the face said again, this time in what was clearly an invitation. It moved aside and Costain stumbled down a single step behind his host. The door and gate creaked behind him and he stood blinking in a small foyer. It took him a moment to realize that the figure he now stared at was his own reflection in a gigantic pier glass that extended from floor to ceiling. "Atmosphere," he said under his breath and chuckled as he followed his guide to a seat.

He faced Laffler across a small table for two and peered curiously around the dining room. It was no size at all, but the half dozen guttering gas jets which provided the only illumination threw such a deceptive light that the walls flickered and faded into uncertain distance.

There were no more than eight or ten tables about, arranged to insure the maximum privacy. All were occupied, and the few waiters serving them moved with quiet efficiency. In the air was a soft clash and scrape of cutlery and a soothing murmur of talk. Costain nodded appreciatively.

Laffler breathed an audible sigh of gratification. "I knew you would share my enthusiasm," he said. "Have you noticed, by the way, that there are no women present?"

Costain raised inquiring eyebrows.

"Sbirro," said Laffler, "does not encourage members of the fair sex to enter the premises. And, I can tell you, his method is decidedly effective. I had the experience of seeing a woman get a taste of it not long ago. She sat at a table for not less than an hour waiting for service which was never forthcoming."

"Didn't she make a scene?"

"She did." Laffler smiled at the recollection. "She succeeded in annoying the customers, embarrassing her partner, and nothing more."

"And what about Mr. Sbirro?"

"He did not make an appearance. Whether he directed affairs from behind the scenes or was not even present during the episode, I don't know. Whichever it was, he won a complete victory. The woman never reappeared, nor, for that matter, did the witless gentleman who by bringing her was really the cause of the entire contretemps."

"A fair warning to all present," laughed Costain.

A waiter now appeared at the table. The chocolate-dark skin, the thin, beautifully molded nose and lips, the large liquid eyes, heavily lashed, and the silver-white hair so heavy and silken that it lay on the skull like a cap, all marked him definitely as an East Indian of some sort, Costain decided. The man arranged the stiff table linen, filled two tumblers from a huge cut-glass pitcher, and set them in their proper places.

"Tell me," Laffler said eagerly, "is the special being served this evening?"

The waiter smiled regretfully and showed teeth as spectacular as those of the majordomo. "I am so sorry, sair. There is no special this evening."

Laffler's face fell into lines of heavy disappointment. "After waiting so long. It's been a month already, and I hoped to show my friend here—"

"You understand the difficulties, sair."

"Of course, of course." Laffler looked at Costain sadly and shrugged. "You see, I had in mind to introduce you to the greatest treat that Sbirro's offers, but unfortunately it isn't on the menu this evening."

The waiter said: "Do you wish to be served now, sair?" and Laffler nodded. To Costain's surprise the waiter made his way off without waiting for any instructions.

"Have you ordered in advance?" he asked.

"Ah," said Laffler, "I really should have explained. Sbirro's offers no choice whatsoever. You will eat the same meal as everyone else in this room. Tomorrow evening you would eat an entirely different meal, but again without designating a single preference."

"Very unusual," said Costain, "and certainly unsatisfactory at times. What if one doesn't have a taste for the particular dish set before him?"

"On that score," said Laffler solemnly, "you need have no fears.

I give you my word that no matter how exacting your tastes, you will relish evey mouthful you eat in Sbirro's."

Costain looked doubtful, and Laffler smiled. "And consider the subtle advantages of the system," he said. "When you pick up the menu of a popular restaurant, you find youself confronted with innumerable choices. You are forced to weigh, to evaluate, to make uneasy decisions which you may instantly regret. The effect of all this is a tension which, however slight, must make for discomfort.

"And consider the mechanics of the process. Instead of a hurly-burly of sweating cooks rushing about a kitchen in a frenzy to prepare a hundred varying items, we have a chef who stands serenely alone, bringing all his talents to bear on one task, with all assurance of a complete triumph!"

"Then you have seen the kitchen?"

"Unfortunately, no," said Laffler sadly. "The picture I offer is hypothetical, made of conversational fragments I have pieced together over the years. I must admit, though, that my desire to see the functioning of the kitchen here comes very close to being my sole obsession nowadays."

"But have you mentioned this to Sbirro?"

"A dozen times. He shrugs the suggestion away."

"Isn't that a rather curious foible on his part?"

"No, no," Laffler said hastily, "a master artist is never under the compulsion of petty courtesies. Still," he sighed, "I have never given up hope."

The waiter now reappeared bearing two soup bowls which he set in place with mathematical exactitude, and a small tureen from which he slowly ladled a measure of clear, thin broth. Costain dipped his spoon into the broth and tasted it with some curiosity. It was delicately flavored, bland to the verge of tastelessness. Costain frowned, tentatively reached for the salt and pepper cellars, and discovered there were none on the table. He looked up, saw Laffler's eyes on him, and although unwilling to compromise with his own tastes, he hesitated to act as a damper on Laffler's enthusiasm. Therefore he smiled and indicated the broth.

"Excellent," he said.

Laffler returned his smile. "You do not find it excellent at all," he said coolly. "You find it flat and badly in need of condiments. I know this," he continued as Costain's eyebrows shot upward, "because it was my own reaction many years ago, and because like yourself I found myself reaching for salt and pepper after the first mouthful. I also learned with surprise that condiments are not available in Sbirro's."

Costain was shocked. "Not even salt!" he exclaimed.

"Not even salt. The very fact that you require it for your soup stands as evidence that your taste is unduly jaded. I am confident that you will now make the same discovery that I did: by the time you have nearly finished your soup, your desire for salt will be nonexistent."

Laffler was right; before Costain had reached the bottom of his plate, he was relishing the nuances of the broth with steadily increasing delight. Laffler thrust aside his own empty bowl and rested his elbows on the table. "Do you agree with me now?"

"To my surprise," said Costain, "I do."

As the waiter busied himself clearing the table, Laffler lowered his voice significantly. "You will find," he said, "that the absence of condiments is but one of several noteworthy characteristics which mark Sbirro's. I may as well prepare you for these. For example, no alcoholic beverages of any sort are served here, nor for that matter any beverage except clear, cold water, the first and only drink necessary for a human being."

"Outside of mother's milk," suggested Costain dryly.

"I can answer that in like vein by pointing out that the average patron of Sbirro's has passed that primal stage of his development."

Costain laughed. "Granted," he said.

"Very well. There is also a ban on the use of tobacco in any form."

"But, good heavens," said Costain, "doesn't that make Sbirro's more a teetotaler's retreat than a gourmet's sanctuary?"

"I fear," said Laffler solemnly, "that you confuse the words *gourmet* and *gourmand*. The gourmand, through glutting himself, requires a wider and wider latitude of experience to stir his surfeited senses, but the very nature of the gourmet is simplicity. The ancient Greek in his coarse chiton savoring the ripe olive; the Japanese in his bare room contemplating the curve of a single flower stem—these are the true gourmets."

"But an occasional drop of brandy or pipeful of tobacco," said Costain dubiously, "are hardly overindulgences."

"By alternating stimulant and narcotic," said Laffler, "you seesaw the delicate balance of your taste so violently that it loses its most precious quality: the appreciation of fine food. During my years as a patron of Sbirro's, I have proved this to my satisfaction."

"May I ask," said Costain, "why you regard the ban on these things as having such deep esthetic motives? What about such mundane reasons as the high cost of a liquor license, or the possibility that patrons would object to the smell of tobacco in such confined quarters?"

Laffler shook his head violently. "If and when you meet Sbirro," he said, "you will understand at once that he is not the man to make decisions on a mundane basis. As a matter of fact, it was Sbirro himself who first made me cognizant of what you call 'esthetic' motives."

"An amazing man," said Costain as the waiter prepared to serve the entrée.

Laffler's next words were not spoken until he had savored and swallowed a large portion of meat. "I hesitate to use superlatives," he said, "but to my way of thinking, Sbirro represents man at the apex of his civilization!"

Costain cocked an eyebrow and applied himself to his roast, which rested in a pool of stiff gravy ungarnished by green or vegetable. The thin steam rising from it carried to his nostrils a subtle, tantalizing odor which made his mouth water. He chewed a piece as slowly and thoughtfully as if he were analyzing the intricacies of a Mozart symphony. The range of taste he discovered was really extraordinary, from the pungent nip of the crisp outer edge to the peculiarly flat yet soul-satisfying ooze of blood which the pressure of his jaws forced from the half raw interior.

Upon swallowing he found himself ferociously hungry for another piece, and then another, and it was only with an effort that he prevented himself from wolfing down all his share of the meat and gravy without waiting to get the full voluptuous satisfaction from each mouthful. When he had scraped his platter clean, he realized that both he and Laffler had completed the entire course without exchanging a single word. He commented on this, and Laffler said: "Can you see any need for words in the presence of such food?"

Costain looked around at the shabby, dimly lit room, the quiet diners, with a new perception. "No," he said humbly, "I cannot. For any doubts I had I apologize unreservedly. In all your praise of Sbirro's there was not a single word of exaggeration."

"Ah," said Laffler delightedly. "And that is only part of the story. You heard me mention the special, which unfortunately was not on the menu tonight. What you have just eaten is as nothing when compared to the absolute delights of that special!"

"Good Lord!" cried Costain, "what is it? Nightingale's tongues? Filet of unicorn?"

"Neither," said Laffler. "It is lamb."

"Lamb?"

Laffler remained lost in thought for a minute. "If," he said at last, "I were to give you in my own unstinted words my opinion of this dish, you would judge me completely insane. That is how deeply the mere thought of it affects me. It is neither the fatty chop, nor the too solid leg; it is, instead, a select portion of the rarest sheep in existence and is named after the species—lamb Amirstan."

Costain knit his brows. "Amirstan?"

"A fragment of desolation almost lost on the border which separates Afghanistan and Russia. From chance remarks dropped by Sbirro, I gather it is no more than a plateau which grazes the pitiful remnants of a flock of superb sheep. Sbirro, through some means or other, obtained rights to the traffic in this flock and is, therefore, the sole restaurateur ever to have lamb Amirstan on his bill of fare. I can tell you that the appearance of this dish is a rare occurrence indeed, and luck is the only guide in determining for the clientele the exact date when it will be served."

"But surely," said Costain, "Sbirro could provide some advance knowledge of this event."

"The objection to that is simply stated," said Laffler. "There exists in this city a huge number of professional gluttons. Should advance information slip out, it is quite likely that they will, out of curiosity, become familiar with the dish and thenceforth supplant the regular patrons at these tables."

"But you don't mean to say," objected Costain, "that these few people present are the only ones in the entire city, or for that matter in the whole wide world, who know of the existence of Sbirro's!"

"Very nearly. There may be one or two regular patrons who, for some reason, are not present at the moment."

"That's incredible."

"It is done," said Laffler, the slightest shade of menace in his voice, "by every patron making it his solemn obligation to keep the secret. By accepting my invitation this evening, you automatically assume that obligation. I hope you can be trusted with it."

Costain flushed. "My position in your employ should vouch for me. I only question the wisdom of a policy which keeps such magnificent food away from so many who would enjoy it."

"Do you know the inevitable result of the policy *you* favor?" asked

Laffler bitterly. "An influx of idiots who would nightly complain that they are never served roast duck with chocolate sauce. Is that picture tolerable to you?"

"No," admitted Costain. "I am forced to agree with you."

Laffler leaned back in his chair wearily and passed his hand over his eyes in an uncertain gesture. "I am a solitary man," he said quietly, "and not by choice alone. It may sound strange to you, it may border on eccentricity, but I feel to my depths that this restaurant, this warm haven in a coldly insane world, is both family and friend to me."

And Costain, who to this moment had never viewed his companion as other than tyrannical employer or officious host, now felt an overwhelming pity twist inside his comfortably expanded stomach.

By the end of two weeks the invitations to join Laffler at Sbirro's had become something of a ritual. Every day, at a few minutes after five, Costain would step out into the office corridor and lock his cubicle behind him; he would drape his overcoat neatly over his left arm, and peer into the glass of the door to make sure his Homburg was set at the proper angle. At one time he would have followed this by lighting a cigarette, but under Laffler's prodding he had decided to give abstinence a fair trial. Then he would start down the corridor, and Laffler would fall in step at his elbow, clearing his throat. "Ah, Costain. No plans for this evening, I hope."

"No," Costain would say, "I'm footloose and fancy-free," or "At your service," or something equally inane. He wondered at times whether it would not be more tactful to vary the ritual with an occasional refusal, but the glow with which Laffler received his answer and the rough friendliness of Laffler's grip on his arm forestalled him.

Among the treacherous crags of the business world, reflected Costain, what better way to secure your footing than friendship with one's employer? Already, a secretary close to the workings of the inner office had commented publicly on Laffler's highly favorable opinion of Costain. That was all to the good.

And the food! The incomparable food at Sbirro's! For the first time in his life, Costain, ordinarily a lean and bony man, noted with gratification that he was certainly gaining weight; within two weeks his bones had disappeared under a layer of sleek, firm flesh, and here and there were even signs of incipient plumpness. It struck Costain one night, while surveying himself in his bath, that the rotund Laffler himself might have been a spare and bony man before discovering Sbirro's.

So there was obviously everything to be gained and nothing to be lost by accepting Laffler's invitations. Perhaps after testing the heralded wonders of lamb Amirstan and meeting Sbirro, who thus far had not made an appearance, a refusal or two might be in order. But certainly not until then.

That evening, two weeks to a day after his first visit to Sbirro's, Costain had both desires fulfilled; he dined on lamb Amirstan, and he met Sbirro. Both exceeded all his expectations.

When the waiter leaned over their table immediately after seating them and gravely announced: "Tonight is special, sair," Costain was shocked to find his heart pounding with expectation. On the table before him he saw Laffler's hands trembling violently.

But it isn't natural, he thought suddenly: two full-grown men, presumably intelligent and in the full possession of their senses, as jumpy as a pair of cats waiting to have their meat flung to them!

"This is it!" Laffler's voice startled him so that he almost leaped from his seat. "The culinary triumph of all times! And faced by it you are embarrassed by the very emotions it distills."

"How did you know that?" Costain asked faintly.

"How? Because a decade ago I underwent your embarrassment. Add to that your air of revulsion and it's easy to see how affronted you are by the knowledge that man has not yet forgotten how to slaver over his meat."

"And these others," whispered Costain, "do they all feel the same thing?"

"Judge for yourself."

Costain looked furtively around at the nearby tables. "You are right," he finally said. "At any rate, there's comfort in numbers."

Laffler inclined his head slightly to the side. "One of the numbers," he remarked, "appears to be in for a disappointment."

Costain followed the gesture. At the table indicated, a gray-haired man sat conspicuously alone, and Costain frowned at the empty chair opposite him.

"Why, yes," he recalled, "that very stout bald man, isn't it? I believe it's the first dinner he's missed here in two weeks."

"The entire decade more likely," said Laffler sympathetically. "Rain or shine, crisis or calamity, I don't think he's missed an evening at Sbirro's since the first time I dined here. Imagine his expression when he's told that on his very first defection, lamb Amirstan was the *plat du jour*."

Costain looked at the empty chair again with a dim discomfort. "His very first?" he murmured.

"Mr. Laffler! And friend! I am so pleased. So very, very pleased. No, do not stand; I will have a place made." Miraculously a seat appeared under the figure standing there at the table. "The lamb Amirstan will be an unqualified success, hurr? I myself have been stewing in the miserable kitchen all the day, prodding the foolish chef to do everything just so. The just so is the important part, hurr? But I see your friend does not know me. An introduction, perhaps?"

The words ran in a smooth, fluid eddy. They rippled, they purred, they hypnotized Costain so that he could do no more than stare. The mouth that uncoiled this sinuous monologue was alarmingly wide, with thin mobile lips that curled and twisted with every syllable. There was a flat nose with a straggling line of hair under it; wide-set eyes, almost oriental in appearance, that glittered in the unsteady flare of gaslight; and long sleek hair that swept back from high on the unwrinkled forehead—hair so pale that it might have been bleached of all color. An amazing face surely, and the sight of it tortured Costain with the conviction that it was somehow familiar. His brain twitched and prodded but could not stir up any solid recollection.

Laffler's voice jerked Costain out of his study. "Mr. Sbirro. Mr. Costain, a good friend and associate." Costain rose and shook the proffered hand. It was warm and dry, flint-hard against his palm.

"I am so very pleased, Mr. Costain. So very, very pleased," purred the voice. "You like my little establishment, hurr? You have a great treat in store, I assure you."

Laffler chuckled. "Oh, Costain's been dining here regularly for two weeks," he said. "He's by way of becoming a great admirer of yours, Sbirro."

The eyes were turned on Costain. "A very great compliment. You compliment me with your presence and I return same with my food, hurr? But the lamb Amirstan is far superior to anything of your past experience, I assure you. All the trouble of obtaining it, all the difficulty of preparation, is truly merited."

Costain strove to put aside the exasperating problem of that face. "I have wondered," he said, "why with all these difficulties you mention, you even bother to present lamb Amirstan to the public.

Surely your other dishes are excellent enough to uphold your reputation."

Sbirro smiled so broadly that his face became perfectly round. "Perhaps it is a matter of the psychology, hurr? Someone discovers a wonder and must share it with others. He must fill his cup to the brim, perhaps, by observing the so evident pleasure of those who explore it with him. Or," he shrugged, "perhaps it is just a matter of good business."

"Then in the light of all this," Costain persisted, "and considering all the conventions you have imposed on your customers, why do you open the restaurant to the public instead of operating it as a private club?"

The eyes abruptly glinted into Costain's, then turned away. "So perspicacious, hurr? Then I will tell you. Becuase there is more privacy in a public eating place than in the most exclusive club in existence! Here no one inquires of your affairs; no one desires to know the intimacies of your life. Here the business is eating. We are not curious about names and addresses or the reasons for the coming and going of our guests. We welcome you when you are here; we have no regrets when you are here no longer. That is the answer, hurr?"

Costain was startled by this vehemence. "I had no intention of prying," he stammered.

Sbirro ran the tip of his tongue over his thin lips. "No, no," he reassured, "you are not prying. Do not let me give you that impression. On the contrary, I invite your questions."

"Oh, come, Costain," said Laffler. "Don't let Sbirro intimidate you. I've known him for years and I guarantee that his bark is worse than his bite. Before you know it, he'll be showing you all the privileges of the house—outside of inviting you to visit his precious kitchen, of course."

"Ah," smiled Sbirro, "for that, Mr. Costain may have to wait a little while. For everything else I am at his beck and call."

Laffler slapped his hand jovially on the table. "What did I tell you!" he said. "Now let's have the truth, Sbirro. Has anyone, outside of your staff, ever stepped into the sanctum sanctorum?"

Sbirro looked up. "You see on the wall above you," he said earnestly, "the portrait of one to whom I did the honor. A very dear friend and patron of most long standing, he is evidence that my kitchen is not inviolate."

Costain studied the picture and started with recognition. "Why," he said excitedly, "that's the famous writer—you know the one, Laffler—he used to do such wonderful short stories and cynical bits and then suddenly took himself off and disappeared in Mexico!"

"Of course!" cried Laffler, "and to think I've been sitting under his portrait for years without even realizing it!" He turned to Sbirro. "A dear friend, you say? His disappearance must have been a blow to you."

Sbirro's face lengthened. "It was, it was, I assure you. But think of it this way, gentlemen: he was probably greater in his death than in his life, hurr? A most tragic man, he often told me that his only happy hours were spent here at this very table. Pathetic, is it not? And to think the only favor I could ever show him was to let him witness the mysteries of my kitchen, which is, when all is said and done, no more than a plain, ordinary kitchen."

"You seem very certain of his death," commented Costain. "After all, no evidence has ever turned up to substantiate it."

Sbirro contemplated the picture. "None at all," he said softly. "Remarkable, hurr?"

With the arrival of the entrée Sbirro leaped to his feet and set about serving them himself. With his eyes alight he lifted the casserole from the tray and sniffed at the fragrance from within with sensual relish. Then, taking great care not to lose a single drop of gravy, he filled two platters with chunks of dripping meat. As if exhausted by this task, he sat back in his chair, breathing heavily. "Gentlemen," he said, "to your good appetite."

Costain chewed his first mouthful with great deliberation and swallowed it. Then he looked at the empty tines of his fork with glazed eyes.

"Good God!" he breathed.

"It is good, hurr? Better than you imagined?"

Costain shook his head dazedly. "It is as impossible," he said slowly, "for the uninitiated to conceive the delights of lamb Amirstan as for mortal man to look into his own soul."

"Perhaps," Sbirro thrust his head so close that Costain could feel the warm, fetid breath tickle his nostrils, "perhaps you have just had a glimpse into your soul, hurr?"

Costain tried to draw back slightly without giving offense. "Perhaps," he laughed, "and a gratifying picture it made: all fang and claw. But without intending any disrespect, I should hardly like to build my church on *lamb en casserole*."

Sbirro rose and laid a hand gently on his shoulder. "So perspicacious," he said. "Sometimes when you have nothing to do, nothing, perhaps, but sit for a very little while in a dark room and think of this world—what it is and what it is going to be—then you must turn your thoughts a little to the significance of the Lamb in religion. It will be so interesting. And now," he bowed deeply to both men, "I have held you long enough from your dinner. I was most happy," he nodded to Costain, "and I am sure we will meet again." The teeth gleamed, the eyes glittered, and Sbirro was gone down the aisle of tables.

Costain twisted around to stare after the retreating figure. "Have I offended him in some way?" he asked.

Laffler looked up from his plate. "Offended him? He loves that kind of talk. Lamb Amirstan is a ritual with him; get him started and he'll be back at you a dozen times worse than a priest making a conversion."

Costain turned to his meal with the face still hovering before him. "Interesting man," he reflected. "Very."

It took him a month to discover the tantalizing familiarity of that face, and when he did he laughed aloud in his bed. Why, of course! Sbirro might have sat as the model for the Cheshire cat in *Alice!*

He passed this thought on to Laffler the very next evening as they pushed their way down the street to the restaurant against a chill, blustering wind. Laffler only looked blank.

"You may be right," he said, "but I'm not a fit judge. It's a far cry back to the days when I read the book. A far cry, indeed."

As if taking up his words, a piercing howl came ringing down the street and stopped both men short in their tracks. "Someone's in trouble there," said Laffler. "Look!"

Not far from the entrance to Sbirro's two figures could be seen struggling in the near darkness. They swayed back and forth and suddenly tumbled into a writhing heap on the sidewalk. The piteous howl went up again, and Laffler, despite his girth, ran toward it at a fair speed with Costain tagging cautiously behind.

Stretched out full-length on the pavement was a slender figure with the dusky complexion and white hair of one of Sbirro's servitors. His fingers were futilely plucking at the huge hands which encircled his throat, and his knees pushed weakly up at the gigantic bulk of a man who brutally bore down with his full weight.

Laffler came up panting. "Stop this!" he shouted. "What's going on here?"

The pleading eyes almost bulging from their sockets turned toward Laffler. "Help, sair. This man—drunk—"

"Drunk am I, ya dirty—" Costain saw now that the man was a sailor in a badly soiled uniform. The air around him reeked with the stench of liquor. "Pick me pocket and then call me drunk, will ya!" He dug his fingers in harder, and his victim groaned.

Laffler seized the sailor's shoulder. "Let go of him, do you hear! Let go of him at once!" he cried, and the next instant was sent careening into Costain, who staggered back under the force of the blow.

The attack on his own person sent Laffler into immediate and berserk action. Without a sound he leaped at the sailor, striking and kicking furiously at the unprotected face and flanks. Stunned at first, the man came to his feet with a rush and turned on Laffler. For a moment they stood locked together, and then, as Costain joined the attack, all three went sprawling to the ground. Slowly Laffler and Costain got to their feet and looked down at the body before them.

"He's either out cold from liquor," said Costain, "or he struck his head going down. In any case, it's a job for the police."

"No, no, sair!" The waiter crawled weakly to his feet, and stood swaying. "No police, sair. Mr. Sbirro do not want such. You understand, sair." He caught hold of Costain with a pleading hand, and Costain looked at Laffler.

"Of course not," said Laffler. "We won't have to bother with the police. They'll pick him up soon enough, the murderous sot. But what in the world started all this?"

"That man, sair. He make most erratic way while walking, and with no meaning I push against him. Then he attack me, accusing me to rob him."

"As I thought." Laffler pushed the waiter gently along. "Now go on in and get yourself attended to."

The man seemed ready to burst into tears. "To you, sair, I owe my life. If there is anything I can do—"

Laffler turned into the areaway that led to Sbirro's door. "No, no, it was nothing. You go along, and if Sbirro has any questions send him to me. I'll straighten it out."

"My life, sair," were the last words they heard as the inner door closed behind them.

"There you are, Costain," said Laffler, as a few minutes later he drew his chair under the table, "civilized man in all his glory. Reeking with alcohol, strangling to death some miserable innocent who came too close."

Costain made an effort to gloss over the nerve-shattering memory of the episode. "It's the neurotic cat that takes to alcohol," he said. "Surely there's a reason for that sailor's condition."

"Reason? Of course there is. Plain atavistic savagery!" Laffler swept his arm in an all-embracing gesture. "Why do we all sit here at our meat? Not only to appease physical demands, but because our atavistic selves cry for release. Think back, Costain. Do you remember that I once described Sbirro as the epitome of civilization? Can you now see why? A brilliant man, he fully understands the nature of human beings. But unlike lesser men he bends all his efforts to the satisfaction of our innate natures without resultant harm to some innocent bystander."

"When I think back on the wonders of lamb Amirstan," said Costain, "I quite understand what you're driving at. And, by the way, isn't it nearly due to appear on the bill of fare? It must have been over a month ago that it was last served."

The waiter, filling the tumblers, hesitated. "I am so sorry, sair. No special this evening."

"There's your answer," Laffler grunted, "and probably just my luck to miss out on it altogether the next time."

Costain stared at him. "Oh, come, that's impossible."

"No, blast it." Laffler drank off half his water at a gulp and the waiter immediately refilled the glass. "I'm off to South America for a surprise tour of inspection. One month, two months, Lord knows how long."

"Are things that bad down there?"

"They could be better." Laffler suddenly grinned. "Mustn't forget it takes very mundane dollars and cents to pay the tariff at Sbirro's."

"I haven't heard a word of this around the office."

"Wouldn't be a surprise tour if you had. Nobody knows about this except myself—and now you. I want to walk in on them completely unsuspected. Find out what flimflammery they're up to down there. As far as the office is concerned, I'm off on a jaunt somewhere. Maybe recuperating in some sanatorium from my hard work. Anyhow, the business will be in good hands. Yours, among them."

"Mine?" said Costain, surprised.

"When you go in tomorrow you'll find yourself in receipt of a promotion, even if I'm not there to hand it to you personally. Mind you, it has nothing to do with our friendship either; you've done fine work, and I'm immensely grateful for it."

Costain reddened under the praise. "You don't expect to be in tomorrow. Then you're leaving tonight?"

Laffler nodded. "I've been trying to wangle some reservations. If they come through, well, this will be in the nature of a farewell celebration."

"You know," said Costain slowly, "I devoutly hope that your reservations don't come through. I believe our dinners here have come to mean more to me than I ever dared imagine."

The waiter's voice broke in. "Do you wish to be served now, sair?" and they both started.

"Of course, of course," said Laffler sharply, "I didn't realize you were waiting."

"What bothers me," he told Costain as the waiter turned away, "is the thought of the lamb Amirstan I'm bound to miss. To tell you the truth, I've already put off my departure a week, hoping to hit a lucky night, and now I simply can't delay any more. I do hope that when you're sitting over your share of lamb Amirstan, you'll think of me with suitable regrets."

Costain laughed. "I will indeed," he said as he turned to his dinner.

Hardly had he cleared the plate when a waiter silently reached for it. It was not their usual waiter, he observed; it was none other than the victim of the assault.

"Well," Costain said, "how do you feel now? Still under the weather?"

The waiter paid no attention to him. Instead, with the air of a man under great strain, he turned to Laffler. "Sair," he whispered. "My life. I owe it to you. I can repay you!"

Laffler looked up in amazement, then shook his head firmly. "No," he said; "I want nothing from you, understand? You have repaid me sufficiently with your thanks. Now get on with your work and let's hear no more about it."

The waiter did not stir an inch, but his voice rose slightly. "By the body and blood of your God, sair, I will help you even if you do not want! *Do not go into the kitchen, sair*. I trade you my life for yours, sair, when I speak this. Tonight or any night of your life, do not go into the kitchen at Sbirro's!"

Laffler sat back, completely dumbfounded. "Not go into the kitchen? Why shouldn't I go into the kitchen if Mr. Sbirro ever took it into his head to invite me there? What's all this about?"

A hard hand was laid on Costain's back, and another gripped the waiter's arm. The waiter remained frozen to the spot, his lips compressed, his eyes downcast.

"What is all *what* about, gentlemen?" purred the voice. "So opportune an arrival. In time as ever, I see, to answer all the questions, hurr?"

Laffler breathed a sigh of relief. "Ah, Sbirro, thank heaven you're here. This man is saying something about my not going into your kitchen. Do you know what he means?"

The teeth showed in a broad grin. "But of course. This good man was giving you advice in all amiability. It so happens that my too emotional chef heard some rumor that I might have a guest into his precious kitchen, and he flew into a fearful rage. Such a rage, gentlemen! He even threatened to give notice on the spot, and you can understand what that would mean to Sbirro's, hurr? Fortunately, I succeeded in showing him what a signal honor it is to have an esteemed patron and true connoisseur observe him at his work first hand, and now he is quite amenable. Quite, hurr?"

He released the waiter's arm. "You're at the wrong table," he said softly. "See that it does not happen again."

The waiter slipped off without daring to raise his eyes and Sbirro drew a chair to the table. He seated himself and brushed his hand lightly over his hair. "Now I am afraid that the cat is out of the bag, hurr? This invitation to you, Mr. Laffler, was to be a surprise; but the surprise is gone, and all that is left is the invitation."

Laffler mopped beads of perspiration from his forehead. "Are you serious?" he said huskily. "Do you mean that we are really to witness the preparation of your food tonight?"

Sbirro drew a sharp fingernail along the tablecloth, leaving a thin straight line printed in the linen. "Ah," he said, "I am faced with a dilemma of great proportions." He studied the line soberly. "You, Mr. Laffler, have been my guest for ten long years. But our friend here—"

Costain raised his hand in protest. "I understand perfectly. This invitation is solely to Mr. Laffler, and naturally my presence is embarrassing. As it happens, I have an early engagement for this evening and must be on my way anyhow. So you see there's no dilemma at all, really."

"No," said Laffler, "absolutely not. That wouldn't be fair at all. We've been sharing this until now, Costain, and I won't enjoy this experience half as much if you're not along. Surely Sbirro can make his conditions flexible this one occasion."

They both looked at Sbirro who shrugged his shoulders regretfully.

Costain rose abruptly. "I'm not going to sit here, Laffler, and spoil your great adventure. And then too," he bantered, "think of that ferocious chef waiting to get his cleaver on you. I prefer not to be at the scene. I'll just say goodbye," he went on, to cover Laffler's guilty silence, "and leave you to Sbirro. I'm sure he'll take pains to give you a good show." He held out his hand and Laffler squeezed it painfully hard.

"You're being very decent, Costain," he said. "I hope you'll continue to dine here until we meet again. It shouldn't be too long."

Sbirro made way for Costain to pass. "I will expect you," he said. *"Au 'voir."*

Costain stopped briefly in the dim foyer to adjust his scarf and fix his Homburg at the proper angle. When he turned away from the mirror, satisfied at last, he saw with a final glance that Laffler and Sbirro were already at the kitchen door; Sbirro holding the door invitingly wide with one hand, while the other rested, almost tenderly, on Laffler's meaty shoulders.

Thomas Flanagan

The Fine Italian Hand

As he padded down the stone-flagged passage beside the tall erect figure of Count Montagno, the Duke's messenger looked meager and inadequate, his thin body hunched in a frayed crimson robe of court, the yellowed skin of his face stretched across sharp cheekbones and slim shrunken chin.

The corridor, cold with the bone-piercing wind of North Italy, was lit by the wavering torches of the servants who preceded them down the hall.

The Duke's messenger looked with grudging admiration at Count Montagno, the Wolf of the North, the greatest of the *condottieri*. The Duke's messenger, who had known the sallow lupine face of the king of France, who had watched the heavy sullen tread of the Hapsburg, had never felt such fear in the presence of a man. Never but once, and that was the time when he had first met his lord and duke, the terrible Cesare Borgia.

The racing, shadowy flames from the pitch torches showed him now the Count's tall sinewy body, his jutting wolflike head. The Duke's messenger longed for the quiet of his small room, for the comforting feel of vellum between his fingers. He longed to resume his translation of Livy. In the turmoil of Fourteenth Century Italy, nothing, the duke's messenger knew, was needed so badly as quiet, unexciting scholarship. And yet (the Duke's messenger shrugged) here he was running errands between the wolf of the north and the lion of the midlands.

He heard the harsh, soldierlike tones of the man beside him. "You can easily see, my dear sir, that not only your great master but I myself and those within my liege are placed in hazard by this theft. France waits beyond the mountains—waiting for the thinnest of excuses with which to justify to the Holy Father an invasion of all Italy—and now this."

By contrast, the voice of the Duke's messenger was cracked and pedantic, flecked with the dust of a hundred libraries. "You could write to his majesty of France. You could explain the theft."

The Count turned and by the glaring light looked down upon the thin messenger. "We have maintained the sovereignty of these states, your master and I, by creating the legend of our strength, of our cunning. And you wish us to tell France that we permitted a footsoldier, or a majordomo, or a servant, to make off with Borgia's gift to the majesty of France?"

"It would be so simple. Simple and direct. One should never be afraid to confess mistakes. That is a sign of strength, not of weakness."

They had entered the large banqueting hall, where tapers, fixed to the walls, shed a fitful light across the flagging, across the broad oaken tables.

"That is a sign of copybook strength," the Count said, and the low vaulted room echoed with his voice. He held up his thick, sinewed arm. "This is the strength which rules Italy."

The messenger smiled apologetically. "One may learn much from copybooks. Have you read Livy? A very clever man."

The Count raised his heavy confident shoulders and turned away. "We were feasting in this hall," he said, "I and the Marquis of Villefranche, who was to receive Borgia's gift, and our retinues. I toasted France, with the wine and the words sticking in my throat, and then together, Villefranche and I, we descended the stairs to where the treasure lay under guard."

"Had Villefranche seen the treasure earlier?"

"Yes. That afternoon, before the feast. We had looked at it together and marveled at—" the Count's eyes raked the Duke's messenger slantwise "—at Borgia's great concern to please France with such gifts."

The messenger shrugged. "Or perhaps wondered at Borgia's great wealth that he should carelessly leave a treasure in cut emeralds under the guard of a border captain."

The Count smiled in angry acknowledgement of the thrust. "You know the rest," he said. "We descended the stairs and found the treasure gone. One of the soldiers guarding it had been killed, and the second wounded."

"Perhaps you should have had more men guarding it."

"Perhaps. Perhaps. You are not a soldier, I take it?"

The messenger smiled primly, pulling down the corners of his thin lips. "Dear, no. I am a man of thought."

"Yes. If you had been a soldier, you would know my position. I have only a few hundred men at Castello Montagno. The rest are foraging the countryside, hunting for food, should we have to sustain a spring attack from France. This is a poor province and my noble ally, your great master, is not as generous with his friends as he is with his enemies."

The messenger slipped his frail blue-veined hands into the sleeves of his robe.

"One gains only the Known from one's friends. One's enemies possess the Unknown and hence should always be courted. But the guards?"

The soldier stared in blunt perplexity at the wizened peasant whom Borgia had sent to receive his report. "Because of this, my dear sir, I used every man as a member of my personal bodyguard, or as a guard at the portcullis, that Villefranche might see them as he rode up. Might see them and be deceived. I even pressed some of the scullery boys into armor."

"That was truly cleverness," the Duke's messenger said. "But had you anticipated a theft, your cleverness might have risen to wisdom."

"I am not a huckster nor a diplomat, nor, pardon my bluntness, a toadying courtier. I know one thing, and I know that well. I know how to fight. When I have sword in hand, when I stand upon the field of action—"

"Your prowess has won you the respect of all Italy," the messenger interrupted. "But it is because of the emeralds that my master has sent me here. He has himself regaled me with tales of your prowess."

"Indeed?"

"Indeed and indeed." As the messenger looked upon the heavy wolf's-head face, it came to him again how ill-suited he was anywhere but among his books. He shuddered delicately, and drew his robe about him.

"It seemed safe," Montagno said, "and it will seem safe to you." He walked toward a low stone door.

"I had three men standing here on guard. Even should they have been overpowered, the thieves would have emerged in full sight of Villefranche and myself and all of our staffs as we sat feasting. Can you not see that?"

"Indeed and indeed," the messenger said.

Montagno flung open the door and signaled to the two torch-bearing attendants. With the messenger following timorously behind, they descended a steep staircase, cut, the messenger guessed, from the very mountain on which Castello Montagno rested. When he had reached the foot of the staircase, he found himself in a low, dark, windowless room, lit only by the torches which they had brought with them.

"This was the room," Montagno said, "and there is but one other entrance to it."

"Ah," the messenger said.

Montagno glared at him contemptuously and walked with his quick wolf's tread to the far side of the room, with the guards scurrying after him. It seemed to the messenger that he had descended into some infernal pit, into the lair of some animal. He glanced apprehensively behind him, but the door leading to the staircase had been slammed shut from above.

Montagno had placed his strong thick arms on the second door, which was of stone and had been set inconspicuously into the wall, and pushed outward. Instantly the room was flooded with sunlight, and the messenger, as he walked toward it, understood the Count's snort of contempt.

For the door opened onto space, onto the sky and the sun, and beneath it was a sheer, straight drop of a thousand feet. The messenger found himself staring south where, hidden by the mist and by many miles, his brutal master, Cesare Borgia, was even now waiting for his report. The messenger shuddered, and fingered his long throat apprehensively.

"There you are," the Count said with gloomy satisfaction. "Through the first door, the thieves *did not* leave. Through the second door, the thieves *could not* leave."

"That is impossible," the Duke's messenger said. He backed away from the window, overcome by a fit of giddiness, and seated himself on a low stone bench.

"It *is* impossible, my dear sir—but it happened."

"It is impossible and Villefranche will report that it is impossible," the messenger said in a low toneless voice. "He will report that the emeralds had never been intended for the majesty of France."

"Yes," the Count said. "That is what he would like to report. It is the news which the majesty of France would wish dearly to hear. But you and I know that it is not so."

"Then—" the messenger looked up sharply, and his face, the Count noticed in some alarm, was that of a fox "—then it was a miracle. The emeralds vanished. They were an offering made jointly to the Virgin by Borgia and France. Another order of being, superior to the mortal, entered temporarily into our field of knowledge and then left it, leaving confusion where, had we but been immortal, there would have been pure reason. It is thus, barring my own lamentable ineptitude for metaphysics, that Saint Thomas defines a miracle."

He smiled deprecatingly, and the Count, slamming the door shut, walked toward him.

"Would it not please France to learn," the messenger asked, "that his jewels, above all others, had been marked for heavenly appropriation?"

"No," the Count said forcefully. "It would not."

"I was afraid not," the messenger said disconsolately.

"You are a fool," the Count said, seating himself beside the messenger. "Borgia has sent me a fool."

"In the sight of God the foolish are often the wise. Italy, cursed by war, famine, and plague, has cried for a miracle, and here we may give it to her."

"In the field of war," the Count said, "there is no room for the miraculous. Listen. If the thieves could not or did not leave by either of the doors, then *they did not leave!*"

"But the emeralds—"

"The emeralds left," the Count said. "Not the thieves, but the emeralds. They did not leave by the stairwell door, for that door was well guarded. They must have left by the wall door. They were lowered on rope, on one thousand feet of rope, to the foot of the mountains, and there they were carried off by the accomplices of the thieves."

"But if the thieves did not leave—"

"Then they remained. Is it not clear to you now, book-mouse? When we went into the treasure room, the two guards, and no one else, were in the room."

"But you said that the guards were dead."

"No. One guard was dead. His head had been severed from his body. The other guard was wounded, but he was not dead. He is not dead now."

The messenger smiled bemusedly at the Count. "Then the second guard, the living one, was the thief?"

"Perhaps, but not of necessity. In war, we examine carefully each possibility. When this room is unlighted, you notice that it is in total darkness. Now, is it not possible that the thieves slipped past the guards, attacked them, lowered the emeralds from the wall-door, then remained in the room until Villefranche and I descended with our staffs, and then, in the confusion, mingled themselves among us."

"Only," the messenger said slowly, becoming aware of the Count's meaning, "only if the thieves were men wearing either your livery or Villefranche's."

"Exactly. There are, then, three possibilities. Either the guards lowered the jewels from the window and then, for a reason which we may learn, fought each other, or else the thieves were men under my orders—or Villefranche's."

"How simple, it becomes so simple," the messenger said. "And this second guard?"

"He was found beside his dead comrade, wounded and almost crazed."

"Too crazed to talk."

"No, not too crazed to talk if he could."

"What do you mean?"

"Nofrio has been with the Montagno family from the moment of his birth. And from that moment he has been a deaf-mute."

The messenger stared at him.

"And now," the Count said, "we may prepare to meet the Marquis of Villefranche and offer to him our solution."

"You have a solution?" the messenger asked, and then stopped to grin. Unlike his usual expression of doleful misery, as though he sucked always upon a persimmon, his grin was oddly youthful. "Of course," he said. "Nofrio can write." He nodded. "We can direct our questions to him and he can write his answer."

"No," the Count said, standing up, and signaling the servants. "He cannot write a word. But still we have our solution."

"Truly," said the Duke's messenger, "one must have the cunning of a wolf."

The Marquis of Villefranche played fretfully with a pompom saturated with scent. He could not stand the bestiality of North Italy, nor the savagery of even the nobility. This blunt, grim-visaged warlord, Montagno, for example. Even the tiny shriveled clerk was preferable. He listened attentively, however, to Montagno's words.

If the words were not well chosen, Summer might find Castello Montagno in the hands of the majesty of France. A bagful of emeralds was a small price to pay for a legitimate provocation to war. Perhaps (the Marquis blanched), perhaps it might even be his duty to take Montagno's place in this mouldering tomb.

"And such, Villefranche," Montagno was saying, "such is the nature of the problem. You will forgive my suggestion that the theft might have been committed on your orders and by your men, but then, I have accused myself equally. As a man of logic, you will realize that it is merely a formal exercise in which we indulge."

"Yes," said Villefranche languidly, "and all of it depends upon the testimony of an illiterate deaf-mute and a dead man."

Montagno leaned toward him. They were in the room of justice of Castello Montagno. The Count was seated in his chair of state, which had arm-rests carved in the images of avenging wolves. Villefranche sat beside him, and to one side the Duke's messenger sat docilely upon a plain oaken bench.

"Yes," Montagno said, "the mute is illiterate, but he is not blind."

The pompom dropped from Villefranche's hand and rolled to the floor. The Duke's messenger leaped up obsequiously, picked it up, and returned it. Villefranche snatched it petulantly. "What do you mean?"

"Just this. I have had Fra Dominico paint for me a series of pictures. Each picture portrays one of the possibilities. He has merely to signify before us the correct way in which the theft occurred and we will have our solution. Fra Dominico, who has long known the youth, has managed to convey to him, through signs, the nature of the test. And so, you see, we have no problem."

Villefranche bit his lip, and the Duke's messenger, watching him closely, wondered whether or not his nervousness was caused by fear or indecision.

"But—" Villefranche said finally, "—but he would never incriminate himself."

Montagno grinned that terrible wolfish grin and Villefranche drew back, not through fear but through detestation of the vulgar.

"Nofrio has been prepared. You will see. Nofrio will be glad to speak the truth and end his misery one way or the other."

He nodded to the soldier behind him, who returned presently with a stout, brown-clad monk, who bore with him a number of sketches.

"These are the paintings?"

"The sketches, may it please your lordship." The monk, his art having demanded exactness of speech, drew back apprehensively. The protecting arm of Rome did not reach to the mountains of Castello Montagno.

"The sketches, then." The Count looked up toward the door. When the guards returned, they brought with them what might once have been a man. The guards supported his sagging body. His chest was crisscrossed with lashes and a terrible scar disfigured his face, running up into the blood-matted hair. Montagno grinned and looked toward Villefranche. "He has been—prepared."

The messenger winced and turned his eyes away, but Villefranche merely placed the pompom against his nostrils.

"I remember," Montagno said, and his voice was heavy and solemn in the room. "I remember when Nofrio was a child playing in the courtyard with the children of Castello Montagno. If he is innocent but can point to the guilty, I will protect him, whomever it incriminates." He gazed steadily at Villefranche. "I want that understood."

"It is understood," Villefranche said.

Montagno nodded to the monk, who drew forth the first sketch and held it toward Nofrio. It showed Nofrio and his dead comrade backed against the wall of the treasure-room, while soldiers, dressed in the Montagno livery and with drawn swords, carried the sack of emeralds to the wall-window.

"Poor Nofrio must think carefully," the Count said, "for if he nods, then I will have all of my banquet squad executed."

Nofrio pushed his squat, heavy head forward, his wide staring eyes fixed. Then, slowly, he shook his head.

The messenger relaxed, but Villefranche gripped the sides of his chair nervously.

The Count looked carefully at Villefranche, and then motioned again to the monk. The second sketch portrayed much the same picture, save that the soldiers were dressed in the livery of France, the livery of the retinue which had accompanied the Marquis of Villefranche.

"Now here, you see," Montagno said, "we have an interesting situation. An embarrassing one, potentially."

"By God," Villefranche said, "this is an insult not to me but to all France. If your peasant—"

"The innocent fear nothing before God or man," the messenger said in his rusty, pedantic voice, "and they never bother to protest."

Villefranche, his nostrils distended, glared for a moment at the messenger, and then all three men turned toward the prisoner.

"Watch Nofrio," the Count said smoothly. "If the men were French he will nod—and there will be war."

But Nofrio was slowly, positively, shaking his head from side to side.

Villefranche relaxed then, and smiled at Montagno, but the Count's face was that of a man accepting tragedy. Wordless, he nodded to the monk, and Fra Dominico held up the third portrait.

It was very different, for in this sketch Nofrio could clearly be seen standing at the wall-window, carefully lowering the sack of emeralds down the perilous mountainside to his unseen accomplices. It was the picture which would represent Nofrio's confession.

"Perhaps," Montagno said, "perhaps for Nofrio this is best of all, for it will end his troubles. He will escape the lash and the boot and the torture by water." The Duke's messenger, watching the Count, saw the face of a man who had looked upon much sorrow.

"Yes," Montagno said. "Nofrio will be set free." He took the torch from a servant behind him and, with the messenger, walked toward the prisoner. Villefranche, and the monk, carrying the third sketch, followed him. He held the torch a scant foot from the staring eyes.

Fra Dominico walked slowly to the prisoner and held the sketch before his wide, vacant, pain-drugged eyes.

The Count rubbed the back of his hand across a forehead which was sweating in the cold room. "Nofrio will be free," he said.

And then, slowly, sadly, without moving his eyes from the picture before him, Nofrio nodded.

"Man's justice has been done," the messenger said.

Villefranche turned to the Count. "I had not thought to find such wisdom in a soldier."

"One must have the cunning of a wolf," the messenger said, his scrawny hands thrust into the folds of his robe.

Montagno placed his hand on the prisoner's shoulder and then drew it away hastily, as though ashamed of such sentimentality.

He turned to the guards. "Take him out," he said. "See if he will reveal his accomplices. And if he will not, then kill him." He walked ponderously to the chair, his heavy shoulders sagging.

He kept his back turned, but the messenger, the marquis, and the monk stared with terrified fascination as the Count's hand was replaced by the impersonal fingers of the guards.

They carried him backwards from the room and his heels scraped on the cold stone. But before they had carried him more than a few feet, his mouth moved, and the Duke's messenger found himself staring into Nofrio's distended mouth, with its ragged stump of a tongue. Then, suddenly and horribly, the man released the hideous, jagged scream of the mute, half animal and wholly inhuman. It emerged for an instant and then Nofrio was silent and limp, and was taken away.

The Count sat hunched in his chair, his shoulders sagging. Suddenly he was not a great *condottiere* but a middle-aged man, a landlord. "He played when he was a child in the courtyard of Castello Montagno."

The Marquis, for once stripped of affectation, placed his hand on the Count's. Then, realizing that he had seen the gesture performed recently, he jerked the hand away.

"The majesty of France will know of this," he said, "and that you executed a thief whom you loved in order to demonstrate the integrity of your dealings with France."

He turned and walked from the room, and the Duke's messenger slipped out with him.

"This is a good country," the marquis said, freeing himself from terror by small talk.

"It can become a great one when it is freed from terror," the messenger said. He pressed his lips primly together. "When it is no longer the prey of wolves."

The marquis looked to the north, and in his mind he saw, beyond the mountains, the court of his sovereign. "It will become great when it is unified beneath the banner of France."

But the scrawny messenger looked, with mingled hatred and admiration, toward the south, toward the brutal corrupt court of his master, the lion of the plains, Cesare Borgia. "By an Italian," he said softly.

Villefranche, once again himself, smiled disdainfully and fingered his pompom. "You are a scholar," he said, "and live only with the abstract. Only strength is important."

"Yes," said the messenger sadly. "Only the strength of the lion and the cunning of the wolf."

"I deprecate," Villefranche said, to show that he, too, though a gentleman, was a scholar, "this growing idea of the nation. So long as there is strength and order it does not matter whether the unifier is French or Italian."

"No," the Duke's messenger said. "Not yet."

Villefranche looked back at the room behind them. "I will report this," he said. "It is not an incident for war."

"Man's justice was done," the messenger said.

"But not God's?"

The messenger shrugged his narrow sloping shoulders. "How may man, being mortal, know the justice of the Infinite?"

Seated once more in his own study, with his scholar's cloak drawn about him, the Duke's messenger felt a strange peace. Beside him,

on his writing table, lay his vellum-bound edition of Livy, and fresh
paper and quills. Perhaps there would be a day, the messenger
thought, when his name would echo through history as the greatest
of all the translators of the Latin historians.

But in the meantime—he shrugged—in the meantime he must
waste himself on the dirt and dross of corruption, writing reports
which would be read by his cunning bestial master and then forgotten. And the Duke's messenger was growing old and time was
eluding him, and he saw himself slipping into the oblivion of ser-
vitude, into that silence in which, to the ears of history, he would
be not even an echo beside the sound of those resounding syllables,
Cesare Borgia.

He took a sheet of foolscap, wet his pen, and began to write. To
even these stilted, hateful documents he lent the full weight of all
his scholarship, feeling as he did the irony of his position. The facts
behind his report no longer had meaning to him. He inscribed them
with the dry perspicuity with which his beloved Livy had spoken of
the growth of Latium.

He wrote: "To my beloved and worshipped lord and master, Cesare
Borgia, Duke Valentin, Lion of Italy, Strong Sword of Christ. Greet-
ings.

"Knowing full well the discrepancy which exists between the public and the private act, I beg leave of these few words to give to you
a thought or two which my public report omitted. You may perhaps
remember that in that report I expressed what I am sure is your
own admiration for the effective way in which that wolf of the north,
that scourge of the mountains, Montagno, Count of Castello Montagno, avenged the theft of your precious gift to the majesty of
France.

"And yet, that pedantry of mine, of which you have often spoken
with such winning humor, that pedantry, I say, forces me to add to
this picture.

"I traveled to Castello Montagno with but one thought in mind.
The theft of the emeralds must, under no circumstances, be used by
the French as the moral excuse for an invasion. Such an excuse,
Count Montagno deprived them of. And so, in that sense, my mission
was accomplished for me. I had not thought the Count so clever.

"At first it seemed to me that he was not being clever at all. But
then he knew that popinjay of a Villefranche as I did not. He knew
knew that Villefranche would not question the wisdom of placing
a deaf-mute on guard duty. He knew that Villefranche would not

question Nofrio's ability to distinguish between French and Italian livery in a pitch-black room. And those were his only risks. He made one mistake, it is true, but, fortunately, it passed Villefranche unnoticed. And the conception of the sketches was a master stroke, worthy of so redoubtable a strategist.

"And yet, not once, but twice was Montagno given away—once through his folly, and once through that instability of the human spirit which all great princes would be well advised to take within their thought. But of this Villefranche knew nothing.

"If you would care, after reading this report, to do me the honor of rereading my public report, you will notice that what so impressed poor Villefranche was the terrible scream of the deaf-mute. Truly and unmistakably, it was the scream of a man possessing no normal powers of speech. Yet so tender were Villefranche's nerves that he did not notice, as I did, the mutilated stump of Nofrio's tongue. A torn, jagged stump of a tongue in the mouth of a man born a deaf-mute? Perhaps, but much more likely we saw in Nofrio a man whose tongue had been plucked out late in life. And were that so, it was at least possible that Nofrio, if he could not speak, could hear and understand.

"I must confess that I had expected something of the kind, and yet, misjudging Montagno's nature, I had feared for something more crude. This was, indeed, polished and jeweled. For all the case hung about one man, a man from whom Montagno had removed the power of speech. Since he was illiterate, he lived, save for his eyes, in a world where communication with his fellows was impossible. He could comprehend, but he could not speak back.

"But no, we have a method, Montagno told us, the matter of the sketches, and had it not been for Montagno's mistake, I would have to this moment merely suspected without knowing. Yet now that I know, it seems the act of a child, wilful and clever, and because it was so I can recognize it as the work of a man with great powers of mind. If you will turn once again to your public report (and here I must again thank you for the great honor which you have done me in affixing *your* august signature to it), you will observe carefully the manner in which the test was made.

"The Count had instructed us that Nofrio had been informed of the nature of the test and hence, naturally, we had no desire to have the terms recapitulated when Nofrio was brought before us; and the Count did not do so. But mark—neither did he, at any time when Nofrio was in the room, so much as mention the sketches. True, as a deaf-mute it would have availed Nofrio nothing, but you and I now have reason to suspect that Nofrio was not deaf.

"Now mark further: When the first picture was brought forth, what did the Count say. Did he say, 'Mark well this picture, wretched Nofrio.'? No, he said merely that if Nofrio's comrades-in-arms had taken the emeralds they would be executed. And hearing those words, naturally Nofrio shook his head, for he knew his comrades were guiltless.

"And when the second picture was shown, again Montagno did not mention it. Merely he said that if the French had taken the jewels there would be war. And again Nofrio, the unfortunate, shook his head.

"But observe: when the third picture, which was to be his confession of guilt, was produced, Nofrio heard these strange words from the Count: 'Nofrio will be free,' and eagerly, incredulously, the fool nodded yes—and, in nodding, sealed his fate.

"But Nofrio had not taken the jewels. The jewels were, as you may have surmised, taken by the wolf of the north, Montagno of Castello Montagno. Presumably, sometime during the day, he walked past the outer guards, killed Nofrio's comrade, and wounded the already muted Nofrio. We shall undoubtedly soon hear of those jewels appearing on the markets of England and the Germanies.

"How else, indeed and indeed, account for the Count's elaborate ruse? Now were you not as clever as you are, you might by now be asking, 'Why did Nofrio nod when he saw the third picture?' But such a question were madness coming from the lips of the tiger of the plains. You have realized, of course, the purpose of the maimed tongue, the purpose of the test, the purpose of the careful phrases. The lamentable fact is that *Nofrio never did admit his guilt*. Nofrio never saw the pictures. *Nofrio was blind*.

"I suspected this when I saw his vacant, staring eyes. I was almost sure when I saw that Fra Dominico placed the pictures before his eyes, rather than letting him turn his eyes toward them. And I was certain, indeed and indeed, when the Count made that pointless, rash mistake: *when he held the torch a mere foot from those unflinching, unknowing eyes.*

"I like to think that Nofrio was blind from birth, and that the Count's only cruelty had been a certain degree of cruelty, in which, of course, we all indulge, and then the matter of the tongue. And, indeed, how much more blind was Villefranche, for the truth was before him and before his sighted eyes, and he saw it not.

"I did not speak, not even to Montagno when I left, of the matter, for he had served his purpose, and Nofrio his, and France was deceived. It would have been amusing to have observed his stunned discovery that someone knew his secret, but it would have been unprofitable, and one of the rules of statescraft is that one does not do the unprofitable. And after, he would have swelled only the more that another had observed his cleverness.

"But more important, he has unwittingly delivered into our hands the proof of his potential perfidy, and of his financial insecurity, and of his desire to risk even the wrath of France in order to arm his barren, poverty-stricken lands without our knowledge. Perhaps, indeed, he even contemplates using his new arms and men against your own person and power, but we are now forearmed. His cleverness has delivered him into our hands, and we may use him merely so long as we wish.

"It was, in truth, one of those affairs where all profited, a situation so unique as to merit your study: for the Marquis had his explanation, and the Count had his emeralds, and your Grace has now this knowledge which is so much more valuable than jewels. Only poor Nofrio suffered, and we must, indeed, take comfort in the thought that not even a sparrow may fall to the ground without Someone taking cognizance of his death.

"As always, your Grace, I throw myself prostrate at your feet, worshipping your wisdom and your strength.

"Your servant,
Niccolo Mächiavelli"

"Q"

William Link & Richard Levinson

Whistle While You Work

T he sun was striking along the edge of the blinded windows as Reber Shelley finished dressing. On the night-table the thin hands of his alarm clock pointed to 7:20. His wife still lay asleep on the small double bed.

He had finished transferring change from an old pair of pants when a sleepy moan came from behind him. "You up already?" his wife mumbled. She looked at him from the quilted cocoon of blankets. "Seems like every morning you get up earlier."

"Go back to sleep." Shelley walked toward the kitchenette, hoping she would stay in bed. "I'll get my own breakfast, Melba," he called out to her.

There was no answer from the tiny bedroom. The man in the kitchen started the coffee percolator and poured some cereal into a chipped bowl. He lifted a window shade and gazed out on the hot pocket of the little town. Heat waves were already shimmering up from the pavements, but the surrounding mountains looked cool and remote. The mercury line in the windowsill thermometer already touched 85.

Shelley grumbled to himself as he poured the coffee. He could see his thin face distorted by the chrome percolator fixtures—the cracked, sun-browned skin stretched tight under the eyes, the dull gray hair matted and uncombed.

If only she stayed in bed. If just this one morning he could get out without her coming in and ruining it.

"Looks like another hot day, Reber." She stood in the doorway, drawing a dressing-gown cord tighter about her dumpy body. He hadn't heard her footsteps on the worn carpet.

"Yeah. Hate like hell to carry the mail in weather like this."

"Makes you sick, that job, doesn't it?"

He didn't look at her, but he could feel his face getting flushed. "Please, Melba. Please don't start that again."

"I am not starting anything again." She came around to glare at him.

Her round face was hollow and without character. "Let's thrash this thing out. Right now. All your life you been a mail carrier here.

Every day you lug that bag—morning after morning—and what have you got? Look at you. Fifty-four and you look over sixty."

"I can't help it," he defended himself. "I work hard."

"You listen! What have you got to show? Other people got nice homes and cars. Not us. We're still living here, but you don't care. Oh, no, not you! Up every day, put on the pack, walk down the road. Like an animal, that's what you are. They could have hired an animal to do the same job."

He raised a placating hand, but it didn't stem her flow of bitter words.

"And it's changed you too. You used to be happy, you used to whistle. I could tell you felt good 'cause you always whistled. But you don't whistle any more."

He slipped one brown-leather strap of his mailbag over one arm, not listening to her at all. She clawed at his shoulder with one hand but he shrugged it off as he opened the door. Slowly he walked down the stone steps, his wife's voice storming out into the hot morning air.

"Go on!" she screamed from the doorway. "Start another day just like the rest! Just like an animal—go on!"

Walk . . . walk . . . walk . . . The road dropped steadily before him, slanting down to the dusty gray pile of stores that made up the center of town. High above, the sun had cleared the hazy rim of the mountains. His shadow was etched sharply on the hard-packed earth. Heat. Dryness. Walking. Always walking.

The post office loomed up. It was the first in the line of store fronts, a red-brick building, neat and compact. He entered and said good morning to Lou Rolfe, a tall wilted man who was the town's other postman. Pop Avery sat behind the stamp window with their two piles of mail stacked before him. "Hot day," he said.

The two carriers made a rapid assortment of the mail, then transferred it to their respective bags. They said goodbye to Avery and went outside.

Shelley watched Rolfe move off toward the opposite end of town before he heaved his bag on his shoulders. The brown pouch was like a heavy weight pressing down on his back. Ahead the road stretched past the post office and on past the five stores that comprised the row. A cloud of dust rose up and choked him as he started to walk. He coughed harshly and wiped his tearing eyes with the back of a chapped hand.

Walk.

The first stop was Tashman's grocery. Through the dirt-caked window he could see Tashman's loose white-smocked figure bent over the produce scales. The store didn't look the same without the grocer's lanky son, who had helped his father behind the counter. The boy was now in Korea, and Shelley looked through the three letters addressed to Tashman to see if any were from his son, but there were no foreign stamps. The mailman dropped the three oblongs through the door slot and walked on.

Olsen's barber shop. Olsen was shaving an early-morning customer. Above the pyramid of hair-tonic bottles an electric fan purred softly. It's cool in there, thought Shelley. I could drop in for a few minutes and chat with him and stand next to his fan. But no, I'd waste time, might even get into the habit of doing it. Better drop my letters and go on.

He passed the other three shops in the same mechanical procedure. Look in, think about the folks inside, slip the mail in the slot, walk on. The bag felt heavier on his back, so he shifted its position. The private homes came after the stores on his route. He followed the dirt road as the sweat began to break out on his neck and stain his shirt. Walk over the road, the dirt road. He could do it with his eyes closed. Walk.

Think about something besides the heat and Melba. Think about anything except those two. Letters. Thousands and thousands of letters all delivered by him. A never-ending chain of sealed papers that would probably stretch for miles if laid end to end. Letters of love, of grief, of birth, of death. *Wish you were here. Will be home in two weeks.* And telegrams. *Your son is missing in action.* All coming here to Cooper, Colorado. A hot, dry little town (population 276). A town with one sheriff, two deputies, four firemen and two mailmen. Letters. Letters and letter boxes. Outside each home: a stenciled metal can with a red metal flag. A flag burning with the heat of the sun. Here comes the mailman. Red flag up, red flag down. Each the same. Red flag up, red flag down. Heat. Melba. Walk.

He stopped at the first house, took off his bag, and rested briefly. It was a shrunken house, resting lazily on its foundations. The second house was slick and modern, freshly painted and gleaming with glass like an aquarium. All different, but in one respect each the same. Every one had its metal mailbox. Red flag up, red flag down.

And so the morning passed as he tramped up the climbing roads. Past playing children. Past talking housewives and friends he knew.

Higher and higher on his twisting route, as if his last silver box lay somewhere in the sky. He journeyed on and the sun went with him.

Finally one house left. The realization flashed through his mind as he turned and looked down the countryside. Below stretched the homes he had left, linked in a chain of bright red flags.

One house left. It sat on top of the hill against a backdrop of mountains. Charles Bywood's house. Bywood was the wealthiest man in Cooper; he commuted every day to his mill in the north. But most important, he always gave the mailman three dollars at Christmas time.

Shelley removed the last letter from his bag and turned into the sweeping driveway. He enjoyed delivering mail to this particular house. Probably it was because the load was now gone from his back and the route was over at last. He liked to walk over the crushed white stones of the driveway and watch the circlets of spray from the spinners on the parched lawn.

A slight breeze, fanning out from beyond a row of trees, cooled his face. It seemed that only the rich could afford the wind. The rest of Cooper seemed trapped far below, in the dusty bowl of the valley.

This morning he could see Mrs. Bywood lying on a chaise longue on a flagged patio in the rear. The silver frames of her dark glasses glinted in the sun. Shelley had almost reached her when a gust of wind flicked the letter from his hand and floated it across the lawn. It landed beneath one of the sprinklers. The mailman swore, stooped quickly, and retrieved the letter. Fortunately, only the back was wet, as he saw at a glance. The envelope was blue, with a black border, and addressed in a queer slanting handwriting. Rather guiltily he wiped the envelope on his shirt and dropped it in the mailbox. Maybe it would dry, he thought, before Mrs. Bywood came for it.

Then he walked down the hill, watching the rays of the sun strike at the terraced homes. He knew the temperature must be well up in the 90's by now. His muscles ached and his neck burned. Down he walked and the town came up to meet him. At last his route was over—and he was going home to Melba.

The next day was just as hot. His wife lashed out at him as she had done the previous morning. Everything seemed the same, yet there was a subtle change. As Shelley went into the post office, he noticed the excitement. Pop Avery did not greet him with the usual "Hot day." The old gentleman was holding court in a group of towns-folk. He turned to the other mailman.

"Hear the news, Reber?" Rolfe didn't wait for an answer. "Mrs. Bywood was murdered last night!"

Shelley was puzzled more than he was surprised or shocked. Murders didn't happen in Cooper, Colorado. Cooper wasn't the setting, it was too small, too hot, too—well, they just didn't happen there. The only bit of violence he could recall happened four years ago when some kids had tossed a brick through Tashman's front window. But murder!

The mailman collected his pouch of letters and started out. The dusty street was not empty as it usually was. Small knots of people stood together, hungry for conversation. The barber shop had an overflow of customers, the bakery was full of talking women. Shelley pieced together what had happened from vagrant sentences he heard as he progressed. Mrs. Bywood had been lured to a secluded spot near the main highway, and there she had been strangled with a silk scarf. That was all. No one knew why she had gone to the secluded spot. No one had witnessed the act. The little mailman was disturbed by the fact that he had seen her the previous afternoon. She was so healthy then, so well tanned and healthy. And now she was dead.

There were several letters for Charles Bywood, so he trudged up the hill to the house. The sprinklers stood idle on the lawn as a dry wind rustled the blades of grass. Behind the house, on the stone patio, the chaise longue was empty. A fleet of cars, their windshields marked with the stickers of northern newspapers, was parked in the driveway.

The mailman was rounding the bend of the walk when the sheriff came out with two other men and called hello to him. Shelley waved, dropped the letters in the box, and started back down the hill.

It was 5:30 and he had almost reached the center of town when he made a discovery. There was still one letter in his bag, half hidden by an overlapping piece of leather. It was a blue envelope with a black border. The handwriting was unusual. Shelley looked at the address and dropped the letter in the mailbox of the modern house as he passed by.

Melba was unbearable that night. Shelley sat, head lowered, at the supper table while she taunted him about his job. He was glad when the meal finally ended and he could retreat from Melba's accusing eyes. He settled down comfortably in his favorite armchair next to the open window and opened the evening paper.

At eight o'clock the doorbell jangled and Melba led three of her friends into the tiny living room. The visitors bid cold good evenings to the mailman and followed his wife eagerly into the kitchen. For a solid hour, while Shelley tried to concentrate on the paper, the four women discussed the murder. Their shrill voices seemed to grow louder as the discussion progressed and soon an argument broke out.

One of the women ardently defended her conception of The Strangler, as she called him; she envisioned him as a sex fiend, a man thwarted in love, who took out his hatred on defenseless women. Melba disagreed, saying he was probably Mrs. Bywood's secret lover who had killed her in a fit of anger. The argument raged stronger, the voices welling up against the warm walls of the kitchen. Shelley, his head aching with the sound, threw down his paper and left the house.

It was quiet outside. A hot, bright moon soared above the mountains, and there was a pulsing of crickets. A few stars hung in the sky. The mailman began walking, and his feet automatically led him over the same route he traversed every day. Houses glowed against the quiet hills and light fingers of wind curled through the sparse, dry vegetation.

Up ahead was the modern house, gleaming in the night like a mirrored box. Shelley stood thoughtfully under a tree and stared at it. He had dropped the letter there that afternoon. Strange. There had been another letter just like that one. Where had he seen it? Oh, yes, now he remembered. The one to Mrs. Bywood's home, the one that had got wet. But his thoughts were suddenly cut short. The front door of the modern house opened and the woman who lived there came out. She locked the door and moved off into the deeper shadows of the road.

Shelley stood transfixed, watching her tall lithe figure disappear beyond the brow of the hill. The little road looked empty but he felt another presence. He didn't see anyone under the hot glow of the moon, but he felt something, something, close at hand. And then the feeling was gone, as if whatever had caused it had followed the woman up the road.

The next day, Shelley discovered that she had been murdered. Strangled with a silk scarf. The town was now in a virtual uproar. One murder was interesting; it had conversational value. But two murders left a strong feeling of horror. The woman who owned the

modern house—her name was Kent—had been found earlier that
morning in a nearby meadow. She had been a quiet soul, an elderly
teacher of Latin at Cooper High School. She had had a few friends,
but no known enemies. And yet she was found dead in a dark thicket
with the silken noose around her throat.

As Shelley made his rounds he became more and more bothered
by something. Not the fact that he had probably seen her walking
to her death, but by something else. He couldn't pin it down. There
were too many other thoughts in his mind—mostly the result of
Melba's early-morning tirades. Shelley was sick of them, sick of his
own existence. He walked on his rounds.

But as he walked he continued to think. He thought about Mrs.
Bywood and Miss Kent. He became so engrossed that he forgot the
aching agony of the bag on his back. He walked past the row of
houses beyond the stores, not seeing any of them.

His legs carried him on his worn route as they had done every
day for the past thirty years. But the silver letter boxes remained
unopened by him on this particular morning. A mailman neglecting
his boxes. No red flag up, red flag down this morning. Letters. They
were the key to the problem, he knew. Suddenly he took off his bag
and peered into its depths. Way down at the bottom was a blue
envelope, a blue envelope with the unusual handwriting and the
black border. Yes, there in his own mailbag was the answer.

Those letters were somehow connected with the murders. They
were lures. On some excuse they got the women out of their homes
to a quiet place where an unknown man with a scarf could meet
them. That was it, of course! Whatever else the man wrote, he probably told his victims to bring the letters with them, and he destroyed
the letters just as he destroyed the women.

Shelley paused. Yes, there was another blue envelope in his bag.
And he was carrying it. No, he wasn't the murderer, but he was the
carrier of death. To his mind came dim memories of the Bible he
had studied in the cool cloisters of the town's church. Something
about the Angel of Death swooping over.

The little mailman palmed sweat off his neck. He had figured it
out. And in that letter in his pouch was probably the name of the
murderer. He could take it to the sheriff, he could get a small amount
of fame in Cooper because of his cleverness. Maybe some of those
reporters might even write him up, put the story of his life on the
front pages of their big northern papers. He could sit in his chair

next to the window some night and read all about himself in the paper. Think of it! For once, he would be important.

If he delivered that letter, it meant certain death to the recipient. He, Reber Shelley, was the channel through which the murderer reached out with his silk scarf. He was an assistant to the Angel of Death.

He groped in his bag, turned over the blue envelope, and saw that it was addressed to *Mrs. Melba Shelley.*

For a long minute the mailman stood still. Then he walked quickly up the hot streets of Cooper, a small figure, sharp in the bright sunlight. He paused for only a moment when he reached his own house, then slipped the letter into his mailbox.

He hefted his bag and started back on his route. He was whistling softly. It had been a long time since he had whistled while he worked.

Robert Twohy

Never Anything But Trouble

The girl lay back on the white sofa. She said, "Pour me another martini, Floydy."

"Pour your own martini."

The languid smile slipped from her face, and she looked at him with apprehension. He was holding a cigar tight in his thick lips, and scowling at a racing program.

"That damn billygoat. An animal like that, they ought to take him out and shoot him."

"Did you drop a lot, Floydy?"

"Eight thousand bucks, that's all. I told you that ten times."

"You need something to change your luck."

He looked at her. She smiled, parting her lips.

The white telephone on the stand by the table tingled.

She said, "Let it ring."

He said, "For Pete's sake, I'm a businessman."

He got up from his chair and moved heavily to the phone.

"Yeah?"

"This Floyd Weber?"

"Yeah?"

"You don't know me. I've got something to talk to you about."

"So talk."

"This phone tapped?"

"How the hell should I know?"

"Hang up, Floydy," said the girl. She had reached over to pour herself another drink from the shaker on the near table. She waved the glass gently to and fro and smiled at the shining liquid. "Hang up," she said softly. She was pretty. Ten years ago she had been even prettier. Ten years ago she was going to be a great and beautiful actress and handsome men would look at her yearningly.

"Listen," said the sharp, clear voice into Weber's ear. "This is important. There's a bar near your apartment—The Glass Slipper. Know it?"

"Yeah."

"Be there in twenty minutes. They have a phonebooth. I'll call you there."

"Listen, who the hell—"

Weber pressed his lips together and stared at the dead phone, then put it back in its cradle. He walked to the center of the room, hooked his thumbs in his belt, and scowled at the rich beige rug under his feet.

"Who was that, Floydy?"

He didn't answer.

She drank the gin, put the glass down, and smiled at him fuzzily.

"Was it a girl? Was it another girl?"

He said harshly, "You're just about washed up."

"What? What, Floyd?"

"They come and they go. You've just about had it."

The phone call had jarred him. What was it—more trouble for him? Never anything but trouble, he thought bitterly. Never any peace or safety. He felt small, oppressed, beset by enemies—and he laughed harshly at this woman, who was weaker than he. "You got a complexion beginning to look like an old blotter," he said. "It figures—the way you soak it up. Why is it girls start out nice, then turn into soaks?"

She stared at him, seeing herself, what she had become in his eyes. Then she closed her eyes. "Just yours, Floyd," she whispered. "Just *your* girls."

When she opened her eyes, he had his hat and coat on.

She said dully, "Where are you going?"

"Out."

"We were going to dinner."

"That's right. You're so right. We were."

He tossed a couple of bills at her.

"Buy yourself a steak. Or a quart of gin. And lock the door before you go out of here."

He went out—a short, fat, scowling man in rich clothes. The rich odor of his brown cigar hung behind him in the apartment.

The phone jangled. Weber growled at the bartender, "It's for me."

"Yes, sir, Mr. Weber."

He closed the door of the booth.

"Weber?"

"Yeah."

"All right. Now listen good, I'm going to kill a guy for you."

Weber took the phone from his mouth and stared at it. Then he grated, "What is this, a joke?"

"No joke. Hyde. I'm going to kill Jack Hyde for you."

Weber breathed deeply a moment. Then he said, "What are you, a cop?"

"No. Listen, I know where Hyde is."

"Where is he?"

"You'd like to know." The voice laughed. "You'd love to know. You've been looking for him the past three months. So have the cops. It's a race. Well, you win. Because I'm going to kill him for you."

"You sound like some hopped-up punk."

"I want ten grand for the job."

"You're crazy."

"That's all right. You don't have to say anything—Thursday night, tomorrow night. About midnight. You and your top men, you be out in public somewhere. Have plenty of witnesses. They won't be able to touch you."

"How about you?"

"I'm all right. I'm just a guy down the street. Just a neighbor. There's no reason I'd want to kill him."

"You must be some particularly dumb cop. Or a reporter. You a reporter?"

"You'll read about it in the papers. A month or so, I'll contact you. Arrange for the money."

"I get it. It's a gag. All right, I can go along with a gag. How'll I know you?"

"I'll say Jack Hyde recommended me."

"It's funny. It's the funniest thing I've heard for five minutes."

"Read your Friday papers," said the voice, and the phone clicked.

Weber put the receiver slowly back on the hook. He stood there a few seconds. Then he went back to the bar.

"Scotch and water."

Ten thousand, he thought. Did the guy mean it? Sounded like it. Voice sharp, hard, sure of itself. It would be worth ten thousand. Worth ten times ten thousand—because if the cops got Hyde first, he, Weber, would burn.

Hyde—he should have finished Hyde a long time ago, Weber said to himself. Hyde had been going soft. Hyde wanted out. Too old for the rackets. Weber had seen it coming. Should have acted then. But he'd delayed. Hadn't wanted to—Hyde was an old hand. Once he'd been useful.

When Hyde had got that Grand Jury subpoena three months ago,

Weber had decided to act. But it was too late. Hyde had taken off, lost himself. A lot of people had been hunting for him since. Nobody but Weber knew how desperately he had hunted. The smart news-paper boys had got wind of it, and hinted. This guy, whoever he was, that had just called must have picked up the hint. Smelled the money, the money he could make. Well, lucky for him. And lucky for Weber.

Weber smiled. Money. You had the money, and the luck followed. So it was, so it would always be. Nothing was ever going to happen to Weber.

Lou Pease slept late. He was on a short vacation. Yesterday he had returned from a week's trip and tomorrow—Friday—he was slated to take another trip. There was a lot of traveling in Pease's job. He was an insurance investigator. Once he had been a cop, but that had been years ago. He had a couple of souvenirs from the old job—a scar on the side of his neck from a bank robber's bullet; and a gun.

Pease woke up, smelled bacon frying in the kitchen, and heard Claire moving around in there. Today was the day, he thought. He didn't feel nervous. Alert, but not nervous. A job was a job. This was a job.

He thought of Jack Hyde. He wondered how Hyde was feeling this morning. Any uneasiness, any vague foreboding?

Probably not. Probably Hyde was feeling fine.

Because Hyde thought he had it made. Three months he had lived in the neighborhood. He'd rented a small cottage, four houses south of Pease, and across the street. The neighborhood knew him as John Wilson. He was clean-shaven, sandy-haired, wore thin rimless glasses, and was developing a paunch. He looked like a moderately prosperous, retired businessman. In his sober gray suit he was the acme of respectability. Who would take him for a gunman hiding out?

Pease hadn't. He'd seen him, off and on, for over a month, without taking any interest in him. He wouldn't have recognized him at all—if it hadn't been for chess.

Pease, lying in bed, remembered the morning that Wilson had strolled up to him as he was watering the neat, tablecloth-sized lawn in front of his house.

"You're Mr. Pease, aren't you?"

"That's right."

"I'm John Wilson."

Wilson had stretched out his hand. Pease had taken the soft white hand bristling with short dark-brown hairs.

"I hear you're a chess player."

"That's right," said Pease, and wondered where Wilson had heard it. Pease didn't have much to do with his neighbors. But neighbors had a way of knowing things you'd never suspect were known outside your own home. "I play a little," he said.

"Like to play me sometime? I'm crazy about the game."

"Sure. I travel a lot, and I'm going away this week, but when I come back—"

"Anytime. I'm alone and up late every night. Just ring anytime."

Pease recalled that first meeting, and he smiled thinly up at the ceiling. I'll ring tonight, he thought. And I'll have a friend with me.

A few nights after Wilson had introduced himself, Pease played chess with Wilson, in Wilson's house. Pease was a good player, but he was beaten three times running.

He said, "You play a fine game."

"I'm rusty. Used to play a lot."

Wilson had stretched out his hand, to gather in some stray pieces to put in the box. His shirt-cuff rode up slightly and Pease saw a small blue star tattooed on the soft white flesh of Wilson's wrist.

The investigator's eyes narrowed; his brain tried to churn up a recollection. Who did he know with a blue star on his wrist? Someone—he knew someone.

Later that night Pease had sat in the dark, smoking, working up the recollection. It came in fragments. The star. Somehow chess was tied in. A man with a tattooed star and a passion for chess—a dark man, because, though Wilson's hair was light, the bristly hair on his hands and the shadows on his cheeks at night were dark. A man who had come into the neighborhood three months before—

On the third cigarette the memory came through. The newspaper picture of Hyde that had been run in the papers quite steadily after his disappearance, until it ceased to be news and the papers got tired of running it, floated up, clear and detailed, into Pease's mind.

And the lines of print under it: "Wanted by the police for questioning. 6 feet 1, 190 pounds, dark-brown hair, brown mustache, small star tattooed on left wrist. If you see this man, contact your local . . ."

Pease put aside the bedcovers and got up. I could have been a civic hero, he said to himself, and got my picture in the paper. Too bad. But I'd rather be anonymous—and rich.

He went into the bathroom, and was annoyed to see that Claire had left the top off the tube of toothpaste. There was a smear of toothpaste on the washbowl too and he wiped it out with a piece of toilet paper. Damn Claire! Pease hated sloppiness.

He shaved, studying his thin bony face in the mirror. His pale eyes looked back at him blandly. No strain showing. Why should it? He felt no strain.

Weber was probably feeling strain this morning. You couldn't blame him. He didn't know Pease. If he knew Pease, he wouldn't be worrying.

Once before Pease had killed a man. That was when he was a cop. Not the robber that had creased him—that one had got away. The other was a kid, nineteen or so, Pease had surprised in a burglary attempt. The kid had bolted from the store. Pease hadn't shouted after him. He'd just stood still, let the kid get up to the head of the alley, let him silhouette himself against the streetlight, and then, feeling a surge of exhilaration, squeezed the trigger. He'd told the Commissioner that he was shooting for the leg and had missed. But he hadn't missed. He'd been right on target. Right in the small of the back.

He put his shaving things away and went back to the bedroom and dressed, putting on jeans and a flannel shirt. He strolled into the kitchen. Claire was just setting his breakfast on the table. It was a good one, eggs and bacon and toast done just right, and he complimented her on it. She looked surprised, then gave him a nervous little smile. She looked pretty, he thought, appraising her—except that her robe was wrinkled and her silver-blonde hair had some loose strands—but she was a nice-looking woman. Then he smiled to himself, because there were plenty of nice-looking women—and a lot younger than Claire.

He thought he'd leave her five hundred. That would do her all right—she could get a job, she'd worked before. She'd probably be glad, after he had gone. Maybe hook up with someone more her style.

Pease grinned. She'd never liked the rough stuff—always a little scared of him, never knew why he'd be nice, then suddenly pull the rough stuff. Why? He didn't know why. He just liked to. It was his way. What was the fun having a woman if you didn't rough her up?

He'd travel, Pease thought—take a trip to South America. A smart

Yankee who had leisure to settle down, look around, make some connections, ought to do all right down there.

When he was having his coffee and cigarette, he told Claire that he thought he'd take a little trip that day.

"Oh. I thought you didn't have to go till Friday."

"I'm going up to Sid's cabin at Silver Lake. I'd like to get in a little fishing." Sid was his brother, a storekeeper in a town upstate.

She said hesitantly, "I don't have any clean stuff ready for you."

"That's all right. I'll be back tomorrow. Maybe even tonight, if it's too cold up there."

He'd be back tonight, all right, but she wouldn't see him. Nor would anyone else who knew him. Except Hyde.

He went back into the bedroom, got shorts, socks, and pajamas from his drawer, put them in a small leather bag. Then, from way back on a high shelf in his closet, he took down a shoebox. He took out the glistening .38 and the box of ammo. Wrapping them in a towel, he tucked them down among the clothes in the bag. He put the shoebox back on the shelf.

"So long," he said to Claire, passing through the living room where she was vacuuming.

"You think you might be back tonight?"

"I might be. Tonight or tomorrow."

He drove the forty miles to the cabin leisurely, stopping on the way for lunch, and it was early afternoon when he got to the cabin. As he had known, Sid wasn't there—he never used the place this time of year.

Pease got the key from under the step and let himself in. He had a can of beer that he had bought at a grocery near the lunch stop and then he lay down on the cot in the bedroom with a magazine and spent the rest of the afternoon in the cabin.

It was a quiet, rough-hewn place on a steep, wooded hillside. There were no cabins nearby and no one to say what time he had arrived or departed.

When it got dark, Pease brewed himself some coffee—that was all he wanted. After he'd drunk it, he loaded the pistol.

He went through a closet where he knew Sid kept old clothes and found an old brown overcoat and a gray hat and decided that they would do fine. He laid them out on a chair, and then there was nothing to do but wait.

He turned on the radio, got some pleasant music, went back to his magazine. His mind wandered from the story he was reading, but he forced himself to keep at it. If he didn't read he'd think, and there was nothing to think about—it was all planned on rails. At this stage thinking just made you jumpy and you began to worry about consequences. He just sat still in his chair, reading the magazine and half listening to the radio, and at last his watch said 9:30.

He drove back to town, driving carefully, alert to every signal marker on the highway. It was a cool dark night, with no moon. The center of town was jazzy with lights, fighting the dark. Out in the suburbs there were only the streetlights and scatterings of light from the houses he passed.

It was 11:00 o'clock now. With tomorrow a working day and a school day, the families in the neat stucco houses had gone to sleep, or were getting ready to. Pease figured he was a bit early, so he drove around for a while. When his watch said 11:20, he headed for his own neighborhood.

He parked in front of a vacant lot three blocks from his home. All the houses on the block were dark—no lights showing, everyone asleep. With the old gray hat pulled low and the overcoat buttoned up, Pease stepped out toward his own block.

He walked casually. If anyone should happen to be glancing out, he was a casual stroller who'd taken a walk and was now returning home. On the three blocks he walked the only lights he saw were two streetlights on each block. Except one. Hyde's light was on—Pease saw the lighted shade from half a block away.

He went up the walk to the porch, pressed the bell, and stood there, hands in his pockets. After about twenty seconds he heard Hyde's voice through the door.

"Who is it?"

"Pease."

The door opened a crack—it was on a chain. A slice of Hyde's pale face showed. Pease stood quietly. Then the chain slid off.

"Come in."

Pease stepped into the hall.

"I thought you'd gone to the country." Hyde was in shirt, slacks, and slippers. Looking beyond him into the living room, Pease saw a highball by a chair, and a downturned book.

"I came back. Too cold. Wondered if you'd like a game. You said anytime."

"Sure."

Pease lingered in the hall as Hyde went on into the living room. As Hyde's back was turned, Pease took out the gun. He moved to the door of the living room and, with the gun pointed at Hyde, waited.

Hyde had gone toward his chair and got his glass. He turned, saying, "What can I fix you?" His eyes went wide and he stared at the gun. His mouth twitched slightly. "Is this a gag?"

"It's real." Pease was enjoying Hyde's look.

Hyde breathed hard, but he didn't move. He stood stiffly, as if by not moving he would stay alive. He watched the gun. After a few moments he whispered, "You gone crazy?"

"No."

Hyde said carefully, "Pease, you're making a mistake. It's not what you think. This won't do any good."

"It won't do you any good, that's for sure," said Pease, and he laughed softly.

He was watching for it, and as he saw the sudden tightening in Hyde's shoulder, the tightening of his fingers on the highball glass, Pease fired. Hyde's intended lunge became a fall. The highball glass hit the rug and rolled to Pease's feet.

Pease watched Hyde, on his knees, come up, one hand grabbing at the chair, as if to drag himself up. Pease calmly squeezed the trigger again, blasting another bullet into Hyde's chest. Hyde fell over on his face and lay still.

Pease slipped the gun into his pocket and, switching off the lamp, so he wouldn't be silhouetted, he went to the door. He lingered a couple of seconds, listening, and then he opened it and stepped out.

He walked toward the curb, then turned toward his car three blocks away. He walked swiftly, but he didn't run. When he was a block away he looked back. Light showed in a couple of houses, one on the corner, one across the street from Hyde's house. Ahead of him was a quiet, sleeping block.

Pease kept on at the same swift, but not hurrying, pace and two minutes after he had squeezed the second shot into Hyde he was in his car, had it in gear, and was driving smoothly away.

A little after 1:00 A.M. he pulled into the clearing next to the cabin. Stars winked down at him from a blue-black sky.

He entered the cabin, and the first thing he did was roll the gun and ammunition box back up in the towel and put it in the leather bag. Then he hung the coat back in the closet and put the hat where it had been on the shelf.

Then he got Sid's whiskey bottle from under the sink and poured himself a long shot, not so much as a nerve steadier—his nerves were all right—but as a reward.

He drank with enjoyment, and because he had not eaten since noon it began to hit him pretty fast. He felt a little woozy but relaxed and peaceful when he pulled on his pajamas and climbed onto the cot. "The dope," he muttered. Hyde hadn't even had a gun on him. A guy like that—he'd really done him a favor. Hyde was too stupid to live.

"Wake up, Pease."

Pease snapped over in the bed, then pushed himself up. Two men stood in the room. Big men. One of them had something in his hand that glittered. A gun.

It was morning, but early. The sky was barely light and he could hear the drowsy call of night birds. But the light was on in the main room of the cabin and he could see the two men clearly.

He'd slept hard. He cursed that long nightcap. Even so, they must have come up very quietly. Who were they? Weber's men?

"You'd better get dressed," said one of them.

"What is it?"

"Police. You're under arrest."

"What'd I do?"

"Murdered Jack Hyde."

Pease's head was spinning. This was ridiculous, this was a nightmare. What an odd way the guy was holding the gun. With a pencil through the trigger guard. Suddenly Pease's mouth went dry, because he'd recognized his own gun. "Recently been fired." The cop looked at it thoughtfully. "You should have thrown it away."

"I don't know what you're talking about." His voice was a croak.

"Come off it, Pease. We've got you cold. Gun, motive, everything. You want to tell us the story?"

"I don't know any stories." It was a lost game, he knew it inside. But what had gone wrong? He stalled. "*Who* is it I'm supposed to have killed?"

"Jack Hyde. Only you knew him as Wilson. We wanted him. Had things to ask him."

The other cop said, "First we thought Weber had done it. Or arranged to have it done. Then we looked around the house. We found lipstick, hairpins—other stuff. So we talked to the neighbors. They all knew about it."

"Knew about what?"

The cop with the gun said, "Come off it, Pease. She told us all about it."

The other one said, "You found out about it. You killed Hyde. You didn't know he was Hyde, she didn't either. She thought he was just a nice, gentle guy—they were going to go away together. But why am I telling you all this? You know it already."

Pease stared at them. After a few seconds he began to laugh. The cop said, "Something funny?"

"Hairpins and stuff," said Pease. "I always liked things neat. What can you do when you've got a sloppy wife?"

The phone rang. She was sitting on the white sofa and she got up to answer it. "Hello?"

"Oh—this Florence?"

"Yes."

"I want to speak to Mr. Weber."

"Oh. Well—he can't come to the phone now."

"I just wanted to ask if he's seen the morning paper?"

"Yes, he has."

"Well, I just wanted to be sure he'd read about it. Guess he's pleased, huh?" said the voice guardedly.

"He was pleased," she said. "I guess he was. I know he was sitting in the kitchen reading the paper and laughing when I let myself in."

"You sound funny. Anything the matter?"

"No," she said.

She hung up. She sat a moment and then went to the kitchen door to look at him, sitting in the chair with his head on the newspaper that was spread out on the table. Blood had run onto the paper and some had fallen on the glistening black floor.

She studied the little hole in the back of his head and wondered what his face looked like, pressed flat on the table.

She sighed. She didn't know if she had done a wrong thing or not. But she had worked it all out in her mind before she'd come up this morning, and it had been something she had known she had to do.

She said, in a wooden voice, "There won't be any more for you to turn into soaks."

She went back to the white sofa and sat down—a woman who looked middle-aged, although only ten years ago she was going to be a great and beautiful actress and handsome young men were going to look at her yearningly . . .

Robert L. Fish

The Adventure of the Ascot Tie

In going over my notes for the year '59, I find many cases in which the particular talents of my friend, Mr. Schlock Homes, either sharply reduced the labours of Scotland Yard or eliminated the necessity of their efforts altogether.

There was, for example, The Adventure of the Dissembling Musician who, before Homes brought him to justice, managed to take apart half of the instruments of the London Symphony Orchestra and cleverly hide them in various postal-boxes throughout the city, where they remained undiscovered until the denouement of the case. Another example that comes readily to mind was the famous Mayfair Trunk Murder, which Homes finally laid at the door of Mr. Claude Mayfair, the zookeeper who had goaded one of his elephants into strangling a rival for Mrs. Mayfair's affection. And, of course, there was the well publicized matter involving Miss Millicent Oney, whom Homes refers to even to this day as the "Oney Woman."

But of all the cases which I find noted for this particular year none demonstrate the devious nature of my friend's analytical reasoning powers so much as the case which I have listed under the heading of The Adventure of the Ascot Tie.

It was a rather warm morning in June of '59 when I appeared for breakfast in our quarters at 221B Bagel Street. Mr. Schlock Homes had finished his meal and was fingering a telegram which he handed to me as I seated myself at the table.

"Our ennui is about to end, Watney!" said he, his excitement at the thought of a new case breaking through his normal calm.

"I am very happy to hear that, Homes," I replied in all sincerity, for the truth was I had begun to fear the long stretches of inactivity that often led my friend to needle both himself and me. Taking the telegram from his outstretched hand, I read it carefully. "The lady seems dreadfully upset," I remarked, watching Homes all the while for his reaction.

"You noticed that also, Watney?" said Homes, smiling faintly.

"But of course," I replied. "Her message reads: 'Dear Mr. Homes,

I urgently request an audience with you this morning at nine o'clock. I am dreadfully upset.' And it is signed Miss E. Wimpole."

He took the telegram from me and studied it with great care. "Typed on a standard post-office form," he said, "by a standard post-office typewriter. In all probability by a standard post-office employee. Extremely interesting. However, I fear there is little more to be learned until our client presents herself."

At that moment a noise in the street below our open window claimed my attention, and as I glanced out I cried, "Homes! It's a trap!"

"Rather a four-wheeler, I should have judged," replied Homes languidly. "These various vehicles are readily identified by the tonal pitch of the hub-squeal. A trap, for example, is normally pitched in the key of F; a four-wheeler usually in B flat. A hansom, of course, is always in G. However, I fear we must rest this discussion; for here, if I am not mistaken, is our client."

At that moment the page ushered into our rooms a young lady of normal beauty and of about twenty-five years of age. She was carefully dressed in the fashion of the day and appeared quite distrait.

"Well, Miss Wimpole," said Homes, after she had been comfortably seated and had refused a kipper, "I am quite anxious to hear your story. Other than the fact that you are an addict of side-saddle riding, have recently written a love letter, and stopped on your way here to visit a coal mine, I am afraid that I know little of your problem."

Miss Wimpole took this information with mouth agape. Even I, who am more or less familiar with his methods, was astonished.

"Really, Homes," I said, "this is too much! Pray explain."

"Quite simple, Watney," he replied, smiling. "There is a shiny spot on the outside of Miss Wimpole's skirt a bit over the outside central part of the thigh which is the shape of a curved cut of pie. This is the exact shape of the horn of the new type of African saddle which is now so popular among enthusiasts of equestrianism. The third finger of her right hand has a stain of strawberry-coloured ink, which is certainly not the type one would use for business or formal correspondence. And lastly, there is a smudge beneath her left eye which could only be coal dust. Since this is the month of June, we can elimate the handling of coal for such normal reasons as storage or heating and must therefore deduce her visit to a place where coal would reasonably be in evidence the year around—namely, a coal mine."

Miss Wimpole appeared quite confused by this exchange. "I was forced to leave the house in quite a hurry," she explained apologetically, "and I am afraid that I was not very careful in applying my mascara. As for the jam on my finger, it is indeed strawberry," and she quickly licked it clean before we could remonstrate with her manners. She then contemplated her skirt ruefully. "These new maids," said she, shaking her head sadly. "They are so absentminded! The one we now have continues to leave the flat-iron connected when she goes to answer the door!"

"Ah, yes," said Homes, after a moment of introspection. "Well, it was certain to have been one or the other. And now, young lady, if you should care to reveal to us the nature of your problem?" He noticed her glance in my direction and added reassuringly, "You may speak quite freely in Dr. Watney's presence. He is quite hard of hearing."

"Well then, Mr. Homes," said she, leaning forward anxiously. "As you undoubtedly deduced from my telegram, my name is Elizabeth Wimpole, and I live with my uncle Jno. Wimpole in a small flat in Barrett Street. My uncle is an itinerant Egyptologist by trade, and for some time we have managed a fairly comfortable living through the itineraries which he has supplied to people contemplating visits to Egypt. However, since the recent troubles there, his business has been very slow and as a result he has become very moody, keeping to his own company during the day and consorting with a very rough-looking group at the local pub in the evening.

"In order to understand the complete change in the man, it is necessary to understand the type of life which we enjoyed when itinerant Egyptologists were in greater demand. Our home, while always modest, was none the less a meeting place for the intelligentsia. No less than two curators, an odd politician or so, and several writers counted themselves as friends of my uncle, and the head mummy-unwrapper at the British Museum often dropped by for tea and a friendly chat on common subjects.

"Today this has all changed. The type of person with whom my uncle is now consorting is extremely crude both in appearance and language, and while I hesitate to make accusations which may be based solely upon my imagination, I fear that several of these ruffians have even been considering making advances against my person, which I am certain my uncle would never have allowed at an earlier day.

"While this situation has naturally worried me a bit, I should have passed it off without too much thought except that yesterday in the course of casually arranging my uncle's room I chanced upon a telegram in a sealed envelope sewn to the inner surface of one of his shirts. The nature of the message was so puzzling that I felt I needed outside assistance, and therefore made bold to call upon you." With this, she handed to Homes a telegram-form which she had drawn from her purse during her discourse.

Homes laid it upon the table, and I stood over his shoulder as we both studied it. It read as follows:

WIMPY. WE HEIST THE ORIENTAL ICE SATURDAY. AMECHE OTHERS. HARDWARE NEEDLESS. THE FIX IS IN. WE RIG THE SPLIT FOR TUESDAY. JOE.

A curious change had come over Homes's face as he read this cryptic message. Without a word he turned to the shelf at his side and selected a heavy book bound in calfskin. Opening it, he silently studied several chapter headings in the index, and then, closing it, spoke quietly to Miss Wimpole.

"I wish to thank you for having brought me what promises to be a most interesting problem," he said. "I shall devote my entire energies to the solution. However, I fear there is little that I can tell you without further cogitation. If you will be so kind as to leave your address with Dr. Watney, I am sure that we shall soon be in touch with you with good news."

When the young woman had been shown out, Homes turned to me in great excitement. "An extremely ingenious code, Watney," he chuckled, rubbing his hands together in glee. "As you know, I have written some sixteen monographs on cryptography, covering all phases of hidden and secret writings, from the Rossetti Stone to my latest on the interpretation of instructions for assembling Yule toys. I believe I can honestly say, without false modesty, that there are few in this world who could hope to baffle me with a cipher or code. I shall be very much surprised, therefore, if I do not quickly arrive at the solution to this one. The difficulty, of course, lies in the fact that there are very few words employed, but as you know the only problems which interest me are the difficult ones. I fear this is going to be a five-pipe problem, so if you do not mind, Watney, handing down my smoking equipment before you leave, I shall get right to it!"

I reached behind me and furnished to him the set of five saffron-coloured pipes which had been the gift of a famous tobacconist to whom Homes had been of service—a case which I have already related in The Adventure of the Five Orange Pipes. By the time I left the room to get my medical bag, he had already filled one and was sending clouds of smoke ceilingwards, as he hunched over the telegram in fierce concentration.

I had a very busy day and did not return to our rooms until late afternoon. Homes was pacing up and down the room with satisfaction. The five pipes were still smoking in various ashtrays about the room, but the frown of concentration had been replaced by the peaceful look Homes invariably employed when he saw daylight in a particularly complex problem.

"You have solved the code," I remarked, setting my bag upon the sideboard.

"You are getting to be quite a detective yourself, Watney," replied Schlock Homes with a smile. "Yes; it was devilishly clever, but in the end I solved it as I felt sure I would."

"I was never in doubt, Homes," I said warmly.

"Watney, you are good for me," answered my friend, clasping my hand gratefully. "Well, the solution is here. You will note the message carefully. It says: 'Wimpy. We heist the oriental ice Saturday. Ameche others. Hardware needless. The fix is in. We rig the split for Tuesday. Joe.' Now, disregarding the punctuation that separates this gibberish, I applied the various mathematical formulæ which are standard in codifying, as well as several which have not been known to be in use for many years, but all to no avail.

"For some hours I must confess I was completely baffled. I even tested the telegram-form for hidden writing, applying benzidine hypochloric colloid solution to both surfaces, but other than an old shopping list which some post-office clerk had apparently written and then erased, there was nothing to be discovered.

"It was then that I recalled that Mr. Jno. Wimpole was acquainted with a mummy-unwrapper, and the theory occurred to me that in the course of their many conversations it was possible that the secret of ancient Egyptian code writing had entered their discussions. Beginning again on this basis, I applied the system originally developed by Tutankhamen for the coding of palace laundry, and at once the message began to make sense. Here, Watney, look at this!"

And underlining the letter W in the word Wimpy, he proceeded to underline the first letter of each alternate word, glancing at my startled face with pleased satisfaction as he did so.

The message now read: WHOS ON FIRST.

"Remarkable, Homes," I said doubtfully, "but if you will forgive me, I find I am as much in the dark as before."

"Ah, Watney," said my friend, now laughing aloud. "When I first read this message I also was baffled. But that was some hours ago, and I have not spent this time idly. I am now in possession of the major outline of the plot, and while it does not involve any truly serious crime, still it has been quite ingenious and clever. But there is nothing more to be done tonight. Please send a telegram to our client advising her that we shall stop by and pick her up in a cab tomorrow morning at ten, and that we shall then proceed to the locale where the entire mystery shall be resolved."

"But, Homes!" I protested. "I do not understand this thing at all!"

"You shall, Watney, the first thing tomorrow," said Homes, still smiling broadly. "But no more for tonight. The Weare brothers are at Albert Hall, I believe, and we just have time to change and get there if we are to enjoy the concert."

The following morning at ten o'clock sharp our hansom pulled up before a small building of flats in Barrett Street, and Miss Wimpole joined us. We both looked askance at Homes, but he leaned forward imperturbably and said to the driver, "Ascot Park, if you please, cabby," and then leaned back smiling.

"Ascot Park?" I asked in astonishment. "The solution to the problem lies at a racing meet?"

"It does indeed, Watney," said Homes, obviously enjoying my mystification. Then he clapped me on the shoulder and said, "Pray forgive my very poor sense of humour, Watney; and you also, Miss Wimpole. I have practically solved the problem, and the solution does indeed lie at Ascot Park. Watney here knows how I love to mystify, but I shall satisfy your curiosity at once.

"When I first decoded the message and found myself with another message almost as curious as the first—namely, Whos On First—I considered it quite carefully for some time. It could have been, of course, some reference to a person or company named Whos which was located on a First Avenue or First Street. While I did not believe this to be true, it is in my nature to be thorough, and since New York is the only city to my knowledge with a First Avenue, I cabled my old friend Inspector Queen to take steps. His reply in the negative eliminated this possibility, and I returned to my original thesis.

"Note carefully the last word, which is First. This might, of course, have been an obscure reference to the Bible, in which it is promised that the last shall be first; but in perusing the original message I sensed no religious aura, and I am particularly sensitive to such emanations. No; instead I allowed myself to consider those cases in which it might be important to be first. I do not, of course, refer to queues or anything of that nature. The logical answer, naturally, is in wagering. The various means available to the Englishman of today to place a wager are extremely limited, and after checking the team standings and finding Nottingham still firmly in the lead, I turned to the racing news.

"And there I found, as I had honestly expected to find, that in the second race at Ascot today the entry of the Abbott Castle stable is a three-year-old filly named Whos On First."

He turned to the young woman at his side. "My dear," said he, "I fear that your uncle is involved in a touting scheme, and that the group with whom he has been meeting of late have been using the telegraph-system to send advices regarding probable winners. This is, of course, frowned upon in most racing circles, but as I have so often stated, I am not of the official police and therefore feel no responsibility for bringing people to their so-called justice over minor vices. I shall look forward, however, to the proof of my ratiocination at the track in a few moments."

"Oh, Mr. Schlock Homes," cried Miss Wimpole, clasping his hand in gratitude, "you have relieved my mind greatly. I have been so worried, especially since I have accidentally come across large sums of money hidden in obscure places in the house, and feared that my uncle had become involved with some desperate characters engaged in nefarious practices. Now that I am cognizant of the nature of the enterprise, I can relax and may even replace at least a part of these sums with my conscience at rest, knowing that they were not gained through dubious means. But you must let me pay you for your efforts in this matter. Pray tell me what your fee is."

"No, Miss Wimpole," replied Homes simply. "If my theory is as good as I believe it to be, there shall be no question of payment. I shall take as payment the benefits of the information which you yourself were so kind as to bring to my attention."

Within a few minutes our hansom drew up at the ornate gate of the racing meet, and while Homes went to study the posted odds and speak with some bookmakers with whom he was acquainted, I purchased the latest journal and retired to the stands to await his return. He was with me in a few minutes, smiling broadly.

"It is even better than I had imagined, Watney," said he. "The diabolical genius of these people arouses my admiration. I note that in addition to Whos On First in the second race, this same Abbott Castle has entered a horse named Whats On Second in the first race. And when I spoke to one of the track stewards just a few moments ago, he informed me that because of rumours which have been flooding the stewards' office they propose to combine the two races. Now, at long last, the true nature of this ingenious plot finally emerges!"

"But what might that be, Homes?" I asked in bewilderment. "Can it be that the stewards have heard of the touting scheme and are using this means to circumvent it?"

"Your faith in track stewards is touching, Watney," said Homes dryly. "I am quite convinced that without the aid of one of their members named Joseph, the entire scheme could not have been contemplated. No, no, Watney; the plan is far more intricate. These people know that if they go to a bookmaker with a bet on any one horse to win, the maximum odds which they can expect will be in the nature of five, or at most ten, to one. But think, Watney, think! Consider! What would the odds be against a *tie?*"

At once the devilish cleverness of the entire business burst upon my brain. "What do you propose to do, Homes?" I asked, searching his strong face for a clue.

"I have already done it, Watney," he replied calmly, and showed me five separate betting slips, each for the sum of £20, and each to be redeemed at the rate of 200 to 1 should the race end in a tie.

"Well, Watney," said Homes, when we were once again seated comfortably in our rooms in Bagel Street. "I can honestly state that to my mind this was one of my most successful cases—certainly from the financial standpoint. I feel that the ingenuity involved in codifying the betting information, while leaving out certain obvious information, puts our Mr. Wimpole and his associates in a special category of brillance.

"We must be thankful that they have selected this relatively harmless means of breaching the law, and not something more nefarious. I certainly do not begrudge him his gains, although I must say that in seeing through their clever scheme I feel quite justified in keeping mine."

Homes lit his pipe, and when it was pulling to his satisfaction, spoke again. "And now, Watney, we must look for another case to ward off boredom. Is there any crime news in that journal which might prove to be of interest?"

"Only this," I said, folding the sheet in half and handing it to Homes with the indicated article on top. "Some three million pounds worth of diamonds were stolen last night from the home of the Japanese ambassador. They were known as the Ogima Diamonds, and were considered the most valuable collection of their type in the world. The article says that the police believe it to be the work of a gang, but that otherwise they are without a clue."

"Ah, really?" murmured Homes, his nostrils distended in a manner which I had long since come to recognize as indicating intense interest. "May I see the article, Watney? Ah, yes! Ogima. There is something faintly familiar—"

He reached behind himself to the shelf where the reference books were kept, and drawing one out, opened it to the letter O.

"Ogima in Swahili means pencil sharpener," he said, half to himself, "while the same word in ancient Mandarin meant a type of pick used with the one-stringed guitar. No, I doubt if this is of much help; it would be too subtle."

He returned the reference book to the shelf and studied the article once again. Suddenly his face cleared and he leaned forward excitedly.

"Of course! You will note, Watney, that Ogima spelled backwards becomes Amigo. I shall be very surprised if the answer to this problem does not lie somewhere south of the border. Watney, your timetable, if you please."

Alice Scanlan Reach

In the Confessional

Blue slipped in through the side door of St. Brigid's and stood motionless in the shadow of the confessional. Opposite him loomed the statue of the Blessed Virgin treading gently on a rising bank of vigil lights. Blue's eyes, darting to the ruby fingers of flame flickering around the marble feet, saw that the metal box nearby with the sign *Candles—10¢* had not yet been replenished. Only a few wax molds remained. Had the box been full, Blue would have known he was too late—that Father Crumlish, on depositing a fresh supply, had opened the drawer attached to the candle container and emptied it of the past week's silver offerings.

So all was well! Once again, all unknowingly, the house of God would furnish Blue with the price of a jug of wine.

Now, from his position in the shadow, Blue's red-rimmed eyes shifted to the altar where Father Crumlish had just turned the lock in the sacristy door, signaling the start of his nightly nine-o'clock lock-up routine.

Blue knew it by heart.

First, the closing and locking of the weather-weary stained-glass windows. Next, the bolting of the heavy oaken doors in the rear of the church. Then came the dreaded moment. Tonight, as every night, listening to Father Crumlish make fast the last window and then approach the confessional, Blue fought the panic pushing against his lungs—the fear that the priest would give the musty interior of the confessional more than a quick, casual glance.

Suppose tonight it occurred to Father Crumlish to peer into the confessional's shadow to see if someone were lurking—

Blue permitted himself a soft sigh of blessed relief. He was safe! The slow footsteps were retreating up the aisle. To be sure, there were torturing hours ahead, but that was the price he had to pay. Already he could almost feel his arms cradling the beloved bottle, his fingers caressing the gracefully curved neck. He could almost taste the soothing, healing sweetness.

It was almost too much to bear.

Now came what Blue, chuckling to himself, called "the floor show." Extinguishing the lights in the rear of the church and thus leaving it, except for candlelight, in total darkness, Father Crumlish, limping a little from the arthritis buried deep in his ancient roots, climbed the narrow winding stairway to the choir loft.

Blue, hearing the first creaking stair, moved noiselessly and swiftly. In the space of one deep breath he flickered out of the shadow, entered the nearest "sinner's" door of the confessional, and silently closed it behind him. Then he knelt in cramped darkness, seeing nothing before him but the small closed window separating him from the confessor's sanctuary.

By now Father Crumlish had reached the choir loft and the "show" began. Believing himself alone with his God and Maker, the descendant of a long line of shillelagh wielders ran his arthritic fingers over the organ's keys and poured out his soul in song. Presently the church rafters rang with his versions of "When Irish Eyes are Smiling," "Come Back to Erin," and "The Rose of Tralee."

It was very pleasant and Blue didn't mind too much that his knee joints ached painfully from their forced kneeling position. As a matter of fact, he rather enjoyed this interlude in the evening's adventure. It gave him time to think, a process which usually eluded him in the shadowy, unreal world where he existed. And what better place to think than this very church where he had served as an altar boy forty—fifty?—how many years ago?

That was another reason he never had the slightest qualm about filching the price of a bottle from the Blessed Virgin's vigil-light offering box. "Borrowing," Blue called it. And who had a better right? Hadn't he dropped his nickels and dimes in the collection basket every Sunday and Holy Day of Obligation from the time he was a tot until—?

The Blessed Virgin and Father Crumlish and the parishioners of St. Brigid's were never going to miss a few measly dimes. Besides, he was only "borrowing" until something turned up. And someday, wait and see, he'd walk down the center aisle of the church, dressed fit to kill, proud as a peacock, and put a $100 bill in the basket for the whole church to see, just as easy as you please!

A small smile brushed against Blue's thin lips, struggled to reach the dull sunken eyes, gave up in despair, and disappeared. Blue dozed a little.

He might more appropriately have been called Gray. For there was a bleak grayness about him that bore the stamp of fog and dust, of the gray pinched mask of death and destruction. His withered bones seemed to be shoved indifferently into threadbare coat and trousers; and from a disjointed blob of cap a few sad straggles of hair hung listlessly about his destroyed face. Time had long ceased to mean anything to Blue—and he to time.

All that mattered now was the warm, lovely, loving liquid and the occasional bite of biscuit to go with it. And thanks to St. Brigid's parishioners, thanks to his knowledge of Father Crumlish's unfailing nightly routine, Blue didn't have to worry about where the next bottle was coming from. The job was easy. And afterward he could doze in peace in the last pew of the church until it came time to mingle with the faithful as they arrived for six o'clock morning Mass, and then slip unnoticed out the door.

Now, kneeling in the confines of the confessional, Blue jerked his head up from his wasted chest and stiffened. Sudden silence roared in his ears. For some unseen reason Father Crumlish had broken off in the middle of the third bar of "Tralee."

Then, in the deathly pale quiet, the priest's voice rang out.

"Who's there?"

Sweet Jesus! thought Blue. Did I snore?

"Answer me!" More insistent now. "Who's there?"

Blue, his hand on the confessional doorknob, had all but risen when the answer came.

"It's me, Father—Johnny Sheehan."

Sinking back to his knees, Blue could hear every word in the choir loft clear as a bell, resounding in the shuttered, hollow church.

"What's on your mind, Johnny?"

Blue caught the small note of irritation in the priest's voice and knew it was because Father Crumlish treasured his few unguarded moments with "The Rose of Tralee."

"I—I want to go to confession, Father."

A long pause and then Blue could almost hear the sigh of resignation to duty and to God's will.

"Then come along, lad."

Now how do you like that for all the lousy luck, Blue thought, exasperated. Some young punk can't sleep in his nice warm beddybye until he confesses—

Confesses!

Blue felt the ice in his veins jam up against his heart. Father Crumlish would most certainly bring the repentant sinner to *this* confessional since it was next to the side-door entrance. Even now Blue could hear the oncoming footsteps. Suppose he opens *my* door instead of the other one? Dear God, please let him open the first door!

Trembling, Blue all but collapsed with relief as he heard the other door open and close, heard the settling of knees on the bench, and lastly, the faint whisper of cloth as Father Crumlish entered the priest's enclosure that separated himself from Blue on one side and from Johnny Sheehan on the other by thin screened windows.

Now Blue heard the far wooden window slide back and knew that Johnny Sheehan was bowing his head to the screen, fixing his eyes on the crucifix clasped in the confessor's hands.

"Bless me, Father, for I have sinned . . ."

The voice pulled taut, strained, and snapped.

"Don't be afraid to tell God, son. You know about the Seal of Confession—anything you tell here you confess to God and it remains sealed with Him forever."

Confess you stole a bunch of sugar beets and get it over with, Blue thought angrily. He was getting terribly tired and the pain in his knees was almost more than he could bear.

"I—she—"

She! Well, what do you know? Blue blinked his watery eyes in a small show of surprise. So the young buck's got a girl in trouble. Serves him right. Stick to the warmer embrace of the bottle, my lad. It'll keep you out of mischief.

"I heard your first confession when you were seven, Johnny. How old are you now? Sixteen?"

"Y—yes, Father."

"This girl. What about her?"

"I—I killed her!"

In the rigid silence Blue heard the boy's body sag against the wooden partition and was conscious of a sharp intake of breath from the priest. Blue was as alert now as he ever was these soft, slow days and nights, but he knew that sometimes he just thought he heard words when actually he'd only dreamed them. Yet— Blue eased one hurting kneecap and leaned closer to the dividing wood.

Father Crumlish shifted his weight in his enclosure.

"Killed?"

Only retching sobs.

"Tell me, Johnny." Father Crumlish's voice was ever so gentle now.

Then the words came in a torrent.

"She laughed at me—said I wasn't a man—and I couldn't stand it, Father. When Vera May laughed—"

"Vera May!" the priest broke in. "Vera May Barton?"

Even in the shifting mists and fog of his tired memory, Blue recognized that name. Who didn't these past few weeks? Who didn't know that every cop in the city was hunting Vera May Barton's murderer? Why, even some of Blue's best pals had been questioned. Al was ready to hang a rap on some poor innocent.

Blue rarely read newspapers, but he listened to lots of talk. And most of the talk in the wine-shrouded gloom of his haunts these past weeks had been about the slaying of sixteen-year-old Vera May Barton, a choir singer at St. Brigid's. Someone had shown Blue her picture on the front page of a newspaper. A beautiful girl, blonde and soft and smiling. But someone—someone with frantic, desperate hands—had strangled the blonde softness and choked off the smile.

Blue was suddenly conscious once more of the jagged voice.

"She wasn't really like they say, Father. Vera May wasn't really good. She just wanted you to think so. But sometimes, when I'd deliver my newspapers in the morning, sometimes she'd come to the door with hardly any clothes. And when I'd ask her to go to a show or something, she'd only laugh and say I wasn't a man."

"Go on," Father Crumlish said softly.

"I—she told me she was staying after choir practice that night to collect the hymnals—"

The priest sighed. "I blame myself for that. For letting her stay in the church alone—even for those few moments—while I went over to the rectory."

"And then—then when she left," the halting words went on, "I followed her out in the alley—"

Blue's pals had told him about that—how one of St. Brigid's early-morning Mass parishioners found Vera May lying like a broken figurine in the dim alley leading from the church to the rectory. She wasn't carrying a purse, the newspapers said. And she hadn't been molested. But her strangler, tearing at her throat, had broken the thin chain of the St. Christopher's medal around her neck. It had her initials on the back but the medal had never been found.

"What did you do with the medal, Johnny?" Father Crumlish asked quietly.

"I—I was afraid to keep it, Father." The agonized voice broke again. "The river—"

The weight of the night pressed heavily on Blue and he sighed deeply. But the sigh was lost in the low murmuring of the priest to the boy—too low for Blue to catch the words—and perhaps, against all his instincts, he dozed. Then there was a sudden stirring in the adjoining cubicles.

Blue knelt rigid and breathless while the doors opened, and without turning his head toward the faint candlelight shimmering through the cracks in the door of his enclosure, he knew that Father Crumlish had opened the side entrance and released Johnny Sheehan to the gaunt and starless dark.

Slowly the priest moved toward the first pew before the center altar. And now Blue risked glancing through the sliver of light in his door. Father Crumlish knelt, face buried in his hands.

A wisp of thought drifted into the wine-eroded soil of Blue's mind. Was the priest weeping?

But Blue was too engrossed in his own discomfort, too aware of the aching, ever-increasing, burning dryness of his breath and bones. If only the priest would go and leave Blue to his business and his sleep!

After a long time he heard the footsteps move toward the side door. Now it closed. Now the key turned in the lock.

Now!

Blue stumbled from the confessional and collapsed in the nearest pew. Stretched full length, he let his weary body and mind sag in relief. Perhaps he slept; he only knew that he returned, as if from a long journey.

Sitting upright, he brought out the tools of his trade from somewhere within the tired wrappings that held him together.

First the chewing gum—two sticks, purchased tonight.

Blue munched them slowly, carefully bringing them to the proper consistency. Then, rising, he fingered a small length of wire and, leaving the pew, shuffled toward the offering box beneath the Blessed Virgin's troubled feet.

Taking the moist gum from his mouth, Blue attached it to the wire and inserted it carefully into the slot of the box. A gentle twist and he extracted the wire. Clinging to the gummed end were two coins, a nickel and a dime.

Blue went through this procedure again and again until he had collected the price of a bottle. Then he lowered himself into the nearest pew and rested a bit.

He began to think of what had happened in the confessional. But it had been so long since Blue had made himself concentrate on anything but his constant, thirsting need that it took a while for the rusted wheels to move, for the pretty colored lights to cease their small whirlings and form a single brightness illuminating the makings of his mind.

Finally he gave up. The burning dryness had gripped him again and he began to yearn for the long night to be over so that he could spend, in the best way he knew, the money he held right in his hand this minute.

Two bottles! I should have two bottles for all the trouble I've been through tonight, Blue thought. They owe it to me for making me kneel there so long and robbing me of my sleep. Yes, they owe it to me!

And so thinking, he took out the gum once more and, bringing it to his mouth, chewed it again into pliable moistness.

The first try at the offering box brought him only a dime, but the second try—God was good—another dime, a nickel, and a dollar bill!

Too exhausted to drag himself to his customary last-pew bed, Blue stretched out once more on the nearest wood plank and slept.

Some time later, the unrelenting dryness wakened him. This "in-between" period was the only time Blue ever approached sobriety. And in the sobering, everything seemed terribly, painfully clear. He began to relive the events of the night, hearing the voices again with frightening clarity. Father Crumlish's and then the kid's—

Blue's own voice screamed in his ears.

"Out! I've got to get out of here! Nobody knows but me—nobody knows about the murder but me. I've got to tell. But first I'll have to have a little sip. I need a little sip. And then I'll tell—"

In a flurry of cloth and dust Blue rushed to the side door. He had never before tried to let himself out this way and had no idea if the door was locked. But the knob gave easily, and in an instant he had closed the door behind him and, leaning heavily against it, was breathing the night's whispering wind.

It had been a long time since Blue had been out alone in the deep dark, and suddenly, with the night's dreadful knowledge inside him, it was overpowering. Shadows rushed at him, clawed at his face and fingers, and crushed him so bindingly that he could scarcely breathe.

In an agony to get away, he plunged into the blackness and began to run.

And in his urgency Blue never heard the shout behind him, the pounding feet on the pavement. He never heard the cry to halt or risk a bullet. He only knew that he was flying, faster and faster, yet not fast enough, soaring higher and higher, until a surprisingly small jagged thrust of sidewalk clawed at him and brought him to his knees.

The bullet from his pursuer, meant to pierce his worn and weary legs, pierced his back.

Suddenly it was calm and quiet and there was no longer any need for speed. He lay on his side, crumpled and useless, like a discarded bundle of rags.

A wave, a wine-red wave, swept over him and Blue let himself rock and toss for a moment in its comforting warmth. Then he opened his eyes and, dimly, in the fast-gathering darkness, recognized Father Crumlish bending over him.

"Poor devil," Blue heard the priest say. "But don't blame yourself, officer. The fellow probably just didn't know you'd be suspicious of his running away like that. Particularly around here, now, after the Barton girl. The poor devil probably just didn't know."

Didn't know? Blue didn't know? He knew, all right! And he had to tell.

"Father!"

Quickly the priest bent his ear to Blue's quivering lips. "I'm listening," he said.

"I—was in the confessional too."

"The confessional?"

The wave rushed to envelop him again. Before he could speak the urgent words, he heard the officer's voice.

"He came out of the church door, Father. I saw him."

"I don't see how that's possible," the priest said bewilderedly.

Blue forced the breath from his aching lungs.

"I heard—the kid confess. I have to tell—"

"Wait!" Father Crumlish said sharply, cutting Blue off. "You have nothing to tell. Maybe you heard. But you don't know about that boy. The poor confused lad's come to me to confess to every robbery and murder in this parish for years. You have nothing to tell, do you hear me?"

"Nothing?"

Blue almost laughed a little. For the pain was gone now and he felt as if—as if he were walking down St. Brigid's center aisle, dressed fit to kill, proud as a peacock, and putting a $100 bill in the collection basket for the whole church to see just as easy as you please.

"There's something—"

His voice was strong and clear as he brought his fumbling fingers from within the moldy rags and stretched out his hand to the priest.

"I was 'borrowing' from the Blessed Virgin, Father. Just enough for a bottle, though. I need it, Father. All the time. Bad! She caught me at it. And she was running to tell you. But if she did, where in the world would I ever get another bottle, Father? Where? So I had to stop her!"

Fighting the final warm, wine-red wave that was washing over him, Blue thrust into Father Crumlish's hand a St. Christopher's medal dangling from a broken chain and initialed V.M.B.

"I've been saving it, Father. In a pinch, I thought it might be worth a bottle."

William North Jayme

I Will Please Come To Order

Trevor MacIntosh was wearing a dinner jacket. He was making his way up the curved marble staircase to the great domed library where the monthly meeting of the One Hundred Club was about to take place. There, in just a few minutes, with only a stained-glass canopy separating him from the heavens, MacIntosh would launch his amazing plan.

True, the plan was improbable, preposterous, outrageous—as MacIntosh himself would have been the first to admit. You're out of your mind, the others would have said. It can't be done.

That is what the other members would have said. But they were not even aware of the scheme. In all the months since the idea first occurred to MacIntosh, he had not shared it with anyone. As a result, finding out if it *could* be done had become as important to his continued existence as water.

He wished he had some water. Now that the crucial moment was near, he found himself somewhat nervous. Tugging at a recalcitrant garter, he almost pitched into the club president, who was just ahead of him on the stairs.

It was not that MacIntosh wanted the $20,000,000 endowment of the club. A successful portrait painter, he had received more commissions this past year than ever before. There had been seventeen actually, averaging $2,000 apiece. In a small and deliberately select circle, his work was greatly admired. Only that morning Eldon Varner's wife had telephoned. After innumerable attempts another well known artist had given up trying to "get" her famous eyes. Would MacIntosh be willing to try?

He had refused, of course. Ethics would not permit him to trespass on the oils of another painter. But the invitation, coming as it did from a woman who had ruled artistic society in New York for a half century, was pleasing evidence of his increasing reputation. In a different way, so was his election last month to the presidency of the National Federation.

No, it was not the money. Nor did MacIntosh bear anyone malice. He was an agreeable, easy, friendly man. Although still comparatively young to have a great deal in common with most of his fellow members, he genuinely enjoyed being with them and he especially looked forward to the camaraderie generated by these monthly affairs.

The real reason was something quite different. It was a collector's desire to acquire an object that was absolutely perfect. And there was no doubt that the One Hundred Club was perfect.

MacIntosh had first noticed it almost a decade before, when Steese Clayson had taken him there as a guest. An architectural historian, Clayson was the ideal guide. The tour had ended in the dining room, and it was while MacIntosh was wiping from his lips the traces of a delectable Welsh rarebit that he became aware of how perfect the place was.

Its perfection did not lie in its beauty. The façade, modeled after the Great Banqueting Hall which Inigo Jones had built for James the First in Old Whitehall, looked anachronistic and shabby in new Manhattan. Over the years it had come to be supported on either side by two towering, white-brick office buildings. Together, the three structures gave the impression of two massive bookends dwarfing a faded miniature.

Inside, the Great Hall had no business having been imported, intact, from the Earl of Stratford's summer castle at Shottley-in-Welting, for which it had been designed 400 years ago. The Hall was wildly out of scale with the club's other proportions. Even the treasured chair in which the visiting Prince of Wales, later Edward the Seventh, had once been served a nine-course dinner, had no real aesthetic significance. A thoroughly ordinary wooden chair, it was unusual only because the fruits, soup, fish, meat, fowl, vegetables, salad, cheeses, ices, and biscuits the prince had consumed were listed by their French names on a plaque set square in the middle of the seat. Predictably, the placement gave rise to a ribaldry whenever visitors were shown through the dining room.

Nor was the club perfect because it was practical. Built in a day when men were shorter but ceilings taller, it wasted space on a grand scale. Cleaning the floors and stairs alone required the nocturnal ministrations of eight charwomen. They were the only persons of their sex ever accorded the privilege of mounting above the first floor.

No, the club was not beautiful. It was not practical. But it was perfect—as the Place des Vosges is a perfect Parisian square, as

Man o' War had been a perfect horse, as Queen Victoria had been a perfect monarch.

There was the famous dinner service capable of accommodating five hundred people. It included fish knives, fish forks, oyster forks, demitasse spoons—even toothpicks, all in solid gold.

There were the menus for guests, printed without prices so that only the member-host ever knew how much anything cost.

There were the six lavatories. Each had two bathtubs placed side by side, separated only by a low table. On each table at all times was laid out a chessboard with four rooks, four knights, four bishops, two queens, two kings, and sixteen pawns, ready for play.

There was the tiny post office just off the club's entrance. It had been especially authorized in 1891 by an Act of Congress so that the membership, which then included President Benjamin Harrison, might have a convenient place to buy stamps. Except for the first of the month, when bills went out, no more than a dozen pieces of mail a day passed through its wicker window. Yet the branch still commanded a full-time postmaster.

And there was the long, hidden tunnel that led off from the wine cellar. It emerged, eleven city blocks away, at the Hudson River. Most visitors assumed that it had been constructed during Prohibition so that members could escape raids by the police. They were wrong. It had been built just before the Civil War so that in the event of a Confederate invasion the club's employees, traditionally Negroes, would have a means of saving their skins. The tunnel had cost $840,000.

That day with Clayson, MacIntosh recognized that the One Hundred Club was the most wondrous and civilized object he had ever beheld. It represented everything in this world that was enjoyable and worth preserving. He knew he wanted the place. The only question was how to go about getting it.

Clayson and another member, Campbell Guthrie, a muralist now deceased, had proposed MacIntosh for membership. There had been no problem getting the thirty letters which the Admissions Committee required. At least a dozen members already knew MacIntosh from school days or from having sat for him. In addition to volunteering their own recommendations, they were conscientious about getting friends to write. At the end of three years, the normal waiting period, MacIntosh found himself elected, and he rapidly became a popular figure at the window table where members dined, *en famille*, when they were not entertaining guests.

The place came to fascinate MacIntosh as a mirror intrigues a puppy. He spent whole afternoons getting to know every room, every piece of furniture, every objet d'art, every book, every fixture. He even discovered the speaking-tube, obediently sealed off during the Twenties, which enabled the doorman to forewarn the bartender of a member's approach so that the man's drink might be waiting.

As MacIntosh's love for the place deepened, so did his apprehensions that one day it might all be lost. What if a new breed of members were to come along—members who might not recognize the club's perfection? Members who might want to install ping-pong tables, television sets, air-conditioning, automatic elevators, hand dryers?

What if some future Board of Governors were to decide to sell the property, say, to a car-parking concession? And what if they were then to use the proceeds to erect on whatever street had come into fashion a new club, constructed of aluminum and glass and containing complete gymnastic facilities?

MacIntosh was by no means opposed to progress in the outside, everyday world; but when it came to the One Hundred Club he saw in progress a distinct peril. He began to realize that some plan of action was called for, and soon. Once a club began to go, he knew, it went fast. Look at the old Van Cortland. A decade ago, it rivaled the Athenaeum in London. Today, the Van Cortland was a police station for the Eleventh Precinct.

MacIntosh's discovery of how he could acquire the place was accidental. He had been waiting for Gauss Fox one day in the library, idly admiring an illuminated manuscript of the Articles of Incorporation. Suddenly, in paragraphs H, I, and J, there it was, exactly what he had been searching for. He had listened to these bylaws dozens of times at monthly meetings, where reading the paragraphs was part of the ritual. But until now he had never realized their possibilities.

From that moment the *voice* of the plan, as MacIntosh came to think of it, grew. By now, neither love for his friends nor the fear of being found out nor logic was strong enough to silence it.

It was a voice that MacIntosh had heard before. As a boy he had been an acolyte in the Protestant Episcopal Church. One Sunday he had walked out with a small communion bowl. He had concealed it upside down under his altar cap because it fitted his skull exactly.

His father, a man of patience if not imagination, had explained that a communion bowl was for everyone to share. Since the time of Joan of Arc, who was believed to have accepted wine from it in Reims, this bowl had represented man's abiding fellowship.

Precisely, young MacIntosh had argued. That's why he had taken it. Simply ornamented, perfectly proportioned, the silver bowl was too beautiful to share. He wanted it for his very own. Besides, if others used it, the bowl might become damaged. In the end he had obediently returned it to the Rector—but not without reluctance.

This was the same obsessive voice to which MacIntosh was listening tonight as he moved in the slow, disorderly procession toward the topmost floor of the club. The library was nearly full by the time he reached the door. Standing on tiptoe, he looked around for a seat where he might be less subject to observation. He was doubly rewarded. As he had hoped, there was a place in the last row. Moreover, the seat was next to Haverstraw Goode, who was almost completely blind. He moved as quickly as the gathering would permit.

"It's Trevor MacIntosh," he said, touching Dr. Goode on the elbow so as not to startle him.

"Good evening," Dr. Goode replied. "Did your dessert have raisins?"

"Raisins?" MacIntosh repeated blankly. He had almost no recollection of what had been served during the dinner. Excitement and nervousness had erased the meal from his memory.

"Raisin pudding, by definition, is made with raisins," Dr. Goode stated emphatically. "I've spoken to the dining-room manager about it several times. But apparently, if I want raisins, and I do, I shall have to supply them myself. Tell me, how have you been?"

"Splendid, splendid," MacIntosh replied absently. "And you?" He noticed that Goode had put on his cummerbund upside down.

On the platform the business part of the evening was getting under way. Labadie Dana, the president, was rapping for order. MacIntosh and Goode leaned forward.

"As is customary in these meetings," the president began, "we start by taking stock of ourselves, and I am saddened to report that during the month of October the club lost one member through removal to another city, and six members through death.

"Memorials to these departed members are now being prepared, and when completed will appear in the Bulletin. We shall miss them all. To paraphrase Dr. Franklin, 'Others may take their place, but none can really replace them'."

The president, a distinguished amateur cellist, was by profession an estate lawyer. The oratorical flourishes of the courtroom did not make MacIntosh feel any easier. His idea was foolproof, he knew. Discreetly, without revealing his purpose, he had checked with various lawyer friends to determine whether there might be any possible flaw. There was none. Nevertheless, MacIntosh continued to be uncomfortable.

"To look upon the brighter side," the president was saying, "we are now entitled to add new friends to our fellowship, and this we shall proceed to do forthwith, before the entertainment portion of our evening begins.

"As of November first our membership stands at ninety-three. This means, of course, that we are privileged to elect seven new members tonight to bring our group back to the full strength of one hundred. As Noah distributes. copies of the printed ballot, let me read aloud the names of the candidates, as required."

MacIntosh looked uneasily around the room. Every eye was on the president.

Dana picked up a piece of paper. "First," he said, "we have Mr. Negley Johnson Truitt, lawyer, painter, proposed by Hoyt Stevens and Klots Houghton. Next, Dr. Harrison M. Dow, university president, author, proposed by Mummery Gore and Shenton Gregg. Third, we have Mr. Charleston Richards the Second, archaeologist, pamphleteer, proposed by Lynes Cox and Haverstraw Goode."

Thump! went Dr. Goode's cane on the floor, and then thump! thump! thump! It was a way he had of expressing pleasure. MacIntosh kept time with his heart. In his eagerness to sit somewhere safe, he had forgotten that Dr. Goode had a candidate up for election that evening. In fact, MacIntosh himself had written a letter for Richards. He felt a twinge of conscience.

Before Goode began losing his eyesight, MacIntosh had spent many enjoyable hours playing bezique with him and he had become fond of the old man. Only two months ago MacIntosh had attended a testimonial dinner honoring Goode's ninetieth birthday. Moreover, he knew it had taken Goode nearly five years to get his candidate in. Richards' youth was the difficulty: he was only fifty.

Well, it was sad, but it could not be helped. The path to heaven, MacIntosh knew, was paved with hell. Even for a friend like Goode, he could not afford to compromise.

The list of candidates droned on. It included the former Suffragan Bishop of the Diocese of New York, an atomic scientist who had won last year's Nobel Peace Prize for experiments on fallout, a retired general who had been the chief labor advisor to a President of the

United States, a journalist whose column, "The Crow's Nest: Being One Man's Point of View," was read by nearly every literate person in America and by most English-speaking people abroad, an agronomist who had recently been decorated by Italy for his work with the soil of Somaliland, a sculptor who only last month, as part of the cultural exchange program, had been commissioned to do a heroic statue of the premier of a foreign power, and a man named Robert C. Martin whose chief qualification seemed to be that he was Chairman of the Board of a large steel corporation.

"The dagger which you will notice before Mr. Martin's name," the president explained, "is, as you know, our private way of designating candidates who, although not involved professionally in the arts and sciences, have 'by word or deed measurably advanced the principles for which this club stands.' I am certain that any members fortunate enough to have attended the opening last month of the splendid new Renaissance Museum in Central Park will agree that a businessman of Mr. Martin's demonstrated affection for the arts should be made to feel very much at home in this Society."

"Businessman!" snorted Dr. Goode. "The whole idea of this club is to escape the world of commerce! But I don't suppose there is any use in protesting."

MacIntosh smiled in reply, although he did not feel like smiling. Martin was exactly the kind of member he too feared for the club. Like most businessmen, MacIntosh reasoned, Martin would probably be a crusader. But $7,000,000, the figure *The New York Times* said the new museum had cost, was an expensive bid for acceptance even in this hallowed institution. MacIntosh broke his promise to be uncompromising. He allowed himself a moment of sympathy for Mr. Martin.

"Finally," the president was saying, "we come to Sullivan Wylie Hughes, proposed by Anderson Gordon-Gordon and Felker Pease." Dana paused and removed his glasses.

"I do not imagine it is necessary to note," he noted, "that Mr. Hughes, who is modestly identified on our ballots as a diplomat, only last week was named by the President to a special post in the Department of State. I think that in these worrisome times, it is singularly fitting that this distinguished gentleman, upon whose shoulders lie so many hopes of the Free World, comes recommended to our group by our member whose surname is Pease."

The pun was acknowledged by exclamations of hear! hear! MacIntosh wiped his palms against his trouser legs.

By this time Noah had reached the back of the room. The elderly steward handed MacIntosh two ballots. One was for Dr. Goode and MacIntosh passed it along.

"I believe," the president began again, "that you have all received ballots. Before folding and passing them along to the aisle, we are beholden to give a hearing to Article Seventeen, paragraphs H, I, and J, dealing with Procedures of Election."

MacIntosh stiffened. The fateful moment was at hand. The president recited the bylaws perfunctorily, as he had at every meeting during his twenty-three years in office.

"H," he said. " 'If, for any reason, a member shall object to any candidate, he shall so indicate by drawing a line through the candidate's name on the ballot.' I. 'One such objection shall be sufficient to exclude.' J. 'Ballots shall be left unsigned.' "

The president sat down and began chatting with Rumsey Henning, the naturalist, who was seated beside him on the platform. As soon as the ballots had been gathered, Dana would introduce Henning, who was to deliver an illustrated talk on "The Secret Fauna of Cordillera Isabel," a range in Nicaragua.

Noah began slowly down the aisle of the great room, collecting ballots in the brass box that had been used in elections since 1842.

MacIntosh looked at Dr. Goode. The nonagenarian was leaning forward on his cane, talking with Trimble Slattery in the row ahead. Even if Goode's eyesight had been perfect, his position would have prevented him from observing what MacIntosh was about to do.

MacIntosh started at the top of the ballot. He hesitated momentarily when he came to Dr. Goode's candidate, and then again at Martin, the millionaire industrialist. But each time he went on.

Last on the list was the new member of the Department of State. Then, finished, MacIntosh folded his ballot.

All eleven names had lines through them.

Waiting for Noah, MacIntosh looked around the room at his fellow members. Ten years? Would it take that long? Probably not, he thought, considering all the gray heads and the increasing frequency with which the club's flag flew at half mast.

Five years was more like it—yes, five years would do it.

MacIntosh saw himself on the platform, rapping the cherrywood gavel with which Cromwell had once opened Parliament.

"I will please come to order," he was saying to the otherwise empty room.

James Powell

The Friends of Hector Jouvet

The old man came up the path that sloped between the benches and flowerbeds, but he stopped short of the edge of the cliff where Brown stood waiting. Instead, he sat down on a bench a few yards away, drew a folded newspaper from his coat pocket, and began to read.

Brown hesitated. His French wasn't really that good and for a moment he couldn't think of the verb "to follow." When he remembered, his chin started to tremble, and throwing his cigarette over the edge he went up to the old man.

"Why are you following me? Is it good to follow people? I do not like being followed. Do you like being followed?" These were all the forms of the verb Brown could muster and rather than start over again, he stopped.

The old man, who had been listening attentively, slipped the newspaper back in his pocket and smiled. "I am afraid you are mistaken, young man. I am not following you." His English was meticulous and the quiet conviction of his words told Brown it was the truth.

"Oh," said Brown, and stepped back in confusion.

"Actually," said the old man, as if to cover the other's embarrassment, "I come here quite often. The sea is blue; the rocks are white. I have always thought that this would be the ideal place for a visitor like yourself to see our gay, carefree little principality for the first time. Regrettably, that is impossible, for to come upon this prospect first, one would have to scale the cliff."

"Maybe a good place to see San Sebastiano for the last time, then," said Brown with a half smile.

"Ah, you are leaving us?" asked the old man sadly. "Well, I hope you have seen more of our happy, light-hearted city than the inside of the Casino."

"I guess that was about as far as I got," admitted Brown.

"But that is terrible, terrible," said the old man, throwing up his hands in mock horror. "But all is not lost and if you will permit me I can still point out a few highlights from here."

He led Brown back to the edge of the cliff. "Below us, of course, is the harbor and over there, the romantic old quarter. Its reputation is exaggerated, I assure you. Our women are not promiscuous; songs have been written about that. On the left you have our celebrated Reptile Museum founded by Prince Adalbert, an ardent herpetologist and the grandfather of our present prince. My father had many stories of the misadventures of the good Prince Adalbert who prowled the streets of San Sebastiano at all hours hunting snakes with his forked stick, returning the salutes of the policemen and chatting quietly to himself.

"And there, behind the Cathedral, you can see the roof of the Casino into which, you are perhaps aware, the citizens of the principality are not allowed to enter. That is quite appropriate. A good host does not laugh at his own jokes."

Brown took a wristwatch out of his pocket, looked at it, and put it back.

"Am I keeping you? I hope not," said the old man. "Actually I cannot stay much longer myself. I must see a friend off on the train—the 4:45."

"You don't have much time," warned Brown.

"Enough for a bit more of our history," said the old man, leading Brown back to the bench. "Were you aware, for example, that our mineral waters were held in high esteem as early as the days of the Romans? One might wonder why, since it is quite sulphurous and abominable. Perhaps they had more horrible diseases in classical times than we do today.

"Within the memory of my grandfather, the elderly and infirm flocked to San Sebastiano to take our waters. They sat on park benches and scowled at our pigeons; they let themselves be pushed along our promenades in wicker chairs; they pulled wry faces and sucked at our mineral waters. But we were more than a spa. We were renowned for personal sobriety and dignified compassion toward those who frequented our life-giving waters.

"Yes, believe it or not, the gay, carefree people of today's San Sebastiano were all that. In the generation preceding the Franco-Prussian War acute depression of the liver was fashionable and our waters were highly recommended.

"Those were the fat years for us, years of building and, as it later turned out, of overbuilding. For with the close of the war an epidemic of disorders of the spleen swept across France and non-Germanic Europe. Less carbonated waters came into style and almost overnight our little city was as deserted and forlorn as an overgrown cemetery. Today one is at the top, tomorrow at the bottom."

Brown's mouth worked soundlessly. Then he said, "Life is a real double-crosser."

"Why, that is quite philosophical for someone so young, and an American at that," smiled the old man.

"Canadian," said Brown.

"A Canadian, how delightful," said the old man, still smiling.

"You're going to miss your train," said Brown.

"I still have a bit more time," said the old man. "Now let me see, where were we? Ah, yes. Now, as it happened, a modest, unassuming little Casino had been established on an out-of-the-way street to accommodate the younger, faster set which frequented our little principality at the height of its popularity. A mere accommodation—"

Suddenly the old man clapped a hand to his forehead. "I have just thought of something I should have thought of before," he said. "Perhaps you can help me. The Canadian and the American dollar are worth the same, are they not?"

Brown stared at him for a moment. "No," he said finally.

"Then the Canadian dollar is worth more?" said the old man.

"Less," said Brown.

"Ah, I am sorry," said the old man. "Forgive me for dwelling on it but would you happen to know the exact—"

"The Canadian dollar is worth between ninety-two and ninety-three cents," said the young man.

"Let us say ninety-three," insisted the old man graciously. He pursed his lips and calculated. "Fine. Fine," he said. "I have just had what you would call a false alarm. But let us get back to what we were talking about. Imagine the city fathers' surprise when at the very time the attraction of our waters declined, the revenue from the Casino showed a healthy increase, due, in part, to our abundance of economical hotels and hungry waiters.

"It soon became obvious that San Sebastiano was at a crossroads. Should we wait, sober, compassionate, with tightened belts for the prodigal elderly and infirm to return? Or should we cut a new path through the history of San Sebastiano, expand the Casino, become gay, hurdy-gurdy, and carefree?

"It was decided to have a referendum. Feelings ran high. A man walking down the street laughed with pure delight at some enchanting thing his daughter, a child of five, had said. He was jumped upon and severely beaten by a group of mineral-water supporters who believed him to be demonstrating in favor of the Casino. A crowd of Casino supporters, returning in an ugly mood from a mass rally, came upon a funeral procession in the street and interpreted it as a counter-demonstration by the mineral-water faction. The ensuing clash provoked three solid days of rioting. Et cetera. Et cetera. The outcome of the referendum you know, for it is as you see us now."

"You know, you've missed your friend's train," said Brown.

"Why, then I'll see him off on the next," said the old man. "As I was about to say, San Sebastiano, with its expanded gambling facilities, entered what has been described as its 'laughing years.' In 1909 an entirely new Casino, constructed in the style of the Ottoman Turk, was opened amid fireworks, balloon ascents, and a magnificent sailboat regatta.

"On the opening day Casimir Vaugirard in his tri-wing Prentis-Jenkins Hedgehog flew from Perpignan to San Sebastiano in a matter of hours. He circled the dome and minaret of the Casino, dropping projectiles trailing the colors of the Vaugirards and San Sebastiano, then dipped his wings in a majestic salute to the cheering crowd and crashed into the side of this very hill.

"What might have spelled disaster for us—since tragedy was hardly the mood we hoped to associate with our little principality—became instead a supreme gesture of love when, in the cockpit, his body was found locked in the embrace of his mistress, the celebrated beauty known as Lola.

"Well, missing one train is no excuse for missing the next," said the old man, "and a few formalities still remain. I trust what I have said will enable you to appreciate what is about to happen."

"Formalities?" said Brown.

"May I see your passport?" said the old man. Brown stared at the outstretched hand. Nodding toward it, the old man said, "I am the police, you see. Your passport, please."

Brown handed it over.

The old man skimmed down the vital statistics, shook his head sympathetically over the photograph, then thumbed through the pages, turning the passport this way and that to read the frontier stamps.

"But I haven't done anything wrong," said Brown.

The old man shrugged genially and without pausing in his examination of the passport, drew an envelope from his pocket and passed it to the young man.

"Mr. Brown, here you will find one second-class railway ticket, San Sebastiano to Paris, and banknotes to the sum of fifty new francs—ten of your dollars, more or less. I would appreciate your checking to see that this is exactly as I say, for I am required to ask you to sign a receipt."

In the midst of counting the bills, Brown stopped. "But this is crazy. I haven't done anything."

The old man closed the passport and handed it back. "Mr. Brown, let me say directly what both you and I know: your coming here this afternoon was for the purpose of doing away with yourself."

"A lie—an out-and-out lie," said Brown indignantly.

"No, it is not," said the old man calmly. "You are not being honest with me."

"Honest?" shouted Brown. "You're a fine one to talk about honesty. Didn't I ask you if you were following me and didn't you say"—he switched into a falsetto—" 'I am afraid you are mistaken, young man'?"

"You are not being quite fair, Mr. Brown. Granted I did walk behind you from the Casino. But I was not following you. Except for my superiors' primitive attitude regarding expenses, I could have come by taxi and arrived here well ahead of you."

The old man shrugged at Brown's look of disbelief. "Mr. Brown," he said, "have you ever considered the possibilities of suicide open to a tourist? He does not have a gun—his intention in coming abroad is rarely to shoot himself. Our pharmacies confuse him and he does not know the name in our language for the poison he might have used with every confidence at home. He distrusts our hotel furniture, and rightly so. Will a chair that looks as though Louis XIV sat in it hold his weight as he ties a rope to the chandelier? And in what store would he buy the rope?

"No, if you think about it, Mr. Brown, there is only one way—to throw oneself from a high place. Here in San Sebastiano there is really only one spot high enough to do the job without risking half measures. And here we are."

"Look," said Brown with a facsimile of laughter, "you've really made a mistake. I came here to try my luck at the Casino and now I'm off to Florence or someplace. I'm making a kind of grand tour."

The old man smiled patiently.

"Look," said Brown, "the whole trip is a reward for my graduating in dentistry from McGill University—that's in Montreal. When the trip's over I go back home to Drumheller, Alberta, and go into practice with my father. A guy with his future all cut out for him would be the last person to commit suicide. What I mean is, you don't have any motive."

The old man sighed and took a notebook from his pocket. " 'On August 15 last,' " he read, " 'the Eighth Bureau of the Judiciary Police' "—he half rose and tipped his hat—" 'was alerted by the local American Express office that one Brown, Norman, had that day cashed in the return portion of a first-class airplane ticket, Paris–Montreal–Calgary. Subsequent routine investigation revealed that on the preceding day the subject had checked into the Hotel de l'Avenir and the same afternoon at the Casino had lost chips amounting to $520.

" 'The afternoon following the subject's visit to American Express he lost chips amounting to $450. That evening he sent the following cablegram to a Miss Annabella Brown, Drumheller, Alberta: DEAR AUNT BELLA, MONEY AND RETURN TICKET LOST IN FIRE THAT DE-STROYED MY HOTEL. BEST NOT TO WORRY NORMAN SENIOR. $1000 SHOULD COVER IT NICELY. NORMY.

" 'August 16, subject loses chips amounting to $1000.' Miss Brown is very prompt. 'Subject leaves Casino and walks to the Parc de la Grande Armée'—which is where we are now—'and stands in contemplation at edge of cliff, then leaves park and sends following cablegram: DEAR AUNT BELLA, HOTEL FIRE NO ACCIDENT. HAVE STUM-BLED ON VAST INTERNATIONAL PLOT LINKING JAPANESE BEETLES, DIS-APPEARANCE OF AMELIA EARHART, AND RADICAL CHANGES IN WEATHER THESE LAST FEW YEARS. CONFIRMS YOUR SUSPICION, WAS NOT SUN-SPOTS. HAVE CONTACTED DISILLUSIONED FOREIGN AGENT. NEED $5000 AS PROOF OF MY GOOD FAITH. LET'S KEEP THIS TO OURSELVES. NORMY.

" 'August 17, subject's losses: $5,000. That evening sends following cablegram: DEAR AUNT BELLA, WE ARE REALLY ONTO SOMETHING. AGENT AGREES TO BE ON OUR SIDE AND SAP THEM FROM WITHIN. HE SAYS DOUBLE AGENTS GET DOUBLE PAY. SOUNDS FAIR ENOUGH. NEEDS ANOTHER $5000. MUM, DON'T FORGET, IS THE WORD. NORMY.

" 'August 18, subject's losses: $5,000. Sends following cablegram: DEAR AUNT BELLA, THINGS COMING TO A HEAD. NEED $5000 FOR INCI-DENTAL EXPENSES—MICROFILM, INVISIBLE INK, SECRETARIAL HELP, ETC., ETC. ITEMIZED LIST TO FOLLOW. KEEP THIS UNDER YOUR HAT. NORMY.' "

The old man looked up from his notebook. "Might I ask you about this Miss Brown?"

"She doesn't happen to be any of your darn business," said Brown through clenched teeth. The old man waited. At last Brown said, "You might say that I'm her favorite nephew. You might say that the money was her life savings."

"I meant is she a bit—potty? Do you still say 'potty'?"

" 'Peculiar' might be better," said Brown.

"I must jot that down," said the old man, scribbling in his notebook. "And now where were we?

" 'August 19, by 5 P.M. subject's *winnings* total $38,000; by midnight, $88,000; by closing time, $123,000. Subject returns to hotel where, in answer to inquiry, is informed that next train for Paris is at 1:47 P.M.

" 'August 20, subject checks out of hotel at 10:37 A.M., leaves bags at station, wanders through streets looking in store windows. Noon finds subject in front of Casino. Subject smiles as if pleasantly surprised, and with glance at wristwatch, enters Casino.' "

The old man closed his notebook and looked up. "By 2:30 you had lost $56,000, and by 3:30, $123,000. And here we are. I must add in conclusion that San Sebastiano for several years now has requested in the most vigorous terms that the railway provide us with a morning service to Paris. Now perhaps we had better go," he said, preparing to rise.

"Hold on a minute," said Brown, and he began to slap the palm of one hand with the back of the other. "I have certain rights. You can't just put me on a train and run me out of town. Nothing you've said would hold up in a court of law."

The old man settled back on the bench. "Ah, now I can understand your hostility," he said. "Believe me, there was never a question of a law having been broken. Consider for yourself how odd it would look if gay, carefree, light-hearted San Sebastiano had a law making it a crime to attempt suicide. What would people say? Why would anyone even dream of committing suicide here?"

"You mean that technically speaking," said Brown, "I could jump off this cliff this very moment and you could do nothing?"

The old man nodded. "It would be perfectly legal. But law is a funny thing, Mr. Brown. If some future historian, for example, were to try to understand the people of the Twentieth Century from a study of their books of law alone, would he, do you think, see them as they were, or as they feared they were, or as they hoped they might be?

"A particular case: what would this future historian of ours think of a certain law in force in San Sebastiano which says that our police must clean their revolvers daily—nothing unusual in that—but, the law continues, in a secluded yet public place in the open air? Legend has it that one Sub-Inspector, Auguste Petitjean, discharged his revolver as he was cleaning it while seated in his bath. The tub and walls, as it happened, were marble, and Sub-Inspector Petitjean was shot seventeen times in as many places by that single ricocheting bullet.

"By some miracle he recovered and returned to the force only to be subsequently discharged when it was discovered that he had developed a psychological block against firing his revolver—or, as another version of the story has it, against taking a bath. Whichever version is correct, the law is there nevertheless. Were you to try to jump, I would be obliged to clean my revolver in public and it might accidentally discharge, the bullet striking you in the left calf. Conveniently enough, the hospital is located right next to the railway station.

"I had intended, by the way, to say before that I am sorry your train ticket is second-class. By all rights it should be first-class, but the authorities view the situation otherwise. You see, our Eighth Bureau, dealing exclusively in cases such as yours, is organized into three divisions based on the amount of money lost by the subject—not winnings that happen to be lost again, you understand, but his own personal investment.

"The first division, headed by Inspector Guizot, deals with amounts of $5,000 or less: the butcher, the baker, and the candlestick maker. Traditionally his subjects travel third-class.

"My own division, the second, deals with amounts of $5,000 to $50,000. By the way, we use American dollars as a standard out of simple convenience. That was why I received quite a start a while back when I realized that in your case we were dealing in Canadian dollars. For a moment I was afraid, forgive me, that you might be in Guizot's division. In any event, traditionally my subjects go second-class.

"The third division, under Baron de Mirabelle, deals with sums in excess of $50,000. His subjects, of course, go first-class.

"However, a few years ago the railways did away with third-class. It was decided that Guizot's would go second-class. What else could they do? Fine, I said, but then I humbly submit that mine should go first-class. But the authorities were blind to the justice of it, and de Mirabelle, though sympathetic, kept smiling in that cultured way of his.

"A very distinguished person, the Baron: always in evening dress and with a black patch, sometimes over one eye, sometimes over the other. I often tell the story of how the Baron acquired his eye patch. I like to think it makes my own subjects' losses appear less significant.

"One day around the end of the last war a large burly soldier arrived in San Sebastiano. He had a system for roulette, as we all do, and $200,000—the accumulated combat pay and savings of his entire regiment, which he had promised to increase a hundredfold.

"This he promptly proceeded to do. His system was based on what he called his 'lucky lower-left bicuspid.' He would survey the roulette table, from number to number, until his bicuspid throbbed. That number he would bet. And he would win astronomical sums—millions—night after night.

"Finally the day arrived when the Casino, short of a miracle, would open its doors for the last time. The soldier dined alone beforehand at Chez Tintin. At the end of the meal there was an altercation. The waiter accused him of overtipping. The soldier threated to ram a wad of banknotes down the waiter's throat and moved toward him with a bobbing and weaving motion, the result, we were later to learn, of considerable experience in the ring, where he was known as—"

The old man thought for a moment. "Breaker Baker, or something like that," he said. "Politely but firmly, the waiter struck him on the head with a bottle, Chateau Pommefrit, 1938.

"The soldier regained consciousness to find his celebrated tooth on the floor in front of him. He rushed to the Casino and, with the tooth clenched in his fist, surveyed the table. Nothing happened.

"But then, as his eye passed number 14, something in his jaw throbbed faintly—his lower-*right* bicuspid! He bet and lost. Again the bicuspid throbbed, more insistently. He bet again and lost. And so on into the night. By closing time he was penniless and the right side of his jaw was swollen, throbbing as indiscriminately as any common toothache.

"The next day, when the soldier tried to take his life, Baron de Mirabelle, of course, was waiting. But at the railway station the soldier grew belligerent and came at the Baron, bobbing and weaving, catching the Baron with a right cross to the eye. Finally two Travelers' Aid people had to force the soldier onto the train. Not a moment too soon either, for at the news of his losses his regiment had mobilized and units had already reached the outskirts of San Sebastiano, thirsting for his blood. The Baron's eye had a fine bruise for a week. He fancied himself in the eye patch and has worn it to this day."

"Let's get back to me," said Brown. "What if your bullet didn't stop me? What if I crawled to the edge and with my last breath threw myself to my death?"

"Believe me," said the old man, "that is just not the way it is done. The suicide, above all others, wants to leave life erect, not on his hands and knees. He wants to savor that last moment. He stops to smoke a final cigarette, to gather his thoughts together into an epigram of one sort of the other, to—and this happens more frequently than you might imagine—to remove his wristwatch. Placing it where? Of course, in his pocket.

"How 'peculiar' we are and how lovable, eh, Mr. Brown? And here is something equally convenient for me in my work: how many turn to say, 'Why are you following me?' As if it should make any difference to them if I were to leap over the cliff right behind them. No, Mr. Brown, man always wants to pause a bit before spitting in life's eye, before jumping, before becoming both the spitter and the spittle."

Brown rested his head in his hands and without looking up, said, "I guess you win." Then his chin began to tremble again. "I just want you to know that I can see right through you people," he said. "You don't give a darn if I kill myself or not as long as I don't do it here. I can lose my aunt's life savings in your Casino, oh, sure. But I can't jump off your gay carefree little cliff." He rubbed his eyes. "Well, I say the hell with you all."

The old man moved to put his hand on the young man's shoulder, then thought better of it. He leaned forward. "Mr. Brown, we must all set a boundary on our compassion or we would turn our faces to the wall and not get out of bed in the morning. San Sebastiano's humble frontiers are the limits of mine. You must forgive me if I find that quite enough. Before, when I told you something of our history, I hoped to prepare you to understand why we cannot allow you and the others to carry out your little plans. For what would be the result? A suicide rate, a per capita statistic so misleading and grotesque that it would reflect on the whole tenor of life in light-hearted, hurdy-gurdy San Sebastiano.

"Besides, aren't you being a bit severe? The railway ticket and the money will take you to Paris where your Embassy will arrange modest transportation home. Confess your little indiscretion. Give Aunt Bella the pleasure of forgiving her favorite nephew."

"And what about my father?" said Brown. "Did I tell you he's got fists like hams? Like hams!" Brown stared down at his shoes and shook his head back and forth.

After watching him for a few moments, the old man looked down at his own shoes and said in a quiet voice, "You know, Mr. Brown, soon I will be retiring and I have often thought these last few years of all the people I have taken to the train. What are they doing? How are they getting on? How many children do they have? Do they, I wonder, ever remember the day Hector Jouvet—that is to say, myself—put them on the train? I am not being sentimental. I tell you this because I want to describe for you a silly daydream of mine, solely because it might amuse you.

"In my daydream it is the day of my retirement. I enter my favorite café. Georges, the owner, stands behind the bar reading a newspaper. 'Good day, Monsieur Jouvet,' he says. 'Would you step out back with me for a moment?'

"Puzzled, I follow him out to the back where they have the large room they rent out for banquets. Everything is dark. Suddenly the lights blaze on. I am taken aback. I am surprised. The room is filled with half remembered faces—stockbrokers, bank tellers, church wardens, trustees of estates of widows and orphans. Across the front wall is a large banner: THE FRIENDS OF HECTOR JOUVET. FIRST ANNUAL CONVENTION.

"Amid applause and well wishes I take my place at the head table beside those special people, whoever they might be, who had gone on from their visit to San Sebastiano to positions of eminence in their own countries—a statesman, a bishop, a magnate or two, and—who knows, Mr. Brown?—perhaps even a famous dentist.

"We eat and at the end of the meal I am presented with a gold cigarette lighter. I could show you the very one in a shop window not far from where I live. It is inscribed: *To our friend Hector Jouvet from The Friends of Hector Jouvet.* Then in six different languages they sing 'For He's a Jolly Good Fellow,' and end by pounding on the tables.

"I stand up. I am deeply moved. I always feel this particular moment most vividly and how deeply I am moved. Then I speak. In my mind's eye, I see all this very clearly. But though my mouth is moving I cannot hear what I am saying. I only feel my own astonishment at the wisdom and simplicity of my words. They are saying everything I had wanted to say to each person in the room on his particular day. But I cannot hear the words. I can only see their faces smiling and nodding."

The old man stopped abruptly and cleared his throat. "But of course all this nonsense takes place only in my imagination. The people I have taken to the train do not know each other. Oh, one or two might meet by chance. Perhaps in his cups, while talking of youthful indiscretions, one might mention Hector Jouvet. 'What?' the other might say, 'you knew Jouvet too?' And they might talk of afternoons at the cliffside in San Sebastiano or even of forming a club. But it would come to nothing because they were only one or two.

"How regrettable, Mr. Brown, because I have all their names and they wouldn't be so hard to locate—except, you understand, it would be out of place for me to take the initiative. As a matter of fact, I carry the list with me should the same idea occur to someone or other as I take him to the train. You might be interested in seeing the list, Mr. Brown. I think I have it here somewhere."

As the old man fumbled through his pockets, he laughed nervously and said, "I don't imagine, Mr. Brown, that you would care to be the first president of The Friends of Hector Jouvet?"

Brown looked up from his shoes. "Did I tell you my father was heavyweight champion of the Canadian Army? Did I tell you what they called him because of those big fists of his?" said the young man with a shudder. "They called him The Buster."

The old man looked puzzled. "Buster Brown. Buster Brown," he said thoughtfully. "But of course, of course—it was Buster Brown, not Breaker Baker. How stupid of me and how delightful! Buster Brown was the name of the soldier who gave the Baron his eye patch."

"You mean the one who lost all those millions was my father? The one with the lucky lower-left bicuspid?" said Brown with an astonished and broadening grin.

The old man nodded. "How appropriate he should have turned to dentistry. Your father was the man who almost broke the bank at San Sebastiano. A popular song was written about him at the time. As we walk to the station I will teach it to you, if you like."

Brown jumped to his feet. "I'll say I would!" he said. "Even just enough to hum the tune every once in a while!"

"I'm sure that would be very useful, Mr. Brown," smiled the old man. "Ah, it is a great day for the Eighth Bureau. First the father and now the son. And after that who knows, eh, Mr. Brown? A fine-looking young man like yourself. Well, come along or we will miss our train."

He took Brown by the elbow and they started down the path. "Mr. Brown," said the old man as they went, "do you recall my mentioning The Friends of Hector Jouvet? It occurs to me that if such a club were ever formed it might offer your father an honorary membership. I don't imagine he's being invited to many regimental reunions."

Jon L. Breen

The Crowded Hours

The city in these pages is real.

The characters are drawn directly from life.

The police procedure is strictly a product of the author's imagination.

The city.

She.

They'll all tell you the city's a female. To some she's a laughing girl, to some a full, ripe woman; to some a lady, to some a dame, and to more than a few a bitch. But she's a female to all of them—just as she is to you, whether you grew up in a swank penthouse in Tewart Towers or a slum tenement in downtown Itolja, whether you graduated from the plush country club of Elizabethtown High or survived the hard knocks of North Manual Trades—or even if you met her only as a mature man and felt you'd known her always.

A female, this city, a she, whether she's warm and comforting or cool and exhilarating or hot and making you drip sweat, or cold and unfriendly and chilling—she can be any of these, and she'll be all of them at some point to every man, even you who love her. At noon her tall spires implore heaven like arms of shimmering brilliance, gazing with haughty magnificence at the clear waters of her harbor. She exudes exuberant life. The curves of her shoreline, the patterns of her streets and freeways can be graceful or provocative or cute—their charm can obscure the midriff bulge of her slums. She's home to more Swiss than the city of Geneva, more Canadians than Toronto and Vancouver combined.

When you love her—if you love her, and how could one not love her?—her small flaws don't repel you but make you love her all the more, this sweetheart of your youth, this mistress of your best years, this comforting friend of your old age.

She's a female, this city, your female.

And you love her.

But you wish she'd change her deodorant and take a bath, because she's dirty and she stinks.

The squadroom was hot, August hot, and Melvin Melvin's bald pate glistened with sweat.

Melvin Melvin was a good cop. He was proud of being a good cop, and he thought he knew why he was a good cop. He was patient. Melvin Melvin thought he was one of the most patient men in the world, certainly one of the most patient cops. One of Melvin's father's ill-advised practical jokes—one of his more permanent jokes—had left Melvin with a name that was bound to draw gags, taunts, and boyhood beatings, like corpses draw insects. Melvin was thankful his name had at least taught him tolerance and patience and left no visible scars except a totally bald head that had been devoid of hair since he was twenty-eight.

Melvin's philosophical bent made him thankful for another small blessing regarding his nomenclature—no one had ever found out his middle name.

It was Melvin.

Melvin Melvin Melvin.

Ridiculous.

"Say, Melvin," said Mascara, from the clerical office.

"What is it?" said Melvin. "Can't you see I'm busy?"

"Do you want coffee?"

"Sure I want coffee. I got nothing better to do in this lousy precinct but drink your lousy coffee. All I do is sit around all day and guzzle your coffee, because all you do all day in that crumby clerical office of yours is make coffee. And for a guy who makes coffee all day, you sure make the goddamnedest putrid coffee, you know that, Mascara?"

"Sure, Melvin. You want coffee?"

"Yeah, I want coffee. Didn't I say so?"

"I guess so. You know what, Melvin?"

"What?"

"You should try to be more patient."

"More patient? I'm the patientest cop in this whole stinking 97th precinct. Doesn't everybody say so?"

"Yeah, they do, Melvin. I never could figure that out."

"Ah, you're just like my father."

The phone on Melvin's desk rang.

"Ninety-seventh. Melvin."

"This is Ella Anders speaking. My husband Phil has just been murdered. Can you send someone over here right away?"

"Certainly, ma'am. Just take it slow. Now, what's the address, please?"

The Anders address was a plush apartment in Itolja, overlooking the River Vix. The body of Phil Anders had been found on a rubdown table in a makeshift gymnasium opening onto the hallway. There was a knife in his chest.

Curt Bing and Houghton Claws were the two 97th detectives sent to investigate the murder. For the two of them to be paired was a rare occurrence in the 97th squad, for both were given to making the wrong moves, and each usually needed the steadying influence of Steve Berella to function successfully. On this occasion it was hoped they would act as a steadying influence on one another.

Bing, who was the youngest of the squad's detectives and looked even younger than he was, frequently antagonized suspects with his crude, tactless interrogation style. Houghton Claws, a huge, handsome man with streaks of red and black in his blond hair, was of so sporting a nature in dealing with dangerous criminals that he had frequently gotten his fellow detectives almost killed.

"What happened, ma'am?" Claws asked the widow.

"I was giving him a rubdown," said Ella Anders. "I give him a rubdown every day at two-thirty. I had gone in the next room to get a towel. I was gone just a few seconds. When I came back, there he was. With that thing in his chest."

"Was he dead when you came back into the room?"

"No, he was still alive, gasping for breath."

"Did he say anything?"

"Yes. He said, 'Teddy Bear.' That was all. Then he died, and I called you."

" 'Teddy Bear,' " repeated Claws musingly. "Does that mean anything special to you, Mrs. Anders?"

"No, it doesn't. I don't understand what he meant."

"I see. Did your husband have any enemies?"

"No. No one. Everybody loved him."

"Come on, lady," said Curt Bing. "He's dead. Somebody killed him. He must have had one enemy. Unless you killed him. Did you kill him, Mrs. Anders?"

"How can you say such a thing?" said Ella Anders. "How can he say that?" she asked Claws.

"Let me handle this, will you, Curt?"

"Why did you kill him, Mrs. Anders? Jealousy?" Bing persisted.

"Curt, shut up! Can't I take you anyplace? Go out and wait in the car."

"Aw, come on, Houghton. That's no fun!"

"Just wait in the car, Curt."

"Aw, you're just like my father," Bing whimpered and ran out.

"I apologize for my partner, ma'am. He's young and has known great tragedy."

"I think I understand," said Ella Anders.

"Isn't there anyone your husband has quarreled with lately?"

"Well, there was one person. A Mr. Bridger was here yesterday, a Mr. Norville Bridger. He was ghostwriting a book for my husband about strength and health, but they couldn't agree about what should be included in the book. Phil was threatening to fire Bridger and get another ghost."

"It sounds like a slim motive for murder, but we'll look into it. Do you know Bridger's address?"

Ella Anders gave the address of a well known magazine publisher in the skyscrapered business district of Itolja.

"Thank you. One more thing, Mrs. Anders. How did the murderer get into the room?"

"Anyone could have. The door that opens onto the hallway was unlocked. But there is one thing I cannot understand."

"What is that?"

"Why did the murderer take such a chance? I was talking to Phil from the next room all the time I was getting the towel. Why did the murderer take the chance of killing my husband when he knew there was a witness in the next room who might walk in on him at any moment?"

"That's a good point. We'll keep it in mind."

As the technicians and photographers worked with the body, Houghton Claws said goodbye to Ella Anders, giving her hand a comforting squeeze. He had fallen hopelessly in love with the widow the moment he had entered the makeshift gym, but his innate sense of decency, ingrained in him by his father, who was a minister, made him decide to wait a couple of days after her husband's murder before going to bed with her.

Houghton Claws was that kind of a cop.

Houghton Claws was a gentleman.

"All you Chinese look alike to me," said Melvin Melvin.

Handsome, dark, oriental-looking Steve Berella smiled good-naturedly. "You know I'm Italian, Melvin."

"Well, all you Chinese Italians look alike to me."

"Yeah. We make spaghetti that you're hungry half an hour after."
Steve got to his feet. "I'm going home, Melvin, before you find some reason to keep me here."

"If I could go home to what you got to go home to," said Melvin, "I wouldn't be sitting around making ethnic jokes about bald Eskimos."

"Eskimo? I thought you were Jewish, Melvin."

"Sure, my wife makes chicken soup in our igloo. Say, Steve, you heard about this Anders case?"

Berella was nearing the door of the squadroom. "Sure, I heard about it."

"It's a hilariously funny case."

"Funny? How?"

"It's a dying-massage case. You never heard of a dying massage?"

"You're a riot, Melvin. See you."

"So long, Steve," said Melvin patiently.

Norville A. Bridger, as the door of his office proclaimed, appeared to be doing very well as an employee of the biggest magazine chain in Itolja. Well enough that it seemed doubtful he'd kill a man who threatened to fire him from a not-too-promising ghosting job.

As Houghton Claws was talking to Bridger, he was hoping to cut the interview short and get back to Bridger's secretary, with whom he'd fallen hopelessly in love at first sight and whom he hoped to seduce by nightfall.

"Now just what is it you do here, Mr. Bridger?"

"I cut novels. Several of our magazines regularly run condensations of new novels before their publication in hardcover form."

"And this is a full-time job, Mr. Bridger?" asked Claws, interested despite his other preoccupation.

"You might be very surprised at what a demanding job it is, Mr. Claws. Cutting books is an art. I had a friend who was in this business and could never get the hang of it. He cut mystery novels for a slick-paper women's magazine. There was one of their regular writers whose books were fairly easy to cut—for a pro, I mean. He usually had about fifteen hundred words worth of plot which he'd beef up to novel length with all kinds of descriptions and character analyses. Well, this friend of mine fell in love with the guy's prose so much that he'd leave in the descriptive passages and cut out half the plot instead. In one story it turned out that the murderer wasn't even a character in the story—my friend had cut him out completely."

"That must have made it confusing to the reader."

"It did."

"What's your friend doing now?"

"He was with *Reader's Digest* briefly, but after the fire—"

"What fire?"

"He ran amok and burned the complete works of Evan Hunter one night. It was the biggest conflagration in the history of Pleasantville, New York."

"I see. Well, this is all very interesting, Mr. Bridger, but I'd like to hear about the quarrel you had with Mr. Anders."

"Oh, it was nothing at all. I just couldn't make his fool book long enough for him. It's my training here, I guess. He had only about fifty pages worth of ideas and I had it all said in twenty. Ghosting books is a dirty business. I much prefer being a cutter."

Steve Berella was bleeding and wondering why.

Not why he was bleeding. He was bleeding because someone had smashed the side of his head in with a bottle. And his belly ached because someone had kicked him there repeatedly.

The feel and taste and smell of blood were easy to explain. So was the aching gut.

But Steve Berella was wondering why he had become a cop. Was it his job to collect the city's human trash? Was it his duty to clean the stains off her shimmering spires? Was it his job to maintain the Chamber of Commerce's façade of respectability? Was it his job to get bottles smashed over his head and get kicked in the gut? Repeatedly? In his own apartment?

Steve Berella thought about it and decided he was glad he was a cop.

But he wished he could stop bleeding.

On the carpet.

He kept bleeding for a while.

Blood is messy.

Curt Bing sat in the squadroom, drinking Mascara's coffee and examining the contents of Phil Anders' billfold. There was no lead to Teddy Bear.

Bing fingered Anders' social-security card, his oil-company credit card, his Diners Club credit card, his American Express credit card, his five department-store credit cards, and his library card.

(NOTE: *Insert here facsimiles of Anders' social-security card, oil-company credit card, Diners Club credit card, American Express credit card, five department-store credit cards, and library card.)*

There was no lead.

"There's no lead, Melvin. I don't understand it."

"Be patient, kid, like I am."

"This is getting us nowhere. I feel I should be out questioning somebody."

"*No!* Not that. You can do better here. Keep mulling over that billfold and something will come to you."

Bing pouted thoughtfully.

Mascara poked his head out of the clerical office. "More coffee, Melvin?"

"Mascara, you want me to tell you what you can do with your lousy coffee?"

"Okay, if you don't want any, say so. Melvin, with everybody else you're so patient. Why can't you be patient with me? Huh?"

"Mascara, you just can't make coffee, that's all." Besides that, Mascara reminded him of his father. "Why don't you go to some friendly neighborhood market and get some friendly little old grocer to tell you what you're doing wrong, huh? That's what my wife did."

"Sure, Melvin. More coffee, Curt?"

"I don't think—hey, wait a minute! I've got it! I just cracked the Anders case!"

Curt Bing reached for the telephone and began dialing the Anders apartment. Melvin cringed.

"Hello, Mrs. Anders? This is Detective Bing of the 97th squad. Who is this? Houghton? What the hell are you doing there? What do you mean it's none of my business? Well, put Mrs. Anders on. I won't insult her, Houghton. Honest. Oh, all right. Ask her if she's sure all her husband said when he died was 'Teddy Bear.' Were those his exact words? This is very important."

There was a lengthy pause.

"Yeah? That's not quite all he said? He said her name too? He said Ella? That's just what I was hoping, Houghton. I'll explain later, Houghton. You and Mrs. Anders can get back to whatever it was you were doing. Goodbye."

Bing hung up the phone and leaped out of his chair.

"Do you get it, Melvin? He said, 'Teddy Bear, Ella'—at least that's what she thought he said. But she thought the Ella part was just her name, so she dropped it from the message when she told us about it. But it *was* part of the message. What he really said was—"

"Teddy Berella?" said Melvin incredulously. "You mean Steve's deaf-and-dumb wife? *She* did it?"

"Sure. That's why she didn't hear Mrs. Anders talking in the next room. She's deaf and dumb. She didn't know danger was nearby. It all fits, Melvin!"

"But, Curt, she has no connection with the case. She hasn't even come into the thing. And why did she do it, Curt?"

Curt Bing shrugged his youthful shoulders. "I don't know, Melvin. I guess we'll just have to wait until the hardcover edition comes out this fall."

Melvin nodded his bald head, wiped the perspiration from his brow, and gave thanks for his patience.

Richard A. Selzer

A Single Minute of Fear

She had sat wrenlike on the edge of an old ladderback chair—small, thin, white-haired, with blue eyes and a startlingly youthful voice. It had struck him that if he had heard that voice without seeing her he would have expected a young girl. The voice was clear, light, with a bit of boldness in it. For an instant he had a vision of a beautiful young girl imprisoned in an old woman's body.

"Yes, it is a big house, I suppose, but it's home," she was saying. "I was born here and never lived anywhere else. From up here on the hill you can see the lights on the water in the harbor. Come, I'll show you."

They walked up the curving staircase to the library. From the window the lights far below darted and zipped, like phosphorescent bugs. It was so quiet. That was what he liked best—he could study here, undisturbed. Warren was older than the other students and needed to regain the discipline of studying. Five years of solitude in the Forestry Service had depleted his drive. Passive and shy at his return to the world, he needed the isolation he saw here.

When they returned to the living room she had said, her blue eyes pale and unswerving, "Of course, no girls in the house. And no liquor."

"May I smoke?"

"In your room."

They arranged for him to work out his rent in chores, giving her eight hours of work each week. She always took in Forestry students, she said. "They understand hedges and grass. You really can't get much out of a Classicist." She had made that mistake once and that year had ended up hiring a gardener.

His room was on the third floor, really more than he had hoped for. The walls were dark walnut, rather somber, but less distracting than wallpaper. There was a bathroom with ancient porcelain fixtures and a naked bulb at the end of a string. One window was darkened by the middle branches of a pine tree. The other window looked down over the steep curving drive of the private road.

He had meant to keep his distance, do his chores, and stay in his room. For a while it worked out that way, and days would go by

150

when he wouldn't see her. Once or twice, while mowing or raking on the grounds, he had the feeling he was being watched, but when he turned to look up at the house all the windows were blank.

Then one night she met him at the door.

"Won't you have dinner with me tonight?"

"Yes, thank you, Mrs. Pierson. I can't stay long, I have so much to do, but I'd like it very much." He was downstairs at six and went to the kitchen.

"Sit down in the dining room and I'll serve in a minute."

At dinner they had talked of many things. She was an aggressive conversationalist, initiating each subject and asking questions. She seemed far more interested in his history than in recounting her own. Not quite in character, he thought. He was pleased, nevertheless, and enjoyed telling her of his experiences in the Forestry Service.

At the end she said, "I'm glad you're here, Warren. I feel safe. These days it's not good for an old woman to live alone in a big house. There are too many burglars."

After that first dinner he found himself spending more and more time in her parlor. It became a matter of course that they would eat dinner together. Warren reluctantly admitted to himself that he enjoyed her company. Actually, she knew many things and could talk intelligently on a number of subjects, from jury duty to conservation. Unlike other women he had known, she had an earnestness, an open strength of mind that appealed to him. After the years of solitude he relished her company and, no less, the semblance of family life she offered.

After his classes he did not adjourn to the coffee shop with the other students but went home, more and more eagerly, and always with a sense of impending comfort. There was the night she talked of her father.

"He was a hunter—not great, but certainly avid." She smiled in nostalgia. As for herself, she admitted a reluctance to shoot animals for sport. "In fact, after he died, I removed stuffed birds and beasts from every mantel and cabinet in the house and put them in the attic. Why, there was even a great horned owl on the piano, if you please. No wonder I hated to practise, with those reproachful eyes on me. Would you like to see his gun collection?"

"I would indeed, Mrs. Pierson. I know a bit about guns myself."

"I'm sure you do. Well, after dinner I'll show them to you."

Later she unlocked a large breakfront in the library and he took one gun after another from its rack, feeling the polished barrels, the rich wood. They still had a faint odor of oil about them. She stood aside and watched him expertly cock a rifle. She seemed immensely pleased at his excitement.

"There are boxes and boxes of shells of all sizes in the drawers. See?"

She opened a drawer and he noted the carefully labeled, neatly stacked boxes.

"Have you ever shot a gun?" he asked her.

"Heavens, no! I'm not strong enough for that."

"It doesn't take much strength if you know how. Someday I'll show you."

"I'd love to watch you shoot. There's plenty of room on the back lawn."

"Good. I'll set up a target and we'll have some fun."

What had started as a game quickly assumed a more and more central focus in the time they spent together. They would meet in the library and after a brief consultation at the gun cabinet would walk together down the great staircase to the back of the house.

One day she said, "May I try?" There was timidity in her voice.

He had stood behind her. It was all so gentle. Outside, on the far end of the lawn, in front of a cluster of copper beeches, the targets he had set up stared up at them like bloodshot eyes. His left hand helped her support the weight of the rifle, his right guided her eye to the sight, her finger to the trigger.

"Now," he had whispered in her ear. The tiny body jerked once beneath his steadying grasp, but remained straight, defiant, before the recoil. She learned quickly. He felt all the pride of the trainer, the tamer of beasts, the drawer forth, the realizer of potential. She was elated at her progress, ran to examine the target, and kept her score with a scrupulousness that was almost fanatical.

At dinner they talked of guns and bullets.

"I must learn to protect myself," she said. "An old woman like me all alone. There are burglars throughout the neighborhood. They know we're helpless. Now we can fight back, can't we, Warren? Thanks to you, we can give a good account of ourselves."

She seemed then to imagine the very confrontation itself, and discovery of the intruder, the gun raised, the report, the impact, the stung body's crumple and fall.

"Well, I doubt you'll ever need to use it," laughed Warren. "I suppose it doesn't hurt a bit to let them know you've been target-practising. But it's fun."

"Yes, it is," she said, with a voice that seemed not to have finished the sentence.

Warren had lived in Mrs. Pierson's house for eight months. It was November and the big house seemed darker than ever. After five o'clock in the evening there was virtually no light from the outside.

For the past few weeks he had been increasingly restless, bored. His rehabilitation at school was complete. He was tired of the old lady's company now, tired of her constant talking of guns and shooting. She was obsessed with it. He began to get home later and later in the afternoon. Often it was too late and too dark for any practise, and on those days she seemed quieter, not glum but disappointed, and he ate quickly and went upstairs to study.

There was a girl who worked as a secretary in the Forestry School, and he had begun to watch her. One day she sensed his gaze, looked up, and smiled. For Warren that smile was a kind of liberation. They had talked, eaten lunch together, and he had taken her to the movies. Later he had kissed her, feeling the warm sweet-smelling body through her thin blouse. From then on he was with Paula every day.

"I won't be home for dinner tonight, Mrs. Pierson."

"Why? Is anything wrong?"

"No, I—I have some work to do in the library." Somehow he couldn't tell her about the girl. She had looked at him for one moment extra.

"We'll have coffee when you come home, then."

"I think I'll be too late tonight. Thanks, anyway."

That was the first time. In the beginning he would tell her each morning that he wouldn't be home for dinner, but when it happened every day he stopped telling her. The more he saw of Paula—and that "more" had developed into a love affair, his first—the less he saw of Mrs. Pierson.

For the past week he had merely lived there in the big dark house. They had not had occasion to speak and he tried to avoid her when possible, waiting until he heard her in the kitchen before he came quickly downstairs and ran out the front door. He felt a certain guilt in the abrupt way he had terminated their relationship, but it only bothered him when he saw her standing, tiny and silent, at the library window upstairs. The rest of the time he did not think about it.

And now tonight. He had left Paula at six o'clock. They had arranged to meet at ten for a beer. As he walked up the long steep driveway he thought he saw Mrs. Pierson at the library window. He looked again, but saw nothing.

He was stopped in his tracks by the sound of the shot and the spray of pebbles that kicked up not five feet in front of him. He was nailed to the spot. Raising his hand to shield his eyes, he peered up at the dark house. Another shot rang out and the paved driveway bore a gouge several feet to his left.

Galvanized, he ran, half crouching, to the safety of the garage. Now she couldn't see him. He knew it was she, beyond any doubt. He unlocked the door of the garage that led to the basement and went inside. I've got to get to her, he thought, before she hurts herself. Crazy old bitch. I'll sneak up behind her and grab the gun. Then out I go, out of here permanently.

He noted that the house was in complete darkness, and thought, Better not turn on any lights. He crept up the back stairs to the kitchen, flattening along the wall, then into the great hall and up the curving staircase. It was completely dark and utterly quiet. At the door to the library he stopped. The shots had come from there.

Should he run in, flick on the light, and rush her? Or creep in on the floor? He slipped off one shoe and, stepping well out of range, threw it into the library. There was a resounding crack and zing which echoed for a few moments. His skin crawled with tension.

The gun cabinet! He had to reach it and get a rifle. He had to meet her on more equal terms, so that if she were truly insane or wouldn't talk to him, if worse came to worst, he could shoot, not to kill but to disarm.

The gun cabinet was at the far end of the room, near the back entrance to the library. A frontal assault was out of the question. Retreating, he slipped off the other shoe and threw it into the library. There was another shot, followed by the tinkle of shattered glass. At the same time he raced lightly and silently through a side hall to the other entrance of the library. The cabinet was now no more than three feet away.

He dropped to his haunches and inched his stockinged feet toward the cabinet. For what seemed an hour he crouched there, staring out into the blackness, then reached up to try the glass cabinet door. It was open! He had thought to quickly smash it and snatch a weapon through the broken glass. He knew which ones were already loaded. She must have forgotten, in her nervousness, to close and lock the door.

"Take one," came the youthful voice.

He froze.

"Take one. I won't shoot while you're there."

He waited. His eyes were accommodating to the darkness and he saw her as a small mound of blackness between the large windows in the far wall. He reached for a rifle and quickly slid it from the cabinet. An open box of shells stood on the lower shelf and he took a handful and dropped to the floor. Crablike, he scuttled backward to the doorway and out of the room. No sooner had he left the library than two shots in quick succession flew across the room. He heard the glass of the gun cabinet shatter.

"Please, Mrs. Pierson, this is crazy. Can't we stop and talk about it? Someone can get hurt."

He tried to keep it light, give her a chance to quit, laugh, agree that it was only a game, and that it was now time to stop and have dinner. She answered with a shot that cracked at the other end of the dark room, spending itself in metallic echoes. Warren knelt at the turn of the hall leading out of the library.

"You need help, Mrs. Pierson. You're sick. Come on, put down the gun. Come out where I can see you. I won't shoot and I won't hurt you. I'll get you a doctor, and when you get well we'll forget the whole thing."

His voice was too loud, he knew, but it was hard to control. He was frightened.

"Mrs. Pierson," he called. "Please. Mrs. Pierson, let's stop this. Calm yourself. Why are you doing this? Why do you want to kill me? You're upset, and maybe I—I don't blame you. But surely we could talk about it."

A pause. "Can't we?"

There was no answer.

"Look, Mrs. Pierson." He made his tone firm, slightly menacing. "If it comes to that, you can't outshoot me. I taught you a lot but not everything." And then more gently, "I don't want to hurt you.

"Answer me, damn it!" he shouted. Still no answer. "Okay, that's it."

He hated her now, hated her for frightening him, threatening him. Hated her as much as she must hate him. He could feel her hatred and his own like two dark clouds filling the house, insinuating poisonous strands into each other's substance. It amazed him how immediately hatred arose, full-grown. All it took was a single minute of fear. Good lord, how he hated her now!

What had she expected? A lasting emotional attachment? Warren could not imagine the basis for her desire to possess him. All right, they had both been lonely, but that was certainly not new to her, and he had honestly enjoyed her company. At what point did reason and propriety snap? When did she announce, in silent authority, her ownership of him? It was only thwarted possession that could produce such a murderous jealousy. Even now the irony of having been the instrument of his possible destruction did not escape him.

Maybe there was time to get out of the house. He rose halfway and backed into the side hall. A shot. He ducked and fled into the library again, coming out the front entrance. Good! She had gone down the side hall, thinking he was still there. He crossed the hall and raced into a bedroom. He knelt there next to the doorway, rifle ready. At the very first sound he was going to shoot. Maybe that would scare her and make her surrender.

He stared out into the blackness. Then, on the other side of the stairwell, he saw the dim shape floating toward him. He raised the gun to his shoulder, took aim at a point just behind the shape, and fired. She did not so much as start or change her speed.

I've got to get out of here or get her. He rose to his feet, fired two shots in the direction of her shape, then plummeted down the stairs to the first floor. As he reached the bottom he heard the crack of a rifle and simultaneously felt a breathtaking pain in his left hip. There was a moment of terror, when he wanted to slump to the floor and give in to his wound; but, steeling himself, he plunged on, feeling his trousers grow warm and wet from the blood.

He was sweating heavily. That shot had been too close for comfort. She couldn't be that good, she couldn't! He was forced to admit that she had improved a great deal in the last weeks of their practising. The thought crossed his mind for the first time: What if she gets me?

True, he was a better shot, but she knew this house—it was like an extension of her own body. For over sixty years it had surrounded her like a carapace. Surely that would count in her favor.

Don't be careless, Warren, he thought.

He had never wanted to kill anything so much as he wanted to kill her. The hate was like a hot branding iron in his head. He twisted and clenched to contain it, but each minute that it went unslaked was torture. He felt his brain draw itself together like an animal, grow dark and concentrated, sitting poised on the floor of his skull, ready to spring. Was he to pay for a lifetime of her spinsterhood?

The bullet didn't hit the bone, or I couldn't run, he reasoned.

He raced across the open expanse of the living room into the solarium. This was a long narrow room with a French door at each end. It was completely windowed and full of plants. He flattened against a wall and waited for her. He knew now that he would have to shoot—to shoot to kill. And he wanted to kill her.

Then he knew she was there in the room with him, at the other end. He couldn't see her but her presence was palpable. He had to kill her with the first shot or she would kill him by learning the origin of his blast. His hip was throbbing unbearably and his right sock was sticky with blood. He had to kill her soon.

From where he crouched, Warren watched with mounting alarm as slowly, icily, the moon slid across the windows, frosting the dark leaves of the plants with a sinister shine. Here and there on the walls tapers of its cold glare threatened to dilute the thick darkness to a vulnerable dusk. In another moment he would be revealed.

Then suddenly, absurdly, the telephone rang. His muscles jumped in fright, making his hip throb anew. It rang again and again and then again. In the middle of the fourth ring it stopped and he heard the youthful voice say, "Hello?"

Lurching forward, he fired shot after shot in the direction of the telephone. It stood on a small table at the other end of the solarium. When he stopped, another shot screamed into his ear, hard, grating at first, then purifying into a single silver sound that filled his head.

My God, she was at the other phone!

From the extension in the living room he heard, or thought he heard her say, "Police—hurry, I've just killed a burglar."

"Q"

John Coyne

A Game in the Sun

Betsy was not allowed to play croquet with her husband and the Reverend, so she sat in the shade of the trees at the top of the mound. The mound overlooked a lush rainforest which grew thick and dense to the edges of the Mission Compound. The view was compelling and frightening to Betsy. The close steamy jungle made her feel insignificant, and as she half listened to Mrs. Shaw's chatter she watched the bush as if it were alive.

The Reverend and Mrs. Shaw had started the Mission twenty years before. Landscaping woods near a village of mud and cattle-dung huts, they cut into the underbrush, leaving only the ancient acacias and gum trees for shade, and planting lawns and gardens. The African laborers had instructions to keep the lawns neatly trimmed during the rainy season, well watered the remainder of the year.

The Shaws had been the only white people in the district until Betsy and her husband arrived with the Peace Corps to teach in the government school. It was their second year in-country and as Betsy had calculated that morning, she had only eighteen more Sundays left in Africa.

"You really won't know Africa for ten years. It takes that long to get a feel of the land," the Reverend had said when he first dropped by to say hello and welcome them to the village. He had crowded himself into their doll-like house, held onto his father's straw hat, and looked with alarm about the inadequate place. "The Peace Corps's not giving you much cooperation, are they?" He shook his head, frowning over the lack of facilities.

He was a big fleshy man, dressed in worn jeans, a tight-fitting plaid shirt, and heavy-duty boots. His face was burnt from the long self-appointed days in the African sun. Only his forehead, protected by the straw hat, was chalky. His eyes were tiny and squinted against the sun. Dark lines clustered at their corners. The rest of his face was soft and slightly moist. He kept a white handkerchief folded in the palm of his hand and continually wiped the running sweat off his red cheeks, as if he were polishing them.

"Look, kids, I want ya to come to our place anytime. Anytime.

Come tomorrow for lunch, a game of croquet." He glanced again about the house. "You're going to need all the comforts of home you can get. But with the help of God—with the help of God."

Before the game the Shaws' houseboys, barefooted and in starched white uniforms, moved like tropical birds among them serving iced tea. The two men talked about the week, the news from the school and Mission, while Mrs. Shaw took Betsy through the gardens, the beds of exotic flowers which grew in the heat and humidity, brilliant and thick.

Mrs. Shaw wore farm gloves and with a gardener's eye clipped flowers and presented them to Betsy. Mrs. Shaw was also concerned about Betsy and her husband living in the village, in a mud-and-dung house, in among the Africans. The flowers were to pretty up Betsy's life.

Mrs. Shaw lay her scissors on the lawn table and pulled off her gloves, then she rubbed baby lotion thoroughly into her hands. The scent was stronger than the flowers and reminded Betsy of her home, of growing up as a little girl.

"I learned years ago that baby lotion was the answer. Just ordinary baby lotion keeps me just fine. The weather is so cruel on people, women especially." Unlike her husband, Mrs. Shaw looked as if she had never been in the African sun. Her skin was milky under the protection of a wide-brimmed bonnet and deep in the shadows her eyes flashed like those of a cornered animal. "After a while you learn these little hints. It takes time, of course, but with the help of God." Her voice bore inward like a drill.

Betsy was no longer listening. She had closed her eyes and was leaning back in the lawn chair, resting. She knew she must not begin to cry in front of these people. She must not be vulnerable. There were, after all, only eighteen Sundays left in Africa. She had gone that morning into the bedroom, to her homemade calendar behind the door, and crossed off another day. Briefly she had felt lighthearted, gay, but that exhilaration had slipped away in the hot bedroom, in the heat of the day. Betsy sighed and then, unexpectedly, shivered.

"Are you all right, dear?" Mrs. Shaw reached over. Betsy could feel the damp fingers, the baby lotion sticky on her own arm.

"No—nothing. I'm fine." She gathered herself together, managed a thin smile, blinked away a rush of tears, said quickly, shading her eyes and looking over the lawns, "Are they finished?"

"You've been remembering your quinine, haven't you, dear?" Mrs. Shaw wouldn't let go.

"Oh, of course, it's nothing really, Mrs. Shaw. We'll be into the rainy season soon. Perhaps I'm feeling the first chills. You know how cold it suddenly seems?" She talked rapidly.

"Yes, perhaps even in the hot sun one can feel chilled." And Mrs. Shaw let the subject slip away, as if it were an error.

On the lawns before them the game was drawing to a close. The Reverend was ahead as always, banging his mallet against the wooden ball, moving quickly from one wicket to the next, looking awkward, too huge for the grass game.

"I've gotcha, Jesse. I've gotcha again." His voice was buoyant.

Jesse behind him, struggling, hit the ball. It bounced erratically across the grass, hapless. He followed, thin and undernourished. Jesse had lost weight in Africa and now his trousers were baggy. He laughed at his miscalculations, amused by his inability. She watched him with eyes bled of color, gray and watery, studied him with detachment, as if watching a stranger. Who was this person? she wondered.

The game was over. They came to her through the heat, haze, and sun, their bodies shimmery. Perhaps she was sick. Tentatively she touched herself, felt the clammy skin of her forearm. Her fingers were cold and around her the lawns and gardens were airless.

"Had enough for one day, boys?" Mrs. Shaw grinned. "I'll have lunch ready in minutes." She clapped once, like a single piano note, and the dark houseboys stepped from the shadows and carried food to them on the lawn.

"How's the little lady?" the Reverend asked and spread himself into the lounge chair beside Betsy. "You're lookin' peaked, honey."

"I was just saying so myself, Walter. She doesn't look at all well. Don't you agree, Jesse?"

They wouldn't let her alone. All of them gauged her with worried looks. Her husband stared. His mouth had flopped open, as if half his mind had been blown away. He touched her and she jerked away.

"Betsy, why don't you lie down a while, until the day cools?" Mrs. Shaw was at her side.

Betsy would have to get away from these people. Part of her mind told her she did not know them. And these lawns, the enclosing rainforest, had not happened to her. She would go somewhere cool, somewhere out of the heat. She could hardly breathe. Why won't it rain? The smell of baby lotion again and the touch of warm flesh.

She let herself be guided from the hot gardens into the house where curtains were drawn and there was a bit of air. The bedcovers were soft silk, not the coarse linen from the village. They let her sleep.

The rains began the next day. Standing at the windows of the Third Form, Betsy watched it soak into the dry football field. She reached out the window and the cool water soaked her arm. It felt refreshing and she smiled for the first time in weeks.

That afternoon Betsy was going to tell Jesse she wanted a divorce, but he had come home after school—wet and muddy into the tiny house—said something silly about her hair, something she knew was meant to cheer her up, and she had gone into the bedroom, slammed the door, and cried herself to sleep.

It was raining again when she woke. The rain pounded on the tin roof deafeningly. She jerked the sheets around her without getting up, and slept. When she woke a second time it was dark. He had lit the lamp and made her soup.

"You'll feel better after this." Jesse held out the cup like an offering. His face carried a blankness, like a birthmark. He did not comprehend subtleties, or his wife. She took the soup without speaking, without looking at him, and sipped it. The cup in her fingers was as warm as a small bird and she kept both hands tight around the porcelain, afraid to let it go.

Jesse kept talking, incessantly, afraid of the silence. He had met the Reverend in the village and the Shaws asked about her, wanted to know if Betsy would like to move into the Mission for a few days until she felt better.

"I feel better."

"Yeah, sure. I told the Reverend you were okay. Told him it was just the heat, you know—Sunday." Jesse perched tentatively, as if he didn't belong, on the edge of her bed.

They had requested a double bed from the Peace Corps early in their tour, but it had never come, and now she was glad of the privacy. If she could only be alone. That was the problem: she couldn't get away.

"I want to sleep." She handed back the cup, careful so their fingers did not touch.

"Again?" He sounded lonely.

She did not respond, but pulled the sheets around her and turned away, dismissing him with silence. This time, however, she did not

sleep, only watched the dark room, the dung walls whitewashed
with lime. Jesse left with the shaky yellow lamplight. Betsy could
hear him in the other room trying to be quiet, moving carefully, not
making noise. She sobbed into the sheets.

Betsy did not go to school the rest of the week. Every morning
after he left for school she would wrap herself in a robe and, wearing
boots, slip and slide through the mud to the outhouse and throw up
whatever little she had eaten into the deep smelly pit. And then,
trembling, she'd sit there among the cobwebs and the stink of the
tin outhouse until her strength came back and she could make it
again through the slush.

Betsy woke from another faulty daytime sleep and found the Reverend and Mrs. Shaw at the foot of her bed, filling the room like
massive furniture. They stood tensely, afraid to touch the surround-
ings. Mrs. Shaw had a giant bouquet of flowers, flaming like a torch
in the dark room. The room was as disheveled as a drunk—drawers
left open, clothes scattered. It also had a close stale smell. The smell
of unwashed bodies.

"My dear, my dear!" Mrs. Shaw rushed through the mess to Betsy,
felt her temperature, began fussing with the linen.

"I'm fine—I'm fine. It's just the weather, that's all. I'm feeling
better every day." Betsy slipped a smile on and off her face.

The Reverend, with one hand mopping sweat from his red cheeks,
said from the end of the bed, as if calling from a great distance, "We
want to see you Sunday. Gotta get you in a game."

Betsy did not respond. She let Mrs. Shaw wipe the perspiration
from her face and neck.

"Walter, you go ahead. I'll stay a while with Betsy." She smiled
at her patient, then began with busy efficient hands to tidy the
covers and make Betsy presentable.

When Betsy woke again, Mrs. Shaw was gone, the room straightened, and her husband home from classes, moving about in the other
room. He seemed to bang into everything. Why was he so inept?
How did she not know that about him, she wondered. He appeared
in the narrow doorway, cautious as a child.

"Bring me the calendar," she ordered, though her weak voice
lacked authority. Jesse was happy to help. He hurried to find her
magic marker and homemade posterboard.

She took the calendar without thanking him, though he waited
for the words, hoped to hear a bit of kindness. She couldn't say

thanks, couldn't give him a civil remark. Why didn't he take control, be demanding, take care of her? She slashed black lines through the dates while he stood beside her bed like one of Mrs. Shaw's houseboys.

"I want you to beat the Reverend at croquet," she said, finishing with the calendar.

"Beat the Reverend?" Jesse frowned, moved to look at her face. "But I can't beat him!" His voice touched the edge of alarm.

"You never try. That's your problem." She tossed the calendar aside and continued not to look at him, but to gaze across the room, eyes locked onto a small patch of wall where a chunk of dung had swollen and the whitewash had peeled away, like a scab. "If you had tried we wouldn't need to be in Peace Corps. You could have gotten out of Vietnam another way."

"It's not a question of trying!" Jesse stuck his small hands into the pockets of his baggy trousers and began to pace. "And you wanted to go too, remember."

"I'm sick of going out there, week after week, talking to that old woman, watching you get beaten—"

"It's a game, Betsy, for God's sake!" He moved about at the end of the bed to catch her eye, but she kept turning away. "You know he likes to win. Croquet is his big deal—the way he takes care of those lawns, sets the wickets."

"You could beat him just once, that's all, but no! You're such a damn weak sister!" The sentence spilled out, uncontrolled. She watched him hunch up against the words. "Him and his dumb wife, God! How have I stood all of you?" Tears stopped her and she clamped both hands across her mouth to keep from screaming.

Jesse's arms went tentatively around her. He smelled of sweat and the local soap. She did not like his odors. He only washed casually, one bath a week. It was too much trouble hauling and heating water, taking a sponge bath in the kitchen, using the metal tub. There lingered about him a close stale odor, reminiscent, she suddenly realized, of the young sweaty boys in her classes.

"Get away." She pushed him. "Why don't you wash?"

He left, slamming the door. Later, before falling to sleep for the hundredth time that day, she heard him heating and pouring water into the washtub.

Betsy stared across the lawns toward the rainforest, watched the close, creepy jungle while Mrs. Shaw wrapped a shawl about her shoulders, made her comfortable in a lawn chair. Mrs. Shaw's voice rang in her ears. She was full of chatty news from the village, stories of conversions to Christ. Betsy turned her head slowly in the direction of the voice, and Mrs. Shaw's face shimmered.

Betsy felt cold and clammy and the wool shawl was a damp cloth on her shoulders. There was again the oily smell of baby lotion, mixed with the scent of carnations and roses. A gift of flowers, wet with rain, lay abandoned on the table. There were seventeen Sundays left in Africa and Betsy knew now she could not make it.

Bright-colored balls shot over the lawns, trailing sprays of water, and the two men followed from wicket to wicket, halting, swinging fiercely, then hurrying to catch up. The Reverend was ahead, banging the painted balls, shouting, poking fun at Jesse fumbling behind.

Mrs. Shaw leaned over the flowers and whispered, "Dear, are you with child?"

Betsy could feel the breakfast of eggs and toast, of weak tea and lemon, catch like gas in her throat. Mrs. Shaw pressed forward, like a parent. "You're showing all the signs. I told the Reverend. I said, Betsy is with child. I know. I've an uncanny knack for such things." Her eyes flashed.

Tentatively Betsy touched her abdomen, sensed it growing there like fungus inside of her. The Peace Corps had not sent the pills. Days and weeks had passed. She'd kept away from him, begged to be left alone while he panted like a stray dog. It was she who woke one humid night in the single bed, stripped herself naked in the heat, and padding through the house to the refrigerator, drank a cold glass of water that cooled her like rain. She touched the tip of her breast with her wet fingers and shivered. Then she went to Jesse's bed, pulled away the sheet, and woke him with her hands and mouth seeking.

"I've gotcha, Jesse!" The Reverend smashed the ball against the final pole, then turned to her husband still among the pattern of hoops. The Reverend wiped his cheeks with the handkerchief and, laughing, took off the straw hat. He waved to her. "I've got'm, Betsy. I've got'm again. In ten years maybe, in ten years—"

She came running wildly down the soft slope, her face flaming with rage. They dropped the mallets, glanced at each other as if there was some mistake, raised their hands to justify, but she had reached them with the scissors.

Francis M. Nevins, Jr.
Open Letter to Survivors

"There was the case of Adelina Monquieux, his remarkable solution
of which cannot be revealed before 1972 by agreement with that
curious lady's executors."

ELLERY QUEEN, *Ten Days' Wonder* (1948)

The book was conceived only in part. The rest of it was still
struggling for conception inside him. A large and vicious neighborhood cat, some lines from Jung, a long wait in a subway station
in the stifling postmidnight hours of a torrid summer were all parts
of the organism fighting for birth. But something was missing, some
vital element. And when he realized that what he and the book
needed was total immersion in the postwar international nightmare,
he picked up his phone and called Burt Billings, who was his attorney, his friend, and, as he happened to know, the attorney for
Adelina Monquieux.

The indomitable, the inimitable, the incredible Adelina—or, to
use her professional name (though she had never married), Mrs.
Monquieux, pronounced Mon-Q, not monkey. She was the last of an
asset-studded line and the foremost political analyst of the generation. Her gargoyle face with its luminously intelligent eyes had
made the cover of *Time* three years earlier, soon after Hiroshima;
the artist had sketched endless cameos of death within the tangles
of her unkempt henna hair.

The feature story in *Time* had chronicled her travels through
Europe and Asia during the Thirties and most of the war years, the
disenchanted brilliance of her many books and articles on international politics, and her unrelieved pessimism about mankind.
After Hiroshima and Nagasaki she had written an essay boiling
with humane fury titled "God Damn Us Every One," had changed
her will so that most of her wealth would be left for the care of the
bomb's victims, and had retired to the family estate to brood and
write.

Billings called back within an hour: the great lady would talk
with him the following Sunday at noon.

He drove out of the city early Sunday morning, the cloudless sky like blue glass and promising thick heat before noon. He had spent Saturday rereading the *Time* story and leafing through some of the woman's books. He had learned that she lived on the estate with the three orphans of World War I she had adopted as her sons and with a niece who did her secretarial work. He had learned that she had come to believe that no man can govern a modern nation-state without raining hideous atrocities on his own people and on his country's neighbors. He thought he had detected a certain oscillation in her between an idealistic anarchism in the Thoreau tradition and a Swiftian disgust with the entire race. All in all, a fascinating woman, combining a large fortune with a desolate philosophy, a dazzling mind with a dumpy body. He looked forward to the meeting with relish.

At 11:00 he spun the new '48 Roadmaster off the Taugus Parkway and the wheels crunched gravel up the steep slope of the drive, which was only five miles beyond where that gas-station attendant had said the turnoff would be. Then suddenly he had crested the peak and a lush cool bed of forest spread below him, with a squarish block of stone seeming no larger than a child's toy in a wide clearing near the center.

Fortress Monquieux.

He descended.

From the radio speaker a voice intoned headlines. Civil war in Greece. Blockade threat against Berlin. Crisis in Czechoslovakia. The infant state of Israel struggling for survival. Truman denounces Stalin. Stalin condemns Truman. God, what a world, he thought. Maybe Adelina's right: who would choose to be born?

On such gloomy reflections he maneuvered the Roadmaster along the curves of the descent and through the tangled green tunnel of forest, finally through a stone archway and into the parking circle at the side of the Fortress. He pocketed his keys and strolled past time-faded classical sculptures in beds of ill-kept greenery. His wristwatch read 11:26 and he hoped he wasn't unconscionably early.

Half a minute after his ring the massive front door opened and he was ushered in by a tall, well built fellow in his early thirties with crisp dark hair. Over shirtsleeves the young man wore an expensive-looking summer gray dressing-gown, monogrammed X at the breast. "Hello and come in," he invited, smiling like a head-waiter. "I am Xavier Monquieux and I've read most of your books at least twice."

"Delighted to hear it. You must be one of Mrs. Monquieux's foster sons."

"Right," Xavier said. "And if you'll step in here—" he led the way into a high-ceilinged room of immense size, filled with books and overstuffed furniture "—you can meet my brothers. This is Yves and this is Zachary."

Two more tall, well built fellows in their early thirties stepped forward from the mahogany bar, each with crisp dark hair, each with a gin-and-tonic in his hand, each wearing an expensive-looking summer gray dressing gown over shirtsleeves. They were as close in resemblance to Xavier and to each other as three prints of the same photograph. Only the gold letters of their monograms distinguished them: one wore a Y, the other a Z.

"I hadn't realized you were identical triplets," he said inanely as he accepted a light Scotch-and-water from Yves.

"Monozygotic is the technical word, or at least it was when I was in med school," Yves corrected. "Identical down to our fingertips. No one but Adelina can tell us apart and God knows how she does it. We're biological rarities but it's sort of fun, switching on dates and things like that."

"And speaking of girls, *mon frere,*" Zachary cut in, "the young ladies ought to be here any minute, so perhaps we should get into our trunks and make sure the liquor cart's stocked up. It was very nice to have met you, sir, and after you've talked to Adelina I'm sure we could find a bathing suit your size if you'd care for a dip." And Zachary and Yves bowed themselves out of the room, the sound of their feet becoming audible a few moments later when they ascended a staircase.

"No sense of the finer things," Xavier clucked disapprovingly. "Imagine preferring a swim to a chat with a famous mystery writer. I'm afraid bookishness has rubbed off only on me. Most of these are mine," he added, sweeping his hand to indicate the crammed shelves.

"Do your brothers have any passions of their own?"

"Oh, yes—we don't have to work for our keep, of course, but all of us got enough boredom in the military during the recent war to ever want to sit around doing nothing again. Yves had a year of medical school before he was drafted and may go back someday, and he's also an amateur concert violinist. Zach is a fanatic stamp collector and he has secret dreams of being a Hollywood star . . . If you'll excuse me I'll go downstairs and tell Adelina you're here." He moved lightly out of the room.

Like most writers and many readers, the guest had an insatiable
urge to inspect the contents of all bookshelves that chanced within
his eye. He was glancing over a large hand-rubbed cabinet devoted
to the modern European novel, with Mann and Sartre and Silone
well represented, when a feminine cough behind him gave notice
that he was no longer alone. A tall blonde in beige was inspecting
him through heavy-rimmed glasses as though he were a signed first
edition of something curious.

"Aunt Adelina apologizes," she said, "but she's all tied up in a
chapter of her memoirs and won't be free for another little while.
I'm Marie Dumont, her niece several degrees removed or something
like that. Also her secretary and all-around drudge. She asked me
to amuse you for a few minutes."

She said nothing more for about thirty seconds, as though she had
no idea how to amuse a male guest. Then, "I understand you want
to sort of pick her brains for political atmosphere on a book you're
doing? I think you might get more mileage out of her crazy will—you
know about that, don't you? When Aunt Adelina dies, the three boys
each get half a million outright and the income from another half
million held in trust. The remaining twenty million or so after taxes
will build and support a hospital to take care of the children we
bombed in Japan. But—and here comes the catch—if the safe in her
office downstairs is opened by anyone, for any reason, sooner than
twenty-four years after her death, all the hospital money is immediately transferred to the Flat Earth Society."

"That *is* a strange will," he commented politely, although something about its terms had already begun to gnaw at him and he was
not sure what. "What's in the safe that would lead her to protect it
that way?"

"Even I'm not sure and I've been her secretary for twelve years.
It's in the manuscript of her memoirs, which she calls *Open Letter
to Survivors*, that's all I know. She's writing it in longhand, you see.
When she's not actually working on it the manuscript is kept in
that safe, and the safe is always locked, whether she's working on
the book or not. Only she and I and her attorney know the combination. When you think how much of the inside history of the past
thirty years must be in those pages, how governments might topple
if the secrets leaked out, you can see why she takes precautions."

"Do you inherit anything under the will?"

She shrugged. "A few hundred thousand, I think. Not enough to
make up for twelve years of stagnation in this place."

"You could have left."

"You can't pull yourself out of the center of a whirlpool," she said. Which he cynically construed as: you don't throw away free room and board and a guaranteed two or three hundred thousand. "Well, I think she may be done by now, it's almost noon. Let's go down to her office and see."

And she led him along a vast foyer full of Victorian statuary and ancestral portraits and down a steep spiral staircase that ended in the center of a sort of anteroom. A functional secretarial desk, piled with papers and folders, stood against the far wall. A few comfortable chairs, occasional tables holding wrought-iron lamps and current magazines, strategically placed smoking stands—it reminded him somehow of a prosperous dentist's waiting room.

Marie Dumont knocked on the door to an inner office, then poked her head in.

"Ready yet?"

"Please show him in," he heard a deep rich voice reply, and a moment later he stood before her teakwood desk in the center of the big windowless room. On the wall to his left, hanging above the squat and forbiddingly shut steel safe, was a tranquil landscape in oils. Adelina Monquieux was seated in a red-leather armchair behind the desk, her henna hair in wild disarray, her spectacles askew on her Roman nose, looking like an intelligent gargoyle.

"I'm so pleased to meet you," she said, touching a thick loose-leaf binder of tough material filled with paper—the only object on the desk except for the blotter, an old-fashioned fountain pen, a small table lamp, and a wicked-looking letter opener. "I'm through writing for the day, and my pen has gone dry anyway. It will take me just a few minutes to read my morning's stint, and then I will be glad to give you all the time you desire. Tell me, do you think our survivors, assuming we have any, will appreciate reading the truth about our time?"

She asked the question with mixed bitterness and resignation, as if being witness to three decades of international politics had burned into her the inevitability of man's greed and stupidity and corruption. When she smiled at him it was like the grin he had seen on the faces of the dead.

It was only after he had closed the door gently behind him that he realized he had not said a word to her.

The silence in the anteroom was oppressive and he needed to make conversation. He turned to Marie Dumont who was seated at her own desk. "Does she do all her writing in there?" he asked, not really concerned to know.

"Ever since she inherited the house and had the basement done over. It's a perfect workroom—soundproof, no windows, no distractions, and that door is the only way in or out. Even the bathroom is outside here."

She suddenly gestured up to one of the windows and he heard the noise of splashing and gay squeals coming, he gathered, from the swimming pool. "The girls must have arrived. Peaceful sounds like that drive Aunt Adelina to distraction when she's working, even though she must have been in a dozen air raids in Europe. That's why she had her office soundproofed. By the way, did you notice the English country scene above the safe? That was painted by Churchill."

They both looked up as light footsteps sounded on the spiral stairs and one of the triplets appeared, barefoot and wearing only dark-blue swim trunks. He did not break stride but went right to the inner door, tossing a casual "Have to see Adelina for a minute" over his shoulder.

The triplet gave a perfunctory knock on the inner door and entered, shutting the door behind him. The cuckoo clock on the wall above Marie Dumont's desk announced that the hour was noon. The wooden bird had just cuckooed his last and retreated behind his tiny door when the big door opened again and the triplet walked out and over to the staircase and mounted.

"I wonder what that was all about."

"I don't know," Marie replied. "But I think Aunt Adelina must be through by now. I'll check."

She knocked lightly, stepped in, closed the door, and in less than a minute was back, her face sick-white.

"My God, she's dead," she kept whispering hoarsely.

A wild thought seized him and he knew what had disturbed him about the will: *If she died with the manuscript still on her desk, what good is that crazy 24-year clause? It will protect not the manuscript but just an empty safe.*

He rushed into the office. Adelina Monquieux lay sprawled in her chair, staring sightlessly through spectacles still askew. Blood ran from her heart. The manuscript of *Open Letter to Survivors* was not in sight and the safe was tight shut: he breathed relief.

Then he noticed that the wicked-looking letter opener was not in sight either . . .

The cuckoo made five noises and popped back into his slot. The body of Adelina Monquieux—according to the medical examiner she had died within a minute after the blade had entered her—had been removed, and when it left most of the police technicians had left too. The office and anteroom had been searched thoroughly and the letter opener had not been found. A few plainclothesmen still roamed the rooms and grounds haphazardly. Cody, the cigarillo-chewing Taugus County detective in charge, crushed his butt into a smoking stand disgustedly.

"What a cool customer we are dealing with, amigo," he said. "I wish I'd had him in my platoon behind Kraut lines in Normandy! He just walked right past you and the girl, stabbed the old lady to death with one blow of the letter opener, marched out past you again with the weapon, calm as you please, and went out to mingle with the girls at the pool. That, amigo, is a man with guts."

"And with a shrewd sense of psychology," the mystery writer added. "He figured that with my brief exposure to the triplets I couldn't tell them apart, and he must have known from experience that Miss Dumont couldn't either."

"That," Cody exploded, "is the hell of it. A big whodunit writer like you, a guy who's cleaned up umpteen cases for the New York force, and you can't even tell me what was the monogram on the killer's bathing suit, an X, a Y, or a Z."

"What bothers me more is that the letter opener that killed Mrs. Monquieux is missing. Why did the killer take it? To deprive us of his fingerprints? But why didn't he simply wipe his prints from the weapon right there in the office? Why did he take the much riskier step of removing the knife from his victim and carrying it past two witnesses in the anteroom? Was it impossible or impracticable for him to follow the safer course? Again—why?"

"Very clever, Mr. Genius," Cody snorted. "But changing the subject don't fool me. You didn't notice what monogram the killer was wearing."

"I don't think it would mean anything even if I did. We can't assume the guilty one didn't simply get hold of a monogram belonging to one of his brothers and sew it over his own, or even wear one of his brothers' bathing suits. By the way, what was the result of that test for bloodstains your technician performed on the three dark-blue bathing suits in the household?"

Cody waved a paper from the sheaf on his lap. "Absolutely no dice. My man examined 'em inside and out, and not a trace of a bloodstain.

None of the old lady's blood splashed onto the killer's trunks. No, we can't solve this one the easy way, amigo. He killed her with one stab, so we'd have no bloodstains. And he's one of triplets, so for all practical purposes we got no one who saw him!" He cursed while taking out another cigarillo.

"Well, we can at least be thankful that Mrs. Monquieux put her manuscript back in the safe before he walked in and killed her. After all, it was much too thick for the killer to have walked past us with it unnoticed, and there's no way he could have destroyed it in the office itself—even the toilet is out here. So it's got to be back in the safe, and whatever Adelina Monquieux knew will stay under wraps for twenty-four years. Adelina? Pandora would have been a better name. By the way, you will keep a guard on that safe overnight till Mr. Billings and the truck come for it?"

"Damn right I will, I—hey, what's the matter with you?" For the distinguished litterateur across from Cody had suddenly risen and was pacing angrily.

"Scars," he muttered. "Look, the brothers mentioned to me this morning that they were all in the service during the war. Didn't any of them get wounded or scratched or marked somehow, even if only in a tattoo parlor? Can't we eliminate one or even two brothers on the ground that neither Miss Dumont nor I saw any marks on the killer?"

"Hell, no," Cody grunted. "Those boys spent their war in a nice safe psychological testing laboratory stateside. Y'see, they've got something between 'em that the eggheads call tele*pathy*—identical twins and triplets have it fairly often, so I'm told—and the Army had some crazy idea of finding out what causes it and using it to help spring Allied troops from enemy POW camps. The whole thing fell through, of course; there's no way of teaching that stuff to someone who ain't got it in the first place. Hell, if God wanted people to read each other's minds He wouldn't have given us vocal cords. Hey, what's got you now?"

"Don't you see?" the writer said. "If each of the triplets can read the thoughts of the others, why can't we simply *ask them* who is the murderer?"

"Oh," Cody rumbled. "Reading your own storybooks again, hey, amigo? Well, first of all, to give you the kinda reason you enjoy, we couldn't rule out that the one guilty brother and one accomplice brother weren't framing the third innocent brother. Second, that tele*pathy* stuff can't be used in court anyway. And third—hell, except for the war I've lived in this community for thirty-seven years. I know those boys. I know they've done everything together their whole lives long. I know as well as I know I'm sitting here that all three of them were in on this murder. They drew straws or some such thing to see who'd do the actual dirty work. But you try to prove that in a court of law, amigo. You storybook writers don't have the first idea in the world the problems of a working cop."

His respect for Cody soared, once the truth of a conspiracy among the brothers had sunk home. How could he not have seen it? From the moment he had rung the bell, every word and every action of those three smiling affable brothers had been as carefully calculated as a Broadway stage performance. Dressing identically, speaking with virtually identical modulations, each one doing or saying nothing that would stamp him as an individual in the mind of their guest. He had been manipulated like a puppet and he didn't like it. He stoked his pipe furiously. Uselessly.

As the sun set he growled a goodbye to Cody and slunk out to his car and drove out of that monstrous valley through a tunnel of darkening forest and mocking bird cries.

Next day he read of the murder in the papers, noting idly the news that Adelina Monquieux's private Pandora's box had been crated up by her executors, the law firm of Billings & Krieger, and transferred to a chilled-steel bank vault in the city. *Open Letter to Survivors* having been made doubly inviolable, he tried to dismiss the whole Monquieux affair from his mind as a fiasco.

It was not until two months later that he saw what he should have seen while Adelina's body was still warm.

What triggered it was a piece of research. He had gone to the County Medical Association Library to look up some data on childbirth that he needed for his own novel-aborning; his serendipping eye had wandered from childbirth to infants and from infants to twins and to the precise differences between monozygotic and fraternal twins.

There it lay, buried in a mountain of medical jargon but unmistakable as a gold nugget in a coalpile.

Monozygotic twins, being genetically identical in every respect, are identical in fingerprints also.

His mind took that fact and raced with it.

Three minutes later he was out of the library with a slam of the door and the glares of several peeved medicos behind him.

He dashed into his apartment and dialed Billings & Krieger, demanding to speak to Mr. Billings at once on a matter a thousand times more urgent than mere life-and-death. When he had the attorney on the line he was brief and to the point. "Burt, can we use your office tonight for a conference on the Monquieux case?"

Billings sounded puzzled. "What's up? Why my office?" Then, after a moment, "Hey, you haven't solved the murder by any chance?"

"In one way I think I have, in another way, no. I'm sorry, Burt, that's all I can say now. Eight o'clock all right with you? I'll need both you and Mr. Krieger, in your capacity as executors. And I'm going to have Cody there too—you remember him? Thanks a million, Burt, see you at eight." He hung up and placed a call to Cody who agreed to attend the meeting.

Shortly after dinner he made an excuse to go out, leaving the dishes to his long-suffering father, and paced the neon-washed streets, marshaling his thoughts, until 7:45 when he hailed a cab. Ten minutes later he stepped into the offices of Billings & Krieger. Burt and Cody were already present, and James B. Krieger, who looked like a starving mouse, came in shortly. Introductions were exchanged, hands shaken, chairs pulled up to the conference room's long table.

He began by explaining the fact of identical fingerprints in monozygotics. "Of course, the great bulk of mystery stories—my own included, I blush to say—have spread the impression that each set of prints is unique, that no one's prints are the same as any other person's. The man in the street accepts without question that every man's prints are exclusively his own, but, as I've indicated, it's just not so. Therefore we must conclude—of course we can verify this with no trouble at all—that Xavier, Yves, and Zachary Monquieux have identical fingerprints. Now, what follows from that?

"First, it reminded me that all three brothers must be aware of this fact; for it was Yves, talking to me, who used the word monozygotic, and even used the phrase 'identical down to our fingertips,' which is quite literally true.

"Secondly, it satisfied me that we had completely misinterpreted the whole matter of the missing letter opener. We had assumed two things: A, that the person who took it out of the office was the murderer; B, that possibly his motive was to deprive us of his fingerprints, which for some unknown reason he could not simply wipe off on the spot. We now know that B is a completely false assumption: all three brothers know their prints are identical and know, therefore, their prints would be of no use to us. So the killer's reason for taking away the knife could not have been what we thought it was. Gentlemen, can any of you suggest another reason?"

Silence. Cody chewed his cigarillo.

"Nor can I. In fact—and I kick myself for missing this two months ago—not only had he no reason, but it was *physically impossible* for the killer to have taken the letter opener with him!

"Marie Dumont and I observed the killer walk out of his victim's office and he certainly wasn't holding the opener in his hands. Could he have concealed it in his clothes? Well, he was wearing only a bathing suit; the letter opener might have been slipped inside the suit. But you told me, Cody, that there was not the slightest trace of a bloodstain on any of the three dark-blue pairs of trunks that could possibly have been worn by the murderer—*inside or out*. Certainly if he had carried out that bloody weapon inside his trunks, you *would* have found traces. Conclusion: the murderer did not, because he could not, take the weapon away."

"Then what happened to it?" Cody demanded. "My men searched that office with a fine-tooth comb and it sure as hell wasn't there!"

"Patience, Cody, patience. Now, let's tackle the problem from another direction. Who had the opportunity to hide or remove the opener between the time I spoke to Mrs. Monquieux a few minutes before her death and the time Marie Dumont and I entered the office shortly after her death and learned that the opener was missing? When I phrase it that way, you can't miss it. *Only one person* set foot in the office during that brief interval. And that was Marie Dumont, who you'll recall was alone in there for almost a minute before she stumbled out to announce that her aunt was dead.

"Now, can the wings of reason bear us any higher? Yes, indeed," he assured his listeners. "Let's go back to your question, Cody—what did she do with the weapon? With me standing right outside the door, would she have concealed it in her clothes and taken a chance she could safely get rid of it later, with the police shortly to invade the premises? Not if she had a safer option, she wouldn't. Was there a safer option in that enclosed office?

"Yes, there was—a safer option, if you'll pardon the pun. Your men searched the entire office, Cody, but in view of the Monquieux will and of your plausible but false conclusion that the killer had taken the opener away with him, you didn't dare tamper with the safe, to which, I remind you, only Mrs. Monquieux and Miss Dumont and you, her attorney, Burt, know the combination.

"And since that safe was under police guard until your truckers removed it to the bank vault, Burt, I'll wager that letter opener is in the safe right now."

"My God," Billings muttered.

"But why would she have hidden the murder weapon like that?" James B. Krieger squeaked.

"If you mean her motive—whether she's in love with the murderer, or hopes to extort money or marriage out of him—I don't know, and its exact nature doesn't affect my analysis. But in a general way her motivation is clear: she intended to protect the murderer. Now, what is presupposed by such intent?"

Again silence.

"Don't you see that it presupposes *she knew which of the triplets* is the murderer?

"Now, did she know prior to the murder itself? Hardly, or she would never have revealed as much information to me as she did. Then she must have learned the truth *after* the murder. But then she had less than a minute, alone in that office, to see the truth, to make a decision, to hide the letter opener in the safe, to return to the doorway. It must have been something instantaneously apparent that revealed the truth to her.

"At this point, gentlemen, we are driven to speculation, but speculation solidly based on facts. Fact: your medical examiner told us, Cody, that Adelina Monquieux lived for perhaps a minute after being stabbed. Fact: Mrs. Monquieux's fountain pen had gone dry shortly before her death, so there was no usable writing implement on her desk. Fact: we don't *know* that it was Mrs. Monquieux herself who put away the manuscript of *Open Letter to Survivors*.

"Hypothesis: In the last moments of her life Adelina Monquieux—the only person on earth who could tell those brothers apart—pulled the knife from her body and slashed into the tough material of the binder of that manuscript the initial—that's all it would take to identify him—of her murderer. X, Y, or Z. This is what Marie Dumont saw when she entered the room. And to protect the murderer she had to conceal that manuscript cover. And being forced to open the safe to place the damning manuscript cover inside, she decided it would be safer to conceal the opener there also. She was counting on being able to remove both objects from the safe later, but circumstances and your truckers, Burt, frustrated her.

"Any questions, gentlemen?"

Cody was now sweating. "Thank God you lawyers moved that safe to where we can still get at the evidence!"

Billings stared at him as if he had mumbled baby-talk. "But you can't get at it," he pointed out. "Mrs. Monquieux's will provides that the safe cannot be opened for any reason until the twenty-fourth anniversary of her death. If you violate that provision, the hospital for atom-bomb victims will not be built. How many lives is it worth to you to procure your evidence, your *hypothetical* evidence?"

Cody went down fighting. "Can't that will be broken? Hell, this isn't the kind of a situation the old lady had in mind when she made that crazy will."

"You can try to break it in the courts," Krieger said. "My considered opinion is that you won't succeed. And our duty as executors under the will, and as human beings, is to stop you."

Billings nodded. "Something even worse, Cody. Suppose the courts *did* rule that the opening of the safe by the police would not defeat the hospital bequest. If the analysis we've just heard is correct, the opening of the safe would disclose proof positive that the safe had *already* been opened immediately after our client's death. And that prior opening would be beyond the court's power to ignore. The end result being God knows how many dead war orphans, and a windfall for the Flat Earth Society."

Cody leveled a long series of curses at the law. No one in the room was hypocrite enough to contradict him.

"Well, as a professional writer," ventured the only professional writer present, "my hands aren't tied by that will. Why can't I publish my analysis of the case and at least let them know that I know, and maybe make them do something insane like attempting to silence me?"

"You want a million-dollar libel suit slapped against you?" Billings boomed. "You forget you've got no solid evidence—not a shred!"

They sat in silence.

When he could take no more of it he rose, stretched his drained and aching body and trudged wearily to the door. "I'm not in my dotage yet," he said, "and neither are they. I can wait; and after all, by waiting, we make sure the great bulk of the Monquieux estate goes to a decent cause. But I swear, Burt, that I will be there when you or your successor opens that safe twenty-four years from now. I'm going to see with my own eyes whether or not I was right.

"Gentlemen, I'll see you in 1972."

David Morrell

The Dripping

That autumn we live in a house in the country, my mother's house, the house I was raised in. I have been to the village, struck more by how nothing in it has changed, yet everything has, because I am older now, seeing it differently. It is as though I am both here now and back then, at once with the mind of a boy and a man. It is so strange a doubling, so intense, so unsettling, that I am moved to work again, to try to paint it.

So I study the hardware store, the grain barrels in front, the twin square pillars holding up the drooping balcony onto which seared wax-faced men and women from the old people's hotel above come to sit and rock and watch. They look the same aging people I saw as a boy, the wood of the pillars and balcony looks as splintered.

Forgetful of time while I work, I do not begin the long walk home until late, at dusk. The day has been warm, but now in my shirt I am cold, and a half mile along I am caught in a sudden shower and forced to leave the gravel road for the shelter of a tree, its leaves already brown and yellow. The rain becomes a storm, streaking at me sideways, drenching me; I cinch the neck of my canvas bag to protect my painting and equipment, and decide to run, socks spongy in my shoes, when at last I reach the lane down to the house and barn.

The house and barn. They and my mother, they alone have changed, as if as one, warping, weathering, joints twisted and strained, their gray so unlike the white I recall as a boy. The place is weakening her. She is in tune with it, matches its decay. That is why we have come here to live. To revive. Once I thought to convince her to move away. But of her sixty-five years she has spent forty here, and she insists she will spend the rest, what is left to her.

The rain falls stronger as I hurry past the side of the house, the light on in the kitchen, suppertime and I am late. The house is connected with the barn the way the small base of an L is connected to its stem. The entrance I always use is directly at the joining, and when I enter out of breath, clothes clinging to me cold and wet, the door to the barn to my left, the door to the kitchen straight ahead, I hear the dripping in the basement down the stairs to my right.

"Meg. Sorry I'm late," I call to my wife, setting down the water-beaded canvas sack, opening the kitchen door. There is no one. No settings on the table. Nothing on the stove. Only the yellow light from the sixty-watt bulb in the ceiling. The kind my mother prefers to the white of one hundred. It reminds her of candlelight, she says.

"Meg," I call again, and still no one answers. Asleep, I think. Dusk coming on, the dark clouds of the storm have lulled them, and they have lain down for a nap, expecting to wake before I return.

Still the dripping. Although the house is very old, the barn long disused, roofs crumbling, I have not thought it all so ill-maintained, the storm so strong that water can be seeping past the cellar windows, trickling, pattering on the old stone floor. I switch on the light to the basement, descend the wood stairs to the right, worn and squeaking, reach where the stairs turn to the left the rest of the way down to the floor, and see not water dripping. Milk. Milk everywhere. On the rafters, on the walls, dripping on the film of milk on the stones, gathering speckled with dirt in the channels between them. From side to side and everywhere.

Sarah, my child, has done this, I think. She has been fascinated by the big wood dollhouse that my father made for me when I was quite young, its blue paint chipped and peeling now. She has pulled it from the far corner to the middle of the basement. There are games and toy soldiers and blocks that have been taken from the wicker storage chest and played with on the floor, all covered with milk, the dollhouse, the chest, the scattered toys, milk dripping on them from the rafters, milk trickling on them.

Why has she done this, I think. Where can she have gotten so much milk? What was in her mind to do this thing?

"Sarah," I call. "Meg." Angry now, I mount the stairs into the quiet kitchen. "Sarah!" I shout. She will clean the mess and stay indoors the remainder of the week.

I cross the kitchen, turn through the sitting room past the padded flower-patterned chairs and sofa that have faded since I knew them as a boy, past several of my paintings that my mother has hung up on the wall, bright-colored old ones of pastures and woods from when I was in grade school, brown-shaded new ones of the town, tinted as if old photographs. Two stairs at a time up to the bedrooms, wet shoes on the soft worn carpet on the stairs, hand streaking on the smooth polished maple bannister.

At the top I swing down the hall. The door to Sarah's room is open, it is dark in there. I switch on the light. She is not on the bed, nor has been; the satin spread is unrumpled, the rain pelting in through the open window, the wind fresh and cool. I have the feeling then and go uneasy into our bedroom; it is dark as well, empty too. My stomach has become hollow. Where are they? All in mother's room?

No. As I stand at the open door to mother's room I see from the yellow light I have turned on in the hall that only she is in there, her small torso stretched across the bed.

"Mother," I say, intending to add, "Where are Meg and Sarah?" But I stop before I do. One of my mother's shoes is off, the other askew on her foot. There is mud on the shoes. There is blood on her cotton dress. It is torn, her brittle hair disrupted, blood on her face, her bruised lips are swollen.

For several moments I am silent with shock. "My God, Mother," I finally manage to say, and as if the words are a spring releasing me to action I touch her to wake her. But I see that her eyes are open, staring ceilingward, unseeing though alive, and each breath is a sudden full gasp, then slow exhalation.

"Mother, what has happened? Who did this to you? Meg? Sarah?" But she does not look at me, only constant toward the ceiling.

"For God's sake, Mother, answer me! Look at me! What has happened?"

Nothing. Eyes sightless. Between gasps she is like a statue.

What I think is hysterical. Disjointed, contradictory. I must find Meg and Sarah. They must be somewhere, beaten like my mother. Or worse. Find them. Where? But I cannot leave my mother. When she comes to consciousness, she too will be hysterical, frightened, in great pain. How did she end up on the bed?

In her room there is no sign of the struggle she must have put up against her attacker. It must have happened somewhere else. She crawled from there to here. Then I see the blood on the floor, the swath of blood down the hall from the stairs. Who did this? Where is he? Who would beat a gray, wrinkled, arthritic old woman? Why in God's name would he do it? I shudder. The pain of the arthritis as she struggled with him.

Perhaps he is still in the house, waiting for me.

To the hollow sickness in my stomach now comes fear, hot, pulsing, and I am frantic before I realize what I am doing—grabbing the spare cane my mother always keeps by her bed, flicking on the light in her room, throwing open the closet door and striking in with the cane. Viciously, sounds coming from my throat, the cane flailing among the faded dresses.

No one. Under the bed. No one. Behind the door. No one.

I search all the upstairs rooms that way, terrified, constantly checking behind me, clutching the cane and whacking into closets, under beds, behind doors, with a force that would certainly crack a skull. No one.

"Meg! Sarah!"

No answer, not even an echo in this sound-absorbing house.

There is no attic, just an overhead entry to a crawl space under the eaves, and that opening has long been sealed. No sign of tampering. No one has gone up.

I rush down the stairs, seeing the trail of blood my mother has left on the carpet, imagining her pain as she crawled, and search the rooms downstairs with the same desperate thoroughness. In the front closet. Behind the sofa and chairs. Behind the drapes.

No one.

I lock the front door, lest he be outside in the storm waiting to come in behind me. I remember to draw every blind, close every drape, lest he be out there peering at me. The rain pelts insistently against the windowpanes.

I cry out again and again for Meg and Sarah. The police. My mother. A doctor. I grab for the phone on the wall by the front stairs, fearful to listen to it, afraid he has cut the line outside. But it is droning. Droning. I ring for the police, working the handle at the side around and around and around.

They are coming, they say. A doctor with them. Stay where I am, they say. But I cannot. Meg and Sarah, I must find them. I know they are not in the basement where the milk is dripping—all the basement is open to view. Except for my childhood things, we have cleared out all the boxes and barrels and the shelves of jars the Saturday before.

But under the stairs. I have forgotten about under the stairs and now I race down and stand dreading in the milk; but there are only cobwebs there, already reformed from Saturday when we cleared them. I look up at the side door I first came through, and as if I am seeing through a telescope I focus largely on the handle. It seems to fidget. I have a panicked vision of the intruder bursting through, and I charge up to lock the door, and the door to the barn.

And then I think: if Meg and Sarah are not in the house they are likely in the barn. But I cannot bring myself to unlock the barn door and go through. *He* must be there as well. Not in the rain outside but in the shelter of the barn, and there are no lights to turn on there.

And why the milk? Did he do it and where did he get it? And why? Or did Sarah do it before? No, the milk is too freshly dripping. It has been put there too recently. By him. But why? And who is he? A tramp? An escapee from some prison? Or asylum? No, the nearest institution is far away, hundreds of miles. From the town then. Or a nearby farm.

I know my questions are for delay, to keep me from entering the barn. But I must. I take the flashlight from the kitchen drawer and unlock the door to the barn, force myself to go in quickly, cane ready, flashing my light. The stalls are still there, listing; and some of the equipment, churners, separators, dull and rusted, webbed and dirty. The must of decaying wood and crumbled hay, the fresh wet smell of the rain gusting through cracks in the walls. Once this was a dairy, as the other farms around still are.

Flicking my light toward the corners, edging toward the stalls, boards creaking, echoing, I try to control my fright, try to remember as a boy how the cows waited in the stalls for my father to milk them, how the barn was once board-tight and solid, warm to be in, how there was no connecting door from the barn to the house because my father did not want my mother to smell the animals in her kitchen.

I run my light down the walls, sweep it in arcs through the darkness before me as I draw nearer to the stalls, and in spite of myself I recall that other autumn when the snow came early, four feet deep by morning and still storming thickly, how my father went out to the barn to milk and never returned for lunch, nor supper. There was no phone then, no way to get help, and my mother and I waited all night, unable to make our way through the storm, listening to the slowly dying wind; and the next morning was clear and bright and blinding as we shoveled out to find the cows in agony in their stalls and my father dead, frozen rock-solid in the snow in the middle of the next field where he must have wandered when he lost his bearings in the storm.

There was a fox, risen earlier than us, nosing at him under the snow, and my father had to be sealed in his coffin before he could lie in state. Days after, the snow was melted, gone, the barnyard a sea of mud, and it was autumn again and my mother had the connecting door put in. My father should have tied a rope from the house to his waist to guide him back in case he lost his way. Certainly he knew enough. But then he was like that, always in a rush. When I was ten.

Thus I think as I light the shadows near the stalls, terrified of what I may find in any one of them, Meg and Sarah, or him, thinking of how my mother and I searched for my father and how I now search for my wife and child, trying to think of how it was once warm in here and pleasant, chatting with my father, helping him to milk, the sweet smell of new hay and grain, the different sweet smell of fresh droppings, something I always liked and neither my father nor my mother could understand. I know that if I do not think of these good times I will surely go mad in awful anticipation of what I may find. Pray God they have not died!

What can he have done to them? To assault a five-year-old girl? Split her. The hemorrhaging alone can have killed her.

And then, even in the barn, I hear my mother cry out for me. The relief I feel to leave and go to her unnerves me. I do want to find Meg and Sarah, to try to save them. Yet I am relieved to go. I think my mother will tell me what has happened, tell me where to find them. That is how I justify my leaving as I wave the light in circles around me, guarding my back, retreating through the door and locking it.

Upstairs she sits stiffly on her bed. I want to make her answer my questions, to shake her, to force her to help, but I know it will only frighten her more, maybe push her mind down to where I can never reach.

"Mother," I say to her softly, touching her gently. "What has happened?" My impatience can barely be contained. "Who did this? Where are Meg and Sarah?"

She smiles at me, reassured by the safety of my presence. Still she cannot answer.

"Mother. Please," I say. "I know how bad it must have been. But you must try to help. I must know where they are so I can help them."

She says, "Dolls."

It chills me. "What dolls, Mother? Did a man come here with dolls? What did he want? You mean he looked like a doll? Wearing a mask like one?"

Too many questions. All she can do is blink.

"Please, Mother. You must try your best to tell me. Where are Meg and Sarah?"

"Dolls," she says.

As I first had the foreboding of disaster at the sight of Sarah's unrumpled satin bedspread, now I am beginning to understand, rejecting it, fighting it.

"Yes, Mother, the dolls," I say, refusing to admit what I know. "Please, Mother. Where are Meg and Sarah?"

"You are a grown boy now. You must stop playing as a child. Your father. Without him you will have to be the man in the house. You must be brave."

"No, Mother." I can feel it swelling in my chest.

"There will be a great deal of work now, more than any child should know. But we have no choice. You must accept that God has chosen to take him from us, that you are all the man I have left to help me."

"No, Mother."

"Now you are a man and you must put away the things of a child."

Eyes streaming, I am barely able to straighten, leaning wearily against the door jamb, tears rippling from my face down to my shirt, wetting it cold where it had just begun to dry. I wipe my eyes and see her reaching for me, smiling, and I recoil down the hall, stumbling down the stairs, down, through the sitting room, the kitchen, down, down to the milk, splashing through it to the dollhouse, and in there, crammed and doubled, Sarah. And in the wicker chest, Meg. The toys not on the floor for Sarah to play with, but taken out so Meg could be put in. And both of them, their stomachs slashed, stuffed with sawdust, their eyes rolled up like dolls' eyes.

The police are knocking at the side door, pounding, calling out who they are, but I am powerless to let them in. They crash through the door, their rubber raincoats dripping as they stare down at me.

"The milk," I say.

They do not understand. Even as I wait, standing in the milk, listening to the rain pelting on the windows while they come over to see what is in the dollhouse and in the wicker chest, while they go upstairs to my mother and then return so I can tell them again, "The milk." But they still do not understand.

"She killed them of course," one man says. "But I don't see why the milk."

Only when they speak to the neighbors down the road and learn how she came to them, needing the cans of milk, insisting she carry them herself to the car, the agony she was in as she carried them, only when they find the empty cans and the knife in a stall in the barn, can I say, "The milk. The blood. There was so much blood, you know. She needed to deny it, so she washed it away with milk, purified it, started the dairy again. You see, there was so much blood."

That autumn we live in a house in the country, my mother's house, the house I was raised in. I have been to the village, struck even more by how nothing in it has changed, yet everything has, because I am older now, seeing it differently. It is as though I am both here now and back then, at once with the mind of a boy and a man...

Joyce Harrington

The Purple Shroud

Mrs. Moon threw the shuttle back and forth and pumped the treadles of the big four-harness loom as if her life depended on it. When they asked what she was weaving so furiously, she would laugh silently and say it was a shroud.

"No, really, what is it?"

"My house needs new draperies." Mrs. Moon would smile and the shuttle would fly and the beater would thump the newly woven threads tightly into place. The muffled, steady sounds of her craft could be heard from early morning until very late at night, until the sounds became an accepted and expected background noise and were only noticed in their absence.

Then they would say, "I wonder what Mrs. Moon is doing now."

That summer, as soon as they had arrived at the art colony and even before they had unpacked, Mrs. Moon requested that the largest loom in the weaving studio be installed in their cabin. Her request had been granted because she was a serious weaver, and because her husband, George, was one of the best painting instructors they'd ever had. He could coax the amateurs into stretching their imaginations and trying new ideas and techniques, and he would bully the scholarship students until, in a fury, they would sometimes produce works of surprising originality.

George Moon was, himself, only a competent painter. His work had never caught on, although he had a small loyal following in Detroit and occasionally sold a painting. His only concessions to the need for making a living and for buying paints and brushes was to teach some ten hours a week throughout the winter and to take this summer job at the art colony, which was also their vacation. Mrs. Moon taught craft therapy at a home for the aged.

After the loom had been set up in their cabin Mrs. Moon waited. Sometimes she went swimming in the lake, sometimes she drove into town and poked about in the antique shops, and sometimes she just sat in the wicker chair and looked at the loom.

They said, "What are you waiting for, Mrs. Moon? When are you going to begin?"

One day Mrs. Moon drove into town and came back with two boxes full of brightly colored yarns. Classes had been going on for about two weeks, and George was deeply engaged with his students. One of the things the students loved about George was the extra time he gave them. He was always ready to sit for hours on the porch of the big house, just outside the communal dining room, or under a tree, and talk about painting or about life as a painter or tell stories about painters he had known.

George looked like a painter. He was tall and thin, and with approaching middle age he was beginning to stoop a little. He had black snaky hair which he had always worn on the long side, and which was beginning to turn gray. His eyes were very dark, so dark you couldn't see the pupils, and they regarded everything and everyone with a probing intensity that evoked uneasiness in some and caused young girls to fall in love with him.

Every year George Moon selected one young lady disciple to be his summer consort.

Mrs. Moon knew all about these summer alliances. Every year, when they returned to Detroit, George would confess to her with great humility and swear never to repeat his transgression.

"Never again, Arlene," he would say. "I promise you, never again."

Mrs. Moon would smile her forgiveness.

Mrs. Moon hummed as she sorted through the skeins of purple and deep scarlet, goldenrod yellow and rich royal blue. She hummed as she wound the glowing hanks into fat balls, and she thought about George and the look that had passed between him and the girl from Minneapolis at dinner the night before. George had not returned to their cabin until almost two in the morning. The girl from Minneapolis was short and plump, with a round face and a halo of fuzzy red-gold hair. She reminded Mrs. Moon of a Teddy bear; she reminded Mrs. Moon of herself twenty years before.

When Mrs. Moon was ready to begin, she carried the purple yarn to the weaving studio.

"I have to make a very long warp," she said. "I'll need to use the warping reel."

She hummed as she measured out the seven feet and a little over, then sent the reel spinning.

"Is it wool?" asked the weaving instructor.

"No, it's orlon," said Mrs. Moon. "It won't shrink, you know."

Mrs. Moon loved the creak of the reel, and she loved feeling the warp threads grow fatter under her hands until at last each planned thread was in place and she could tie the bundle and braid up the end. When she held the plaited warp in her hands she imagined it to be the shorn tresses of some enormously powerful earth goddess whose potency was now transferred to her own person.

That evening after dinner, Mrs. Moon began to thread the loom. George had taken the rowboat and the girl from Minneapolis to the other end of the lake where there was a deserted cottage. Mrs. Moon knew he kept a sleeping bag there, and a cache of wine and peanuts. Mrs. Moon hummed as she carefully threaded the eye of each heddle with a single purple thread, and thought of black widow spiders and rattlesnakes coiled in the corners of the dark cottage.

She worked contentedly until midnight and then went to bed. She was asleep and smiling when George stumbled in two hours later and fell into bed with his clothes on.

Mrs. Moon wove steadily through the summer days. She did not attend the weekly critique sessions for she had nothing to show and was not interested in the problems others were having with their work. She ignored the Saturday night parties where George and the girl from Minneapolis and the others danced and drank beer and slipped off to the beach or the boathouse.

Sometimes, when she tired of the long hours at the loom, she would go for solitary walks in the woods and always brought back curious trophies of her rambling. The small cabin, already crowded with the loom and the iron double bedstead, began to fill up with giant toadstools, interesting bits of wood, arrangements of reeds and wild wheat.

One day she brought back two large black stones on which she painted faces. The eyes of the faces were closed and the mouths were faintly curved in archaic smiles. She placed one stone on each side of the fireplace.

George hated the stones. "Those damn stonefaces are watching me," he said. "Get them out of here."

"How can they be watching you? Their eyes are closed."

Mrs. Moon left the stones beside the fireplace and George soon forgot to hate them. She called them Apollo I and Apollo II.

The weaving grew and Mrs. Moon thought it the best thing she had ever done. Scattered about the purple ground were signs and symbols which she saw against the deep blackness of her closed eyelids when she thought of passion and revenge, of love and wasted years and the child she had never had. She thought the barbaric colors spoke of those matters, and she was pleased.

"I hope you'll finish it before the final critique," the weaving teacher said when she came to the cabin to see it. "It's very, very good."

Word spread through the camp and many of the students came to the cabin to see the marvelous weaving. Mrs. Moon was proud to show it to them and received their compliments with quiet grace.

"It's too fine to hang at a window," said one practical Sunday-painting matron. "The sun will fade the colors."

"I'd love to wear it," said the life model.

"You!" said a bearded student of lithography. "It's a robe for a pagan king!"

"Perhaps you're right," said Mrs. Moon, and smiled her happiness on all of them.

The season was drawing to a close when in the third week of August, Mrs. Moon threw the shuttle for the last time. She slumped on the backless bench and rested her limp hands on the breast beam of the loom. Tomorrow she would cut the warp.

That night, while George was showing color slides of his paintings in the main gallery, the girl from Minneapolis came alone to the Moons' cabin. Mrs. Moon was lying on the bed watching a spider spin a web in the rafters. A fire was blazing in the fireplace, between Apollo I and Apollo II, for the late-summer night was chill.

"You must let him go," said the golden-haired Teddy bear. "He loves me."

"Yes, dear," said Mrs. Moon.

"You don't seem to understand. I'm talking about George." The girl sat on the bed. "I think I'm pregnant."

"That's nice," said Mrs. Moon. "Children are a blessing. Watch the spider."

"We have a relationship going. I don't care about being married—that's too feudal. But you must free George to come and be a father image to the child."

"You'll get over it," said Mrs. Moon, smiling a trifle sadly at the girl.

"Oh, you don't even want to know what's happening!" cried the girl. "No wonder George is bored with you."

"Some spiders eat their mates after fertilization," Mrs. Moon remarked. "Female spiders."

The girl flounced angrily from the cabin, as far as one could be said to flounce in blue jeans and sweatshirt . . .

George performed his end-of-summer separation ritual simply and brutally the following afternoon. He disappeared after lunch. No one knew where he had gone. The girl from Minneapolis roamed the camp, trying not to let anyone know she was searching for him. Finally she rowed herself down to the other end of the lake, to find that George had dumped her transistor radio, her books of poetry, and her box of incense on the damp sand and had put a padlock on the door of the cottage.

She threw her belongings into the boat and rowed back to the camp, tears of rage streaming down her cheeks. She beached the boat, and with head lowered and shoulders hunched she stormed the Moons' cabin. She found Mrs. Moon tying off the severed warp threads.

"Tell George," she shouted, "tell George I'm going back to Minneapolis. He knows where to find me!"

"Here, dear," said Mrs. Moon, "hold the end and walk backwards while I unwind it."

The girl did as she was told, caught by the vibrant colors and Mrs. Moon's concentration. In a few minutes the full length of cloth rested in the girl's arms.

"Put it on the bed and spread it out," said Mrs. Moon. "Let's take a good look at it."

"I'm really leaving," whispered the girl. "Tell him I don't care if I never see him again."

"I'll tell him." The wide strip of purple flowed garishly down the middle of the bed between them. "Do you think he'll like it?" asked Mrs. Moon. "He's going to have it around for a long time."

"The colors are very beautiful, very savage." The girl looked closely at Mrs. Moon. "I wouldn't have thought you would choose such colors."

"I never did before."

"I'm leaving now."

"Goodbye," said Mrs. Moon.

George did not reappear until long after the girl had loaded up her battered bug of a car and driven off. Mrs. Moon knew he had been watching and waiting from the hill behind the camp. He came into the cabin whistling softly and began to take his clothes off.

"God, I'm tired," he said.

"It's almost dinnertime."

"Too tired to eat," he yawned. "What's that on the bed?"

"My weaving is finished. Do you like it?"

"It's good. Take it off the bed. I'll look at it tomorrow."

Mrs. Moon carefully folded the cloth and laid it on the weaving bench. She looked at George's thin naked body before he got into bed and smiled.

"I'm going to dinner now," she said.

"Okay. Don't wake me up when you get back. I could sleep for a week."

"I won't wake you up," said Mrs. Moon.

Mrs. Moon ate dinner at a table by herself. Most of the students had already left. A few people, the Moons among them, usually stayed on after the end of classes to rest and enjoy the isolation. Mrs. Moon spoke to no one.

After dinner she sat on the pier and watched the sunset. She watched the turtles in the shallow water and thought she saw a blue heron on the other side of the lake. When the sky was black and the stars were too many to count, Mrs. Moon went to the toolshed and got a wheelbarrow. She rolled this to the door of her cabin and went inside.

The cabin was dark and she could hear George's steady heavy breathing. She lit two candles and placed them on the mantelshelf. She spread her beautiful weaving on her side of the bed, gently so as not to disturb the sleeper. Then she quietly moved the weaving bench to George's side of the bed, near his head.

She sat on the bench for a time, memorizing the lines of his face by the wavering candlelight. She touched him softly on the forehead with the pads of her fingertips and gently caressed his eyes, his hard cheeks, his raspy chin. His breathing became uneven and she withdrew her hands, sitting motionless until his sleep rhythm was restored.

Then Mrs. Moon took off her shoes. She walked carefully to the fireplace, taking long quiet steps. She placed her shoes neatly side by side on the hearth and picked up the larger stone, Apollo I. The face of the kouros, the ancient god, smiled up at her and she returned that faint implacable smile. She carried the stone back to the bench beside the bed, and set it down.

Then she climbed onto the bench, and when she stood she found she could almost touch the spider's web in the rafters. The spider crouched in the heart of its web, and Mrs. Moon wondered if spiders ever slept.

Mrs. Moon picked up Apollo I, and with both arms raised took careful aim. Her shadow, cast by candlelight, had the appearance of a priestess offering sacrifice. The stone was heavy and her arms grew weak. Her hands let go. The stone dropped.

George's eyes flapped open and he saw Mrs. Moon smiling tenderly down on him. His lips drew back to scream, but his mouth could only form a soundless hole.

"Sleep, George," she whispered, and his eyelids clamped over his unbelieving eyes.

Mrs. Moon jumped off the bench. With gentle fingers she probed beneath his snaky locks until she found a satisfying softness. There was no blood and for this Mrs. Moon was grateful. It would have been a shame to spoil the beauty of her patterns with superfluous colors and untidy stains. Her mothlike fingers on his wrist warned her of a faint uneven fluttering.

She padded back to the fireplace and weighed in her hands the smaller, lighter Apollo II. This time she felt there was no need for added height. With three quick butter-churning motions she enlarged the softened area in George's skull and stilled the annoying flutter in his wrist.

Then she rolled him over as a hospital nurse will roll an immobile patient during bedmaking routine, until he rested on his back on one-half of the purple fabric. She placed his arms across his naked chest and straightened his spindly legs. She kissed his closed eyelids, gently stroked his shaggy brows, and said, "Rest now, dear George."

She folded the free half of the royal cloth over him, covering him from head to foot with a little left over at each end. From her sewing box she took a wide-eyed needle and threaded it with some difficulty in the flickering light. Then, kneeling beside the bed, Mrs. Moon began stitching across the top. She stitched small careful stitches that would hold for eternity.

Soon the top was closed and she began stitching down the long side. The job was wearisome, but Mrs. Moon was patient and she hummed a sweet, monotonous tune as stitch followed stitch past George's ear, his shoulder, his bent elbow. It was not until she reached his ankles that she allowed herself to stand and stretch her aching knees and flex her cramped fingers.

Retrieving the twin Apollos from where they lay abandoned on George's pillow, she tucked them reverently into the bottom of the cloth sarcophagus and knelt once more to her task. Her needle flew faster as the remaining gap between the two edges of cloth grew smaller, until the last stitch was securely knotted and George was sealed into his funerary garment. But the hardest part of her night's work was yet to come.

She knew she could not carry George even the short distance to the door of the cabin and the wheelbarrow outside. And the wheelbarrow was too wide to bring inside. She couldn't bear the thought of dragging him across the floor and soiling or tearing the fabric she had so lovingly woven. Finally she rolled him onto the weaving bench and despite the fact that it only supported him from armpits to groin, she managed to maneuver it to the door. From there it was possible to shift the burden to the waiting wheelbarrow.

Mrs. Moon was now breathing heavily from her exertions, and paused for a moment to survey the night and the prospect before her. There were no lights anywhere in the camp except for the feeble glow of her own guttering candles. As she went to blow them out she glanced at her watch and was mildly surprised to see that it was ten minutes past three. The hours had flown while she had been absorbed in her needlework.

She perceived now the furtive night noises of the forest creatures which had hitherto been blocked from her senses by the total concentration she had bestowed on her work. She thought of weasels and foxes prowling, of owls going about their predatory night activities, and considered herself in congenial company. Then, taking up the handles of the wheelbarrow, she trundled down the well defined path to the boathouse.

The wheelbarrow made more noise than she had anticipated and she hoped she was far enough from any occupied cabin for its rumbling to go unnoticed. The moonless night sheltered her from any wakeful watcher and a dozen summers of waiting had taught her the nature and substance of every square foot of the camp's area. She could walk it blindfolded.

When she reached the boathouse she found that some hurried careless soul had left a boat on the beach in defiance of the camp's rules. It was a simple matter of leverage to shift her burden from barrow to boat and in minutes Mrs. Moon was heaving inexpertly at the oars. At first the boat seemed inclined to travel only in wide arcs and head back to shore, but with patient determination Mrs. Moon established a rowing rhythm that would take her and her passenger to the deepest part of the lake.

She hummed a sea chanty which aided her rowing and pleased her sense of the appropriate. Then, pinpointing her position by the silhouette of the tall solitary pine that grew on the opposite shore, Mrs. Moon carefully raised the oars and rested them in the boat.

As Mrs. Moon crept forward in the boat, feeling her way in the darkness, the boat began to rock gently. It was a pleasant, soothing motion and Mrs. Moon thought of cradles and soft enveloping comforters. She continued creeping slowly forward, swaying with the motion of the boat, until she reached the side of her swaddled passenger. There she sat and stroked the cloth and wished that she could see the fine colors just one last time.

She felt the shape beneath the cloth, solid but thin and now rather pitiful. She took the head in her arms and held it against her breast, rocking and humming a long-forgotten lullaby.

The doubled weight at the forward end of the small boat caused the prow to dip. Water began to slosh into the boat—in small wavelets at first as the boat rocked from side to side, then in a steady trickle as the boat rode lower and lower in the water. Mrs. Moon rocked and hummed; the water rose over her bare feet and lapped against her ankles. The sky began to turn purple and she could just make out the distant shape of the boathouse and the hill behind the camp. She was very tired and very cold.

Gently she placed George's head in the water. The boat tilted crazily and she scrambled backward to equalize the weight. She picked up the other end of the long purple chrysalis, the end containing the stone Apollos, and heaved it overboard. George in his shroud, with head and feet trailing in the lake, now lay along the side of the boat weighting it down.

Water was now pouring in. Mrs. Moon held to the other side of the boat with placid hands and thought of the dense comfort of the muddy lake bottom and George beside her forever. She saw that her feet were frantically pushing against the burden of her life, running away from that companionable grave.

With a regretful sigh she let herself slide down the short incline of the seat and came to rest beside George. The boat lurched deeper into the lake. Water surrounded George and climbed into Mrs. Moon's lap. Mrs. Moon closed her eyes and hummed, "Nearer My God to Thee." She did not see George drift away from the side of the boat, carried off by the moving arms of water. She felt a wild bouncing, a shuddering and splashing, and was sure the boat had overturned. With relief she gave herself up to chaos and did not try to hold her breath.

Expecting a suffocating weight of water in her lungs, Mrs. Moon was disappointed to find she could open her eyes, that air still entered and left her gasping mouth. She lay in a pool of water in the bottom of the boat and saw a bird circle high above the lake, peering down at her. The boat was bobbing gently on the water, and when Mrs. Moon sat up she saw that a few yards away, through the fresh blue morning, George was bobbing gently too. The purple shroud had filled with air and floated on the water like a small submarine come up for air and a look at the new day.

As she watched, shivering and wet, the submarine shape drifted away and dwindled as the lake took slow possession. At last, with a grateful sigh, green water replacing the last bubble of air, it sank just as the bright arc of the sun rose over the hill in time to give Mrs. Moon a final glimpse of glorious purple and gold. She shook herself like a tired old gray dog and called out, "Goodbye, George." Her cry echoed back and forth across the morning and startled forth a chorus of bird shrieks. Pandemonium and farewell. She picked up the oars.

Back on the beach, the boat carefully restored to its place, Mrs. Moon dipped her blistered hands into the lake. She scented bacon in the early air and instantly felt the pangs of an enormous hunger. Mitch, the cook, would be having his early breakfast and perhaps would share it with her. She hurried to the cabin to change out of her wet clothes, and was amazed, as she stepped over the doorsill, at the stark emptiness which greeted her.

Shafts of daylight fell on the rumpled bed, but there was nothing for her there. She was not tired now, did not need to sleep. The fireplace contained cold ashes, and the hearth looked bare and unfriendly. The loom gaped at her like a toothless mouth, its usefulness at an end. In a heap on the floor lay George's clothes where he had dropped them the night before. Out of habit she picked them up, and as she hung them on a hook in the small closet she felt a rustle in the shirt pocket. It was a scrap of paper torn off a drawing pad; there was part of a pencil sketch on one side, on the other an address and telephone number.

Mrs. Moon hated to leave anything unfinished, despising untidiness in herself and others. She quickly changed into her town clothes and hung her discarded wet things in the tiny bathroom to dry. She found an apple and munched it as she made up her face and combed her still-damp hair. The apple took the edge off her hunger, and she decided not to take the time to beg breakfast from the cook.

She carefully made the bed and tidied the small room, sweeping a few scattered ashes back into the fireplace. She checked her summer straw pocketbook for driver's license, car keys, money, and finding everything satisfactory she paused for a moment in the center of the room. All was quiet, neat, and orderly. The spider still hung inert in the center of its web and one small fly was buzzing helplessly on its perimeter. Mrs. Moon smiled.

There was no time to weave now—indeed, there was no need. She could not really expect to find a conveniently deserted lake in a big city. No. She would have to think of something else.

Mrs. Moon stood in the doorway of the cabin in the early sunlight, a small frown wrinkling the placid surface of her round pink face. She scuffled slowly around to the back of the cabin and into the shadow of the sycamores beyond, her feet kicking up the spongy layers of years of fallen leaves, her eyes watching carefully for the right idea to show itself. Two grayish-white stones appeared side by side, half covered with leaf mold. Anonymous, faceless, about the size of cantaloupes, they would do unless something better presented itself.

Unceremoniously she dug them out of their bed, brushed away the loose dirt and leaf fragments, and carried them back to the car.

Mrs. Moon's watch had stopped sometime during the night, but as she got into the car she glanced at the now fully risen sun and guessed the time to be about six thirty or seven o'clock. She placed the two stones snugly on the passenger seat and covered them with her soft pale-blue cardigan. She started the engine, and then reached over and groped in the glove compartment. She never liked to drive anywhere without knowing beforehand the exact roads to take to get to her destination. The road map was there, neatly folded beneath the flashlight and the box of tissues.

Mrs. Moon unfolded the map and spread it out over the steering wheel. As the engine warmed up, Mrs. Moon hummed along with it. Her pudgy pink hand absently patted the tidy blue bundle beside her as she planned the most direct route to the girl in Minneapolis.

"Q"

Michael Talbot

Oddity Imports

" 'Charlie Chaplin sat on a pin. How many inches did it go in? One, two, three, four—' " How much fun they seemed to be having, Marie thought as she wiped the glaze of her breath off the window.

" 'Five, six, seven, eight—' " Old Mr. Trumble was twirling the rope and Miss Macfarlane was having the time of her life doing peppers.

Marie didn't know whether to feel sad about the people in the yard. There were two dozen of them cloistered from the outside world by the hurricane fence and the shade of the large chestnut trees. Their age averaged in the late thirties, but some, like old Mr. Trumble, would never see sixty again. And yet ask them their age and they would answer with a childlike slur, "Five years old." Or perhaps one of them would hold up an age-gnarled hand and gesture shyly with his fingers. Was it really so tragic? Of course, they had to be taken care of like children, but they were enjoying life. They were young again.

Marie sometimes wondered what emotional problems made them regress and sometimes, although rarely, she thought about her own mother. When had she stopped worrying about her mother?

Was it that night long ago in the hallway?

No . . . Was it that evening she decided her mother was too much of an albatross around her neck? Or was it that day she first came across the little shop, the one off Abingdon Square?

"There you go, Miss," the man said as he held the door open for her. It startled Marie. She blinked naively and pulled her raincoat a little tighter. He was a large man with oddly narrow features and a squinty grin.

She had just stepped under the awnings to escape the rain when the sign on the door attracted her attention. *Oddity Imports*, the impressive little bronze plaque read. She had been peeking in, or at least trying to peek in, when the man opened the door.

He was clutching a small package and when he saw her staring he tucked it quickly under his coat. Well, she had to go in now. She certainly couldn't just stand there letting the rain pour through the open door.

"Thank you," she said briskly. The man smiled and tipped his Homburg. The inside of the shop was more like a salon on the *Queen Mary*. No wonder she couldn't see through the windows. From this side she could tell they had been frosted. Not only that, but thick green-velvet curtains shrouded them like the anteroom of a funeral parlor.

"May I help you?" said a voice from the back. Marie turned and saw a veritable shadow of a woman, very thin, very old.

"The rain," Marie stammered. "I just came in to get out of the rain."

"Perhaps you would like it to stop." The old woman smiled in an odd way.

"I sure wish it would," Marie replied.

"Five dollars for a fifteen-minute lapse, thirty dollars and the whole storm will stop."

Marie chuckled, not grasping the sincerity in the woman's voice. The prospect of purchasing the weather as if it were a pair of shoes made her grin.

"Perhaps you would like to see a few items." The old odd woman turned and vanished through a doorway. Outside, a peal of thunder shook the windows and the honk of an automobile returned a muted answer.

This was certainly an odd place, Marie thought, and then laughed. It had been an unintended reminder of the name of the shop—*Oddity Imports*. Within moments the woman returned, loaded down with boxes.

Marie felt a little uneasy at being the focal point of what was obviously going to become an intense sales pitch. She wondered why there wasn't any other visible merchandise as the old woman placed her armful on the marble-topped counter.

"Now, dear, this is an interesting piece of work." She began wiping the edge of her mouth with a delicate lace handkerchief. From one of the boxes she withdrew a large form wrapped in silk. As she lifted the veil Marie gasped.

"Why, it's beautiful. But surely I couldn't afford something like this."

"I'm sure we could work out some sort of arrangement," the woman said. There on the counter sat a crystal vase of roses. Not only was the receptacle made of glass, but the flowers as well. Each stem, each thorn, each shimmering leaf and gossamer petal was of the clearest crystal.

"And that's not all," the old woman murmured, carefully reaching down into the bunch of almost invisible flowers. There was a click and then a whir of machinery as the petals began to spread and as each tiny bud bloomed.

"Would you like to see more?"

Marie's smile broadened as she quickly nodded. From another ornately carved wooden box the woman brought out a tiny glass case. Carefully she rested it on the counter and motioned for Marie to look at it more closely. Inside was a miniature room, a study. The walls were covered with books no larger than pinheads, and a fireplace the size of a fingernail burned brightly in the corner. In the middle was a tiny desk equipped with microscopic pencils, papers, scissors, pens, and everything else a desk should have. Marie gazed intently at the little room when suddenly her attention was pulled toward a diminutive couch in one of the corners.

Abruptly a figure no larger than a tiny insect stood up from behind it. It was a maid complete with a minute feather duster and white cap. There was an almost imperceptible squeak as a door near the couch opened and in walked a wee little man. Marie almost grinned as the maid rushed toward him and the two passionately embraced. The door opened once more and another figure entered, this time a woman. She was obviously the lady of the house, dressed in a long silk gown. She threw herself into a Lilliputian fit of rage and pulled a tiny gun from beneath her dress. A barely audible report rang out as the two figures fell dead, still embracing, and the woman turned the gun on herself.

Marie straightened quickly with an expression of horror on her face as the old woman cackled. "It takes you by surprise, doesn't it?" she said and returned the miniature room to its box.

She then proceeded to show Marie other oddities, all with pure P. T. Barnum showmanship. There was a small golden birdcage with a mechanical bird that sang any song requested. Other boxes revealed such treasures as a dancing ballerina made of fishbone and parchment; a large and brightly colored crepe butterfly that actually fluttered around the room; a bottle with a ship in it and a miniature storm that tossed the little vessel about; marvelously detailed oil paintings no larger than postage stamps; delicate little insects carved from precious stones; and perfumes with such scents as morning, surprise, and silence.

There were books that read themselves, dolls that imitated every human movement, and mirrors that only reflected a person while he was smiling.

"You mentioned the weather," Marie said as the woman carried away the last of the boxes. "You said you could make the rain stop."

"Yes," the woman said blankly and brushed off her hands.

"Well, can you?" Marie asked excitedly.

"The weather is one of the items in our intangible line," the old woman replied. "Instead of selling a pill that makes you sleep we sell you sleep itself. Instead of selling a drug that makes you dream we sell you the dreams directly. That way you can buy ten minutes of sleep or ten hours of sleep, not just something that makes you unconscious."

"And dreams?"

"We can sell you dreams in any size, shape, or form. We can sell you a happy dream, a dream about puppies, a dream about riches, a ten-minute dream or a ten-year dream. In a dream you could be a princess or a bird flying free through the heavens—" The old woman traced a wide arc with her hand and Marie shuddered. She hated birds.

The old woman leaned closer. "We also sell emotions, dear, like love and happiness." She paused for a moment and then spoke in a lowered voice. "We occasionally have been known to sell death too."

"You mean someone comes and murders—"

"No!" the woman corrected harshly. "Remember, I said we sell directly. There is no middle man, no assassin, just the product itself—death."

For a fleeting moment Marie thought of her mother and then mentally reprimanded herself. Just because she seemed to dictate Marie's life from that—that awful chair.

"I think," Marie said, "I think I'll purchase a fifteen-minute pause in this storm."

"Five dollars," the woman blurted out. Marie fumbled in her purse and pulled out a bill.

"There is a guarantee, of course?" Marie asked when the woman motioned with her hand toward the window. There was another crash of lightning as the rain seemingly melted in the cool gray sky.

Considerably unnerved and with an excited feeling in her stomach, Marie made her way home quickly. Just as she was climbing up the dark stairs to their second-floor apartment she heard the rain begin to beat on the windows again.

"Fifteen minutes to the second," she said aloud, after glancing at her watch.

"Is that you, Marie?"

"Yes, Mother."

"Who are you talking to?"

"Ah—the neighbor's cat."

"Well, please hurry. I'm hungry."

Marie struggled momentarily with the key and then entered the apartment. It wasn't anything elaborate, except for the birds. They were everywhere, in cages and out of them. Parakeets, doves, pigeons, lovebirds, finches, and one fat ebony mynah with amber eyes. A cacophony of voices greeted her.

"Shut the door, Marie," her mother called from the other room. "That terrible cat the neighbors have will sneak in. Don't cook anything greasy tonight either. My stomach has been talking to me all day and I just know anything greasy would—"

"Yes, Mother, I won't." Marie took off her coat and flopped down on the couch. Before she realized what she was doing she looked behind it to see if the maid was still dusting with that tiny feather duster. She tried not to think of the little shop off Abingdon Square, and then she suddenly thought: I should buy a dream. No, Marie, she checked herself, it's all nonsense.

But the rain had stopped for exactly fifteen minutes.

"My dinner, Marie!"

"Right away, Mother." She sighed and forced herself to stand. With a plaintive cry, an azure-breasted parakeet swooped down from the curtains and narrowly missed her. She wanted to throw something at it, but her mother would wonder what the noise was.

Since her mother never did any of the work, Marie considered the kitchen to be the one room completely her own. It wasn't much—a sink, a stove that would only work when you kicked it, an old and noisy refrigerator that leaked rivers onto the cracked linoleum. Two enameled louvered doors kept the birds out. She had once put a Japanese paper lantern over the lamp, but it got too hot and burned, leaving a scorched halo on the ceiling. She had also plastered the refrigerator with self-adhesive flowers, but some had come off and left gray scars where they had peeled the paint away.

Still, she really didn't mind it. The only thing she minded about the kitchen was that she could see her mother through the cracks in the louvered doors. Like a shadowy icon, her mother's form grew out of the familiar outline of the chair. She sat there in the darkness, a gray hulk with her back toward Marie. During the day her mother watched the pigeons and the flies while her birds softly cooed around her. At night she watched the midge swarms dance in the weird bluish light of the mercury-vapor lamps.

That was her mother's life. And Marie's.

Tonight they would have brussels sprouts, boiled potatoes, and Polish sausage. Her mother would complain about the lack of salt in the sprouts, the starchiness of the potatoes, and the spiciness of the meat. The night came slowly.

Marie saw it only a week later while she was fixing breakfast. As usual, her mother was already up and in her chair. Marie almost didn't hear it prance across the floor over the crackle of frying eggs, but the warped linoleum gave it away.

Marie screamed.

A large well fed rat glared at her from a corner. "What is it?" her mother cried and Marie could hear her struggle to turn in her chair.

"A rat," Marie answered and grabbed the broom. "A filthy dirty rat that does nothing but sit around and eat our food." She beat it again and again and then realized what she had said.

"Don't forget to wash your hands, dear," her mother warned as Marie took the dark gray form and wrapped it in an oily piece of butcher's paper. "I'm glad you caught the ugly thing. He was probably after my baby finches. And, Marie, would you fix me some poached eggs? My stomach has started talking to me and you know what grease—"

"Yes," Marie interrupted sharply.

She visited the little shop the next day. The same withered woman came out to greet her.

"So it's you again. Wait until you see the shipment of puppets we just got in." Before Marie could say anything, the old woman had once more disappeared into the back room. When she returned she had an armful of small wooden figures.

"May I?" the old woman asked, and reached over to fasten several heavy black cords on Marie's arms. Marie backed up.

"I'm sorry," the woman said.

"It's just that I'm not in the mood," Marie said.

The woman smiled. "You see, instead of you operating the puppets, they operate you. We've already sold two of them to one of our regular customers." She paused. "But that's not what you came for, is it, my dear?"

"No." Marie forced a smile. "I really enjoyed all the things you showed me the last time, but I don't need any of them."

The woman nodded knowingly.

"What I would like to know is—" and Marie stopped. "What I would like to know is the price of the dreams."

"It depends on the dream."

"What do you mean?"

"It depends on the dream. Nightmares are cheaper than good dreams and daydreams are very expensive. There are so few of them on the market nowadays. Also the length of the dream causes the prices to vary. A ten-minute nightmare will cost you only a dollar, but a ten-minute dream of ecstasy will cost you much more. Pipe dreams are a dime a dozen."

Marie let her eyes fall from the woman's gaze and stared down at the marble counter.

"And death?" she asked timorously.

" 'To sleep: perchance to dream: ay, there's the rub: For in that sleep of death what dreams may come, When we have shuffled off this mortal coil, Must give us pause . . .' " The old woman's eyes narrowed. "So you did not really want a dream at all." Marie regained her courage and peered into the woman's eyes.

"Death, like dreams, comes at many prices. We can sell you a horrible death, a hellish death that distorts and tortures the mind of the victim. That would be very expensive."

"Oh, no," Marie objected.

"We can sell you a lingering death that slowly consumes or we can sell you a death as quiet as a cat that steals upon the victim and silently pounces. If someone were to buy death for me I would ask them to get the quiet death." She threw her head back regally.

Marie handed over one hundred dollars and the old woman brought out a tiny gold box.

"Death is inside this little box?" Marie asked nervously.

"Yes," the old woman replied in a hush. "This box contains enough death for one person," and with that she became silent.

Marie left quickly, returned home, and rushed up the stairs.

"Is that you, Marie?" her mother called.

"Yes."

"Don't fix much for me tonight. I'm not very hungry."

Marie tried not to look at the small, exquisitely carved gold box that contained death. She went into the kitchen and rattled a few pans. Marie wasn't very hungry either.

She stared at the scorched circle on the ceiling and the ugly gray patches on the refrigerator where the paste-on flowers had been. She looked at the small crimson stain on the linoleum floor where she had killed the rat. And then she looked at the box.

Finally night came.

Her mother was still sitting in the chair like a lifeless automaton when Marie crept softly into the hallway. The mercury-vapor lamps silhouetted the woman in a ghostly blue aura. Marie took a deep breath and then opened the box in the darkness.

It moved. She could sense it. Warm and silent, it moved. The room seemed a shade darker as her mother shifted her weight and the chair creaked. A murmuring chorus arose from the birds. Like a pool of ink it surrounded her mother, who absorbed it like a blotter. Her head slowly drooped to one side.

Coronary arrest, the doctor said the next morning.

That was the story, or at least most of it. For the first few weeks Marie forced herself to celebrate, but too many images began to haunt her mind.

Is that you, Marie?—a voice called from the darkness. She would often find herself staring at the burnt ceiling, at the old and rumbling refrigerator, and, sitting in her mother's chair, she would even watch a midge swarm in a shaft of light.

At last, in desperation, she sold the meager furnishings of the apartment and went back to the little shop off Abingdon Square.

"You said I could buy emotions," she asked the old woman. "Perhaps I could purchase some peace of mind?"

Another box, this one carved of ivory. Marie opened it and peered into the velvet-lined interior. It seemed empty, but it was not.

The box brought her here.

The nurse came in and placed a tray of food on her bed.

"And how are we this morning, Marie?" the nurse smiled.

"Fine," Marie answered in a childish giggle.

" 'Charlie Chaplin sat on a pin. How many inches did it go in?' " Old Mr. Trumble and Miss Macfarlane were having so much fun. After Marie finished dressing and the nurse put her hair up in pigtails she would go join them.

S. S. Rafferty

Murder by Scalping; or, The Invisible Indian

(The following is transcribed from the papers of Wellman Oaks, a former English bond slave, who lived in Connecticut between 1713 and the late 1750s. Some liberties have been taken with Oaks's original syntax, spelling, and the use of obscure colloquialisms to make his work more meaningful to the contemporary reader.)

It was the first time in my remembrance that Captain Cork and I were abroad in these Colonies without it costing him money for expenses, food, and travel. For once, *we* were guests, and we were not, thank Jehovah, involved in one of those "social puzzles" which so often divert the Captain's attention from profitable enterprise. Captain Cork calls them social puzzles; I label them nonlucrative excursions into the solution of murder, mayhem, and other forms of criminal skulduggery.

Ironically, our present sojourn at the Rhode Island home of Squire Norman Delaney was owing to a former case in which the Captain had ingeniously recovered the Squire's famous horse, the Narragansett Pacer. Eager to show his appreciation, Squire Delaney had written several times, urging a visit to his "ranch," as he called it. When the Captain finally accepted, I knew his motives were not vocational. Of late he had theorized that the Colonial diet could be improved if the present descending priorities of raising cattle for hide, tallow, and lastly, for meat, were reversed. No, Cork accepted Delaney's bidding because he loves good food and a chance to talk to an expert in any field.

The Delaney ranch was more like a plantation of the Carolinas than a New England farm. Located a few knots down from Point Judith, it featured acres of pasture land, an imposing Center Hall mansion, and, believe it or not, four separate houses of office. The Squire was a jocose Irishman with a plump wife and seven brawny sons who operated the ranch. This gave the Squire the leisure he required for the gentlemanly arts, with time left over for such minor municipal duties as keeping the peace between the Indians beyond the tree line and the frontier farmers.

The last about Indian affairs reminds me that I have forgotten to mention Tunxis, which is not easy to do. Tunxis is a tamed Quinnipiac, whose main employment is to serve as the Captain's shadow, even when the sun is not out. He goes everywhere with us. On the few occasions he has spoken to me, it has been in perfect English, but he is always jabbering away to Cork in aborigine. This usually leaves me in the dark about many matters, but I have learned to live with it. Just as I have learned to accept the fact that Tunxis will not sleep indoors at any time and that he takes a daily swim, even in mid-winter, which is a sight to shiver your liver. Needless to say, Tunxis was also a guest at Delaney's ranch—an outdoor guest by choice.

It was our third evening of relaxation at the ranch. We had supped well on a delicious bear's paw sauced in cranberries and had settled in for a cozy October night's conversation with pipes and bowl and glasses of usquebaugh, a Scotch-Irish corn liquor as potent as the Captain's own concoction, Apple Knock. I sat back and listened to these two fertile minds run the gamut of politics, enterprise, soldiering, women, and finally, as with all stout hearts well warmed by liquor, of philosophy.

"It is well to talk of good and evil," the Squire said, trickling the smoke from aside his clay stem, "but it's another thing to control it. Take crime, for example. Much of it in these Colonies is undetectable. I wouldn't hazard to guess how many culprits have committed foul deeds along this frontier and had them entered in life's ledger as accidents—people lost on the trail or taken by Indians. What stands in the criminal's way in these rude climes, I ask you, sir?"

"I do," Cork said. And he said it without pride or prejudice. "If all of us do in theory, some of us must do in practice."

I was thinking "practice and no profit" when Madame Delaney entered the parlour and announced a Mr. Goodman Stemple. It was prophetic that the discussion of the theory of crime should be interrupted by the reality of it. Stemple was a split-rail of a man, made all the coarser by his buckskins and moccasins. But his back-country appearance was belied by his educated speech. Although he was obviously agitated, he had himself under control and addressed himself to the Squire. His tone was cool, but his tale was horrifying.

"It's a scalping, Squire, right in my own home—my own future son-in-law. There's talk among the trappers and frontier folk about raising a punitive expedition against the Tedodas, and I'm afraid the talk is getting out of hand."

I must say I admired Delaney's ability to sustain a shock and to rebound from it in a logical state. Indian uprisings were considered a thing of the past in these parts, a dark, bloody thing long forgotten.

"Let's have the details," the Squire said, bidding Stemple to a chair. He first introduced the Captain and myself, and the flicker in the frontiersman's eyes at Cork's name was an unspoken awareness of my employer's reputation.

As it turned out, Goodman Stemple was no light under a bushel in his own right. He was the owner of Stemple's Redoubt, a prosperous trading post that serviced upcountry trappers and farmers in barter, or truck, as it is called.

Although the Redoubt flourished and Stemple's family grew, his children were all female. Eight daughters and not one son. It was this dilemma that had led to the scalping.

Stemple's eldest daughter, Faith, was, at eighteen, beyond average marrying age, but her father had steadfastly refused offers for her hand from local farmers and woodsmen. Since he was without a male heir and was likely to remain so, he wanted his affairs to pass to a son-in-law of some brainpower. His wishes seemed hopeless, however, until the arrival of Donald Greenspawn, the son of a distant cousin who had settled and fared well in the Maryland Colony. Greenspawn brought with him a letter from his father, which explained in vague terms that the young man had gotten into a bit of trouble in the South, and that a new start in the North was advisable.

As Stemple saw it, one father's misfortune was another's gain, for Stemple planned to marry off Faith to the newcomer. The trader admitted to us that Greenspawn indeed had some faults. Like many of his kind, he was a dandy, with a superior attitude which did not sit well with Stemple's customers, but Stemple felt that time would temper the situation.

In the two months that Greenspawn had been at the Redoubt, there had been several problems with the Tedoda tribe, whose medicine man, Shellon, had accused the Southerner of short-counting pelts. This Stemple ignored, since he too had had run-ins with Shellon from time to time.

With this background, the trader brought us to the night of the tragedy, which proved to be more mysterious than we first had suspected. Greenspawn had been killed and scalped in a closed room, and the only person who could have done it was Faith Stemple herself—or an Indian who could walk through walls. Either conclusion was patently ridiculous, but no other was in the offing.

Just two days before his death, Greenspawn had agreed to take Faith in marriage. As is the custom, a period of courtship was begun, which, of course, included bundling. Now I must interpolate here that bundling is often misunderstood at home in England. Lascivious minds might smirk at the idea of an unmarried couple sharing a bed, with only a wide wooden board between them. However, the custom is quite practical and innocent.

Since the couples are occupied at chores all day, there is left only nightfall for private conversation. Cabins on the frontier usually have only one fireplace, in the main room, and that is reserved for the parents. Small children are tucked into unheated attics, and the only place left for an affianced couple is an unheated side room. Thus, on these cold winter nights, it was logical to send Faith and Greenspawn to bundle, fully clothed and protected from temptation by the bundling board and by Providence.

On the eve of the tragedy, the trader went on, a certain Vicar Johnson was visiting the Stemples and was asked to spend the night before continuing his journey north. He accepted, and was bedded down in the main room on a pallet just outside the room where Faith and Greenspawn had bundled. The Vicar, it so happened, was stricken with gumboils, and, unable to sleep, spent the night reading a volume of Cotton Mather's sermons by the light of the dying embers in the fireplace. This good man of the cloth could answer that no one entered or left the side room all night save Faith and Donald.

"And yet, by Moses, gentlemen, when my daughter woke, there was Donald Greenspawn dead in his side of the bed, his head stove in, and his scalp gone." Stemple's composure failed as he spoke, and Delaney quickly poured another usquebaugh and bid him to quaff it.

"Thank you, sir," he said, tossing it back to his gullet. "There he was, all bloody pated and covered with gold dust."

"Gold dust!" Cork sprang from his chair.

"Yes, Captain, gold dust. All over his chest, the bed, and across the floor to the north wall. It was as if some spirit from the nether world had entered, done the foul deed, then left a trail of lucre behind him. It could only have been Indian magic, I swear. My little Faith would not harm a flea, much less scalp the man she was betrothed to."

"Astounding, eh, Cork?" the Squire said, relighting his pipe.

"What passes for astounding is often merely curious."

"You parry in the adjectival, Captain. If it's Indian trouble, I don't like it."

The comfortable appointments of the Delaney domicile were but a memory after twelve hours in the saddle. From long before sunup to almost dusk we had ridden through a panorama of this American country. We had left the beach and pushed inland past well plotted farms and villages and beyond into rude woods pocked with oasis-like clearings where hearty tillers of soil had thrown down the gauntlet to Nature.

As our journey had progressed, the woods thickened, the trails thinned, and I had the ominous feeling that I was riding closer and closer to the unknown. Finally, we broke through a cluster of elms to find ourselves in touch again with humankind. Ahead was the Redoubt, enclosed by a twelve-foot-high stockade. Over its huge gate was a weather-worn handpainted sign that read:

STEMPLE'S
GOODS AND WARES
FOR CASH OR TRUCK
THAT WILL ANSWER

Within the main enclosure was a large building and several smaller ones, all of log and mud-chinking construction. The large building, which served as Stemple's home, was a one-and-a-half-story house with a sloped roof wing attached. The wing was windowless, and I assumed it was behind these solid walls where Donald Greenspawn had met his Maker.

As we rode into the enclosure of the stockade we saw a cluster of thirty or forty men milling around one of the outbuildings which served as the trading post. They were woodsmen and farmers, all armed to the teeth with steel muskets and powderhorns. The sight of Squire Delaney brought them forward as we dismounted.

"It was the militia you should 'a brung, Squire," said one of them, a bearded man with a tomahawk at his belt. "Them Tedodas don't need a talkin' to, just a good lickin'." His statement brought grunts of approval from the group.

"Let's not get a lather up before we see what the trouble is, Delly Tremont, and that goes for the lot of you." The Squire continued with his chiding, which was proving to be a fine piece of diplomacy, when I noticed Cork disappear through the door of the main house.

Withdrawing from the group as inconspicuously as I could, I followed him and entered what was the main room of the Stemple abode.

It was not unlike the rooms in other backwoods cabins. To the left there was a dining board, and to the right several chairs were scattered near the fire. Two women sat holding each other's hands, while a man read to them from the Good Book. I had no trouble deducing that these were Goodwife Stemple, her daughter Faith, and the Vicar Johnson, although the latter startled me. I had expected a wizened old clergyman, infirm from gumboils, and yet here was a strikingly handsome youth no more than two or three years out of Divinity School. Goodwife Stemple's head was bowed at the holy words, but Faith looked straight into the Vicar's face, as if drawing warmth from his aesthetic countenance.

An open door to the far right led us into the murder chamber, where Cork became busy examining the body and Tunxis prowled around on all fours, like a bloodhound.

The sight of Donald Greenspawn in death was not pleasant. But even had he been lying there alive and unwounded, I would have been taken aback.

Where Stemple had led us, or at least me, to believe that Greenspawn was a lad, such was not the case. Despite his disfiguration, I could see that he was a grown man in his late thirties. His body, now rigid in death, had in life been dissipated and flaccid.

While I stood mutely in the background, Cork directed his attention to the gold dust on the earthern floor. He fingered it for a few seconds and then said something to Tunxis in aborigine. The Indian nodded and left the room. I swear by heaven I am going to learn Indian talk one of these days and surprise the two of them. But Indian talk or not, I had some suspicions of my own.

"Perhaps we had better examine someone to see if he really has gumboils," I said slyly to the Captain.

"Excellent idea, Oaks," he responded. "Perhaps I could get the Vicar to sing us a psalm or two while you peek into his mouth."

I knew he was jibbing me, but I let it pass. I thought at the moment that he was a bit ruffled that his own yeoman had so quickly come to the heart of the matter.

Cork left the bundling chamber and strode across the main room without stopping, until he was outside the house. And as always, I was right behind him.

The Squire's early diplomacy was eroding into anger as he held off the verbal attacks of the countrymen. The mob quieted, however, as Cork walked into its midst. Most groups do, because a six-foot-six giant with a grandee's barba and a plumed Cavalier's hat always commands attention.

"Goodman Stemple," he asked the trader in a loud voice, "who among these gathered here has ever asked for your daughter's hand?"

There were groans and a giggle or two from the group.

"Practically every man Jack of them, Captain. Jeb Howard there, and his brother Pete, Win Goulding and Tappins here. Just about everyone, even old Delly Tremont." As Stemple pointed to the bearded man, hoots were heard from the rest. Tremont did not like it and gripped his musket as if to menace one and all.

"Seems to be you're all turned mighty merry when we got murderin' Injuns about," he said.

"You are right, Mr. Tremont," said the Captain. "This is no time for jollity. You look like a man who knows his way with the redman, Tremont."

"He should," Stemple said. "That's how he got his name. Lived with the Delawares for five years, didn't you, Delly? Best trapper in these parts."

The bearded man relaxed a bit under the flattery and Cork went on, "The Delawares! Well, my compliments, sir. You learned a great deal along that great river's banks, did you not? I'll wager you are quite a fisherman, Tremont."

It all happened so quickly that it still boggles my mind to reconstruct the scene. As Cork talked, I didn't notice Tremont's trigger finger, but as he swung to fire on the Captain, Tunxis's knife smashed into Tremont's chest, deflecting the muzzle blast to the ground. I later estimated that the Indian had hit his target from at least twenty feet.

"Tremont's method was obvious from the first," Cork told us later that day as Goodwife Stemple served us a piping-hot corn pudding and generous cups of hard cider. "He was enraged at the thought of being spurned by Faith and sought vengeance on Greenspawn."

"But such an elaborate plan for a crude backwoodsman!"

"I don't think it was a plan, Squire. It was luck and everyone's ignorance that brought the Indian scalping into it. Tremont lurked about that night, and when all was quiet he removed some of the dry mud-chinking from between the logs of the north wall. It could easily be replaced and be dry by morning. Using an arrow attached to a tag line, he killed his victim as the Delawares catch fish, harpoon fashion.

"But when he tugged his line to retrieve the arrow from Greenspawn's head, he found he had caught more than death. You see, a close examination of Greenspawn showed me that this vain man was somewhat bald, and wore a wig piece, as is fashionable on the Continent. When the arrow was retrieved, the wig came with it—hence, the look of a scalping."

"And the gold dust, Captain?" Stemple asked.

"I suggest that you examine your strong box, Stemple. I think you'll find that your coins have been cleverly shaved since Greenspawn's arrival. And what better place to hide his ill-gotten gains than in the lining of a wig nobody even suspected he wore."

"So when everyone jumped to the conclusion that it was a scalping and Indian magic, Tremont just sat back and let the mystery grow," Stemple said.

"Yes, just as you jumped to the conclusion that Greenspawn was a man of quality. I think after Faith's harrowing experience, you might consider a man of the cloth for her."

Many months later I read of the couple's wedding in the Boston *Weekly Gazette*. When I showed it to Cork, he unkindly reminded me that I had suspected the Vicar. It was one of those times when I wished I spoke aborigine and he didn't. Cork and Tunxis would have got an earful.

Kay Nolte Smith

Reflected Glory

There was no need to wait another minute. His afternoon class had seemed to take place in slow motion, and then the drive home from the college had been prolonged by a wait at the liquor store; but all that was behind him now, while in front of him was a tall drink and a weekend in which to savor the magazine.

He opened the magazine, thinking that millions of copies were spreading across the country—that hundreds would reach the college alone—and found the article. He stared incredulously at a color photograph of himself that filled an entire page. The picture had been taken on the patio, seated just as he was now, and shot from such an angle that his figure, short and plump in actuality, seemed to dominate the house and the grounds. It was only when his breath returned that he realized how great was his relief. A smile inflated his pink round cheeks and his eyes, imprisoned in cages of tiny lines, shone for a moment like blue beads.

He looked, finally, at the page that faced his photograph and read the title: "A Visit with Jasper Kryler's Son." He read the subtitle: "As youth discovers the literary lion of the '30s, his son reminisces." Everything drained from his smile, leaving only the shape. He took a long drink and began warily to scan the text.

The first paragraph described him as a Professor of Creative Writing at Bentham College, appointed on the publication of his memoir about his famous father. He was relieved that neither his own age nor that of the memoir was given; it had appeared twelve years before, when he was still in his thirties, and was his only published book. He never could think of it without remembering his father's agent, who had edited the memoir, insisting on a virtual rewrite; his mouth tightened, but he reminded himself that the agent was now dead, and he smiled.

He turned back to the text, to a description of the town of Bentham and of "the handsome house in the New England hills where Jasper Kryler lived until his death." There was a discussion of the new generation of college students who formed "the Kryler cult," but there was no mention of his own classes, so he hurried on, skimming through the story of his father's career: the early struggle and the

213

escapades in Paris, the war years, the writing of the trilogy, the Nobel Prize, and the fatal solo flight across the mountains. Exit the old man, he thought impatiently, turning the page. But the article had ended. He had been quoted less than a dozen times, and always on the subject of his father's life. The quotation marks trailed through the text like ants.

He had known, of course, that he was being interviewed because he was Jasper Kryler, Jr. But still, he thought, the familiar phrase locking into place in his mind, serving as a bar to its own completion. He recalled the interview: the excellent lunch he had provided, the description he had given of his classes, and the book reviews he had written. Why had none of that been mentioned?

The answer sidled into his awareness. He drained his drink and flung his glass across the patio. It landed with a thud, intact, reminding him that when the old man had thrown glasses around, they had shattered with a splendid ring.

The front doorbell rang loudly. Although he was not expecting anyone, he decided that one of his colleagues must have seen the magazine. He thought of the amused tolerance with which those colleagues treated him; he had counted on the article to conjure respect from their faces, but now he felt paralyzed, unable to answer the door. He forced his legs to move, reminding himself that the article was a glowing tribute to the name of Kryler.

A young man stood on the steps, clutching a package. He wasn't one of the Bentham students, although he was dressed like many of them. A ragged poncho hung on his tall bony frame and his feet were bare. His face seemed bare, too, an expressionless canvas framed by long black hair.

"Yes?" said Jasper guardedly.

"I've got to talk to you. You're the only man I can talk to."

"Oh? About what?"

"Literature."

Jasper hesitated. "Come in."

Seated in the living room, the young man stared at its Art Deco furnishings in silence. "Now then," Jasper smiled, "why am I the only man you can talk to?"

"Because you're his son. You sure don't look it, though."

Jasper shifted in his chair but the young man went on, his pale eyes transfixed by space. "I read his stuff two years ago and it changed everything for me. Before that I didn't know who I was. He made me want to write. So I did. This book." He held out the package he had been clutching. "You've got to read it."

"If you want literary criticism, enroll in one of my classes."

The young man rose and came closer. "You've got to read it. It's like one of his. That's why I brought it to you. I couldn't tell anybody else about it, they'd laugh. I saved it for you."

"Who are you? Did someone send you?"

The young man shook his head, puzzled. "Nobody even knows I was writing it. If people asked me what I was doing, I'd move on to some other place."

"What place? Where are you from?"

"Oh, all over," said the young man vaguely. "L.A., Chicago, New Mexico—New York for a while. Sometimes you find a group, but it's better alone. You take a job, maybe, and then you move on. All you want to do is write. Like him."

"And what makes you think I would care?"

"Well, aren't you his son?"

Jasper rose, a hard red circle blooming on each of his cheeks. "I think you had better leave. Now."

"Sure," said the young man amiably. "I'll stay away till you've read it." He put down the package carefully. "I'll be back soon." He walked serenely to the hall, and then the front door clicked behind him.

"Of all the bloody nerve!" Jasper muttered. "Walking in as if he owned the place." Slivers of admiration sneaked into his anger and fed it. He thought of throwing out the package, and then he thought of something more satisfying: the look that would twist the young man's face when he heard that his book was bad.

Smiling, Jasper carried the package into the study, switched on the reading light, and took out his gold-rimmed glasses. He unwrapped the manuscript, which was not typed but neatly hand-printed. The title page read: *Pursuit of the Hunter* by Luke Blount.

When he reached the end of Chapter One, his smile had faded; when he finally turned the last page his mouth had become a taut seam. Despite his efforts to prevent it, the thought formed in his mind: the boy had written a Kryler book. The sentences were short and punchy; the hero was tough and sardonic; the story was filled with action and ended in defeat. If it weren't contemporary, Jasper thought, it could have been written by the old man.

He turned back to the title page: "by Luke Blount." By a nobody, he told himself. But he knew that the critics could turn Blount into a somebody; they could hail him as a hero who had reconciled the literary past and future. Jasper closed his eyes. Headlines swam into his mind: KRYLER REDIVIVUS . . . KRYLER'S NEW HEIR. Luke Blount appeared, and then the old man; their figures merged into one huge image. He willed it to topple.

He opened his eyes hastily. The room was quiet, unchanged, reassuring. A smile curled in one corner of his mouth. He had been assuming, he realized, that *Pursuit of the Hunter* would be published—but wasn't he the one to say whether that would happen? He began to compose the phrases with which he would send Luke Blount away.

But the phrases died before his memory of the young man's confidence, and the resentment which it evoked. Then everything died in the presence of a new fear: Blount, Jasper realized, could take the manuscript to someone else who might help him find a publisher. And word could get out that Kryler's own son had discouraged the author.

He drummed his fingers on the manuscript. To be or not to be? he thought, finding it unjust that he was confronted by such a choice. There would be no choice to make, he thought bitterly, if he had written the book himself. If *Pursuit of the Hunter* were by Jasper Kryler, Jr.—

He sat up slowly, visualizing the reviews—"Kryler Is Dead, Long Live Kryler!"—and surrendering completely to the fantasy, to the feeling of standing at some high podium with ant hills of crowds below him.

He looked down. There was Blount's manuscript in his lap.

It was some moments before he realized that he was thinking of murder, and he waited for the shock that he ought to feel. The shock was that he didn't feel it. "That's because I don't mean it," he said aloud, quickly, but he got up and began to pace.

Of course, he thought, if Blount really was a loner, a drifter, there would be no one to inquire after him or to care if he was missing.

He paused at his desk and began to doodle on a pad. The scribbles reflected his thoughts, he decided; they were idle and abstract. Impractical.

He sighed and moved to the windows, pulling aside the drapes. It was dawn. Unwilling to leave the room and take up the normal business of a Saturday morning, he stared restlessly at the lawns and gardens. Then his gaze was caught by a strange object near the potting shed. At first he thought it was a log, then he saw that it was someone sleeping—Luke Blount. He began to pace the room again, more slowly.

Two hours later he walked out and shook the sleeper. "Wake up and come in, Luke," he said. "Have breakfast and tell me more about yourself."

Two years later *Pursuit of the Hunter* by Jasper Kryler, Jr. was published.

Several months after Luke's visit, Jasper had taken out the manuscript, made a few minor changes, and then begun slowly to type it, putting out word at the college that he was writing a novel. He had decided against taking it to a literary agent and had approached a new aggressive publishing firm that responded eagerly to the Kryler name, promising him an intensive promotion.

Eventually a clipping bureau had begun to send him sentences and paragraphs about Jasper Kryler, Jr. and the book that would be published in the Spring. He had appeared on several television talk shows and had been invited to a party at which his fellow guests were important citizens of the literary world. It had seemed to him that each of these events was the turning of more and more eyes toward himself; he began to feel that he moved in a spotlight composed of people's glances.

In the Sunday book section of the country's leading newspaper, *Pursuit of the Hunter* was reviewed by a famous novelist. The review was entitled "Dry Sawdust Off the Old Block."

An influential literary magazine dismissed the book as "a puerile pastiche of Kryler Sr.'s works." A Los Angeles review declared: "It Doesn't Run in the Family."

Jasper saw advance copies of some of the reviews at his publisher's. It took him some time to read them, for the words kept jumping in rhythm with his pulse. When he had finished, he turned and denounced the publisher for promoting the book so widely and exploiting the Kryler name.

That night, alone in his study, he reread *Pursuit of the Hunter* and discovered that he had no opinion of it. He strained to recapture his former view; he even tried to feel that the critics were right, but his mind was like a heavy ball of dough.

The ball began to swell with the pressure of a thought: he had believed the book was good, good enough to bear his name. He had called himself a literary critic. What was he to call himself now?

He shoved the question back down into silence by hurling the book across the room. He stared at it and whispered, "But I didn't do it."

When the first of the reviews appeared in print, he stayed away from the college for two days, phoning in to say he was ill. But the secretary's voice held a note of amusement and he decided it would look better if he went in. Several of his colleagues made dry remarks and his students gleefully asked him pointed questions about *Pursuit of the Hunter*. By the end of the week even the most casual glance seemed to him a beacon of contempt. "But I didn't do it," he muttered as he walked away from people.

The clipping bureau sent him copies of new reviews, several of which were favorable. *Pursuit of the Hunter* was equated with the best of Kryler Sr.'s work by a weekly Vermont newspaper, and a sportsmen's journal recommended the book as good reading on a camping trip.

Jasper was certain that his colleagues had planted the reviews to humiliate him and he refused to leave the house again.

He drank steadily, but the liquor seemed to settle in his stomach, bypassing his mind. He sat for hours before the television set, waiting for a torpor that it did not induce. One night he was watching a talk show on which he had appeared a month before. The host and a guest were discussing the upcoming Father's Day. "And then," said the host, "there are kids who want to grow up and be *exactly* like dad. I think it's called the Kryler complex." The studio audience chuckled.

"But I didn't do it!" Jasper cried.

Into his mind, like a cooling salve, crept the memory of the thing he *had* done.

Bentham's chief of police was getting ready to leave the station after a long day when the desk sergeant came into his office.

"Sorry to hold you up," said the sergeant, "but there's a guy out here who says he's got to talk to the man in charge. He's from the college, name of Kryler, and he's acting strange."

"Kryler?" said the chief. "I used to know his family a bit. Read most of his dad's books."

"Shall I bring him in?" asked the sergeant. Chief Corey nodded.

A short pudgy man was then ushered into his office. "I want to prove I didn't do it," he said, sinking into a chair.

Half an hour later Chief Corey was frowning deeply over a story he had extracted with some difficulty. "Now let's see if I've got this straight. You claim that two years ago you killed a fellow named Luke Blount. You don't know where he came from, because he had no family and just drifted around the country. You don't know where his body is, because after you poisoned him with weed killer you put him in the potting shed and set fire to it, and the next day you broke up what remained of the body and scattered it in the weekly garbage, which was hauled away. Then you got some people to clean up after the fire and had a new potting shed built on the same spot."

"Yes," said the little man.

The chief frowned even more deeply and consulted his notes once more. "Then what is it you want to prove that you *didn't* do?"

"I didn't write the book. *Pursuit of the Hunter*—I didn't write it! Luke Blount did, and he brought it to me, but I killed him and stole it!"

Chief Corey's eyebrows shot up. "You mean your book that just came out? You claim somebody else wrote it?"

The visitor nodded.

The chief's lips began to quiver and he bit them. "Professor," he said finally, "my oldest boy tells me that people don't like your book, and I bet that's rough on you. I bet you wish you hadn't written it. But you can't come in here with a story like that and expect me to take it seriously. Confessing to theft and murder just so people won't think you wrote a bad book?"

"But I didn't!" The little man rose and looked off into space, as if he were addressing a crowd. "People have to realize. I didn't write the book at all. I did something much more difficult. I planned and executed a murder." His eyes darted back to the chief. "So you've got to prove it."

"Now how am I going to do that?" Chief Corey stifled a laugh. "The next time you kill somebody, better leave some evidence lying around. Especially the body."

"You can make inquiries, can't you? Luke Blount, he's got to be missing from somewhere!"

"Sure," grinned the chief. "But where?" Suddenly he snapped his fingers. "I thought that name sounded kind of familiar. You made that up out of your dad's books! I remember he had a fellow called Luke Horn, I liked him a lot, and then there was a somebody Blount, Harold or Harley, I think." He looked up at his visitor chidingly. "Now, Professor, couldn't you make up something more original than that?"

The little man's eyes closed, as if an inner weight had pulled them shut.

"I'll tell you what," said the chief genially, patting him on the shoulder. "We'll just say that you committed the perfect crime. Okay?"

When the desk sergeant had shown him out, the little man stood for some time on the steps. Then he moved uncertainly up the street. He thought he saw one of his colleagues approaching and turned aside hastily, pretending to check his reflection in a store window. But dusk had fallen, the light was gone, and there was no reflection to be seen.

Barbara Callahan

The Sin Painter

Retracing the series of events that shattered my tranquil existence is like running a motion-picture film backward. I'm sitting on a bench looking out at the sea, and the film keeps intruding. Images of two lost friends and a weatherbeaten barn skip crazily on the horizon.

Where shall I stop the film? I suppose at the central point. So I'll focus on a sign dangling from two rusty hooks at the Crafts Barn. It reads: Macramé, Découpage, Carvings, Portraits, and Sin Painting. Sin Painting—an intriguing illusion, an X-ray of the soul through the penetration of art, or a novel come-on devised by young artists to peddle their wares?

Sin painting—the silent shill that lured us into the barn. Valerie's husband and Martha's both told us about the sign. They had seen it on the way to a golf course in the New Jersey countryside. They knew of Valerie's unceasing quest for diversion and they thought this would be just her cup of tea.

Valerie is in her forties, heavy-set and good-humored, but restless. She was convinced that in a previous incarnation she had been a gypsy roaming the highways in an unending odyssey of discovery. The problem was how to fit a gypsy soul into the substantial chassis of a wealthy matron.

The unleashing of the gypsy occurred once a week when Valerie cruised to my door in her foreign sportscar. We'd pick up Martha, the wife of Valerie's husband's business partner, then set out for parts unknown. Valerie would conquer the highway, then abruptly turn off to a random side road. We'd pass housing developments fringed with adolescent trees until we'd reach a single-lane road, our corridor into the unexpected.

Once we stopped at a bungalow that housed the powers of Sister Solace who read our fortunes. A flea market snared us another day. Valerie paid $100 for a Portuguese water jug after being solemnly assured it had served Vasco da Gama. She escaped with only sunburn when we stopped at a pick-it-yourself strawberry patch.

Martha and I followed our gypsy to a nudist camp, discreetly tucked off the beaten path, which naturally was our path, where we listened for two hours to the manager's description of health *al fresco*. We chanced on a glassblowing settlement, a horse auction, and a brush fire for which we turned in the alarm and whose dousing we watched like fascinated schoolchildren.

I enjoyed these outings with Valerie, although in a previous incarnation I was probably a settled soul. Valerie's jaunts helped to dispel the depression that had gnawed at me since my husband's death. I don't have enough money to go out on my own when the blues descend, and Valerie, good neighbor and good friend, included me and paid for everything.

Martha, although she never said it, looked forward to our romps with the same enthusiasm one would reserve for two hours of root-canal work. Her lovely face was always drawn when she entered the car. I could understand because less than three months ago Martha planned to run off to Tahiti with Valerie's husband.

The telltale plane tickets were discovered by Valerie while checking John's suits to be cleaned. She began to hyperventilate. Gasping and sobbing, she phoned me and I took her to the hospital. John came immediately. He was grief-stricken and repentant. He confessed and vowed the affair between him and Martha would be over.

Martha's husband, Howard, came to the hospital too, and heard everything. The next day the four of them met and discussed the problem in an adult and civilized manner. The men swore that the business would not be affected. They would remain partners and friends. Valerie kissed everyone and dispensed her forgiveness. Everyone cried, except Martha.

When John told Valerie about the Sin Painting he said, "You don't have any sins, dear, but I thought you and the girls might check it out and bring us back another adventure story."

Valerie clucked delightedly at John's evaluation of her soul. She protested that she might have one or two little sins, and that the Sin Painter might do a "Dorian Gray" job on her.

She related this exchange to us on the way to the Sin Painter's. Martha said nothing. I felt a sense of uneasiness which I attributed to Martha's silence and a gloomy drizzle that runneled the windshield. Several times I wanted to turn back but I was sure Valerie wouldn't consent.

The sign creaked in the wind when we got out on a board that bridged the mud by the barn. There were five young people inside, working in sections of the barn assigned to their craft. A blonde girl tying macramé knots smiled at us.

"Where is the Sin Painter?" Valerie asked.

The girl laughed, and Martha shivered. I think she considered the girl's laughter obscene, as out of place as a joke at a funeral.

"Up there," she grinned, and waved toward the loft.

We walked to the ladder in single file. When we reached it, Martha tried to dissuade Valerie from climbing.

Valerie beamed. "Nonsense, I used to be a good gymnast. Don't let these extra pounds fool you."

Within seconds she had scaled the ladder and beckoned for us to follow.

"Ahab is calling us to the whale," Martha said softly. It was my turn to shiver.

The loft was presided over by a bearded young man. He was completing the face on a ship's figurehead.

"You are the Sin Painter, I presume?" Valerie asked.

He nodded.

"I suppose business is always booming in your line," she chirped. "Here are three vestal virgins to be sacrificed at the altar of truth. Do you need clues, or do you proceed, psychic-like, without any help from us?"

He shrugged. "I just paint what I feel."

"Oh, I see," Valerie said, "it's vibrations."

"No, lady," the artist sighed. "No vibes, no ESP."

"I'll go first," Valerie announced. "You'll pick gluttony as my sin, I'm sure. I *am* overweight."

She grinned as she sat down. "Gluttony should be depicted as a roast pig with an apple in its mouth."

I glanced at the artist, who was scowling. Martha sat down on an old milk can. The young man set up his easel to the accompaniment of Valerie's banter.

"Or gluttony could be a Henry the Eighth type banquet, don't you think, young man?"

"Ma'am, I paint your head and shoulders—no pigs, no banquets."

Valerie looked triumphant. "An instant Dorian Gray!"

"Sit still," the artist hissed. Valerie obliged.

Martha began to pace the loft. She examined more ship's figureheads and a group of tavern signs, all antiqued to look like originals. Wooden weather vanes attracted her next, and she spun them around.

I was tempted to see how Valerie's portrait was coming, but the artist's sullenness discouraged me.

"Okay," he said finally.

Valerie came to life again. "You're finished? You've painted bulbous cheeks and a bloated expression?"

The artist ignored her. She walked to the easel, but he blocked her way.

"When I've finished all of you, then you can look."

"Artistic temperament," Valerie cooed.

When I sat down, Martha was far across the loft staring into space. Valerie went below to browse. I didn't try to guess which sin would appear on my face. The truth was, I felt foolish about the whole affair.

When Martha posed, her face was a study in fear. I wondered how the artist could draw her as anything but a frightened woman. But fear isn't a sin.

I could hear Valerie laughing below and I became uneasy. I realized that all our trips had been agonies for Martha. Valerie was killing her with forgiveness, and today's trip had to be the most humiliating of all. Was Valerie hoping that the right sin would appear on Martha's face?

When the artist finished, he put the third sketch face-down on a table. Valerie's timing was excellent. Her head bobbed through the opening to the loft.

"Let's have a peek into our souls," she said.

"Thirty dollars," he announced.

Valerie feigned indignation. "Thirty dollars before we see the portraits? You must be afraid we'll be so horrified by your evil revelations that we'll run off without paying."

She pulled out three ten-dollar bills. "We can take it, girls, can't we?" she asked.

Neither of us answered. The artist stuffed the money into his jeans and Valerie headed for the pictures. She turned each one over. When she spun around, her face was contorted with anger and she strode over to the young man.

"What is this game you're playing? Do you take us for fools?"

He didn't answer. While Valerie continued her verbal assault, I picked up the sketches. I was stunned. Valerie looked like a middle-aged cherub, absolutely beatific. I looked unlike a penurious widow. My face was aristocratic. And Martha looked like a movie starlet. All her beautiful features were accurately copied. The sketches were flattering. And they were without sin.

Valerie felt she had been cheated by the Sin Painter. Before descending, she stalked over to the easel and knocked it down. The artist handed me the three portraits.

Valerie marched straight to the door. She didn't stop until she reached the board to cross to the car.

"I'm sorry for this cheap come-on," she said. "I'd like to rip that sign down."

She walked off the board and sloshed through the mud to the sign that still rocked in the wind. Suddenly she laughed. I was worried about the mood change.

"Come here," she called.

Martha declined. I struggled through mud oozing over my ankles. I looked at the spot on the sign that Valerie's finger pointed to. Above and between the "i" and the "n" in the word *Sin* was a small "g" which seemed to have been put there as an afterthought. It was painted in light pink while the other letters were in black. What it really said was Sign Painting. From the road we couldn't see the "g," and neither had Howard or John noticed it.

After dropping Martha off, Valerie talked on about how we'd been hoaxed.

"You see, it was a joke. No sign painter worth his salt would leave out a letter, but this one did it to attract attention. Our taciturn artist has a sense of humor. He mocked his craft on the very sign he painted."

"But why didn't he tell us," I interjected, "that it was an intentional mistake?"

"Oh, I guess most people see the real spelling when they get close to the door. We missed it because of the rain. When we got to the loft, we went right to the portrait section. We ignored the tavern signs which could be called sign painting. Oh, all these signs! It's so confusing. But you do understand?"

"No, I don't," I told her.

Valerie laughed. "Our young man does portraits, figureheads, and tavern signs. Each of them is in a different spot in the loft. We happened to settle right at the portrait part, and he assumed that's what we wanted. He must have thought all my chatter about sin painting was just so much aimless talk about the joke-sign outside."

"You're probably right," I said, "but I think he knew the reason we came."

"Why, dear?" Valerie asked.

"Because he seemed uncomfortable about the whole thing."

"I think he was simply an opportunist who didn't want to lose a sale," she said.

When I got home, I took my rolled-up portrait and slid it into the coffee-table drawer. I had had enough of the Crafts Barn and of Valerie. The day had been disturbing. I needed a cup of hot cocoa and a nap.

The phone riddled my sleep. Martha was choking out words I couldn't quite make out and coming over to see me right away. I had a brandy poured by the time she arrived. She didn't want it. Her hand was shaking as she unfurled her portrait.

She put it down on the coffee table and ran her finger over the ruffled collar of the blouse she had on when she posed.

"Look at the collar," she sobbed.

I looked and saw nothing. She grabbed my hand and ran my index finger over the outline of the ruffles. Then I saw it. In darker strokes, almost blended into the contours of the collar, was scripted the word *Adultery*.

Martha reached for the brandy. "Valerie, sweet forgiving Valerie. She put on a good scene for our benefit. She had all this prearranged. After John told her about the Sin Painter, she called him and hired him to do this to me. I knew she wanted to punish me for the affair with John."

I let her sip her brandy. "I can't believe she would be that cruel to you," I told her.

"Then let's compare pictures," Martha cried. "You'll see that yours is sinless."

I opened the drawer and smoothed out my portrait. Martha gasped. She pointed at my barrette which is engraved with my name, Ellen. I squinted at it and saw the *E* clearly drawn, and then I saw the *nvy* that followed. My barrette said *Envy*.

It's disconcerting to see your prime sin staring at you. When it's disclosed so openly, the only thing to do is confess.

"It's true," I told Martha. "I do envy, and I'm not proud of it. I envy your beauty and your wealth, and I envy Valerie her vitality and her wealth. I hope you'll forgive me."

"Please," she said, "there's nothing to forgive. I thought Valerie hated only me. I didn't realize she was so sick she'd lash out at you too."

"Let's burn these things," I suggested.

"No," Martha said, "get your coat."

In a few minutes Valerie, John, Martha, and I stood around Valerie's dining-room table. Martha was in command.

"I'm here to put an end to this cheap charade. There's no sense in pretending we can be friends. John, we've done irreparable damage to Valerie, and she simply can't forget it."

With that she opened up the portraits and indicated the sins. Valerie gasped and John swore softly.

"Our friendship is over," Martha said, "and as for the business—well, John and Howard can decide about that."

She started to leave but Valerie caught her.

"Please," she begged, "I didn't do this. There's some evil force at work. That young man did this on his own."

Martha pulled away.

"Let me get my portrait," Valerie pleaded. "He must have written something on mine too."

She ran to the library and came back with a rolled-up sheet, a sad diploma of our transgressions. We all studied it and John saw it first. He pointed to the outline of the curls piled high on Valerie's head. We followed his finger as he traced the letters V-*e-n-g-e-a-n-c-e*.

Valerie, struck dumb, sank back on a chair.

Martha took to her bed shortly after. She was convinced Valerie had wanted her to see the word vengeance so that she would be eternally afraid of her. She was certain Valerie intended to kill her.

John and Howard retained the business out of economic necessity, but they stopped being friends. Howard believed Valerie had devised the painting scheme to destroy Martha, and he further despised Valerie for bringing my failing into it. John stood by Valerie. He too thought the young man had uncanny perception. He tried to locate him but the Crafts Barn told him the artist had left for another part of the state. They had no forwarding address.

My own theory was that the young man had played a cruel joke, in the same vein as his sign. Valerie's harping on sins had annoyed him. He studied us and had made lucky guesses on our weaknesses.

I did wish I could tell him how his cruel prank ultimately led to Martha's death. Valerie couldn't bear Martha's withdrawal and wanted to be reconciled. She brought flowers one day and brushed past the housekeeper. When Martha saw Valerie, she ran from the room to the staircase, stumbled, and fell down the whole flight. Her body lay broken at the foot of the stairs.

In his grief Howard turned to me. We began seeing each other regularly. Neither of us ever talked about Martha or Valerie until today, as we were strolling on the boardwalk in Cape May. An artist was doing portraits. For a moment I thought it was the same young man, but this one was clean-shaven. I was about to mention it when he said, "Like to have your picture done, Mister?"

Howard shook his head. Then the artist offered him a reduced rate. Howard didn't want to appear cheap, so he consented. When the portrait was finished, the artist handed it to me.

It was quite good. In fact, it was too good. And the final piece of the puzzle fell into place.

When I confronted Howard, he admitted that the beardless painter on the boardwalk and the young man at the Crafts Barn were the same person. He was afraid of arousing my suspicions if he continued resisting the portrait. He hoped to get the painting before I could check it over.

He got off cheaply this time. When he went back to the Crafts Barn after he and John had seen Sin Painting, he paid the artist $300 to do the portraits of the three women who would come in. He described each of us, and named our sins.

Knowing Martha's vanity, he was sure she'd examine the picture carefully and discover *Adultery*. He had *Envy* drawn into mine to make me conscious of it, hoping I'd rid myself of the flaw. He thought I was a cut above Valerie and Martha, and had no reason to be jealous of them. He knew how terrified Martha was of Valerie and was sure *Vengeance* would unhinge her mind.

And Valerie, poor Valerie—she really did forgive and forget. It was the injured husband who could do neither.

I am sitting alone on the bench now. I cannot fault the Sin Painter for his part in this. After all, it was he who kept me from pursuing my relationship with Howard. When I studied the portrait of Howard, my eye had been drawn to the paisley design on his tie, and my finger traced the word *Hate*.

"Q"

Jean Darling

Never To Be Lost Again

Today is the first time the sun shone all this week. That's why I'm sitting here in the window seat. The view from this side of the house is still beautiful. It used to be nice from all the windows before Da sold the back garden. He sold it to property developers, as they are laughingly called, who took simply ages to build that great useless pile of brick and glass. They paid Da a good price for the property, but when it had been ours it had given us flowers and vegetables and birdsong each year. Now the brick monstrosity stands unrented, collecting dead leaves and broken windows.

Ron, the only son of the next-door neighbors, was a squatter before he came home this last time. Oh, not in the building out back, but somewhere right in the middle of town. The only reason he returned at all was because the house he shared with the rest of his commune was raided by the police and condemned as a health hazard. Da is very upset at having Ron living next door again and he'd do something about it if he could, but Da is helpless. Ron's father owns the house next door, so the boy has a perfect right to stay there.

I'm glad Da can't chase him away though. Ron always waves and smiles when he passes my window. And I don't really care if he was or is a mainliner; he's kind to me and I love him for it. I suppose you could sort of say it is a Romeo and Juliet romance—really! Guess what my name is! It's Julie—Julie Benson. My father, Da, is Terence Benson, an author and former Ambassador to various African countries.

Anyway, to get back to Ron. He is tall and slender, like a dancer. That's what I want to be too. I want my legs wound with ribbons, my feet clasped in tiny pink-toed shoes, a tutu swirling around my flying limbs. Someday you'll see me on television floating featherlike across the screen just like the ballet dancer I saw last night. I won't mind the hard work or the practising. Ron and I can be together that way.

We'll get married and keep right on dancing until we become as famous a ballet team as Rudolf Nureyev and Margot Fonteyn. Our clamoring public will throng the stage door each time we give a performance, and like the Red Sea they'll part for us to pass, their hands reaching out just to touch the air we've moved through. A long elegant Rolls-Royce will whisk us home to our "squat" in the building that has usurped Da's back garden.

I suppose you doubt the truth of the things I have been telling you. You should. Sunshine after rain always makes me daydream. I'm not a dancer and Ron is not my boy friend. Seriously though, I'm going to be a nurse. I became interested in nursing when Da was Ambassador to Mali. My ambition is to go where Dr. Schweitzer was—they need people there who are brave and strong like me.

Mother won't hear of it because I want to nurse in Black Africa. She's racist, as you can see. So, unless something drastic happens to make Mother change her mind, I suppose nursing as a career will have to be forgotten, even though Da has no objections. But what else can I do? I wouldn't like to be a secretary or a salesgirl in a boutique, and I must make up my mind. Time is growing short. I'll be twenty-two years old next month.

The sun has gone away, darkening the sky. Soon the clouds will shed large tears—tears almost as large as the ones locked inside my heart where even Da can't find them.

The rain will ruin Da's *Times* again because he won't carry an umbrella, ever. He says it makes him look like a comedy Englishman. He never wears a hat either, just uses the *Times* to protect him from the rain. Mother hates him to get the paper wet and says he looks like an old washerwoman with it clutched over his head. She doesn't really appreciate Da. Or me, for that matter.

But then, you see, she didn't really want me. Oh, there was nothing personal. Mother just didn't want children. She had neglected to tell Da of her aversion to childbearing prior to the wedding, but the dear man had been so smitten by her raven-haired beauty, I suppose he would have married her if she had confessed to being Dracula's daughter.

Theoretically I should have two siblings: I was the last of three pregnancies Da hoped through. The first two were terminated by Mother. Number one, a scant year after the marriage, she was the victim of a fall down the stairs. The second had been lost when Mother had ridden to hounds against Da's explicit wishes. When she miscarried for the second time, Da was heartbroken. More than anything he wanted a family. His brothers and sisters had twenty-seven children between them. Mother had come from a long line of single children, and she had decided the line would stop with her.

Years later, when she found herself pregnant for the third time,

Mother was off again, dancing, riding—she even took up trampolining. Nothing helped: I stayed the course. After I was born, Da gave up trying for a big family, deciding to quit while he was ahead, I suppose.

I'm sure it will come as no surprise if I tell you that Mother and I are not friends. I wouldn't care two cents if she dropped dead tomorrow. All my love is for Da. He is my idol. When I think that maybe someday I'll be without him, my heart almost shatters with the pain. If anything happened to him, I think I'd die too, I love him so much.

There goes the front doorbell. You hear that ugly clumping? That's Mother tripping daintily in her new platform shoes. She looks simply ridiculous stumping along. She always has embarrassed my dear dignified Da with her way-out dress. From beatnik to hippie, she has been "with it" for years. If it were the Twenties, Mother would be dripping fringe and champagne-warped slippers all over pianos in the wee hours of the night. But I shouldn't be unkind. She wasn't always foolish. I've seen pictures of her before my birth and, I must admit, she was beautiful. But no longer, with her bleached piled-up hairdo and platforms worn to dazzle her latest protégé.

The new boy is sallow and acne'd and teaching her Ancient Greek. I wonder if she finds Greek very much different from the modern French or modern Italian she studied in past lessons.

How brazen she is about these grotty little affairs! She flaunts them in my face, knowing I'd never tell Da, that I'd rather die than see him hurt. I try to make it up to him as best I can. He knows how much I love him. But it's difficult when one is grown up. A barrier seems to grow. No longer can I sit clasped tight in his arms, so tight that all feeling of lostness is cradled away. I'm too big for that now.

I remember once, long ago when I was quite small, he took me on a merry-go-round. Mother objected, making some malicious remarks that I recall to this day. I can still hear the cruelty of them and feel the terrible hurt. Da didn't say a word and finally she went away. We stayed on the merry-go-round and the horse went up and down, round and round. Lights flashed, cymbals crashed, music blared, and Da's arms held me so tight I could hardly breathe as he insisted over and over, "It's not your fault, little love. It's not your fault."

Soon after that Da put up the rear garden for sale. Those few months, while it was still ours, were the last happy times Da and I had together. I was on the brink of growing beyond lap size but he could still hold most of me snuggled in his arms. Every evening that long lovely summer he held me close and told me of the "Jumblies" and "The Duck and the Kangaroo." How I wished to be the Duck! To wear socks to keep my feet dry so the kangaroo would take me around the world on his tail, never to be lost or alone again.

If only I could have stayed little, never have grown up. The happy memories are all from those days so long ago when I was a child. Like the Sundays we spent at the beach before the terrible thing happened and we never went again. That last Sunday was just like all the others until Da said he'd go for ice cream. As soon as he was out of sight, Mother took me into the sea and swam swiftly out to the breakers. For a minute or so she held me, riding the waves. Then Mother disappeared.

After the momentary terror of being left alone had passed, I felt quite happy. Gentle waves led me down into a shimmering fairy tale where I'd find playmates—the Little Mermaid, the Water Babies, and other storybook friends. Yearnings would be fullfilled, everything would be as it should be. I was home at last.

Then strong arms snatched away the dream, and I was back to being me again. The sand felt warm and dry, and there was a pleasant hum of voices. Someone was rubbing my hands—Da, of course. He was the first person I saw when I opened my eyes. For a moment I thought he was wearing a wreath, then I saw it was a wreath of faces that haloed his head.

Curious bathers were murmuring concern and nodding encouragement on seeing that the half drowned little girl was going to be all right. Everyone was glad, every one of them, except one—Mother. She returned my gaze with eyes so filled with hostility, with such naked hatred, that all at once I understood. I had defied her once more by unreasonably clinging to life.

There goes the bell again. I wish she'd answer the door. I get nervous listening to it ring while the person outside is getting cold and wet. It's only the doctor, of course, but he's human and should be let in. He comes every Tuesday and Friday at this time, regular as clockwork. Supposedly he's Da's friend, but that doesn't keep him from having a bit of fun with Spring.

Spring is Mother's name. Ridiculous, isn't it? Spring, at her age! I do wish she'd answer, but she won't until she's finished primping. Fluff, fluff, long red claws combing through her recently bleached hair. I don't have to see her to know every move she makes. The flap of the puff against her nose, the wipe of lipstick, the fingers tracing the fine webbing of wrinkles that creep like mildew, blurring the fineness of her cheek.

She wants to go to Switzerland to have her face lifted, but she can't because Da doesn't have the money. She wants a new mink coat too, for all the good that will do her. Everything has gone on doctors' bills. Just this morning Da was on the phone to a real-estate agent. The man didn't seem too hopeful—nobody really wants a Georgian white elephant of a house as large and cold as ours is. So Mother will have to grow older and uglier, colder and poorer. There is no way now for her to avoid the misery that old age will bring to her.

Ah, at last that horrid ringing has stopped and the wet Dr. Madison has finally been admitted. And here they come, straight as arrows into this room. Oh, oh, look who's slinking in their wake. The little Greek protégé. This could be interesting.

I wonder if she has any idea how unwelcome she is, and the doctor, not to mention the Greek. Mother comes near and dabs in my direction with her handkerchief. Dr. Madison glances at me briefly before settling himself by the fire. The Greek boy sulks in the shadows.

An ear-shattering crash of thunder startles the handkerchief from Mother's hand. The storm shades the room with false night. Mother moves toward the light switch, then, changing her mind, she borrows the doctor's lighter. Soon the room springs to life again with the cheerful glow of candles. That's Mother for you, always the poseur.

But in her zeal she makes one unbelievable mistake. She lights the candle that stands on the taboret in front of my window. She's sitting over there beside the doctor, smoking and chattering like a schoolgirl. The Greek boy is watching them, but nobody is paying the least attention to me. Here, at last, is the chance that I have been waiting for all these years, since that Sunday on the beach.

With one bold stroke I will solve all Da's problems. He'll have money from insurance policies, and then maybe he'll marry some lovely young woman who will give him the family he's always wanted.

If only I can knock over the candle without being seen. Oh, please God, help me now to free Da. I hit the candle—it's rocking. Oh, no! The wrong way! Get away from the curtains! Oh, God, what will I do, what will I—

But look! A breeze has fluttered the curtain across the tiny guttering flame, and the curtain has caught fire! Oh, see the hungry fire, the lovely hungry fire! Goodbye, Mother! Goodbye, Dr. Faithless Friend Madison! Goodbye, Foolish Greek Boy! Oh, Da, be happy!

Flames leaped up to welcome the falling roof. Water arched into the gutted shell of the once-beautiful house. Just a moment before, a man had stood black against the flames, and in one sudden thrust shoved a wheelchair out of the inferno to safety. Then he was gone, swallowed in a burst of flame that enveloped the old house.

A patrolman stood talking to a tired fireman lit by the nickelodeon flicker of the fire.

"How'd it start?" asked the cop.

"Crippled kid, Julie Benson, knocked over a candle," answered the fireman.

"Any casualties?"

"One. The crippled kid's father. He got home just in the nick of time to save the girl. Her mother was too hysterical to do anything but scream. Two men saved from the fire, too—a foreign kid and a man who says he's a doctor. They're in pretty bad shape." The fireman's voice was hoarse.

"Some kind of dame to run out and leave her kid, even if she was hysterical." The cop took off his hat and wiped the sweatband with a handkerchief.

"Yeah, some dame! But she sure has all the luck. She's just become a very wealthy widow. The house was insured for over a hundred thousand, and her husband carried a life policy twice that big so that the kid, Julie, would never have to worry. If it's a double indemnity, that woman certainly will be well heeled. But I wonder what will happen to the girl."

The fireman looked over at the blanketed figures being helped into the ambulance.

"She'll have the best care money can buy, I suppose. What luck! And all because that poor helpless kid accidentally knocked over a candle."

The cop put back his hat and started on his beat once more.

"Q"

Etta Revesz

Like a Terrible Scream

Me, I just sit here and wait until the man outside push the little button and the door open with a small click and the Father walk out. The Father, I know him since I be five, which is now eight years. I bet he never think he come to see me in lockup. Kid lockup they call it but look like real grown-up jail to me.

I look out the little window for two days now. All I see is sky and maybe a airplane go by. The bed is clean but the floor is cement stone and hard on my leg. It is the door that I hate with much feeling. It is gray and iron, like the brace I wear on my leg. The little square window is high and I am yet too little to see out it and down the hall. I know a man sits there by a high desk and pushes buttons for many doors like I have to my cell. Yesterday I push up tight against the door because I am afraid. I think maybe I am the only one left here. But all I see is the ceiling of the hall and it is gray and not so clean.

It is hard to sit here and see the Father leave. He try. He try hard to make me tell why I do it.

"Confess, my son," Father Diaz say. "Tell me why did you do that terrible thing? You could not have realized. You were not thinking right!"

The good Father he lean his head way down and I think he cry, but I shake my head. How can I tell him? If I tell him the reason why I have done this it would be all for nothing. So I let him put his hand on my head and I say nothing.

"Kneel, my son," the Father say. "If you cannot tell me, tell God. It will help."

"No, Father," I say. "I cannot kneel."

He look very unhappy then, almost I think he will slap me when he take his hand away from my head. But he does not.

"A boy that cannot kneel and ask forgiveness from God is lost," he say and then go to my iron door and punch the little black button that tell the man at the desk to open up.

Now I sit here on my cot and wait for the Father to leave. My leg is out straight with my iron brace beginning to hurt me. Always at this time when night sounds start, Rita come home and take it off

235

for me and rub my leg. Her hands, always so soft, rub away the
stiffness. She talk to me about things outside. Always she ask to see
my picture that I make that day. It was Rita that buy the paper and
black crayon for me to draw. And last Christmas she bring me a box
of paints! How much I do not guess it cost, but I know it cost much.

I feel in my eyes the water begin, but I want not to cry. I look
again at Father Diaz's black suit. Like a crow he looks, standing
with his arms folded close to his side like wings. I cannot stop my
eyes from making tears. I pretend it is because my leg hurts and I
try not to think of Rita.

I decide to tell Father Diaz that I cannot kneel because my iron
brace does not bend. Then he would not think that all his teaching
about God and the Blessed Virgin was for nothing. But it is too late.
I hear the click and the door pop open and I am alone again.

Soon they will bring me food. I do not like noodles and cheese.
Cheese should be on enchiladas. Noodles and cheese and maybe
wheat bread with edges curled up like a dried leaf. Next to it a
spoonful of peanut butter which I hate. It glues my tongue to my
teeth. I think back to what Rita always bring to me.

Every night before she go to her job she come by the house with
a surprise. First she take off my iron brace and rub my leg and then
she put the brown bag in my lap and we stick both our heads close
to see what big pleasure is there. Sometimes I look up and see her
eyes big on me and smiling when I find a bag of candy or a pome-
granate or even a new paint brush. At such time I feel a big pain
over my heart and my jaw hurt from not crying. Rita she hate for
me to cry. How can she know that it is for love of her that I cry?

Sometimes when only Mama and I are home I stop my painting
and look out the window. We are high, two stairs up, but I can see
the branches of the tree growing from the brown square of land in
our sidewalk. It is not very healthy this poor tree, and has dry brown
limbs with no leaves much. But still I watch the sun on what leaves
are still there. It is when the sun is low and shines even with my
tree that I like it best. Long fingers of white light run sharp from
the center and when the wind blows everything shoots gold and
shining. It is like a sign from God that the day is gone and Rita will
run soon into the room and call out.

"Pepito," she calls, "I am here again. Your ugly old sister is here
again!"

I pretend I do not hear her and then she come and put her hands
around to cover my eyes from behind.

"Guess who it is?" she ask in make-believe man voice.

"My ugly old sister!" I say and then we both laugh. My sister Rita is not ugly. Sometimes she have a day off and she let me draw her picture. She sit by the window quiet while I look at her and put my markings on my paper. Sometimes I forget to move my hand when I look at her. Rita have long black hair and she tie it back so her neck looks very thin. Her mouth is still but when she think I am not watching her lips move a little and I think she is telling secrets to herself. It is her eyes that I cannot draw so well.

When I look once they are laughing and show a joke ready to be said, but when I look again, I feel I must weep. Once I really start to cry at least a year ago when I was only twelve. Rita rush over and hug me.

"My little Pepito." She touch my cheek. "Does your leg hurt? I will work hard and save—oh, I will save so and will take you to a big hospital where the finest doctors will make a miracle on your leg."

"No," I tell her. I can never lie to Rita even when I want pity. "It is my love for you that make me cry. You are like Sunday music."

She just laugh then and the next day when she come she say, "Here is your Sunday music for your ears to hear on Wednesday!"

I love my Mama and Papa almost as much as I love Rita. But Mama sigh often as she count her beads and wears black instead of colors bright and gay like Rita. I remember long time before, when we first come to city, Mama sing always. Sometimes she dance with Papa when Papa say about the big job he going to get.

"No more driving the junk truck for me," say Papa. "Lucerno family will be on easy street soon."

When Papa finish driving truck for Mr. George Hemfield he go to night school. When I wake up at night from the couch where I sleep because my leg hurt, I see Papa sitting at the kitchen table with books. All is quiet. Only sleeping sounds and the tick-ting of the wake-up clock and the hush sound of the books when Papa close them. Then I hear him push back the chair and walk to his bed.

Carlos and Mikos, my big brothers, sleep in the bedroom. They have the big bed and Rita sleep with little Rosa in the little bed. Rosa is very small, only three years, and Rita call her Little Plum. Mama and Papa have the back porch for them. Papa fix it up and when Mama say, "What about the heat, my husband, when the winter come?" Papa he laugh and grab Mama as she pass him to the stove and say, "I will keep you warm—like always!"

"You crazy fellow, not before the children!" And Mama push his hand away like she is mad but I see her lips smile. Mama think I know nothing about life because I stay at home, because I do not run the streets and only walk outside for special days like Easter and Christmas and Cinco de Mayo when the world is spinning to guitar music.

At first when we come to city I go to school but after a while the stairs and long walk is too much. Rita try to carry me but the iron prison on my leg make her tired and once she drop me and the iron bend and cut into my leg. I learn, but not very much. It is hard for me to read the words and the teacher do not call my name very often.

Rita try to help. She is in the high school and she show me to make my letters. But I cannot do well. At my desk I draw pictures of what I want to say. It is much easier and soon the school hall show them on the walls.

One day the Principal give Rita a note for Mama to come and talk with him. Papa he go instead and after a long time in the Principal's office he come out and we walk home. Papa walk very small steps and not even holds my hand from sidewalk to car street. When we get to house Papa pick me up and carry me up to Mama. He hold me very tight and push my face to look behind him but I know he angry, sad angry. He tell Mama that a special teacher is going to teach me at home because they have no place for me at my school.

The teacher come but not for long. After a while another lady come to talk to Mama about budget and say that if Mama bring me to Down-Town I go to special school. Papa get mad and go Down-Town but come back soon. He say nothing and now I stay home and draw much.

I hear the pop of my iron door and a kid like me come in. He is an old one in experience at this place and they let him bring the food. He push open my door with a foot and carry in the tray. I watch him look where to put it.

"Here's your supper, Crip," he say. "Where d'ya want it?"

I sit up and look at what there is to eat but all I see is red jello and two pieces of brown bread poked into a sauce of broken meat. I take off the square paper box of milk and tell him to take the tray. He looks worried at me.

"Look, Mex," he speak low. "Not eating won't help."

I shake my head and lean back on my cot and he leaves. It is almost dark now in my little gray room. I can put on a light. It is held away from me in a wire basket like a muzzle for a dog, but I have nothing to look at anyway. So I stand and press against the stone wall so I see up and out the window into the soon night.

In the sky is fuzzy lines of color, like the cotton when you pull it out of the box and it spread fine in your hand. Somewhere I hear a noise and the red and green light of a airplane pass my eyes. So small it is, like a ladybug. So far away and such a small spot, much bigger looks the bird that flies closer to my window, not knowing that night is close and he should be in his nest. I am all alone now in my darkness.

It is like the darkness that came to our house the day Papa come home from new job hunting. For long days Papa try for new job, after he come home from school and hold high his beautiful piece of paper with gold words saying he is a educated man.

"This is just the beginning," say Papa. "I am just the number one to bring home the High School Certificate. Look, kids," say Papa, "this little piece of paper will be our passport to a new life."

We have a good dinner that night and Mama make a toast. "My man, with all his education, will be *presidente* yet!" Papa kiss Mama then and she let us all watch. Rita dance that day. She was 15 and the next one who would bring home such a paper. But it was not to be.

Papa's paper was only words and no one pull Papa in by the arm and give him a good job. Each day it was harder and harder to see his face at night and each night he have more and more red wine. At last Papa go back to his old job. It was a big truck and Papa was very tired at night after filling it with broken cars and iron and rusty pipes. Soon Mama cry all the time and then Rita stop her school. She come home one day and say she have a fine job that pay much money but she have to work at night. Papa ask who boss is, but Rita say he is Up-Town man and that Papa would not know him.

Rita sleep late now every morning and sometimes she look sad at me when she say goodbye to go for job. Always she look tired and one day she and Mama have big fight. Rita say she move out nearer her job and Mama say, "No," but Rita go anyway. She tell Mama she come every day to see me and bring money every week. The house seem so still now and Mama sit long times with little Rosa on her lap and I hear her say "Little Plum" over and over.

Now for me the day begin when Rita come, for Rita keep her promise. One day she come and after we eat the caramel corn she bring, Rita tell me of a secret she and I will have. It is a plan to make me walk straight without iron brace.

"Pepito," Rita say and put three dollars in my hand, "I want you to hide this and every week I will give you more until there is enough and then we will visit the doctor who fixes legs."

We find empty box that oatmeal come in and cut a hole in the round top big enough to fold money into. It is our secret hiding place and I push the box under the couch where I sleep. Each week Rita add more money, sometimes even more at one time.

Our home is not very happy now. With Rita the smiles have gone. Carlos and Mikos are big now. Carlos is in the high school but want to stop and he and Papa fight now. Carlos say to Papa, "Old man, you live on your daughter's hustling!"

I watch as he pull himself and like a bear try to squeeze the words back into Carlos' mouth. Papa's big hand slap out at Carlos but he is quick and runs out and down the steps to the street. For the first time I see Papa cry, and when Mama come in and ask he will not tell her what hurts him.

I cannot sleep that night. I know what hustling is. It is the walking of the streets that a woman does to offer her body to any man who will pay. I have hear Carlos and Mikos talk when they think I sleep. I hear the names of some girls and then rough words and then small swallowed laughter. I am much older than the pain in my legs. I am as old as the new leaves on my poor tree on the sidewalk.

My pillow is hard that night and I close my eyes against my fear. It is then that Rita's face come before my mind. I see her smooth skin and the quick way her body moves and the softness of her breast. I have watched her grow more beautiful in form as in heart. I have made the curve of her with my crayon on white paper. Do not think I look upon her with more than a brother should. But is it wrong to see beauty when it grows before your eyes? Her name is really Margarita, like the white flower with the golden center.

I cannot bear the evil pictures that pass before my eyes, and I cross myself and insist to my mind that Carlos spoke in anger and said a lie. I prefer it so.

When Rita come that next evening I want to tell her what Carlos say so we could laugh about it together and she could slap his face. But I keep silent. When she ask me why I do not smile I tell her a lie. I say my foot hurt.

"Come," she say, "get our box and let us count the money."

We open the top and count it in her lap. "We need more," Rita say. "I will work overtime."

I nod for I am afraid to ask and afraid not to ask. For the first time I want Rita to leave.

It is weeks before I sleep well and I blame it on my leg but I know it is Rita that worry me. Now I look at her more closely as if I expect to see a sign that all was a lie. Once I start to say something.

"A woman that sells her body." I stutter over the words. "What would one call her?"

Rita look at me quick and pulls her lips tight, then smiles. "Don't tell me that my little Pepito is growing up!"

She put her hand on my head and push my hair off my face.

"You do not answer me," I say.

"A prostitute." She turn away from me and her hand drop.

"That is an evil thing for a woman to do, isn't it?" I say.

"It all depends."

She turns and picks up a big bag. "Look what I brought you tonight."

After we eat the big oranges she lean her head against mine and speaks into the room.

"You must not concern yourself with ugly things. You must see only beauty and put it on paper. I do not know any prostitutes and neither do you."

She leave soon after and before I sleep that night I curse my brother Carlos and his vile tongue.

It goes on as before now with Rita and me. Soon it is her birthday. She is to be 18 in a week and I decide to buy her a present. Mama has said that 18 is a special age for a girl and I want to make it fine for her birthday. The only money I have is under my couch in the oatmeal box. I decide within myself that it would not be wrong to use some of it for Rita's birthday present.

Mama is surprised when I tell her I will go down the stairs and on the street until I explain to her what I want to do. I tell her I have saved some money and I show her the $20 I have in my pocket. She help me down the first steps and watch me as I walk down the street to where the stores are.

The stores are filled with fine things and I move slowly from one window to the other. Before one I stop a long time and almost decide to buy a small radio. But I think maybe a pretty dress would be better for Rita. A white dress to make her hair blacker than the midnight and the white like snow against her golden skin.

Now I look for a dress shop. Across the street is a large store with dresses like a flower garden. At the corner I stand waiting for the street light to change when I hear voices behind me. It is what they say that make me turn and follow them instead of crossing the street.

I do not know all of them but one boy is Luis. He is older than Rita but was in school with her and sometimes Carlos bring him to the house. It is when I hear him say the name Rita that I decide to follow them.

"Yeah, that damn Rita," one boy say, "since she move Up Town into the big time you can't even touch her any more."

"I hear she hooked up with some pimp who is really rolling in clover." They all laugh.

My blood! I feel it leave my body and sink to the sidewalk. Surely the earth will open up and these boys will fall into hell! I cannot walk any more. They turn the corner and disappear. My heart is dead inside of me. No longer can I doubt what I feared. No longer can I doubt.

I feel people shove at me as they pass me and still I cannot move. Long later I take steps, slowly down the sidewalk. All the time in the center of my throat is a sore spot I cannot swallow away. Like a terrible scream that has no sound.

It was when my leg hurt so much that I stop and lean my face against the smooth glass of a store window. Cool it feels on my hot cheeks. My eyes I close tight—so tight it hurts. Colors dance in my head and run to stab my heart. My leg beats out the music of pain.

No longer can I stand the ache, so I open my eyes again. There, under my look, I see the guns. Like soldiers ready to march when the general shout out a command. They wait quietly, these black snails that carry death inside a shell.

For a long time I look at these guns. Has not Father Diaz said that death is only another life? And a better one?

I move to the store door. It is glass with a wire across it, like the knitting Mama does, all looped together. I put two hands on the door handle. It is stiff and cold like a gun, I think. Down I push and shove open the door. I stumble on a mat and my iron brace rips at the rubber as I pull my leg free. A small bell shakes and makes a ringing. I walk in.

When the police ask me I shake my head and when Mama and Papa cry in the courtroom for children and the judge ask me why

I kill my sister on her birthday I still am quiet. They would not understand how hard a thing it was to do. To lose your star when you are thirteen is to walk blind on the earth. Better this way than to see your star fall from the heavens and end in mud. Always to me Margarita will be like her name, pure white on the outside and golden in the center.

And that is why I lie here on this cot with the black of my little room hiding me from the night of nothingness and I am called a murderer.

Dorothy Benjamin

Sound of a Distant Echo

Mereno assumes the perennial boxing stance, his muscles bulging, and jabs the air one-two in my direction.

"El bravo," I sneer, and rear back against the sink as his fist cuts through the air like a sickle.

Lowering his fists he growls, "Where's my lunch?" He opens the refrigerator, pincers his beefy hands around five cans of beer, swings the door shut with an oddly graceful twist of his leg, and slams the cans down on the table.

Hurriedly I grab the bread knife from the sink drainboard, slice in three the hero sandwich I'd made before our fight began, and place the sandwich before him. Mereno scans it, a master architect inspecting a student's practise model, seeking a flaw for which he can gleefully pounce on the hapless student.

"Gonna eat?" His black eyes flick over me as if I'm an addendum to the design. Though my nerves scream no, I nod yes. The better part of valor is to pacify him. He hates to eat alone.

Turning to the sink where the sandwich makings are spread on the drainboard, I glance out the window above, the only one in this dump from which I can glimpse the summer sky, and wonder: What am I doing in this place? I, who love the sky, trees, green grass, who grew up on the land?

I remember the feel of spring earth under my bare toes—my stepmother Ethalyn's herb garden of sage, thyme, rosemary—the green oasis beyond the furrowed field where I'd hide shielded by a canopy of buttonwood leaves, to brood over my constant yearning for approval and affection from my father, a morose bull-necked man given to cuffings and black looks—

"What the hell is takin' you so long?" The cans of beer jump as Mereno pounds the table and I am wrenched back to the reality of the present.

Someone coughs outside our door. That will be Justina, Mereno's babytalking older sister. In a moment she'll waddle in. Her sly cough is a warning not to be caught intimo, Justina's way of letting me know she never forgets I'm not her brother's wife.

"Hawhoa, Ahwison. Just get up?" Justina's eyes, embedded in fat, gleam like jet-black marbles. A twin to her mother, except for Mamacita's matriarchal air of authority.

Tugging at my half-buttoned blouse, I glance into the cracked mirror propped on the windowsill, my reflection split into jagged halves, and make a one-handed stab at smoothing my unkempt hair. My hair is what attracted Mereno in the beginning. He has a thing about blondes, but until me nary a natural one.

So used to his blondes were Mamacita and Justina that when I met them each one asked, "Wha' bottle that color from, eh?" To which Mereno answered proudly, "Her hair is natural." I used to take care of my hair then, brushing the regulation one hundred strokes every night.

Pushing for status, I play the hostess and ask Justina, "How about lunch?"

"H'm—" Her eyes follow the knife as I slice my sandwich. "I had an erwey breakfast." If Justina's had an erwey breakfast it's a sure bet she'll have an erwey lunch.

I begin preparing another sandwich, thinking how ludicrous for a forty-year-old to babytalk. It's as if a mannerism Justina once affected had become routine. It reminds me of the girls I met when I went east to college, who took b*ah*ths in b*ahth*tubs. I suppose their affectations became routine too. Though I wouldn't know. In the throes of first love, by turns on Cloud Nine feeling loved at long last, then in despair over the affair's abrupt end, I didn't crack a book and dropped out, and was too scared of my father to go home.

I reach for the kettle. "Justina, I'll make tea. Okay?" Neither of us drinks beer. Mereno, I notice, has already emptied a couple of cans.

Justina gives me her no-yo-comprendo act. "Coffee, Ahwison. It's not too much troubew—?" She comprendos all right. Mereno doesn't allow me to buy instant so I'll have to brew a whole damn pot for her. I purse my lips and reply, "No trouble at all."

Sitting in his undershirt, as my father always did at the table, Mereno flexes his biceps and grunts a bueno. He can't stand his sister, or his mother for that matter, but they're *his* and woe betide me if I fail to observe what he considers the amenities.

Justina plunks herself down beside Mereno, giggling, and punches his biceps on the arrowed twin heart tattooed there, oblivious of his scowl. Brother and sister like to pass themselves off as pure Spanish, but Mamacita once let it drop that her muchachos are only one-quarter Spanish. Give or take un poco.

At the sink I run water in the pot, dump coffee into the basket, and slap the pot down on the stove. Mereno shoots me a dirty look and I move quickly to the window to keep from making a retort. He has a low boiling point. Someday, sure as I stand here, he will bash my face in. Not that he hasn't already tried.

Once, if a man laid a brutish hand on me, I'd vamoose like a streak of wind. With Mereno I exist on a residue of hope, my rationale for remaining with him. I remember that he gave me a home three years ago Christmas, when I was bitter and broke.

The guy I'd been living with skipped, leaving me with a raft of unpaid bills. I had barely $13 to my name, so I skipped too, vowing the next twosome was going to be legal. Now I just wanted security. At a loss what to do, where to go, I paused in front of a store displaying gift blouses, and over the loudspeaker came a voice singing: "I'll be home for Christmas." With something akin to shock I remembered Ethalyn's last words to me the day I left for college, as if she'd had an intimation of the future: "You'll be home for Christmas?"

"Of course!" I'd cried, so nervous at leaving home at 17 that I couldn't wait to return.

"Come *on*," my father had pushed me, scowling as usual. He drove me to the railroad depot and left without a backward glance after imparting a few words of fatherly advice: "Don't come back a know-it-all." He'd never shown me a bit of affection, so why should I have felt bereft because he didn't show me any then? How he must have taunted Ethalyn when, embroiled in my freshman affair, I wrote I wouldn't be home for Christmas after all. It was Ethalyn who had encouraged me to try for the scholarship.

I'd been ashamed to write her after dropping out, but standing in front of the store I decided to send her a blouse for Christmas, certain she'd need to be saving her old worn one to wear to church, if it were up to my father.

I wanted to write *Mother* on the card accompanying the blouse, but I hadn't called Ethalyn that since I was eleven years old when I discovered she wasn't my real mother. Memory of the long-forgotten sound of Ethalyn's rocker came to me—like the sound of a distant echo. I fled from the store, boarded a bus, not caring where it went, and rode to the end of the line. It was spitting snow, and in the deepening dusk I felt as bleak as the alien neighborhood I found myself in.

Spotting a *Waitress Wanted* sign in the dingy window of an all-night restaurant, I entered, feeling as if I'd been handed a reprieve. I had worked as a waitress. The hard-eyed dame behind the counter snappishly told me I wouldn't do and, let down, I headed for a table in the corner, planning to sit out the night nursing an occasional cup of coffee with the last of my money, and in the morning look for work and a place to sleep.

Several men seated at the counter immediately began behaving like frisky colts. Swiveling on the stools, shadowboxing, laughing uproariously, all the while casting oblique glances at me. A double-B girl—big-breasted and broad-beamed—I was used to that reaction.

The woman came over and glowered at me as if I were polluting the atmosphere. "What'll you have?"

"Coffee, please."

"That all?" she sniffed.

The door opened and the men's attention shifted to the bull-chested man who entered, brushing snow from his wavy black hair. "'Ey, Mereno!" "Que tal, amigo?" "Mer-*ren*-no!"

Flashing white teeth, Mereno swaggered toward them, his glance sweeping sidewise over my hair. The woman brought my coffee, set it down hard, her manner daring me to protest as liquid sloshed over the saucer onto the table.

In two strides Mereno was at the table, exuding charm, and asked her to bring me a fresh cup. Sliding into the chair opposite, he told me that Mereno was his last name, and since his boxing days he preferred it alone—his given names were unpronounceable anyway. I was almost mesmerized by his gorgeous black eyes.

Mereno was his mother's maiden name, I learned. His father had run off when he was ten and he'd beat up any kid who dared call him by his father's name. Remembering my own suffering at eleven, I felt a kinship with that anguished ten-year-old boy.

"Broke?" Mereno asked sympathetically. He lit a cigarette and said softly, "You can stay at my place."

"No, thanks," I said sharply, thinking of my vow.

He took a couple of puffs, eyeing me thoughtfully. "Don' worry. I won' lay a hand on you."

My head went down and I wept as I hadn't wept since the early weeks at college, when I was so lonely and homesick I cried myself to sleep every night, only then understanding why Ethalyn had turned away instead of bidding me goodbye the day I left home. I never saw Ethalyn cry. But many a night from my bed I heard the sound of her rocker in the kitchen as she nursed her wounded spirit.

Grateful for the haven Mereno offered me, I cleaned up his two-room dump—washed the dirty walls, scrubbed the kitchen linoleum till its pattern emerged, hand-stitched a curtain for the window I am now gazing out of. And recall with regret that I forgot my vow and melted into Mereno's arms the night he urged, black eyes glowing with warmth, "Stay, querida. But not like before."

It didn't take long to learn of Mereno's mercurial shifts of temper, his quirky humor, his vanity and possessiveness. I couldn't go anywhere without him. But withal, he was a tender lover. When I began talking of marriage, he shrugged it off. I'd stayed without it, so what was the big deal? I mentioned it once too often and that was the first time I felt his fist. After that, tenderness went down for a count of ten.

Brooding, I turn from the window as Mereno snaps open another beer can. The room has grown strangely shadowy for midday. Beside Mereno, Justina chews contentedly, food her passion since she has no man.

Mereno removes a crushed cigarette package from a pants pocket and digs out his last cigarette. Scowling, he searches his pockets, then growls, "Hey! Gimme a match!" Shouts, "D'ja hear? A match!"

Collecting myself, I pick up a matchbook lying on the stove and toss it to him, and watch as he lights the cigarette, one liquid black orb shut against the spiraling smoke.

Justina takes a walloping bite of her sandwich, runs a crimson feline tongue over her lips to trap every crumb, and plants a pudgy hand on Mereno's arm. I can see the food churning in her mouth as she says, "Mamacita needs—uh—money. The rent—you know?"

I brace myself for an outburst. Mereno is sure to blow his top. This is the third time in as many weeks that Mamacita is asking for rent money. For rent she pays once a month.

It is a measure of Mamacita's shrewdness that she sends Justina to do her dirty work. I have a suspicion the old dame plans to plead ignorance, should Mereno catch on, and throw the blame on Justina. Mereno is pretty sharp, but his filial loyalty has helped create a blind spot where his mother is concerned.

I don't know what Mereno does for a living. He's refused to tell me. Because of his irregular hours I have a hunch it's gambling. And, too, he's either flush or flat.

Mereno drains the can of beer and tosses the can into a pail of empties with a clatter. Taking a deep drag of his cigarette he exhales smoke into Justina's face, ignoring her sputtering cough. He flicks at her hand resting on his arm as at an annoying insect, his expression so reminiscent of the black look I'd get from my father if I so much as chattered at the table.

Only once did I receive anything like an approving look from my father and, despite my constant yearning, it would have been better if I hadn't. That was the day I found a snapshot of a lovely blonde girl and Ethalyn told me it was a picture of my mother who had died when I was a baby.

From babyhood I'd grown up believing Ethalyn to be my mother, and at age eleven was suddenly rendered motherless. Though Ethalyn asked me to forgive her for not telling me sooner—she'd thought of me as *her* baby—I felt betrayed, that I'd been living a lie. And betrayed, I became the betrayer.

At supper I couldn't eat and when Ethalyn said, "Alison, dear, don't play with your food," I burst out, "Don't *you* tell me what to do!" I'd never spoken to her like that before. My father glanced up and I shrank back in my chair, expecting the usual look.

Instead, I caught a glint of amusement in his eyes and, exhilaratedly courting his approval, I spat at Ethalyn, "You have no right! You're not my *mother!*"

Ethalyn sat unmoving, frozen in her chair, her plain face pinched—aging. That night, waking from a fitful sleep, I heard her rocker in the kitchen and pulled the blankets over my head to shut out the sound.

"Ahwison!" Justina calls, giggling. "The coffee."

I stare down at the coffee perking like mad, and seeing, yet unseeing, wonder: Is Ethalyn lighting candles for me in church, praying the glow will illumine my way home? How I wish she knew how sorry I was for the grief I'd caused her, for the years of silence.

She was the only one who ever really loved me. When she so patiently brushed my hair each morning before school, when she stayed up late sewing pretty dresses for me, wearing dowdy ones herself, when she stood between me and my father and received blows meant for me. But fixated on my father, I spent my life pursuing what was denied me.

"The coffee!" Mereno yells.

I glance about bewildered. *Why is my father sitting in his undershirt at the table? Why isn't he out in the fields?*

"Dammit, are you blind?" Mereno roars. There is a hissing sound as the pot boils over. Mechanically I lift the pot, wait for the boiling to subside, then pour out a cup of coffee and bring it to the table.

Mereno gives me a dark look "What the hell is the matter with you?"

He removes a wad of bills from his pants pocket and begins to count, peeling bills off one by one and dropping them on the table where they mound like falling leaves.

"Mereno?" I clear my throat anxiously. "I want—to go—home. To see my mother." I will need money from him to make the trip.

He stares at me suspiciously. "You tol' me your mother was dead."

"My stepmother. Ethalyn."

"Sure, querida." His sudden grin has a touch of malevolence in it, like a cunning conspirator's. "But I go with you."

I think of the one empty room at home. My father would never stand for my sharing it with Mereno. There would most certainly be a brawl. I couldn't do that to Ethalyn.

"Never mind," I tell Mereno, my voice breaking. Someday, I promise myself, I will go home.

Mereno shoves the mound of bills toward Justina. Murmuring "Gracias," she sweeps them into her bag, the coffee untouched, and heads for the door. In almost the same breath as her hasta la vista, she sings out, "Ahwison? Mamacita wants to know why you don' come see her?"

Sly Justina. El toro is becalmed and she waves the red cape. A wary eye on Mereno, I begin clearing the table. Teetering on the hind legs of his chair, he snaps open his last can of beer. "Whensa las' time you visit Mamacita?"

"Oh?" I shrug tensely, force myself to concentrate. "Three, maybe four weeks." At our very first meeting Mamacita pointed a plump finger at me and commanded, "You come see me ever' week. Eh?" She hadn't set foot in Mereno's dump for nearly a year, but hearing from Justina that his new blonde had cleaned the place she came to check, her practised eye inspecting everything, including me. Eager for acceptance, I'd promised to visit her.

Mereno takes a swig of beer. "Why so long?" I drain Justina's cup into the sink before answering.

"She accuses me of fooling you, says I bleach my hair." What I can't tell him is that Mamacita has taken to taunting me that her son will never marry me.

"Big deal." A flash of white teeth. "Go visit her." He wipes a bare arm across his grinning mouth. "No one can fool me. I know your hair is natural."

"Ole."

His eyes narrow. "You go."

"No—I won't." Shaking my head, I shut off the tap and reach for a dish towel.

"Dammit!" Mereno slams the can of beer on the table and leaps from his chair. "I say you go, you go!"

"I'm never going there again! And if *you're* as smart as you think, you won't go either!" Tossing the towel on the drainboard, I turn from the sink. "Don't you realize Mamacita is taking you? Rent money every week. Hah!" An inner voice cautions restraint, yet I can't seem to help myself, as if I am beyond the point of no return.

"You want to be made a fool of?" my voice rises. "Go right ahead, amigo. After all, she's *your* mother—*oh!*" I reel back against the sink, holding my cheek. Blood oozes through my fingers. I quail before the vision of Mereno's face, black as fury.

Trembling, I reach behind me for the bread knife on the drainboard, with a vague notion that my brandishing the knife will force Mereno to give ground and allow me to escape from him.

With a lunge Mereno snaps the knife from my hand, sends it skittering across the linoleum. I drop onto all fours and scrabble after it. Clutching the knife in my fist, I remain crouched on the floor, puzzled by the change in the light. The room is dim now, as though a dense fog has rolled in.

Revolving on my heel, I half rise. Through a haze I glimpse Mereno, his face blurred out of focus, floating toward me in a strange slow-motion movement. I float upward to meet him, feel the knife make contact with his body, watch dreamily as he crumples slowly to the floor.

In the enveloping darkness I hear a woman's voice keening—the sound of a rocker—

Ethalyn, don't weep. We are safe now, you and I. See, my father lies there on the floor. He will never be able to hurt us again. Never . . . Mother . . .

"Q"

Barbara Owens

The Cloud Beneath the Eaves

May 10: I begin. At last. Freshborn, dating only from the first of May. New. A satisfying little word, that "new." A proper word to start a journal. It bears repeating: I am new. What passed before never was. That unspeakable accident and the little problem with my nerves are faded leaves, forgotten. I will record them here only once and then discard them. Now—it's done.

I have never kept a journal before and am not sure why I feel compelled to do so now. Perhaps it's because I need the proof of new life in something I can touch and see. I have come far and I am filled with hope.

May 11: This morning I gazed long at myself in the bathroom mirror. My appearance is different, new. I can never credit myself with beauty, but my face is alive and has lost that indoor pallor. I was not afraid to look at myself. That's a good sign.

I've just tidied up my breakfast things and am sitting at my little kitchen table with a steaming cup of coffee. The morning sun streams through my kitchen curtains, creating lacy, flowing patterns on the cloth. Outside it's still quiet. I'm up too early, of course—difficult to break years of rigid farm habits. I miss the sound of birds, but there are several large trees in the yard, so perhaps there are some. Even a city must have some birds.

I must describe my apartment. Another "new"—my own apartment. I was lucky to find it. I didn't know how to find a place, but a waitress in the YWCA coffee shop told me about it, and when I saw it I knew I had to have it.

It's in a neighborhood of spacious old homes and small unobtrusive apartment houses—quiet, dignified, and comfortably frayed around the edges. This house is quite old and weathered with funny cupolas and old-fashioned bay windows. The front and side yards are small, but the back is large, pleasantly treed and flowered, and boasts a quaint goldfish pond.

My landlady is a widow who has lived here for over forty years, and she's converted every available space into an apartment. She lives on the first floor with several cats, and another elderly lady lives in the second apartment on that floor. Two young men of foreign extraction live in one apartment on the second floor, and I have yet to see the occupant of the other. I understand there's also a young male student living in part of the basement.

That leaves only the attic—the best for the last. It's perfect; I even have my own outside steps for private entry and exit. Because of the odd construction of the house, my walls and ceilings play tricks on me. My living room and kitchen are one large area and the ceiling, being under the steepest slope of the roof, is high. In the bedroom and bath the roof takes a suicidal plunge; as a result, the bedroom windows on one wall are scant inches off the floor and I must stoop to see out under the eaves, for the ceiling at that point is only four feet high. In the bath it is the same; one must enter and leave the tub in a bent position. Perhaps that's why I like it so much; it's funny and cozy, with a personality all its own.

The furnishings are old but comfortable. Everything in my living-room area is overstuffed, and although the pieces don't match they get along well together. The entire apartment is clean and freshly painted a soft green throughout. It's going to be a delight to live here.

I spent most of yesterday getting settled. Now I must close this and be off to the neighborhood market to stock my kitchen. I've even been giving some thought to a small television set. I've never had the pleasure of a television set. Maybe I'll use part of my first paycheck for that. Everything is going to be all right.

May 12: Today I had a visitor! The unseen occupant from the apartment below climbed my steps and knocked on my kitchen (and only) door just as I was finishing breakfast. I'm afraid I was awkward and ill-at-ease at first, but I invited her in and the visit ended pleasantly.

Her name is Sarah Cooley. She's a widow, small and stout, with gray hair and kind blue eyes. She'd noticed I don't have a car and offered the use of hers if I ever need it. She also invited me to attend church with her this morning. I handled it well, I think, thanking her politely for both offers, but declining. Of course I can never enter a car again, and she could not begin to understand my feelings toward the church. However, it was a grand experience, entertaining in my own home. I left her coffee cup sitting on the table all day just to remind myself she'd been here and that all had gone well. It's a good omen.

I must say a few words about starting my new job tomorrow. I try to be confident; everything else has worked out well. I'm the first to admit my getting a job at all is a bit of a miracle. I was not well prepared for that when I came here, but one trip to an employment agency convinced me that was pointless.

Something must have guided me to that particular street and that particular store with its little yellow sign in the window. Mr. Mazek was so kind. He was surprised that anyone could reach the age of 32 without ever having been employed, but I told him just enough of my life on the farm to satisfy him. He even explained how to get a social-security card, the necessity of which I was not aware. He was so nice I regretted telling him I had a high-school diploma, but I'm sure he would never have considered someone with a mere eighth-grade education. Now my many years of surreptitious reading come to my rescue. I actually have a normal job.

May 13: It went well. In fact, I'm so elated I'm unable to sleep.

I managed the bus complications and arrived exactly on time. Mr. Mazek seemed pleased to see me and started right off addressing me as Alice instead of Miss Whitehead. The day was over before I realized it.

The store is small and dark, a little neighborhood drugstore with two cramped aisles and comfortable clutter. Mr. Mazek is old-fashioned and won't have lunch counters or magazine displays to encourage loitering; he wants his customers to come in, conduct their business, and leave. He's been on that same corner for many years, so almost everyone who enters has a familiar face. I'm going to like being a part of that.

Most of the day I just watched Mr. Mazek and Gloria, the other clerk, but I'm convinced I can handle it. Toward the end of the day he let me ring up several sales on the cash register, and I didn't make one mistake. I'm sure I'll never know the names and positions of each item in the store, but Mr. Mazek says I'll have them memorized in no time and Gloria says if she can do it, I can.

I will do it! I feel safer as each day passes.

May 16: Three days have elapsed and I've neglected my journal. Time goes so quickly! How do I describe my feelings? I wake each morning in my own quiet apartment; I go to a pleasant job where I am needed and appreciated; and I come home to a peaceful evening of doing exactly as I wish. There are no restrictions and no watchful eyes. It's as I always dreamed it would be.

I'm learning the work quickly and am surprised it comes so easily. Gloria complains of boredom, but I find the days too short to savor.

Let me describe Gloria: she's a divorced woman near my own age, languid, slow-moving, with dyed red hair and thick black eyebrows. She's not fat, but gives the appearance of being so because she looks soft and pliable, like an old rubber doll. She has enormous long red fingernails that she fusses with constantly. She wears an abundance of pale makeup, giving her a somewhat startling appearance, but she's been quite nice to me and has worked for Mr. Mazek for several years, so she must be reliable.

I feel cowlike beside her with my great raw bones and awkward hands and feet. We're certainly not alike, but I'm hoping she becomes my first real friend. Yesterday we took our coffee break together, and during our conversation she stopped fiddling with her nails and said, "Gee, Alice, you know you talk just like a book?" At first I was taken aback, but she was smiling so I smiled too. I must listen more to other people and learn. Casual conversation does not come easily to me.

Mr. Mazek continues to be kind and patient, assuring me I am learning well. In many ways he reminds me of Daddy.

I've already made an impression of sorts. Today something was wrong with the pharmaceutical scales, so I asked to look at them and had them right again in no time. Mr. Mazek was amazed. I hadn't realized it was a unique achievement. Being Daddy's right hand on the farm for so many years, there's nothing about machinery I don't know. But I promised I wouldn't think about Daddy.

May 17: Today I received my first paycheck. Not a very exciting piece of paper, but it means everything to me. I hadn't done my figures before, but it's apparent now I won't be rich. And there'll be no television set for me. I can manage rent, food, and few extras. Fortunately I wear uniforms to work, so I won't need clothes soon.

Immediately after work I went to the bank and opened an account with my check and what remains of the other. I did that too without a mistake. And now it's safe. It looks as though I've really won; they would have come for me by now if she had found me. I'm too far away and too well hidden. Bless her for mistrusting banks; better I should have taken it than some itinerant thief. She's probably praying for my soul. Now, no more looking back.

May 18: I don't work on weekends; Mr. Mazek employs a part-time student. I would rather work since it disturbs me to have much leisure. It's then I think too much.

This morning I allowed myself the luxury of a few extra minutes in bed, and as I watched the sun rise I noticed an odd phenomenon beneath the eaves outside my window. Because of their extension and perhaps some quirk of temperature, the eaves must trap moisture. A definite mist was swirling softly against the top of the window all the while the sun shone brightly through the bottom. It was so interesting I went to the kitchen window to see if it was there, but it wasn't. It continued for several minutes before melting away, and up here in my attic I felt almost as though I were inside a cloud.

This morning I cleaned and shopped. As I was carrying groceries up the steps, Sarah Cooley called me to come sit with her in the back yard. She introduced me to the other widow from the first floor, Mrs. Harmon. Once again Sarah offered her car for marketing, but I said I like the exercise.

It was unusually soft and warm for May, and quite pleasant sitting idly in the sun. A light breeze was sending tiny ripples across the fishpond, and although the fish are not yet back in it I became aware that some trick of light made it appear as though something were down there, a shadowy shape just below the surface. Neither of the ladies seemed to notice it, but I could not make myself look away. It became so obvious to me something was down there under the water that I became ill, having no choice but to excuse myself from pleasant company.

All day I was restless and apprehensive and finally went to bed early, but in the dark it came, my mind playing forbidden scenes. Over and over I heard the creaking pulleys and saw the placid surface of Jordan's pond splintered by the rising roof of Daddy's rusty old car. I heard tortured screams and saw her wild crazy eyes. I must not sit by the fishpond again.

May 19: I was strong again this morning. I lay and watched the little cloud. There is something strangely soothing about its silent drifting; I was almost sorry to see it go.

I ate well and tried to read the paper, but I kept being drawn to the kitchen window and its clear view of the fishpond. At last I gave up and went out for some fresh air. Sarah and Mrs. Harmon were preparing for a drive in the country as I went down my steps and Sarah invited me, but I declined.

Mr. Mazek was surprised to see me in the store on Sunday. They were quite busy and I offered to stay, but he said I should go and enjoy myself while I'm young. Gloria waggled her fingernails at me. I lingered a while, but finally just bought some shampoo and left.

A bus was sitting at the corner, and not even noticing where it was going I got on. Eventually it deposited me downtown and I spent the day wandering and watching people. I find the city has a vigorous pulse. Everyone seems to know exactly where he's going.

I must have left the shampoo somewhere. It doesn't matter. I already have plenty.

May 20: Today I arrived at the store early. Last week I noticed that the insides of the glass display cases were dirty, so I cleaned them. Mr. Mazek was delighted; he said Gloria never sees when things need cleaning.

Gloria suggested I should have my hair cut and styled instead of letting it just hang straight; she told me where she has hers done. I'm sure she was trying to be friendly and I thanked her, but I have to laugh when I think of me wearing something like her dyed red frizz.

Mr. Mazek talked to me today about joining some sort of group to meet new people. He suggested a church group as a promising place to start. A church group, of all things! Perhaps he thought I came into the store yesterday because I was lonely and had nothing better to do.

Tonight my landlady, Mrs. Wright, inquired if I had made proper arrangements for mail delivery. Since I've received none, she thought there might have been an error. Again I regretted having to lie. Only the white coats and she would be interested in my whereabouts, and I have worked too hard to evade them.

I am restless and somewhat tense this evening.

May 24: My second week and second paycheck in the bank, and it still goes well.

I've realized with some regret that Gloria and I are not going to be friends. I try, but I'm not fond of her. For one thing, she's lazy; I find myself finishing half of her duties. She makes numerous errors in transactions, and although I've pointed them out to her she doesn't do any better. I'm undecided whether to bring this to Mr. Mazek's attention. Surely he must be aware of it.

On several occasions this week I've experienced a slight blurring of vision, as though a mist were before my eyes. I'm concerned about the cost involved, but prices and labels have to be read accurately, so it seems essential that I have my eyes tested.

May 26: What an odd thing! The little cloud has moved from under the eaves in my bedroom to the kitchen window. Yesterday when I awoke it wasn't there, and as I was having breakfast suddenly there it was outside the window, soft and friendly, rolling gently against the pane. Perhaps it's my imagination, but it seems larger. It was there again today, a most welcome sight.

Yesterday was an enjoyable day—the usual cleaning and shopping.

Today was not so enjoyable. Just as I was finishing lunch, I heard voices under my steps where Sarah parks her car. The ladies were getting ready for another Sunday drive and when I looked out they were concerned over an ominous sound in the engine. Before I stopped to think, I heard myself offering to look at it. All the way down the steps I told myself it would be all right, but as soon as I raised the hood the blackness and nausea came. I couldn't see and somewhere far away I heard a voice calling, "Allie! Allie, where are you?"

Somehow I managed to find the trouble and get back upstairs. Everything was shadows, threatening. I couldn't catch my breath and my hands wouldn't stop shaking. Suddenly I was at the kitchen window, straining to see down into the fishpond. I'm afraid I don't know what happened next.

But the worst is over. I'm all right now. I have drawn the shade over the kitchen window so I will never see the fishpond again. It's going to be all right.

I wish it were tomorrow and time to be with Mr. Mazek again.

May 30: Gloria takes advantage of him. I have watched her carefully this week and she is useless in that store. Mr. Mazek is so warm and gentle he tends to overlook her inadequacy, but it is wrong of her. I see now she's also a shameless flirt, teasing almost every man who comes in. Today she and a pharmaceutical salesman were in the back stockroom for over an hour, laughing and smoking. I could see that Mr. Mazek didn't like it, but he did nothing to stop it. I've been there long enough to see that he and I could manage that store quite nicely. We really don't need Gloria.

I have an appointment for my eyes. The mist occurs frequently now.

June 2: The cloud *is* getting bigger. Yesterday morning the sun shone brightly in my bedroom, but the kitchen was dim and there was a shadow on the shade. When I raised it a fraction, there were silky fringes resting on the sill. I stepped out on the landing and saw it pressed securely over the pane. It is warm, not damp to the touch—warm, soft, and soothing. I have raised the kitchen shade again—the cloud blots out the fishpond completely.

Yesterday I started down the steps to do my marketing, my eyes lowered to avoid sight of the fishpond, and through the steps I saw the top of Sarah's car. Something stirred across it like currents of water and suddenly I was so weak and dizzy I had to grip the railing to keep from falling as I crept back up the stairs.

I have stayed in all day.

June 7: I have been in since Wednesday with the flu. I began feeling badly Tuesday, but I worked until Wednesday noon when Mr. Mazek insisted I go home. I'm sorry to leave him with no one but Gloria, but I am certainly not well enough to work.

I came home to bed, but the sun shining through my window made disturbing movements in the room. Everything is so green, and the pulsing shadows across the ceiling made it seem that I was under-water. Suddenly I was trapped, suffocating, my lungs bursting for air.

I've moved my bedding and fashioned a bed for myself on the living-room couch. Here I can see and draw comfort from the cloud. I will sleep now.

June 10: I have been very ill. Sarah has come to my door twice, but I was too tired and weak to call out, so she went away. I am feverish; sometimes I am not sure I'm awake or asleep and dreaming. I just realized today is special—the first month's anniversary of my new life. Somehow it seems longer. I'd hoped

June 11: I've just awakened and am watching the cloud. Little wisps are peeping playfully under my door. I think it wants to come inside.

June 12: I am better today. Mrs. Wright used her passkey to come in and was horrified to find I'd been so sick and no one knew. She and Sarah wanted to take me to a doctor, but I cannot get inside that car, so I convinced them I'm recovering. She brought hot soup and I managed to get some down.

The cloud pressed close behind her when she came in, but didn't enter. Perhaps it's waiting for an invitation. Poor Mrs. Wright was so concerned with me she didn't notice the cloud.

June 13: Today I felt well enough to go downstairs to Mrs. Wright's and call Mr. Mazek. I couldn't go until after noon—Sarah's car was down there. I became quite anxious, sure that he needed me in the store. He sounded glad to hear my voice and pleased that I am better, but insisted I not come in until Monday when I am stronger.

I am so ashamed. Suddenly wanting to be with him today, I heard myself pleading. Before I could stop, I told him my entire plan for letting Gloria go and having the store to ourselves. He was silent so long that I came to my senses and realized my mistake, so I laughed and said something about the fever talking. After a moment he laughed too, and I said I would see him on Monday.

I have let the cloud come in. It sifts about me gently and seems to fill the room.

June 21: Didn't go to the bank today. Crowds and lines begin to annoy me. I will manage with the money and food I have on hand.

Mr. Mazek, bless him, is concerned about my health. I see him watching me with a grave expression, so I work harder to show him I am strong and fine.

I've started taking the cloud to work with me. It stays discreetly out of the way, piling gently in the dim corners, but it comforts me to know it's there and I find myself smiling at it when no one's looking.

Yesterday afternoon I went to the back stockroom for something—I'd forgotten Gloria and another one of her salesmen were in there. I stopped when I heard their voices, but not before I heard Gloria say my name and something about "stupid hick"; then they laughed together. Tears came to my eyes, but suddenly a mist was all around me and the cloud was there, smoothing, enfolding, shutting everything away.

A note from Mrs. Wright on my door tonight said that the eye doctor had called to remind me of my appointment. No need to keep it now.

June 23: Sarah's car was here all day yesterday, so I did not go out.

I don't even go into the bedroom now. I am still sleeping on the couch. Because it's old and lumpy, perhaps that's what's causing the dreams. Today I awoke suddenly, my heart pounding and my face wet with tears. I thought I was back there again and all the white coats stood leaning over me. "You can go home," they chorused in a nasty singsong. "You can go home at last to live with your mother." I lay there shaking, remembering. They really believed I would stay with *her!*

Marketed, but did not clean. I am so tired

June 27: You see? I function normally. I reason, so I am all right. It's that lumpy old couch. Last night the dream was about Daddy choking out his life at the bottom of Jordan's pond. I was out of control when I awoke, but the cloud came and took it all away. Today I fixed my blankets on the floor.

June 28: Dear Mr. Mazek continues to be solicitous of my health.

Today he suggested I take a week off—get some rest or take a little vacation. He looked so troubled, but of course I couldn't leave him like that.

Sometimes I feel afraid, feel that everything is slipping away. I am trying so hard.

Maybe I should be more tolerant of Gloria.

July 5: After several hours inside my blessed cloud, I believe I am calm enough to think things through. I have been hurt and betrayed. I cannot conceive such betrayal!

Today I discovered that Gloria is—how shall I say it?—"carrying on" with Mr. Mazek and has evidently been doing so for years. Apparently they were supposed to spend the holiday yesterday together, but Gloria went off with someone else. I heard them through the closed door of Mr. Mazek's little office—their voices were very loud—and Gloria was laughing at him! The cloud came to me instantly and I don't remember the rest of the day.

Now I begin to understand. It explains so many things. At first I was terribly angry with Mr. Mazek. Now I realize Gloria tempted him and he was too weak to resist. The evil of that woman. Something must be done. This cannot be allowed to continue.

July 8: I found my opportunity today when we were working together in the stockroom. I began by telling her my finding out was an accident, but that now she must stop it at once. She just played with her fingernails, smiled, and said nothing until I reminded her he was a respected married man with grandchildren and she was ruining all their lives. Then she laughed out loud, said Mr. Mazek was a big boy, and why didn't I mind my own business.

July 11: I'm afraid it's hopeless. For three days I've pursued and pleaded with her to stop her heartless action. This afternoon she suddenly turned on me, screaming harsh cruel things I can't bring myself to repeat. I couldn't listen, so I took refuge in the cloud. Later I saw her speaking forcefully to Mr. Mazek; it looked almost as though she were threatening him. What shall I do now?

I am not sleeping well at all.

July 12: I have been let out of my job. There is no less painful way to say it. This afternoon Mr. Mazek called me into his office and let me go as of today, but he will pay me for an extra week. I could say nothing, I was so stunned. He said something about his part-time student needing more money in the summer, but of course I know that's not the reason. He said he was sorry, and he looked so unhappy that I felt sorry for him. I know it isn't his fault. I know he would rather have me with him than Gloria. Even the cloud has not been able to save me today.

July 16: I have not left here for four days. I know, because I have marked them on the wall the way I did when I was there. Tomorrow I will draw a crossbar over the four little straight sticks.

I think I have eaten. There are empty cans on the floor and bits of food in my blankets.

The cloud sustains me—whispering, shutting out the pain.

July 19: It is all arranged. Gloria was alone when I went in this morning for my last paycheck. She seemed nervous and a bit ashamed. We were both polite and she went back to Mr. Mazek's office for my pay.

I felt a great sadness. I love that little store. And I have memorized it so well in the time I was allowed to be a part of it. It is fortunate that I know precisely where everything is kept.

At first she refused my invitation to have lunch with me today. She said she begins her vacation tomorrow. But I was persistent, pleading how vital it is to me that we part with no hard feelings between us. Finally she agreed, and I am calm inside the cloud, and strong and confident again.

She came here to my apartment and it went well. Lunch was pleasant and Mr. Mazek's name was never mentioned. I even told her all about myself, and she seemed no more upset than could be expected.

Tonight I put a note on Mrs. Wright's door saying I'd been called away for a few weeks. I've moved my heavy furniture in front of the door. I must be very still and remember not to turn on lights. There is enough light from the street to write by and the cloud is here to protect and keep me. I have come a long way. This time it is right.

July   : All goes back, goes back. The white coats are wrong. I can't do it.

I saw Daddy again. We stood under the lantern in the big old barn. He showed me all the parts of his old car and how each one of them worked. It felt so safe and good to be with him, and he told me again that I was his good right hand. I wanted

Bad. Oh bad. Everyone said you were crazy. Mean. Your Bible and your praying and church, over and over, your church every night, shouting and praying, never doing anything to help Daddy and me on the farm. Sitting at the kitchen table with your Bible, singing and praying, everything dirty and undone, then into the old car and off to church to shout and pray some more while Daddy and I did all the work.

Never soothed him, never loved him, just prayed at him and counted his sins. Couldn't go to school, made me stay home and work on the farm, no books, books are the devil's tools, had to hide my books in the barn high up under the eaves. Ugly, you're a big ugly child, girl, and you prayed for my soul, prayed for mine and Daddy's souls. Poor sad Daddy's soul.

Took it too hard they said, oh yes, took it too hard, so they sent me away for the white coats to fix and then they made me go back to you, your Bible, and your praying, and everyone said it was an accident, a tragic accident they said, but you knew, you never said but you knew, and you prayed and sang and quoted the Bible and you broke my Daddy's life. In the clouds, girl's always got her head in the clouds, I loved my Daddy and you prayed for souls and went to church every night and every night It is hot in here. It must be summer outside. All the windows are closed up tight and it is very hot here under the eaves. In the clouds

Today: I do not know what day it is. How many days I have been here. Markings on the walls, words and drawings I do not understand. I lie here on the floor and watch my cloud. It sighs and swirls and keeps me safe. I can't see outside it anymore. It is warm and soft and I will stay inside forever. No one can find me now.

Gloria is beginning to smell. Puffy Gloria and her long red claws. Silly foolish Gloria who didn't even complain when the coffee tasted strange. I have set my Daddy free.

I am in the barn. Night. I am supposed to be milking the cow. I am peaceful, serene. I have done it well and now life will be rich and good. The old car coughs and soon I hear it rattling toward the steep hill over Jordan's pond. It starts down. I listen. Content. The sound fades, a voice, the wrong voice, calling my name: "Allie! Allie, where are you?" The light goes out of the world.

Odaddydaddydaddy, where were you going in the car that night? Wasn't supposed to be you   supposed to be her her her

"Q"

Clements Jordan

Mr. Sweeney's Day

I think I was about ten when I found the puzzle in a magazine. It was a page-size summer landscape. There was a huge tree with a profusion of leaves and intricately etched bark. At its foot was a variety of flowers and grass, and close by a rippling brook. Overhead was a blue sky interspersed with puffy clouds. The caption at the top of the page asked: How many faces can you find?

At first I thought there must be a mistake. How could there be faces in a picture that had no people or animals? I was about to turn the page when—I don't know how it happened, whether I turned my head or shifted the magazine—dozens of faces suddenly popped into my amazed view. The leaves on the trees outlined faces; the etched bark limned profiles; on the ground I saw more faces peeping out from among the flowers; still others could be traced in the ripples of the brook and among the clouds. Delighted, I began to look at the page from every angle. I was absorbed until my mother interrupted me by calling me to help her.

Meals, chores, and school intervened so that it was the next afternoon before I could get back to the puzzle. I had thought about it a lot and anticipated the joy of being surprised again. I'd planned to hold the page up and at first see nothing. Then I would tilt the page and move it just a little, then a little more, until suddenly again all those faces would flash out at me. But this didn't happen. I found that after you saw a thing, it was impossible to turn back time and not see it. There could be only one first time.

I can't turn back Mr. Sweeney. Never again will it be that hot summer day when I was five, standing on the strip at the bottom of the fence with my feet between the palings so that I could better see the people and cars passing on the road. Now and then a neighbor in a car waved or someone walking to the store spoke to me. Then a flivver stopped by our gate and Mr. Sweeney stepped out of it into my daddy-craving heart.

How did he look? Let me see. Remember, I was only five. After knowing him a couple of years, I came to realize he was not tall. He didn't have much hair in front, but I remember his eyes. How many adults *see* children? They pat their heads, or chuck their chins, or even kiss them, but do they really take a good look at them? Mr. Sweeney *looked* at me. He reached out and put his hand on my arm and stepped back the length of his own arm and looked at me from head to toe. His eyes glowed. He reached down and picked me up and carried me up the path to the house, his hand warmly gripping my thigh. And all the time he was saying the dearest things.

"Where did a little sweetheart like you come from?"

"I came to live here."

"How nice. For a long time?"

"All the time."

"How did we get that lucky?"—giving me an extra squeeze.

"My mama works. I'm going to stay here with grandpa and grandma." My father had been dead for six months. My mother had decided to remain in the city and work there.

We were on the porch then and he put me down to knock on the door. But I, feeling I had known him for a long time, took his hand and led him inside, calling my grandmother. He kept hold of my hand while he talked to her. With country hospitality, she invited him into the kitchen for coffee and pie. I learned that he was our paper delivery man. He put our paper into the mailbox on the road early each morning and once a month he came into the house to collect money for it.

Mr. Sweeney was not one of those people who only talk to children when there is no adult around. He didn't sit on a chair but on the table bench by me, with one arm around me, and insisted I have some pie too. He squeezed my shoulders at intervals and when he had finished his pie he put his chin on the top of my head so I could feel its movement when he talked to grandmother. I thought this hugely funny. When he left, we walked to the gate hand in hand. He got into the car and waved as long as he could see me as he drove down the road, leaving me already lonely for him.

Grandmother spoke of it to grandfather when he came in from the tobacco field for lunch.

"He sure made a lot over her. Didn't know he was so crazy about children."

"He ought to get married. He's plenty young to have a whole raft of youngsters of his own."

"Mella Wilson set her cap for him. She's right good-looking too. But she never hit it off with him."

"Some don't take to marrying." I was sitting by grandfather on the bench and slid down to nestle at his side. He patted me on the head and said absently, "Watch out. You'll get this fork in your eye."

They loved me dearly, but they were old. Grandfather was considered vigorous for his age and grandmother's step was brisk as she canned and cooked and cleaned, but they had "slowed down," my mother said. They had sold the animals until there were only a hog and some chickens left. Grandfather had to "work on shares" because the tobacco crop was too much for him alone. They both took afternoon naps. I had the feeling I must walk on tiptoe and whisper when I really wanted to stamp, run screaming down hills, and jump hurdles. Most of all I wanted my father. I wanted his honey-pie, bristly cheeked, squeeze-me-tight, toss-me-in-the-air, roll-on-the-rug loving. Mr. Sweeney was the nearest I had found to that in all those lonely months.

I had gone to kindergarten in the city, but there was none here in the country and the nearest house with children was considered too far for me to walk. Only occasionally, when grandfather drove the truck into town, would he drop me off to play at a neighbor's and pick me up on the way home. Between times I made do with cousins who visited frequently in the summer—"watermelon company," my grandfather called them. They might grumble about having to draw water from the well to take baths and complain about the heat in the kitchen when grandmother made a fire to cook, but sometimes a cousin would spend a week with us. They were fun, but there were times, especially around suppertime—daddy time—that the loneliness set in. No man's step in the hall, no man's voice calling, "Where's my little girl doll?"—pretending not to see me just inside the living-room door until, suddenly, he swooped in, grabbed me, and swung me about, shouting, "*Here's* my doll! *Here* she is!" Even when my mother came to visit me, it was not enough, even when we could go down to the orchard and cry a little together.

Only Mr. Sweeney was almost right. I began to get up earlier and go down to the fence to wait for the paper. He would hand it to me from his car window, asking, "How's my sweetie this morning?" And, oh, the days he came to collect. Always the meeting at the gate, always the ride on his shoulders, always the squeezing, hugging, hand holding, the cheek rubbing and kiss goodbye.

Then one winter's day he found me in disgrace. I can't remember what I had done, but shortly before he arrived my "sins had found me out" and I had been spanked. He saw the traces of tears on my cheeks. He knelt down to my face level and said, "My, my, whatever is the matter with my sweetheart?" I confessed with shame and he said, "Oh, my, we'll just have to see about that." He kissed me on each cheek, lifted me up tenderly, and carried me into the house.

Inside he sat down, still holding me, and said to grandmother, "I see that our little girl has been naughty. Now we want her to be a darling angel, don't we? Just the best little girlie in all the world, don't we? I guess I'm just going to have to punish her too." He turned me over, raised my dress, and slapped me lightly on my pants. Then he put me on the floor, holding me against his side with his arm around me, and kissed my cheek again. "Now you let me know when she needs another good whipping. We are going to have us a *good* girl, aren't we?" Grandmother laughed indulgently and said I usually behaved pretty well. I decided to always tell him when I had been bad.

Once when he came I didn't meet him in the yard. I had had a cold with a slight fever and grandmother had forced me to stay in bed. I had cried, thinking I would not see him, but we had our visit. He bounded up the steps and into my room saying, "We can't have my sweetheart feeling sick." He sat down on the bed, raised me up into his arms, and kissed me on the forehead, then lowered me into the bed under the quilt. "Now I'm your own doctor," he said. He put his hand under the quilt and asked, "Where does it feel bad, mmmmm? *There? There? There?*" He had me giggling and playing his game. Each time I admitted to feeling bad, he patted the place and kissed my cheek. For the first time, I remember, I kissed him too. He looked into my eyes, got up suddenly, and went away. But he waved at me from the door. And after that, whenever he left, he would bend down and point with his finger to a place on his cheek for me to kiss.

Then the next August I met him at the gate with sad news. I would be in school the next time he came and not see him at all. "Oh, my," he said. "Now let's see about that." He pulled from his shirt pocket a miniature calendar. "What do you know about that?" he asked, amazed. "The good fairy has put collection day on a Saturday." For the first time that day I noticed that the sun was shining.

I liked school. It was fun to play at recess, to write on the board with colored chalk, to show the teacher how well I could read, to drink water out of the fountain. But Saturdays were the best days. I saved everything for him—the jack-o'-lantern the teacher taught us to make, the picture of the turkey we each drew for Thanksgiving, the secret of whose name I drew for polyanna, the disgrace of "staying in" for talking, for which he spanked me, the good report card for which he kissed me three times—once for each A.

It was the summer I was eight that the brightness dimmed. From smaller than average, I became overnight as though I'd eaten the cake in *Alice in Wonderland*. When grandmother made me new dresses, she kept murmuring, "How she has shot up! Goodness!" One month when Mr. Sweeney came, he hoisted me up to carry me to the house; the next month we had to walk with our arms around each other. I noticed that he was no longer tall. "My, my! My little girl has become a young lady," he kept remarking in an astonished voice. In vain I tried to scrunch down to the size of his little girl.

Another month I pressed up to his side and half sat, half leaned against his knee. He quickly put his arm around me to keep me from slipping. Aunt Bess, who was visiting us, frowned. Later I heard her say to grandmother, "She's just too big to be all over him like that."

"Nonsense," grandmother said sharply, "he doesn't mind a bit. He likes children. He has always made a fuss over her."

"That's not the point, Mother," my aunt said and closed her lips to a line. "She's just too big," she added lamely.

I hated my height and developed a stoop. I became quieter, shyer. I sometimes quarreled with playmates at school. One day I was sent home in disgrace. A group of us girls, big and little, were in the schoolyard near the fence right before bell time, when it was too late to start another game, and Mr. Sweeney drove by. Maybelle Purdy, who was thirteen and wore rouge, snickered and said, "There goes Touch-up Sweeney."

"Who?" asked someone.

"Touch-up Sweeney. He touches you up, get it? Touches you down too." Maybelle giggled and whispered in the ear of her friend, who giggled and grew red in the face.

A wave of anger swept over me. "You take that back! Take it back!" I screamed at her.

"Can't take back the truth without telling a lie. What's the matter? Somebody step on your toes? He been touching you up and down and round and round?"

Screaming, I lowered my head and rammed it into her middle and she sat down on the ground, breathless. The teacher monitoring the yard rushed over. Maybelle and I were both crying but some of the other children pieced together a story for her—not the words we had said, just that she had made me angry and I had butted her in the stomach. Maybelle wouldn't tell the teacher what she had said, just that she "didn't mean nothing." I wouldn't repeat those awful words, so the teacher sent me home to "cool off." All the way the name kept beating in my head: "Touch-up, Touch-up, Touch-up!" Since the teacher didn't send a note, I told grandmother that I'd come home because I didn't feel too good. By now it was true. I felt miserable. I threw up until I was all dried out. I drank some water and threw up again.

I was home from school for two days. When I returned, everything was seemingly as usual. Maybelle and I weren't often in the same part of the yard at recess, so it was not necessary for us to meet. Nobody realized there was any change in me.

The following Saturday was Mr. Sweeney's day, as I knew. Hadn't I always counted the days? On the Monday before, I began my campaign for permission to visit my mother. I had been to see her twice the past year since I had proved myself capable of riding on the bus, taking charge of my suitcase, and getting off at the right station. I could read signs now. I was a "young lady."

The next month we had an unexpected visitor on Mr. Sweeney's day. My youngest aunt arrived in hysterics, holding a sobbing child, my cousin Jennie Sue. They handed her over to me and retired behind closed doors. Worn out with sobbing, Jennie Sue fell asleep almost between sobs. I put her on the sofa and went close to the door, though my aunt's voice would probably have reached me even if I had been another room away. She made it plain that she was determined to get a divorce, that she "had taken all she could," and no one could talk her out of it. My grandparents agreed to keep Jennie Sue while my aunt went west and they talked soothingly to her, expecting her, I believe, to be more rational the next day. She was not and departed on the train for Reno to be gone six weeks.

It was summer vacation and I had almost sole charge of Jennie Sue, sometimes much against my will. She followed me everywhere on her short plump legs, imitating me in everything as best she could—insisting on drying the silver when I washed dishes, putting napkins at places when I set the table, holding a book before her when I read. Once I smacked her hand because she wrote in my book while I was writing on paper.

She was not with me that Saturday when Mr. Sweeney's flivver came in sight because I ran quickly around the side of the house and up to my room, leaving her in the yard. I stared out of the window which was up to let in the morning air, so, of course, I could hear too. Mr. Sweeney opened the gate just in time to meet Jennie Sue who was attracted by the arriving car.

"Well, hello, sweetie pie. Now, who are you?"

"I'm Jennie Sue. I'm four," she confided, holding up four fingers.

He bent, kissed the fingers, swung her up to his shoulders, and marched to the door with her while she giggled delightedly. I heard the murmur of voices below and finally grandmother called to me that Mr. Sweeney was here and wasn't I going to come down and say hello. Reluctantly I went down to find him holding Jennie Sue on his lap, his chin resting on her curls, his arms folded around her middle.

"Hey, where've you been so long? Come here and howdy me," he greeted me, taking one arm from around Jennie Sue and beckoning me with it. "My, I've never seen anyone grow the way you have. It seems just like yesterday when you were the size of this little cutie." He tried to put his other arm around me. I went closer to him but not that close. I realized it would never do to show how near to heaving I was. "I'm going to pour you some coffee," I said, getting a cup and bringing the pot from the stove.

"She's getting to be a real help. She's been taking care of the little one all week," grandmother said.

"Yes indeed, a real young lady. And this one here—a little angel is what she is."

I doubt if he noticed that I didn't go near him, so absorbed was he with Jennie Sue. I could look at him with her and realize how he had been with me, almost as if I were seeing a movie in which I had starred. As for her, she kept putting her fingers over his mouth when he talked so that his words would kiss them and she put her face against his chest. I wanted to yell, "You are not her daddy! She will never have a daddy again! Quit touching her!"

I brooded over her for the rest of the day. Aunt Susan would get a job and leave her here all the time for me to take charge of after school and she would always be here for Touch-up Sweeney's visits. Poor child—to miss a daddy all the time—just having somebody touching her. And grandmother didn't even know. She would *let* him. Well, I wouldn't.

I knew then what I had to do. Jennie Sue was only four and didn't know enough to thank me. She didn't know how long she would have to live without a daddy. She imitated everything I did. Should I put poison in a cookie for her while I ate a good one? It might taste so bad she wouldn't eat it. Should I put a pillow over her face like the lady in the movie? She might wake up and scream, then later when I did it right somebody would remember. Could I push her up real high in a swing so that she would fall out and break her neck? Maybe someone would guess that I did it on purpose.

The thing is, I was still only half serious. Understand, I knew it was the right thing to do, but I wasn't sure I could do it. I had to do it right the first time. You can't do it half one time and half the next. Then everything just sort of fell right for me. The water had been tasting funny, so grandfather had men dragging around in the well to see if something dead was down there and they went home to supper and didn't close the top of the well.

It was dark when I thought of catching lightning bugs around the back. Jennie Sue and I got some mayonnaise jars. Honestly, I hadn't even thought it all out. I stepped up on the well platform and looked down just because the top was open. Jennie Sue just naturally came too and stood on tiptoe looking down.

"Look way down and see the moon shining on the water," I said. She pulled herself up until her feet were not touching the platform at all. I simply up-ended her. She didn't scream or struggle. The hardest part was waiting a while before running in and pretending it had just happened.

No one thought of blaming me. It was so easy that I could hardly believe I had managed it and for a couple of days I found myself still making plans. The only important result to me was the effect it had on grandmother. She blamed herself and claimed she must be getting too old to manage a child, so mother decided to take me back to the city with her. After all, I would be in school most of the time.

Jennie Sue would never suffer—never wake up in the night to find her face wet with tears for her daddy, never have to see her cousins riding away with their daddies, or miss him in the evenings at daddy time, or have secrets that only a daddy would want to know—and not have a daddy to tell them to. Jennie Sue was safe forever. But what about him? It was not fair that he should go on hugging, squeezing, touching everyone. But what could I do?

The answer came to me one night. I woke up knowing what to do. I couldn't get him near a well but I could write, couldn't I? And I knew where to write from the many receipts he had given grandmother. One of the first words I could read was Sweeney, C. L. Sweeney. Later I could read the names of his office and his employer. I never forgot anything about him.

I poured my heart out to his employer on a piece of mother's stationery, but I realized that would not do. Finally I wrote a short note on half a sheet of tablet paper. Addressing his boss, I wrote: "I think you ought to know Mr. C. L. Sweeney touches all the girls on his paper route. He touches them everywhere." And I signed it: "One Who Knows."

A few weeks later grandmother wrote, "You will be sorry to hear that nice Mr. Sweeney doesn't work for the paper any more. He gave up his job and moved away. I don't know where. He never said a word to us."

That was long, long ago. They don't have many wells any more, do they? But we can all help in other ways. We can all write. And the telephone is a godsend. Don't call the person himself. He will just argue and threaten to sue. Find out who his next-door neighbor is or call his boss and call from a drugstore. They might pretend that they don't believe you, but they'll think about it, you bet. I urge you all to pay attention. They might look nice like daddies. But before it's too late, tilt the page. Take another look.

ABOUT ELLERY QUEEN

Ellery Queen is the pseudonym of Frederic Dannay and his cousin, the late Manfred B. Lee, both of whom were born in Brooklyn, N.Y., in 1905. In 1928, attracted by a $7,500 prize in a mystery-novel contest sponsored by *McClure's* magazine, they worked nights and weekends for six months, producing the novel which won the contest.

They celebrated by buying each other a Dunhill pipe monogrammed EQ, then learned that the magazine was going bankrupt and they would not collect the prize after all. Frederick A. Stokes Company, however, took on the novel—*The Roman Hat Mystery*—and its publication (in 1929) was a major historical event in the genre.

For this first collaboration they decided on Ellery Queen as their pseudonym as well as the name of their detective, writer Ellery Queen, hoping readers would find it easier to remember one name than two. Queen's genius for weighing the clues, timetables, motives, and personalities in a complicated murder case until he has discovered the only possible solution dazzled his fans book after book.

For a while his creators lectured, masked, crosscountry, Dannay challenging Lee with intricate crime puzzles. Along with the Queen novels they also wrote four novels as by Barnaby Ross, three classic critical works on the mystery genre, *The Detective Short Story, Queen's Quorum,* and *In the Queens' Parlor,* and two collections of true-crime articles, *Ellery Queen's International Case Book* and *The Woman in the Case.*

In 1940 they interested publisher Lawrence E. Spivak of Mercury Press in the idea of *Ellery Queen's Mystery Magazine,* which first appeared in the fall of 1941. From the beginning, Dannay was its active editor. Davis Publications, Inc., was founded on August 1, 1957, with the purchase of *EQMM* from Mercury Press.

The Ellery Queen books have sold, in various editions published by approximately 100 publishers around the world, a total of more than 150,000,000 copies. Queen books have been translated into every major foreign language except Chinese.

Ellery Queen popularized the mystery drama on radio in a program called *The Adventures of Ellery Queen,* which was on the air for nine years, and in 1950 *TV Guide* gave the Ellery Queen TV program its national award for the best mystery show on television. In 1975–1976 the most recent TV program starred Jim Hutton as Ellery and David Wayne as Inspector Queen.

Ellery Queen has won five Edgars (the annual Mystery Writers of America awards similar to the Oscars of Hollywood), including the prestigious Grand Master award (1960), three MWA Scrolls and one Raven, and twice Queen was runner-up for the Best Novel of the Year award. He also has won both the gold and silver Gertrudes awarded by Pocket Books, Inc. Mystery Writers of Japan gave Ellery Queen their gold-and-onyx Edgar Allan Poe ring, awarded to only five non-Japanese detective-story writers. In 1968 Iona College honored Queen with its Columba Prize in Mystery. In 1978 *And On the Eighth Day* won the Grand Prix de Litterature Policière.

The late Anthony Boucher, distinguished critic and novelist, described Queen best when he wrote: "Ellery Queen *is* the American detective story."

Novels by Ellery Queen

The Roman Hat Mystery	Cat of Many Tails
The French Powder Mystery	Double, Double
The Dutch Shoe Mystery	The Origin of Evil
The Greek Coffin Mystery	The King Is Dead

The Egyptian Cross Mystery
The American Gun Mystery
The Siamese Twin Mystery
The Chinese Orange Mystery
The Spanish Cape Mystery
Halfway House
The Door Between
The Devil to Pay
The Four of Hearts
The Dragon's Teeth
Calamity Town
There Was an Old Woman
The Murderer Is a Fox
Ten Days' Wonder

The Scarlet Letters
The Glass Village
Inspector Queen's Own Case
The Finishing Stroke
The Player on the Other Side
And On the Eighth Day
The Fourth Side of the
   Triangle
A Study in Terror
Face to Face
The House of Brass
Cop Out
The Last Woman in His Life
A Fine and Private Place

Books of Short Stories by Ellery Queen

The Adventures of Ellery Queen
The *New* Adventures of Ellery
   Queen
The Casebook of Ellery Queen
Calendar of Crime

Q.B.I.: Queen's Bureau of
   Investigation
Queens Full
Q.E.D.: Queen's Experiments in
   Detection

Edited by Ellery Queen

Challenge to the Reader
101 Years' Entertainment
Sporting Blood
The Female of the Species
The Misadventures of
   Sherlock Holmes
Rogues' Gallery
Best Stories from *EQMM*
To the Queen's Taste
The Queen's Awards, 1946-1953
Murder by Experts
20th Century Detective Stories
Ellery Queen's Awards, 1954-1957
The Literature of Crime
Ellery Queen's Mystery Annuals:
   13th-16th
Ellery Queen's Anthologies:
   1960-1981

EQ's Double Dozen
EQ's 20th Anniversary Annual
EQ's Crime Carousel
EQ's All-Star Lineup
Poetic Justice
EQ's Mystery Parade
EQ's Murder Menu
EQ's Minimysteries
EQ's Grand Slam
EQ's The Golden 13
EQ's Headliners
EQ's Mystery Bag
EQ's Crookbook
EQ's Murdercade
EQ's Crime Wave
EQ's Searches and
   Seizures
EQ's A Multitude of Sins

The Quintessence of Queen
  (edited by Anthony Boucher)
To Be Read Before Midnight
EQ's Mystery Mix

EQ's Scenes of the Crime
EQ's Circumstantial Evidence
EQ's Crime Cruise
  Round the World

Ellery Queen's Mystery Magazine (42nd Year)

Masterpieces of Mystery (20 volumes)

True Crime

Ellery Queen's International
  Case Book

The Woman in the Case

Critical Works by Ellery Queen

The Detective Short Story   Queen's Quorum   In the Queens' Parlor

Under the Pseudonym of Barnaby Ross

The Tragedy of X
The Tragedy of Y

The Tragedy of Z
Drury Lane's Last Case

"Q"